WEDDING NIGHT

They spent their wedding night in the Old House. Just the two of them; not even a slave was under their roof. He estimated she'd need thirty minutes to get ready. He paced, in torment. He could hear the stroke of blood in his ears. A-swell and a-throb, he stood gripping the edge of the mantel, waiting for deliverance.

When the time arrived, the split second, he leapt to her door. Forced himself to pause.

Because she was virgin, was innocent. Because she'd be covered by a white nightdress which he, by God, would somehow persuade her to remove. He had to be gentle. But he had also to establish that he'd tolerate no prudishness on the part of his wife.

Like a gentleman he opened the door. What he saw snatched his breath. His ears ceased to pound and began to roar . . .

BAYOU

BAYOU

SALIEE O'BRIEN

BANTAM BOOKS

TORONTO · NEW YORK · LONDON · SYDNEY · AUCKLAND

BAYOU
A Bantam Book / March 1979
2nd printing ... April 1985

ISBN 0-553-24806-5

Published simultaneously in the United States and Canada

For

Gene Thurlow III
Auwina Thurlow IV

Author's Note

This is a novel. Characters and events, except for those in history, are imaginary. The Gabriel Leblanc herein portrayed is imaginary, and no relative of Notary Gabriel Le Blanc of history.

To those who helped in research—Miss Peggy Ryder and Mrs. Janet Marseco of the Hollywood, Florida Public Library; Robert H. Land, Library of Congress; Denis J. Weimer, Sr., State of Louisiana Archives, my deepest gratitude.

BAYOU FAMILY TREE

Pierre and Aurora Leblanc
|
b. 1734 Gabriel Leblanc
m. Georgette Babin b. 1734
|
b. 1756 Gabby

Gabriel and Tonton
|
b. 1757 René
m. Catherine Perrault b. 1759
|
b. 1780 Gabe
m. Octavie Gaboury b. 1793
|
b. 1814 Gabriel René

m. Angeline Dupres in 1841;   m. Carita Nuñes in 1854 b. 1832

b. 1842 Euphemie, Eulalie   b. 1855 Dolores
b. 1845 Elena
b. 1850 Emelia
b. 1853 Eliza

René and Olive Rivard b. 1827 began alliance 1845
|
a son born 1856

PART ONE

Carita

1856

ONE

Sunday in New Orleans was the day of days. The city teemed with life, thousands of people, residents and visitors alike, tasting its varied delights.

On Sunday nights there were balls held for the elite gentlemen and their exquisitely gowned ladies, while, in a certain hall not mentioned openly, quadroon beauties in silks and jewels glided and curtsied for other elite white gentlemen while the girls' handsome mothers watched. No Negro men were permitted here, except for the orchestra.

Sunday was a time of gaiety for the slaves, too, and they flowed to the voodoo dances held in Congo Square, the women wearing their brightest skirts—red, yellow, green, blue—their heads draped in tignons; the men in their best hand-me-downs from their masters. The square was full of the swirl of skirts, the lively music of the orchestras; people chattered and called back and forth, and there was a world of laughter. But at nine o'clock, when the cannon boomed, they stopped their dancing and went quietly back to the homes of their masters, for they were not allowed on the street after nine without passes.

On Sunday, too, for the daringly elite and the elegantly bloodthirsty, there were exotic entertainments at the Circus—extraordinary, cruel fights to-the-death between furious animals. The arena where the animals fought was a rotunda 160 feet across, with a stout railing seventeen feet high and a safe circular gallery.

It was in this gallery, amid the throbbing, shouting crowds that René Leblanc was spending this hot afternoon. With him were his young Creole wife, who had been Carita Nuñez y Petain, his friend Pierre Le Fleur, and Pierre's plump and pretty blonde wife Sere-

3

phina of the Creole Segura family, who would be traveling home with the Leblancs.

René couldn't have kept his excitement from showing if he had tried, and there was no reason to try. He had never been more pleased with this exciting city, had never, in his forty-two years, experienced a more rewarding stay, yet, conversely, had never been so eager to leave. For this time, when he returned to Bayou Téche, Olive would be waiting at Rivard, the plantation he had secretly bought for her. She would be moving through the gracious rooms with that marvelous grace, but more slowly since she was now pregnant with his child. She would be there, filled with beauty, tenderness, joy, and that wondrous intelligence and understanding.

Suddenly Carita tugged his arm, and her bright voice sparkled. "Now listen, René darling! I'm not going to read it again!"

He realized that she had been reading from her program to an enthralled Serephina and that he had never seen her look more beautiful or spoiled than she was at this moment. Familiar, indulgent affection welled in him, and he began to chuckle as he watched her.

It was his belief that life was to be enjoyed, and Carita not only enjoyed but reveled in it, taking as her due her jewels and elegant clothes and being mistress of L'Acadie with its showplace mansion and its countless acres and slaves. This pleased him. Now in particular, because of his own elation concerning Olive, he felt even more indulgent than usual toward the petulant, capricious Carita.

"René, now—you listening?"

Chuckling, he nodded.

"Why are you laughing at me?"

"Not *at* you," he protested, smiling. "But because you're perfect."

She tossed her chin, a sassy toss, and waited, her program held daintily, posing, as it were, for him to appreciate her. She was dressed, as always, in turquoise. The skirt of her gown was scandalously short,

4

barely reaching her ankle. Peeking out from under her turquoise bonnet her smooth, pale red hair glistened in the sun. Her eyes were fiercely blue, her skin so fair and her chiseled features so pure that they looked like white marble come to life. He watched the quiver of her delicate lips and, recognizing that she was still a headstrong child though she was twenty-three and the mother of a baby daughter, smiled.

"The third fight!" she said breathlessly, reading from her program, "is a beautiful tigah against a black bear! Oh, Serephina!" she gasped in delighted horror to her equally delighted friend. "Do you s'pose it'll be a *black* tigah? I do simply believe there's nothing more *dangerous* than a black tigah!" She whirled to René and rested her slim hand on the sleeve of his fitted white coat. "Don't you agree, René, darling?"

"If you want it black, it won't dare not be," he smiled.

Her lips curved, and her eyes danced over him. "Don't be jealous!" she teased. "You're the handsomest thing in the *world*! I just wouldn't have anybody but you! So tall and slim, with such a strong build! I vow, you don't look a day ovah thirty!"

"Carita. The program."

She put her head to one side. "I'm pleased that your French coloring got lighter, mixed with your mothah's Creole! Did I evah mention it?"

"Many times, Carita."

"You can't make me hush, so you might as well not try!"

"You forget my mother was also half American," he teased in his turn.

Her eyes flashed. "Hush! I was talking about the tigah!"

Serephina sighed. "It may be fiercer if it's black. Just think, we're maybe going to see two ferocious *black* beasts fightin'!" She smoothed her pale blonde hair toward her bonnet, a glitter of sapphires on her hand. "Those six bulldogs in the last fight, why that Canadian bear killed them before you could say 'scat!' Just put out a paw and killed a dog ev'ry swat!"

5

Pierre Le Fleur snorted. He shifted his long, gaunt frame on the wooden chair. "And you delicate ladies didn't blink," he drawled. "Tell me, René, I found myself wincing, how about you? Yet our beautiful wives—is it because we're older than they by a generation?"

"Oh, you're terrible!" chided Serephina, laying her palm alongside Pierre's lean, dark cheek. "This is diff'rent!"

René laughed. Carita's eyes danced. "Indeed, yes!" she upheld Serephina. "This is entertainment. It's—" She broke off, her attention drawn to the far side of the arena. Some movement there seemed to make her think the entrance of the black bear and the tiger was imminent.

René's eyes met Pierre's, and he winked. At the Circus, Carita and Serephina, like other ladies, could scream with delight at gore and death. But away from the Circus, in the parlor, they could faint over nothing, with facility and grace, and the swoon was genuine. Indeed, Carita had swooned during the birth of her baby a year ago, and they had had a devil of a time bringing her out of it. She also, on occasion, swooned from headaches.

Yet today she had watched, lips quivering, while a strong Attakapas bull was attacked and subdued by six of the strongest dogs to be found. She had seen the bull slashed and bleeding, heard its agonized bellows, seen the dogs gored and bleeding, mouths foaming blood, heard them yawling. She had moaned, squealed, and clasped her hands on René's arm. She had also clung to Serephina, and Serephina had clung to her, both half delirious.

René and Pierre had earlier agreed that their wives were of natures too fragile to endure the Circus, and had instructed their coachman to wait as near the entrance as permitted. It was only sensible, they had agreed, to be prepared, but up to this moment it had not been necessary to rescue their ladies.

Now a cry rose from the crowd as at one side of the ring a great black bear appeared and ambled ponderously into full view. Then, from the opposite side came a big, glistening tiger, ears slicked back, eyes carefully watching the bear.

Carita's voice winged above the moan of the crowd. "It is—oh, it is! It's a *black* tigah! Oh, Serephina,— René, darling,—Pierre—oh, *world*—it's *black*, a real, living, ferocious black wild beast! Look at how his fur shines, how it throws off sunlight. See his tail. He moves it just like a cat—only this is fierce. He's so *big*."

"Weighs a good five hundred pounds," Pierre said.

"So does the bear," René added. "They're evenly matched."

"And if he isn't vanquished by the bear," cried Carita, "he'll be sent alone against the last bull, and if the bull wins, fireworks'll be put on the bull's back, and when they go off—oh, *my*!"

Again she and Serephina clasped each other. Then they leaned forward, lips parted, watching in horrified anticipation.

In the ring, the tiger began to move in a wide, slow circle toward the ponderous, watchful bear who in turn ambled with held-in, slow power away from the big cat.

A hush settled over the gallery. The bear reared up on his hind legs and began to move with slow, ambling grace, in a circle of his own. The tiger half crouching, fangs bared, circled ever less slowly, with terrible purpose.

He sprang so swiftly that he was a streak of black hurtling through sun-flooded space. The bear's left paw struck, and the tiger went flying backward.

The crowd was on its feet, roaring.

The tiger hit the ground and bounded up in one motion. The beasts circled again, cautiously, the tiger hissing once, the bear rumbling in his throat.

The tiger sprang again, fangs drawing a seam of red across the bear's fur. The bear sent him hurtling. The spectators went into frenzy.

"Kill him—kill him!" Carita screamed.

René felt an emptiness in his belly as the death battle continued. He looked at Carita. Her face had become feral. Her lips were pulled back, revealing her teeth. Lost in the blood-lust of the arena, she had forgotten him, Serephina, Pierre, and the shouting spectators.

Weary of gore, René sat down. He became aware that Pierre had resumed his own seat. Their eyes met again, and this time they exchanged no smile.

René realized that Pierre wanted only to escape to the little white cottage on the Ramparts where he kept his mistress Zoe. Pierre had chosen Zoe at one of the quadroon balls, and had made the financial arrangements with her mother, ensuring the placée a lifetime income and freedom for any children she might bear. That was ten years ago, seven years before he had married Serephina Segura.

Pierre had been fortunate. Zoe had borne no children. Serephina, at marriage, had brought him her Creole blood, her blonde beauty, a quarter of a million dollars, and had given him a son in nine months, now two years old and heir to the cotton brokerage Pierre's grandfather had established. Serephina was unaware that Zoe existed; if she did suspect, she held her tongue.

René reflected that both he and Pierre were fortunate. Both had beautiful Creole wives younger than themselves. Pierre also had an heir and Zoe; he himself had a new daughter, a daughter from his first marriage, and Olive, his beloved, due to bear his love-child very soon.

Yet twice, even for René Leblanc who seemed always to get what he wanted, life had flawed. He felt his expression go blank, heard the noise of the crowd as a whisper only, and the black flash and slash of death in the arena misted to nothing.

He was again twenty-six, standing on the New Orleans wharf to board the little vessel, *Linda Starr*, which would take him home to L'Acadie in the bayou country. It was a blowing, sunny morning in June, 1840, and he was looking forward to his return.

TWO

René was eager to see Old René, his grandfather, now eighty-two and also Hippolyte, the old gentleman's wizened, twisted valet. He was even willing to take over the plantation, retaining Ramsey, the competent overseer, to run it.

There were numerous passengers on the boat, but René saw no one he recognized. He and Pierre had toured Europe for several years, and the younger bayou people had grown up and changed. As the vessel made its way through the bayous, René lazed, enjoying the shrill voice of the little boat as she gave out one long and two short toots, repeating them in a raucous little song as she approached each town or village.

Stately oaks and graceful magnolias lined the banks, and the green foliage and snowy blossoms added to the beauty. There were water willows, pecans, and other forest trees as well, making a setting, here, for a pillared mansion, there for a smaller, weathered cypress dwelling, and at still another spot embracing a sprawling, white-painted house. Such dwellings lined Bayou Teche from where it rose well above St. Martinville, down its windings into the other bayous, which, in like manner, were furnished with homes, sugarhouses, and villages, strung like varied baubles on the strong, watery threads of the bayou wilderness.

René was standing at the rail as the vessel noisily approached the St. Martinville landing, eyes searching the crowd and there in the middle of them all, was the most beautiful woman he had ever seen. He stared, entranced, and his passion leapt.

She was tall, supple, and shapely. Her soft, sheer white dress outlined beautiful full breasts and accentuated her tiny waist. Her hair was a dark cloud, her skin the olive of some of the French, her eyes he noted

9

as the boat neared the dock were lustrous and almost black.

It was her eyes that identified her. He had seen her at Mass when his great-grandmother had dragged him to the church. He was maybe eight and she was—three? Those large, lustrous black baby eyes had stared at him, the red baby lips even then hinting at their present gentle, chiseled loveliness.

Angel, he thought, groping. No—Angeline. Angeline Dupree, that was it. The enchanting baby whose parents had died, the little orphan who was taken far away by kinspeople.

And now she was back in St. Martinville. By some magic she was here, and for him she was the only person on the landing. The others, moving about, waving to people on the *Linda Starr*, laughing and calling, were but a living frame for this girl.

She was the right age. He was twenty-six, which made her twenty or so. He knew instantly that she was the woman he was going to marry.

He stood at the railing as the vessel tied up, willing those black eyes to meet his, but they never did. In fact, she stopped looking at the boat and gave her attention to the people she was with. Instant jealousy flamed in René, startling him because he had never experienced it. A handsome man, he had always gotten any girl he desired. He began to sweat as he glanced at her party.

It was all right. She was with another girl and two old ladies. There was no man in their midst. But he realized, they could be meeting a man.

He spun, miraculously not stepping on any toes, made his way across the crowded deck, and found Apollo, his valet, where he had left him with the hand luggage. The valet was very small, almost a miniature slave, and had been René's property since both were five.

"You ready, Mastah René, suh?" Apollo asked.

"I've seen some people on the landing. Get some bucks to load our trunks into pirogues and go on up to L'Acadie. Tell my grandfather I'll be along later, that I'll explain. I've got business to transact."

"Yas, Mastah René," Apollo murmured and was gone.

René made for the gangplank. Rush though he did, he was extremely polite. He was also the first person off the boat.

He went directly to Angeline's group and introduced himself to the old ladies, his eyes on Angeline's eyes, half delirious over the wonder in them, the recognition of fate. The old ladies remembered him as a boy; they knew his family. They presented Angeline and the other girl.

He murmured and smiled, his eyes never leaving hers, and asked permission to call. She nodded, her lips trembling into a half smile, and the old ladies delightedly approved the idea.

"Only it'll have to be soon!" chirped one old lady. "Our darlin's visit is almost finished. She's going home day after tomorrow!"

"This evening, then?" he pressed.

Looking amazed but delighted still, they acquiesced.

He left with a bow and went to L'Acadie, where he greeted Old René and the others. He ate dinner, conversing, scarcely knowing what he said, yet loathe to cut short the evening. It had been so long since he'd talked to Old René he couldn't get enough of it.

Later, at the old ladies' home—they were cousins of Angeline's, it seemed—he again conversed. The cousins laughed and chattered, obviously pleased, but he never really listened to what they said until they excused themselves and went upstairs, leaving him with Angeline.

She was seated on a small, rose-colored divan, and he went directly to her, sitting on the edge of the divan, and capturing her hands when she would have withdrawn them. He held them warmly.

Her eyes were downcast, and there was color in her cheeks.

"Look at me, Angeline," he said tenderly.

Her eyes lifted. "T-that's all I've been doing," she whispered.

"And all I've done is look at you."

"Y-yes."

"Don't you know—don't you understand the reason?"

"I—think so," she whispered.

Gently he drew her into his arms, covered her lips with his own, and with his long and tender kiss spoke of his love for her. He received her new and innocent love in return. Holding her, he restrained his ardor, taking only chaste kiss after kiss.

"We'll be married," he said, his lips on hers.

"Yes—oh, yes!"

"Immediately—tomorrow!"

"Not immediately—but soon . . ."

It was a year before they did marry. Angeline had to return to her kinspeople first and prepare her trousseau. Also, L'Acadie needed to be refurbished, a task that Eleanor Ramsey, the overseer's wife, undertook under the guidance of Aunt Hebert, who lived in St. Martinville.

There was much for René to learn about sugar cane. Through the overseer, his old grandfather kept him on the jump, mentally and physically. He was hard put to study records and methods, and to understand what lay ahead of him.

He spent an occasional social evening with Old René, giving him an edited version of his European travels with Pierre and discovered, from the sudden twinkle in his grandfather's eye, that he knew what was being deleted. Hippolyte, as twisted and bandy-bodied as ever and no larger than René's servant Apollo, sat with them.

"What'll you do while I run L'Acadie?" René asked his grandfather.

"Play serious chess," the old man chuckled. His olive-skinned face, like his lean body, had shrunk and hardened, but it lit up when he smiled.

"I'll have to smarten my game," Hippolyte said.

"And," continued Old René, "I'm going to breed

dogs. Hippolyte and I will converse and read. Also, there are the journals."

"Ah, yes, the family history."

"Begun by my father," Old René said. "Carried on by myself."

René nodded. Careful, he thought. The journals are important to him, and he is a very old man.

"Perhaps," his grandfather said, "I'll ask you to read them when you're forty, but not now. You're getting married, and it's not pressing."

"I have got something pressing—more study," René said, getting to his feet. "And I need a night's sleep." He took his leave knowing his grandfather was ignorant of his assignations three times a week with the widow down near New Iberia. Without her his nights would be untenable, though they robbed him of sleep. He would have to part with her before the wedding, though, and give her a decent settlement.

THREE

René and Angeline spent their wedding night in Old House alone; not even a slave was under their roof. René waited in the front room while Angeline closed herself into the bedchamber to make ready.

He estimated she would need thirty minutes. He paced, feeling tormented. He could hear the blood pounding in his ears. His eyes kept going to the mantel clock; the hand never seemed to move. He stood gripping the edge of the mantel, waiting for deliverance.

When the time arrived, he leapt to her door, then forced himself to pause. He must open the door like a gentleman and walk, not charge, through, for she was an innocent virgin. She would, he imagined, be covered by a white nightdress that he, by God, would somehow persuade her to remove. But he would have

13

to be gentle. Accordingly, like a gentleman, he opened the door. What he saw snatched his breath away. His ears ceased to pound and began to roar.

She was utterly nude. Her chin lifted, her long black eyes met his, and a smile trembled at her lips, then fell away. A flush appeared on her body, enriching the olive-tinted skin over the delicately voluptuous breasts. He stared at her tiny waist, the delectable thighs touched by the amazing fall of her black, floating hair.

Never had he seen a woman like this, not in any country. He tried to speak and could not, tried to swallow and failed.

She was trembling, he saw that now, but her chin was still high. "Maybe I'm brazen," she said, her voice quivering, "but I feel clothed. In this." She touched the band on her finger and again almost managed to smile.

He couldn't respond because he still couldn't speak. And he couldn't move lest she see the bulge in his trousers and be frightened.

"I've been instructed," she said, "that it's a wife's duty to submit. But for a wife to need to submit—how can this word exist if she loves her husband?"

The unholy bulge in his trousers grew. Seeing it, her eyes widened. She held out her arms to him. He tore off his clothes and flung her onto the bed.

She lay spread and waiting. He sprang onto the bed with her. He touched one of her nipples, his fingers unsteady, and the nipple seemed to leap upward. Bending his head, he took the nipple into his mouth, and it stood higher, harder. He stroked his tongue around it, his male part rigid, his mind distantly aware that no matter what his urgency, no matter what her willingness, this girl was one to be treated with care.

He moved his lips to hers, kissing with controlled ardor, letting his tongue gently push into her mouth. Her tongue moved against and around his, an inner embrace.

When he lifted his head, she moaned. "Please—don't stop kissing me—don't stop anything!"

"Of course not," he groaned, then lowered his mouth to her other nipple, caressing it, feeling its rising and its hardness. He kissed the whole enticing breast, then trailed kisses, hot and slow, across the hollow to the other breast. She was moaning constantly now, was stirring, pushing her body closer to his. Her breath was audible, shallow, gasping.

He moved his hand downward, and at the soft dark heart of her thighs, he discovered she was ready.

"When, darling?" she whispered. "You needn't wait, you needn't be gentle. I want you—want you—"

Instantly, he bestrode her. She cried out when he drove in. She was scalding, tight, new. He managed, sweating, to wait an instant longer. Her arms came around him, then hesitantly, yet eagerly, her legs.

And then he was free, free to plunge and ride and gambol. Carried though he was on passion, he could sense her groping, doing her part, gradually at first, later in near-accord. She clung and moaned when he broke within her, and it was then, in that perfect instant, that their love reached full and flaming bloom.

In March, 1842, nine months to the day after the wedding, the twins, Euphemie and Eulalie, were born. That same year Angeline miscarried. She miscarried again in 1843 and still again late in the following year.

As Angeline filled again with child, her beauty increased. This time the baby, though born ahead of time and small, was healthy. They named her Elena.

In a week Angeline was urging René to make a needed business trip to New Orleans. She was propped up on pillows, looking lovely and a bit tired. Elena was sleeping beside her.

"There's no reason for you to stay here," she said. "Elena's here and is going to be as dark and as beautiful as her sisters. Besides, you need a change, poor darling."

"What change do I need?" René demanded.

"A change from babies, from a wife who can't . . . until it's time for you to get home, anyway. You need to escape from the nursery, from constant breeding."

Although he felt guilty, he recognized the truth. "You're the one who needs the change," he countered.

She laughed, indicating the infant. "Another time, darling, another time."

They laughed together.

"What shall I bring you?" he asked.

"Bring yourself, René." She smiled. "And next time I swear to you—and to Grandfather—it will be a boy. In twelve months, my husband, L'Acadie will have an heir!"

Only it was not to be a son at any time, though René had no way to know this.

Once in New Orleans, René began to feel a sense of escape, of freedom. It was a relief to be away from L'Acadie, away from his grandfather, from Ramsey and his consultations, from chattering, screaming children—even from Angeline, who, because of him, had done nothing but breed since they had been married.

He pushed down the disloyalty so vigorously that it never again surfaced, his mind veering to another more urgent matter. Already the week of abstinence was making itself felt. Another month, especially in a city of beautiful women, and he would be more than ready to get home.

But he didn't return, as planned, in a month. The reason he didn't was that he fell in love, completely, astoundingly, and unselfishly, in love.

It happened suddenly. Pierre, on René's first night in New Orleans, talked him into going to a quadroon ball. He had his eye on a particular girl and was ready to discuss terms with her mother.

The Orleans Ballroom was blazing with light, and the sounds of laughter and music floated over it. In a vestibule, René and Pierre handed over their hats and gloves, and Pierre paid the admission of two dollars each. Then they climbed a wide stairway to the ballroom, the music and laughter warm and gay.

They stopped at the edge of the room, and René looked about in surprise. The ballroom was long and gaudy, with a lofty ceiling and balconies that overlooked the gardens behind the St. Louis Cathedral. From the ceiling over the dance floor hung tremendous crystal chandeliers, their brilliance glittering on the fine, highly polished oak of the floor. In tiny wall recesses were nude statues, and on the walls hung original paintings.

Just then the orchestra, on a dais at one end, swung into a lively tune, and the dance floor filled with impeccably clad white gentlemen and finely gowned, beautiful quadroon girls.

Around the sides of the room sat the girls' mothers dressed in satin, handsome, all of them, hair in the latest coiffures and wearing diamonds, rubies, and pearls given them by their protectors, the fathers of the girls being presented. Most of the mothers were mulattoes, though a few were themselves quadroons. Their fingers flashed with jewels as they slowly waved their fans. Sometimes they murmured together, but they never took their eyes from their daughters for as much as a heartbeat.

"These women are like hawks," René muttered.

"You bet they are. For them, the connections the girls make are as honorable as marriage. Sure they watch."

"Well," René asked, "where is she? This girl you want?"

"We'll make the rounds and find her. She's waiting."

They moved slowly, circling the ballroom. The music stopped, and the girls, escorted back to their mothers, watched from behind their fans. As the men completed the first round and came again to the stairway, René stopped, his hand on Pierre's arm.

A cluster of girls were coming up, followed by their mothers. René stared. Never, in any place, at any time, had he seen so many beauties, such grace and delicacy, such purity.

There was one, a white girl, in the center of the group. She was a whisper taller than the others, slimmer, her movements graceful, her beauty of such purity that it was numbing. Her skin was whiter than his own, luminous against the ivory tones of the girls with her. But it was her hair that drew his notice, dark blonde curls, which, unlike the dark ringlets the others wore in front of each ear, fell free on her shoulders.

His first thought was that a man could love her. His second thought was that he, René, loved her now, this moment. His third was that he would always love her, that here was his destined mate, miraculously and always his.

He forgot that Angeline existed. Pierre had vanished. This girl in a soft green gown matching her up-tilted eyes the shade of light green emeralds was the only being, other than himself, in the ballroom.

His heart thundered. She was exquisite. His impulse was to grab her and run.

Instead, he arranged with a man whom he recognized, one Samuel Pitt, to be presented to her.

"Mademoiselle Olive Rivard, Monsieur René Leblanc," Pitt said. "Monsieur Leblanc is from L'Acadie at St. Martinville, Madame Rivard."

The mother, a comely quadroon in ivory silk murmured a greeting. Then, as Olive consented to dance with René and other gentlemen pressed in to ask the remaining girls to dance, the mother joined the watching ranks.

René stood squarely in front of Olive. "What," he asked bluntly, "is a girl like you, a white girl, doing here?"

"I'm not entirely white, monsieur. My mother brought me, at my request. So that I can see for myself and decide whether I'll—enter an arrangement." Her voice was rich and soft.

"That being the case," he told her, "you're dancing with no one but me. You know it's like that, don't you?"

She gazed at him. Her emerald eyes widened.

"It is the custom to arrange such a thing with my mother."

"No disrespect to your mother, but to hell with custom," he said. "I'm no young blade to wait my turn, not tonight."

"And after tonight, monsieur?"

"From this moment," he told her, "you can have anything it is in my power to give you."

Immediately, René purchased a cottage for Olive. He ordered all new furniture which was legally hers. He also ordered the best piano and all the books on her list. Her preferences in fabric and color were relayed to him, and he purchased everything.

He bought a very black, fine-featured woman. This was Nette, twenty-five, intelligent, trained as lady's maid, cook, and housekeeper.

He thought of the months Olive would be alone. She could go for walks and go to the shops. Discreetly. But that was all the wife of a seafaring man who was away from home—this being the story René had concocted—could, with propriety, do. Others wouldn't be apt to call on her, for it was an exclusive area, where there would be no one to introduce her.

"I'll spend hours at the piano," she assured him, "and at reading and study. I'll have my painting and needlework. Also, I design my own clothes and make them. Why, I'll hardly miss you!"

He stared. She laughed, teasing. She almost caught his arm with both hands, then refrained. He began to laugh, too, and color washed up her heart-shaped face and into her hair.

His month in New Orleans expired the day the cottage he bought for the eighteen-year-old Olive was ready. It was located on Prytania Street in the exclusive Garden District, remote from neighbors, looking out on vistas of greenery.

He wrote no lie to Angeline, only that, though his business had been transacted, he meant to stay an additional week. One week, he told himself, was a short enough honeymoon. Brushing aside guilt, he determined that Angeline should never suffer because of Olive.

Pierre, he was sure, knew nothing of her. He had been so busy at the ball with his own plans, he had never noticed that René had met Olive. He had been so busy establishing his Zoe that he had no idea René was similarly occupied. Olive was an absolute secret and would remain so.

She waited alone on their night. He walked from the hotel because he was impatient and knew that if he hired a carriage he would arrive before the appointed time.

Evening was sliding into darkness as he neared the cottage. Light shone in all the windows. His heart began to lunge, and he sprang up the steps and tapped the knocker. The door swung inward—she had been waiting—and he went through, closing it silently, closing them together.

She was wearing green—he had never known her to wear any color but the soft hue of her emerald eyes—a robe that fell in graceful folds. Her hair was loose, curling tenderly about her face, falling below her hips.

His lunging heart went out of control. He yearned to whisper of love, to say tender things, give promises that he would keep, but he couldn't utter a word. The reassurance he so longed to give her now, at their beginning, was locked away, lost in tumult.

"I'm ready, monsieur," she murmured.

In the bed chamber she stood before the bed. "I'd like it, monsieur, if you would remove your clothes. I have never seen a man."

Fumbling, he undressed, then turned to her, knowing that he was bigger, needier than ever before.

Her green eyes slowly traveled over him, paused a trifle at his male organ, then returned to his eyes. "Now," she said, her tone a caress, "would you like to undress me, monsieur?"

He reached her in one stride. He was gentle but clumsy as he unfastened the robe, pushed it away and let it fall. She was nude, her skin smooth, and soft, and very white in the shimmer of light.

20

Her breasts were larger than he had dared to hope, high and round, the nipples flat and unawakened. She had a perfect body—tiny waist, shapely hips and thighs. Her ankles were slender, her feet narrow.

"Don't wait," she said. "Not a moment, not a second."

He heard himself groan, felt the mattress give, felt the wonder of her under him. And then, with a guttural cry of which he would have thought himself incapable of uttering, he plunged into her.

When he had spent his passion, he rolled aside, keeping her in his arms. She was trembling; her breath was quivering. He stroked her shoulder. Caught though he had been in greedy torment, he had known that her body was seeking his rhythm, that it was moving with him, wild and wilder, unlike any other. It was a thing he hadn't expected, hadn't hoped for or dreamed existed. And it was his.

"I hurt you," he murmured.

"It won't hurt again. And even if—"

"I was a selfish brute. I should have—"

Her finger tips lay on his lips, stilling them.

He drew his own fingers through her soft hair. Kissing her, he then put her gently aside and got up. He knew she was sitting, nude and unashamed, as he fumbled through his clothes. He drew the jeweler's box from the pocket of his coat, brought it to her, and placed it in her hands.

"I meant to give it to you at supper, before—"

She smiled, and there was a tilt to her smile, a flash of teasing in her eyes. "Only we didn't wait!" she said, then chuckled.

"Open it," he urged.

She lifted the lid, stared at the large emerald pendant on the gold chain. She gazed at him, her eyes questioning.

He willed his own eyes to reply, to explain that the jewel was a seal upon their love. And somehow, in that wonderful way, she knew.

"Thank you, darling," she said. "If you'll put it on me, I'll never take it off, so long as I live."

When he had fastened the tiny clasp, the chain glistened as he had known it would, and the stone rested in the space between her breasts and moved glowing and rich, with her breathing.

The week they spent alone in the cottage opened for him depths he had never known existed in a woman. He discovered that she had an amazing grasp of what was taking place in the world and that she held sound opinions that she defended, even against him.

They walked, listened to music, and read. He watched the way she ran the cottage, Nette banished for the week, and saw that, were circumstances different, she could manage any household. Some day, he would give her more with which to occupy herself than a six-room cottage and one wench.

Reluctantly, he parted from her to return to L'Acadie.

Angeline miscarried in 1847 and again in 1848.

Olive lost their baby in 1849.

Angeline bore Emelia in 1850, then a stillborn girl in 1851.

She died giving birth to Eliza, their fifth daughter. It was January, 1853.

FOUR

How could it be? René asked, over and over, in his grief.

But he knew. They had been married—God, could it be twelve years? And she had borne five daughters and had how many miscarriages and still births? Dear God, could it be *six*? Had he thrown her at death eleven times? Had he literally worn her out, that beauty, that young girl he had seen standing on the St. Martinville landing?

Losing Angeline was so stunning a blow he couldn't accept it. Only hours ago she had smiled, made light of the first birth pangs, and assured him that this time it would be a son and she would take a vacation from babies.

Now she was on endless vacation. And he had sent her there.

Numbly he accepted Aunt Hebert's prompt arrival. A plump, aging, energetic woman near seventy, she arrived still at a trot, her gray wig, a known secret, very straight and proper.

"My services, René," she said, embracing him. "I'm here to look after things!"

He patted her shoulder. "Thank you, Aunt Hebert. The little girls will need you."

"I've got to make some arrangement," he told his aunt when Eliza was a month old. "I can't expect you to stay here indefinitely."

"Nonsense!" She had taken Eliza from her wet nurse and was rocking contentedly, her wig awry. "You know, that wet-nurse, VeeVee, has a good hand with this baby. I'd say keep her on for Eliza."

"Done," René agreed. He smiled, but a kind of panic took him. What the hell was he going to do? He hadn't even realized that Eliza would require her own nurse. What kind of father was he?

No father, he thought with sudden honesty. The little girls had been like toys, like dolls, beautiful little objects out of Angeline's mold. He loved them, of course, but they weren't people to him. And now, suddenly, they were adrift, needing God knew what.

"Now," Aunt Hebert said, "about running L'Acadie."

"I don't know. I just don't know."

"That Eleanor Ramsey, your overseer's wife."

"Has she been a help?"

"None better. She runs a good house of her own. I've looked into that. She has a way with nigras. They respect her and do her bidding."

"You think she can run L'Acadie."

The old lady pursed her lips. "That's right."

Mrs. Ramsey, then, could run L'Acadie. She could see that it was clean, filled with flowers, could see to menus and his daughters' clothes, manners, and nurses.

"It's settled," Aunt Hebert said. "I've told the woman I'll stay on a bit, through her getting acquainted with the children. She's willing."

"Stay as long as you like," René said. "I'm deeply grateful. But you're not to wear yourself out, understand."

"While I'm here," she said, abruptly changing the subject, "why don't you go to New Orleans? Be with your friends."

Olive.

He hadn't permitted his thoughts to go to her. He had been due in the city a month after the birth of the new baby. Olive was expecting him now; she would be making preparations. But he couldn't go, not yet.

"You're thinking it's too soon," said the old lady. "The sooner the better. I'm not trying to rush you, please understand. It's a duty I have as a woman to speak out. You've got to marry again. You've got to give all these little girls a proper mother, and think as I can, there's not an unmarried girl around suitable in all the necessary—and many—ways."

She was right, of course, but he recoiled from the idea of putting someone else in Angeline's place. And then he tried to forget it.

At last he made his trip to New Orleans. Olive was quieter than usual, warm, sympathetic, generous with the love he so deeply needed. Their hearts touched as never before.

He found himself wishing that his daughters could be loved by her, that he could bring her to L'Acadie. But there was her blood, because of which she would refuse. It had never troubled him; except for that trace of black blood, he could never have won her. What was so terrible about a mere dash of blood? He had always liked the L'Acadie slaves and got along well with them. But Olive wouldn't listen to such reasoning, he knew.

Even so, it had to be Olive, he thought, and his choice was made. Somehow, it was going to be Olive. They would marry nine months from now, at the end of the proscribed year. Three months from now he would speak to Olive, not sooner, lest his haste count against him.

He returned to New Orleans in July. His love for Olive grew. He stayed at the hotel, for the need of secrecy was now urgent, but spent as many nights as possible with her. No one, Pierre included, must suspect that René's bride had been his placée for eight years and had lost his stillborn son.

He spent time with Pierre and Serephina, who, trying her skill at matchmaking, produced beauty after beauty for René's approval. He attended dinners, escorted the girl of the moment to the theatre, to balls. He realized that he had never seen so many beautiful, marriageable girls, all of them, according to Pierre, with big dowries.

But it was Olive, and only Olive he wanted.

But when four weeks had passed and he asked her to be his wife, she refused. She said it was impossible, reminding him of her background and of how long she had been his mistress.

"Background be damned!" he exploded.

"There's the Black Code, darling."

"Damn the code! It's not stopping me!"

"I'm recorded as Olive Rivard, free woman of color."

"We can go away to Havana and be married there."

"It wouldn't work, darling."

"It's working for your brother. He's married white, living white."

"That was Papa's choice, and my brother is in Paris. My choice was left to my mother and myself. It was made when I met you."

"You chose to be my beloved. Now I ask you to be my wife."

"Please."

"Who would know?"

25

"The name Rivard. There was the scandal—Papa being a river boat gambler and killed over a card game."

"We'll use a different name."

"That would be to live a lie, darling. Living as your placée, though we keep it secret, is to live by an honorable custom. So I have been taught, so my mother was taught. And so I have seen for myself, many examples, I'm proud to be your placée; I don't mind if you make it known. I would walk with pride. But not the other, my darling."

"You've never denied me," he said wonderingly.

"And I never will again, except for this."

Argue though he did, he couldn't shake her resolution. She would not go with him to L'Acadie, not even for the sake of his motherless daughters. She would remain here, and would love him until death. But she would never marry him.

FIVE

Because of the situation, René determined to select a wife from among the girls Serephina trotted before him, much as he would select a slave in the marketplace. One day when he and Pierre were eating their noon meal together in the dining room of the hotel, he said, "I've decided to marry."

Pierre raised his eyebrows. "Anybody I know?"

"Perhaps. Serephina will have many candidates at the dinner tonight, I trust?"

Pierre grinned. "You know my wife. She's been prattling about a new girl."

"Fine," René said. "Splendid."

He pretended not to see the sardonic look on Pierre's face.

He arrived at the stroke of seven and was announced by the old mulatto butler. To his surprise the salon was not, as usual, swarming with exquisitely dressed, beautiful women and their gentlemen.

Only three people were present—Pierre, Serephina, and standing at the fireplace, a red-haired girl in turquoise. The girl looked at René with the most dazzling blue—and devilish—eyes he had ever seen.

Pierre's expression was blank, which indicated that the candidate Serephina had produced this time was one of importance.

René bent over Serephina's hand, touched his lips to it, then straightened. He flicked a glance over the new girl, taking in her dazzling beauty. She stood with pride, even arrogance, her gown intensifying the blue of her eyes. A choker of emeralds glittered on her white skin, and her eyes also glittered from behind thick, long lashes.

It was her hair that caught him. It was red, thick, straight, and lustrous. She wore it parted and smooth with bangs across the brow and a large high knot at the back, above which fanned out a tall, emerald-studded Spanish comb that looked like a crown above her delicate, chiseled features. Her lips were faintly arrogant.

"Señorita Carita Nuñez y Petain," Serephina said, "may I present Monsieur René Leblanc? René, Carita has just returned from Europe."

René bowed.

Carita spoke, her voice sparkling. "I've heard about you. Youah Creole."

"Er—yes, I suppose I am, a bit. Through my mother."

"Creole blood is very important," Carita said, and the sparkling voice was arrogant, even spoiled, though charmingly so. "I'm Creole, and Serephina is Creole. It helps to make us dearest friends."

René watched the red-haired Carita and the blonde Serephina smile together. Then Carita turned back to him.

"Youah mothah was half Creole, Serephina thinks."

"H'm'm," René mused, thinking back, "that's right. She was a Gaboury. Her grandfather, Marcel Gaboury, was French, and his wife was Anya Sanchez. My mother's father was Pablo Gaboury."

"He was the Creole, Pablo Gaboury!" Carita exclaimed. "Half French, half Spanish, the true Creole!"

René smiled. "Some would argue that," he said, moved to nettle this beauty.

"Yes," Pierre agreed. "Some insist that a black woman is Creole if she has French blood."

"A nigra is nothing but an animal!" cried Carita. "All nigras are animals!"

"Possibly," said René, holding back his smile. Obviously, there would be no dull moments this evening.

"Youah part American, too, then, way back," Carita said.

He laughed. They had been discussing him thoroughly, Serephina and this redhead. "Guilty," he agreed.

"It shows, I vow it does!" Carita declared. "It's exciting to see how good Creole blood improves a new one, like American! It's lightened youah hair to a nice brown and youah eyes, too!"

"How many Creoles did you find in Europe?" Pierre teased.

"Pierre, youah terrible! In France I was with French relatives on my mothah's side, and in Spain I was with the Spanish my fathah was kin to."

"And in England—Holland—Italy?"

"I didn't waste my time in those places!"

"Pierre," Serephina said, "stop teasing! You know how Carita and I feel. About each othah, too."

"And about ev'ry Creole," Pierre said lightly. He smiled, but René caught the measuring glint in his eye. There was more to this girl than to the others. She was beautiful, but beyond that she was spirited, had fervid convictions, and was not timid about upholding them. She was ancestor-proud, imperious, arrogant, and willful.

And she intrigued him more than any girl had ever done. Further, though he had lain twice with Olive that day, he felt a stir of desire. He decided then and there to marry Carita.

They were alone in the Le Fleur salon the evening she said that she would marry him. "We need to discuss a mattah," though, she said. "And aftah that, you'll need to confer with my guardian, Attorney Herrera."

"I should have spoken to him first."

"No such thing! I wouldn't accept a husband who didn't have the spirit to ask me first or to kiss me, the way you did, and reveal his feelings. Besides, I'll be twenty-one in a month and can do as I please."

René admired her spirit more every day. She wouldn't be timid about taking over as mistress of L'Acadie. She asked about his daughters eagerly. Her brightness would be good for them, for himself.

"You know I have money," she said with directness one day. "And I know you've got scads and leagues and leagues of land. You probably don't even know how much land you have got!"

"Around twelve thousand acres."

"Lots of money, too."

"Considerable. Sugar cane is profitable."

"How much did youah—Angeline—what dowry did she bring you?"

Reluctantly, he told her. "A hundred thousand dollars."

"Well! I don't have to be ashamed of my half million, then! I don't need to take second place in dowry!"

"Nor anywhere, Carita. In anything."

"Aftah all, I'm a Nuñez, a lateral descendent of New Orleans' Spanish govenah, Don Luis Unzaga y Monzaga, did you know that?"

"No, I didn't. I've read about him—"

"Oh, you and reading!"

"He was said to be a good governor."

"He really was good! They said he was cruel, too. But they say that about any man in powah! He has to be firm, has to get things done. And Don Luis—I'll tell you about him one day."

She laughed, beautiful and gay. Touching the emeralds at her neck, she said, teasingly, "I'm glad youah a wealthy man because I want all the emeralds and diamonds in the *world!* I want my wedding ring to be a circle of emeralds! There, is that too bold? Are you displeased ovah a girl who speaks out?" Her voice still held the teasing note, but there was determination in her chin.

Emeralds. They drew him back to Olive. He had spent the day with her. He could still see how the pendant had clung between her breasts.

"You think I'm spoiled!" Carita accused, bringing his attention back to herself, to her beliefs, wants, and demands.

René laughed. "My grandfather says we're a spoiled generation. He says we've never known what it is to want for anything, that it's been put into our hands before we could ask."

She began to laugh, too. "That's what my fathah said when he was alive and we had Natchez at our feet! Belle Verde was the finest plantation of all. If I *am* spoiled, do you want me to change? Do *you* want to change, to be anything diff'rent than what you are?"

His laughter quieted. He studied her from head to toe. She was right, this devilish, beautiful Creole girl was right. His life being as it was, he wanted nothing to be different, nothing whatsoever.

SIX

It was June, 1854, when René took Carita Nuñez to be his wife.

Serephina gave the wedding in her salon. Only a few guests were present, both because René was a recent widower and because Carita had had the sudden whim it would be more exclusive. This pleased René, too, for he believed a crush of people might overstimulate his bride and possibly even cause her to faint.

His concern was sparked by an occurrence at an intimate dinner that only René, Carita, Serephina, Pierre, and Attorney Herrera shared. Carita had been standing at the fireplace with the attorney, demanding that he admire the white roses in the crystal vases at each end of the mantel. Then she began to tease for a necklace she had seen, saying she wanted Herrera to give her some of her money so she could buy it.

"That's not in my power, señorita," Herrera told her, smiling. He was a very handsome old man, his hair more white than black, his Spanish features honed by age.

Carita laughed. "Whatevah do you mean? I'm not asking you to *give* me such a costly bauble! I *need* diamonds. I'm wearing an aquamarine wedding gown, and it simply demands that diamond necklace!"

"But I can no longer manipulate your assets. They're in the process of being turned over as dowry."

"Fiddle on that!" she cried. She had, in a flash, gone deathly pale. "I simply *must* have—"

She wilted onto the carpet.

Instantly René lifted her and carried her to a sofa. He was aware that Serephina was standing next to him, holding a vial, and he stepped aside as she waved it slowly under Carita's nose.

"What is it—what's wrong?" he asked. Why should such a vibrant creature suddenly fall unconscious?

"It's only a swoon," Pierre said.

"Yes," Serephina agreed. "She's such a sensitive creature, she takes ev'rything so hard! When she wants something, she wants it so terribly that it makes her ill. And she did set her heart on that necklace!"

"Why doesn't she revive?" René asked anxiously.

"Be patient," Serephina soothed, continuing with the vial. "It's bettah to go slowly—we don't want to *choke* her."

Carita began to turn her head from side to side. She

opened her eyes and tried to sit up. Waving René back, Serephina assisted her friend.

"There, darling," she murmured. "You swooned, but it's ovah."

Carita lowered her lashes, then lifted them. Her color was returning. "What a silly," she murmured. Glancing around her, her gaze lingered on René. "I vow I'll nevah do it again, René, I promise!"

"You couldn't help it, sweet," Serephina comforted her.

"Forgive me, René, darling?"

"There's nothing to forgive," he said.

"Oh, yes, there is! I just should not permit myself to *want* something like I want that necklace! It's silliness, and for me to get so excited. . . . Why, I'm so ashamed, I vow I could swoon ovah the fact that—" She flung her hands apart slightly.

René hadn't known that she felt so strongly. The hair on the back of his neck prickled.

Later, when Herrera had departed and Pierre and Serephina had retired, Carita was lighthearted and gay, as though nothing had happened. Yet, beneath the gaiety, there was a lingering wistfulness.

It was René who brought up the subject of the necklace. "That bauble you want for your wedding dress," he said. "I'm going to buy it for you. What establishment is it in?"

"Oh, René, darling!" she cried, her face alight. "You *are?* It's that big shop on Royal Street—you know the one!"

He nodded. It was where he had bought Olive's pendant.

"The jeweler knows the one I want. Actually, he's put it aside for me—I told him my guardian would be in to pay. He offered to let me take it, he insisted, but I didn't, proud I was able to handle the temptation. It's just the right length—only six stones on a fine platinum chain. It's just so delicate and in the finest taste! I inherited this choker from my mothah, and I did so want my own *new* necklace for my wedding. You do understand, really."

"I don't know much about gems, I must confess."

"Well, I'll teach you! My mothah left me othah things—rubies, pearls, and diamonds. I don't *love* anything but emeralds and diamonds and just nevah will be able to get enough of them! My mothah said for a lady to have jewels is business. It's like owning land or investing or putting money into a bank. Emeralds and diamonds *are* money, but they're also beautiful and something a lady simply must have!"

René chuckled. She was like an excited child, and he found this aspect, which was only now being revealed, intriguing. She was spoiled and charming, and it would be a pleasure to keep her so.

His desire for her stirred, and he wondered how it was going to be—with her.

Their first night was spent in the bridal suite of the new stern-wheeler, *Bayou Belle*. They boarded at sunset, an hour after the ceremony. Only Pierre and Serephina, at the bride's request, came to see them off.

Alone in their cabins, valet and maid in cubicles somewhere, Carita faced René across the width of their tiny sitting room. She was resplendent in her aquamarine gown, her emerald wedding band, her delicate—and surprisingly costly—new necklace.

"I'm Mrs. Gabriel René Leblanc!" she cried. She spun about. "I'm married to the richest man in the world, and I'm going to have the most beautiful life!"

She whirled to a stop and smiled in such a dazzle of joy that it struck a response where it should not have. Because of this, he made no move toward her. Not yet, caution warned, not yet.

"René, darling," she cried suddenly. "I conduct myself as a lady, but I have something to say, only I want youah solemn word that you won't misunderstand—"

She broke off. Amazed, he saw that she was blushing. "Say anything you want, Carita."

Her color brightened. "It's—I don't know what to do! I don't know what *happens*. Whatevah it is, you'll need to—well, *show* me."

33

She continued to blush, but her chin stayed high and her eyes blazed.

"When?" he asked, unable to control the urgency in his voice.

"N-now," she replied, her eyes on that part he no longer needed to hide.

She was trembling and ineffectual as she tried to help him remove her clothing. She let him take the lead, her clumsiness as he lowered her to the bunk bespeaking her ignorance, her quick compliance, when she understood, revealing her willingness.

"It'll hurt," he warned, hovering.

Even as she said, "It's all right, I'm ready," he lost control and thrust into her with such violence that the last word came out on a sharp cry. She twisted suddenly under him, jerked away, and he slid out.

"You nevah said it'd hurt that much!" she blazed.

Somehow he held back from again plunging into her. "It's because you're a virgin," he groaned. "The worst is over. It won't hurt now."

She held him off, her arms shaking under the strain. "No you don't, René Leblanc! I'll not undahgo—"

"Trust me," he said between clenched teeth. "You won't have to." If she didn't give in soon—in the next seconds—he would never be able to hold back. He would have to rape her, and then there would be hell to pay.

"Youah just saying that! You don't care what it does to me!"

"It's God's truth, I swear it. Soreness. You'll feel soreness, but not the other. Darling, lie back and let me—I promise—"

Her pushing hands fell away, and he seized that as compliance. Swiftly he entered her again. She moaned, but softly, and he began to thrust, slowly.

Unbelievably, after an instant, she began to match his thrusts. Soon she cried out in joy. The boat was moving under them, and again they came together, and the rocking of the boat held them.

SEVEN

Carita was joyful when they arrived at L'Acadie. To their right lay a grassy driveway lined on each side by a double row of giant live oaks that wept Spanish moss. The driveway extended a quarter mile from the levee to the great white house. To their left lay an identical driveway that led to the big, older house of weathered, unpainted cypress. Behind this stood the original kitchen.

North of the kitchen, facing the bayou, was a creation of utter beauty. It was a grape-arbor house of one room. The walls and roof were formed of sun-scented, breeze-rippled vines that in season were studded with sweet purple grapes. There was not only a door opening, but window spaces as well.

Fifty feet from the ends of each great house, stood twin octagonal towers. Each held two rooms, one above the other. These were the garçonnières, or boys' houses, built for the sons of René's ancestors. All this was surrounded by a giant rose garden, backed by a grove of live oaks that extended down two sides of the place, leaving the front open to the bayou. Doves cooed in their shelters, the ivory-billed woodpecker hammered, and hooded warblers tossed their notes upon the soft air. There was, now and again, the flash of a cardinal, and the everchanging song of the mockingbird.

René, eager for Carita to see everything at once, to know all about it, kept up a running commentary as they progressed. He called her attention to the size of the house, to the eight square pillars which reached across the front, and she murmured and smiled.

"You see that the second floor has an outside gallery, extending from one side to the other, while the third floor has no gallery," he said. "Look—beyond those oaks to the north, there is a small cottage we call Honeymoon House. Both it and the Old House yonder are furnished and kept ready for guests at all times. At the back of the grounds is the old schoolroom and, beyond the oaks, so it's out of sight, is the Quarters. There are six rows of whitewashed frame cabins; some of them have been standing nearly as long as L'Acadie has existed, and have been occupied by descendants of the first Leblanc slaves."

"Goodness!" half-whispered Carita, looking all about.

"At the back of the Quarters," René plunged on, "is the overseer's new house and back of that smokehouses, granaries and stables. You'll find fruit trees, a large kitchen garden, and pasture land, where horses and cattle graze. You'll find chickens, geese and ducks in large pens. Then, further than the eye can see there are fields of grain and thousands upon thousands of acres of sugar cane, the lifeblood of L'Acadie. Then, far off, is forest land and swamp and small bayous. Hidden away among a grove of trees is our burial ground."

"It's a kingdom!" Carita breathed. "And it's mine, isn't it, René, darling?"

"All yours," he agreed.

They landed. Slaves, smiling and bowing, lined the drive as they walked to the big house. Apollo and Consuela, Carita's mulatto maid, followed. The L'Acadie Negroes stared at her because, even in the memory of the oldest, no mulatto had lived here.

At the front door, René swooped Carita into his arms, swung her across the threshold, and set her down in the great hallway. Eleanor Ramsey waited at the foot of the broad stairway. With her were the five little girls and their nurses.

The children, as alike as pearls on a string, graduated in size, all in white, stood silently, their eyes wide in wonder, their dark hair falling past their waists.

"Carita," René said, "this is Mrs. Ramsey."

"It's a pleasure," the housekeeper said.

"She's kept things running here, darling."

"Also a pleasure, sir—madame."

"Wash, our butler," René continued, "Myrtle, his wife and our cook." After they bowed and smiled and Carita acknowledged them with a glance, he said, "And these are my daughters. They're too shy to come running for their gifts—you've overwhelmed them."

The faces of the four older girls broke into smiles, enhancing their beauty, and they ran to René, and there was a flurry of embraces. The baby, Eliza, remained in the arms of her nurse. "Now," he declared to his clustered daughters, "you must greet your new mother."

They moved shyly and gathered about Carita as if they were the petals of a dark flower growing from a fiery center. Carita gazed at them, and they smiled and then laughed, their voices rising like bird notes. And suddenly Carita was laughing with them, was permitting them to come into her arms, and René felt intense joy that he had provided them with this mother.

"René," she exclaimed, "they're so *dark*, so lovely!"

"We look like our maman," said one. "I'm Euphemie, I'm twelve, and this is my twin, Eulalie."

Carita gazed from one to the other. "But how can I tell you apart?" she wailed. "René, darling, you said twins, but not that they're exactly alike! They're even dressed alike!"

"All of us are," Eulalie said. "People can tell Euphemie and me apart by this little scar on my forehead, see? It's where I fell on a rock."

Carita nodded and smiled.

"This," Euphemie said, indicating the next in size, "is Elena—she's eight. And this is Emelia—she's four, and very shy. And the baby is Eliza. She's just one year and a half. She—" The child broke off, her dark eyes suddenly moist. "What should we call you, please?" she plunged on. Then, as Carita was momentarily speechless, Euphemie turned to René. "Papa—?"

Before he could respond, Carita laughed. "I have it!" she cried. She embraced all four girls and spoke with enthusiasm. "I'm not old enough to be the real

37

mothah of such big girls. Only to Eliza, actually. So it wouldn't be propah for you to address me as maman or madre—or whatevah you called youah own mothah."

"Maman—we called her maman."

"See! Now, while it might do for you two oldah girls, who could be my young sistahs, to call me Carita, it won't do for the little ones. So, you can call me Missy. That's what my maid calls me, and I'm used to it." She frowned. "Oh, my! I'll have to memorize youah names! All I know is that they all commence with an E. That's the oddest thing!"

"It's Acadian," René explained, "to name the children of a family so. A number of people on Bayou Lafourche have done it."

"I vow!" Carita whispered. Then, to the housekeeper, "I hope you found quarters near me for my maid."

"Yes, ma'am, I did."

"I wouldn't want her in the Quarters. I simply can't turn around without her. I'm just *helpless*."

René reflected, amused, that aboard the *Bayou Belle,* he had scarcely seen the servant. He reflected that, except for her thick lips, the woman was a dark beauty with much the same looks that Carita herself possessed.

"That's settled, then," he said. "I'll take Missy up to meet Grandfather and Aunt Hebert."

He escorted his bride up the stairway to the third floor. She murmured and exclaimed at the richness and beauty of the house, though she mentioned possible changes at the same time. They approached double doors at the end of a cross-corridor.

"This is the master suite," he said. "It's where Grandfather and Hippolyte practically live."

"Who's Hippolyte?"

"Grandfather's valet. They're like you and Consuela."

"Nobody's like me and my maid. Mastah suite—what does that mean?"

38

"These were rooms intended for the master when the mansion was built by my father."

"Then why," Carita demanded, "aren't we to occupy it? What are an old man, tottering on the edge of the grave, and a hundred years old—"

"Grandfather's only ninety-six."

"—and an old black, stinking nigra animal doing in the mastah suite of L'Acadie?"

Before René could speak, the doors swung open, and Hippolyte was bowing. "We hoped it was you, Mastah René," he said, his smiling black face handsome under his close-cut white, woolly hair, his small body looking exceptionally twisted and humped.

"This is Hippolyte, darling," René said. "The new mistress, Hippolyte."

The slave bowed again. Carita nodded.

The sitting room was in its normal condition—clean but cluttered with books, newspapers, and an open chessboard set up for a game. The row of journals over which Old René labored were on their shelf. The bedchamber was visible through open double doors, and it, too, had books stacked in shelves and even on the floor.

Slipping his hand under Carita's arm, René took her to the far side of the room. Here, in front of long windows, sitting in armchairs, were his grandfather and Aunt Hebert, her wig absolutely straight. Old René looked older than usual, the lines in his face deeper, but his dark eyes were as keen as ever. René felt a surge of pride.

"Don't get up," he said to them and performed the introductions. Carita acknowledged them, her head high.

Aunt Hebert's jet brooch winked and her eyes rested on Carita's delicate features. "We've looked forward to meeting you," she said. There was no bubbling to her tone.

"René," Carita said evenly, "has spoken of youah helpfulness. Please accept our gratitude and take youah ease. There'll be no more burden for you."

"It's been a pleasure," Aunt Hebert said. "It's given an old lady a purpose in life."

"You're not old, Apasie," snapped Old René, his dark eyes carefully examining the bride. René noted, uneasily, that his grandfather did not smile. "So," he said deliberately, "you're the new Leblanc. You're wanted here, needed. From the look of you, you'll be a credit to L'Acadie, a Creole mistress to be remembered."

"Thank you, sir," Carita said. "Now," she continued, her voice taking on a silken note, "if you two will pardon me, I'll have my husband take me to our chambers."

René waited uneasily as she inspected their suite. She returned to the sitting room and turned, viewing the blue walls, the white-painted French furniture covered in blue-green, the blending carpet and drapes.

"I had it done in a hurry," he said. "Sent the furniture down by special shipment."

She glanced again into the bedchamber, where Consuela was unpacking, laying out garments on the great tester bed, draping filmy lingerie on chairs. "What you've done fits these rooms," she said. "I'll not change them. This can be a guest suite."

René looked at her in astonishment.

Her lips thinned. "The rooms will be used, René. We'll use them while I do L'Acadie ovah. I'll do ovah the Old House, too."

He tried to hide his consternation but failed.

"But darling!" she cried, seeing. "Surely you realized that I'd want . . . . How could I evah be mistress of L'Acadie unless it breathes of *me*? How could I endure living where anothah woman—?"

She had gone pale, almost as pale as when she had swooned about the necklace. He hastened to reassure her.

"Do whatever you like, darling. Honeymoon House, too."

Her color returned. She came running into his arms.

"I knew you'd understand! I'll be satisfied with these rooms, they'll do until I get the mastah suite fixed!"

His arms stiffened, but she didn't seem to notice and chattered on. "Those rooms are so *big*—and they've got more windows!"

"I told you, Carita. Grandfather and Hippolyte are not to be disturbed."

"Why not?" she quavered. Her lips were trembling. "I'll wait to fix that suite until the very last, and by then the Old House'll be so enticing they won't be able to resist it! Think how wonderful—they'll have a house of their own!"

"You're not serious!" He searched for a teasing look, but saw none. Indeed, she looked remarkably pale and stern.

"You really are serious," he said wonderingly. "Well, so am I. On this one thing I'll not bend."

"So!" she screamed. "You want me to model myself aftah *her*! You order me to do things the way *she* did!"

Tears coursed down her face, which had gone whiter. He made no move to draw her close, for that would lead her to think he was going to relent.

"Understand this," he said. "There's just one thing that can't be changed, and that is the last days of my grandfather's life."

She pulled away from him and went running and weeping into the bedchamber. He followed, not knowing whether to go or stay.

"Consuela!" she sobbed. "I've got a headache. Drop ev'rything and get my hairbrush, the gold one with the emeralds, and brush my hair!"

The maid dropped the garment she had been about to hang away and hastened forward. "You want me to take off youah dress first, Missy? Get youah robe, so you'll be loose and cool?"

"No, *no*! The brush, where's the brush, you no-account wench?" Carita moaned, holding her head.

Consuela scurried about the littered chamber. Every chair and footrest bore piles of silk; a jewel box was on one table and beside it a slim, splendid jeweled dagger, its needlelike point touching a filmy scarf. A jewel-encrusted comb lay beyond the scarf; beside this was a crystal vial of some clear liquid.

But there was no brush. The maid moved quickly, searching for it, her face filled with anxiety.

"Oh, you mis'rable black baggage!" Carita shrilled. "What'd you do with it—where did you *put* it?"

Suddenly Consuela discovered the brush and its hand mirror beneath a stack of folded scarves. With utmost diffidence, she picked it up and approached her mistress, apprehension in every line of her body.

"Consuela found it, Missy," she said, her voice soft, soothing, practiced. "Missy want to sit on a chair?"

Carita snatched the brush from Consuela. Holding it by its jeweled handle, she struck the ornate, emerald-encrusted back across Consuela's cheek. Consuela shrank, but did not move.

Carita struck again, screaming, and the maid stood silently. Even though she dared not strike back, there was a flashing rage in her that matched the rage of her mistress.

René, at first too stunned to move, saw that, except for the difference in blood, they looked almost as much alike as his twins did.

"Flinch from me if you dare!" Carita shrieked. "Make a fool of me, trick me into waiting for service!" She flung away the brush, whirled to the table, snatched up the dagger and started for Consuela.

"No!" René shouted, leaping after her.

"I'll kill you!" she was screaming. "You know I will! You've seen—that yipping dog—that mis'rable little suckah I almost—"

Grabbing her arm, René twisted it, and the dagger fell. She yanked vigorously, but he held her. She struggled and kicked, screaming still. "Let me go!"

Grabbing her other arm, he let her struggle and scream. He got a glimpse of Consuela who, tears mingling with blood, picked up the brush and the dagger and laid them on the dresser. After that he was fully occupied with his hysterical bride who was shrieking without letup, twisting ever more strongly within his hold, trying to bite his hands.

He locked her to him so she couldn't move and felt her strength as she strained against him. He held her tighter, until the rage and the resistance and the screaming ceased, and she went limp. She had swooned.

Afterward, lying in bed, she poured out scalding remorse.

"Consuela, you poor thing!" she cried. "Youah *face*—but it's not deep! Go doctah it before you do anothah thing for me!"

Consuela smiled slightly at her mistress's concern. She lowered her head, then departed.

René understood that somehow, in her own way, sacrificing neither superiority nor pride, Carita had made peace with the maid.

"René, darling," she whispered, "we've had our first quarrel. I can't bear to quarrel. It makes me swoon and do—what I just did."

"It was my fault, Carita. I should have explained about Grandfather long ago."

René was sitting on the edge of the bed. Consuela laid her fingers on his lips, tears filling her eyes. "Still love me?" she whispered, as once Elena had done when she had been naughty.

"Everything's the same," he assured her, with indulgence similar to that which he had felt toward Elena. He was grateful that she seemed not to have realized that he had never, formally, declared undying love for her. She had, in her pride, assumed it could be no other way.

the highest bid. To him — the youngah he'd found the
other evenings, she cuddled against him. He told her
another such her move, and after ten minutes more she
could not persist, and she went limp. She had
won.

EIGHT

One morning at breakfast, which Carita and René
ate in their sitting room, she brought up the subject of
the housekeeper. "I want to keep her on, René, darling."

"She won't be leaving. She's the overseer's wife.
She'll be on the place, in her own house."

"That's what I mean. I want her to stay as she is."

"Whatever for?"

"To run things. The way she's been doing."

"I thought—you're the mistress—"

"Well, youah the mastah, but *you've* got an overseer
who does the actual drudgery. He reports to you, and
youah free to live as a gentleman. So, with Mrs.
Ramsey running L'Acadie and teaching her daughtah-
in-law how to run the servants in the Quarters, I can
live as a lady. And you *said* you wouldn't deny me
anything else."

"It's just that the idea is new."

"Is it settled—can I keep her?"

"If you can talk her into it."

"She's already said yes!" Carita sang out, then ran
around the table and gave him a special kiss.

She threw herself into renovation of Old House. She
had consultations with Oscar, the L'Acadie carpenter,
and spent hours inspecting what he and his crew accomplished. The four older girls, as often as not, were
underfoot, excited and happy when Missy ordered Oscar to give them brushes and let them paint furniture.

"This furniture belongs in Old House," she told
René when he asked if she didn't want new furniture.
"I'm making it pretty and—*young*! The girls are going
wild ovah it, begging to be allowed to spend the night
aftah it's finished!"

"You're spoiling them," he teased.

She looked at him so keenly he wondered if she thought he was being critical. But then she laughed and said the girls were her little sticker burrs, and he laughed, too.

Late in August he devised a plan for going to New Orleans. He hadn't seen Olive since his marriage and longed for her.

"There's land for sale down-bayou," he told Carita one night in bed. "Five hundred acres. I need to go to New Orleans about it."

"Whatevah for?" she asked. "If it's right down-bayou—"

"The owner died, the estate agent is in New Orleans. Correspondence is too slow, and in any event I prefer to deal in person."

"But it's a bad time! I'm so busy with Old House I won't even take time to be presented yet in the neighborhood! I'm so busy—"

"I know. I'm not asking you to go on a business trip. Maybe I can even help your decorating, if you give me a list, descriptions—"

She stiffened. "You'd go *without* me?"

"It's just a dull—"

"Nothing about New Orleans is dull. If you go, I go, and the entiah damn world can just wait! Now see what you made me do, René Leblanc—you made me *swe-ah*!"

He apologized. He tried to reason with her, promising that he would make the entire trip in one week, but she wouldn't listen. Instead, she reminded him, with tears, that he had promised to deny her nothing except about the master suite, and she was holding him to it.

He must wait until Old House was completed. Then, before she started on L'Acadie, they would go to the city. "That way I can make my own selections," she declared. "While you're conducting business, I'll do my buying, and in the evenings we'll have our social life."

It wasn't what he wanted, but at least he'd have the days with Olive. Resignedly, he gave in.

As it happened, they were unable to go to New Orleans as planned. For the day after he and Carita had agreed on the timing of the trip, she fell suddenly ill.

They were standing out in the sun watching Oscar and the slaves working. She looked pale. René frowned, thinking that, if anything, she should be flushed from heat and impatience. Even the little girls had a flush to their olive skin.

"Myrtle's fixed lemonade," he told them all. "She sent a pitcher to Grandfather, and now she's waiting to send one to the children's quarters, and one to our sitting room, darling."

Carita whirled. "René Leblanc, how can you chattah about *lemonade*? These nigras'll nevah—I'll nevah—" One hand fluttered, her pallor increased, and before René could reach her, she crumpled to the grass.

"Papa, Papa, what's wrong with Missy?" cried Euphemie.

All the children clustered as he knelt beside Carita. "She's only fainted," he assured them. "Run ahead, all of you. Tell Consuela I'm bringing Missy."

She had revived, still deathly pale, before Doctor Gilbert, brought posthaste by Apollo, arrived.

"Your boy just caught me," he told René. His dark hair was pasted to his head, and his face looked worn. "I've been delivering babies all night. What seems to be the trouble here?"

René explained. Consuela opened the bedchamber to them, and the doctor hurried to the bed. He listened and tapped, murmured questions and Carita whispered answers, her pallor replaced with blushes. Consuela, standing ready, had a knowing look on her face.

Suddenly Carita went scarlet. For an instant she looked terrified but quickly took on an air of triumph

46

that was instantly erased by an angry glare at René.

He glanced at the doctor, who nodded.

"So," the doctor said to Carita, "stay in bed and rest today. You watch after her, hear?" he said to Consuela. "For some weeks, in fact. I'll leave something for morning sickness."

He turned to René, whose ears were thundering.

"Congratulations. For you—and for me another midnight call in seven months or so."

After he had left, Carita pushed to a sitting position. Consuela settled the pillows, scolding.

"You should lay flat, Missy! No soonah does the doctah turn his back, but youah up! You got to take tendah care of youahself, and the new little mastah!"

"Oh, fiddlesticks!" Carita snapped. "Now go—I want to be alone with the mastah!"

With what approached a pout, making her look like her mistress, Consuela took herself out of the chamber.

Carita's lips were quivering. "Just like that—I'm to have a baby!"

René sat on the bed and took her hand.

"I know youah happy. You want a son."

"That's true. Every man wants a son." Especially a Leblanc with the need for sons bred into him.

"No mattah what it puts on a woman!"

"That part I regret, Carita, believe me."

"But you don't know, you don't re'lize—no man does!"

He did know. He hadn't forgotten Angeline or any of her times of travail. He hadn't forgotten Olive's stillborn son.

Carita's eyes snapped; her lips thinned. "He's got to finish in a week!" she declared.

"Who has got to do what?"

"Oscar. The Old House."

"You're not to step foot in there again or to begin on L'Acadie. Your one obligation now is to take care of yourself."

"That's exactly what I'm going to do, take care of

47

myself. And so I'm putting the five girls and their nurses in Old House!"

He stared, uncomprehending, and she became very irritated. "They're at my *heels* all day long, ev'ry day! I can't go a *step* without four girl children tagging along, always *at* me, 'Missy this' and 'Missy that.' I don't get any peace!"

"They like you—they're coming to love you. And I thought you—"

"Oh, I do. They're darlin' children, but they *are* children, and they do get on my nerves! Even when they do move into Old House—"

"We can set limits, Carita. Tell them about the baby. We don't have to put them out of their home."

"It isn't putting them out!" she wailed. "Old House has always been here, and they're crazy about it. Moving in to live will be a *game* to them, an adventuah! And we'll have them with us for noon dinnah. It's just that they'll sleep in Old House and play and eat the othah meals there. And I won't have to be feeling strain, wondering if *maybe* they'll come breaking in on me when I'm faint ovah this baby, maybe even throw me into a swoon!"

"It doesn't seem right, Carita. People don't move their children out of the house."

"Youah wrong, evah so wrong! All the bayou people move sons to the boys' houses! And the boys like it, you know they do!"

René hadn't liked it, he hadn't liked it at all. And he had been nine, older than his three smallest daughters. But he couldn't say this to Carita, not in her condition.

"Old House is bettah than the boys' houses," she pressed. "And the girls have got their nurses. You've got to say yes, René, you've got to show me that consideration. I'm not asking you to move youah grandfathah out, only that you make it possible for me to have peace and quiet. It's not for me, it's for the baby."

Finally, after talking to his daughters about the projected move and seeing their delight at the idea of playing house thus, he gave in to Carita's demands and their excited pleas. He submitted to what he half-angrily, half-indulgently thought of as blackmail. But he took particular pains to assure his daughters that L'Acadie was their real home.

The plan worked smoothly enough. Carita, deathly ill every morning, swooning frequently, in a bad humor, usually had recovered by noon. She would come to the noon meal, and, though she had lost her sparkle and looked pale, she chattered with the little girls. On their part, they seemed not to feel neglected. Thus reassured, René let them resume their places in his life as charming, beautiful toys.

The more smoothly things went here, the more his mind dwelt on Olive. The trip was still in abeyance, and he worried lest there be an upheaval over it. Carita was too ill to go, but he feared that she would weep, swoon, and become ill if he mentioned the word trip.

As it happened, she herself brought up the subject. "I'm not going to New Orleans with you," she said one afternoon in their sitting room. "I'll not stir until aftah the baby is born. I hope youah satisfied, getting me enceinte so fast! You'll just have to go alone and get me my list of things for the baby. Serephina'll do it for you and add whatevah I miss. Consuela is helping me with the list, but she's nevah had a suckah—nevah will, because I won't allow it. No sense passing on that human blood she's got to othah nigras, put it into suckah aftah suckah—"

"What are you talking about?" René asked.

"Consuela, that's who! Haven't you *seen* it, how much she looks like me, as much as an animal can look like a human being!"

René shook his head. He deemed it prudent not to admit the resemblance.

"She's my own papa's 'git'l'" she snapped. "She's got Creole human blood mixed into that animal nigra, that's why she's so smart! If only she had all human blood, she'd have a *mind*!"

"She's your *sister*?"

49

"Don't be foolish! How can a slave be sistah to a Creole? She's Papa's 'git' is all. Oh deah, the only reason I'm even talking about a slave is so you'll undahstand!"

"We Leblancs consider our slaves human and have kept their blood pure black so as to—er—avoid a situation like Consuela."

"That's not the Creole way!" she declared petulantly. "If you were all Creole youahself, you'd think Creole! Why, it's a known fact that if a white woman lowers herself to willingly bear the suckah of a buck, she can nevah have any but nigra suckahs aftah that, no mattah if the fathah is a white man! *Nothing* could be worse for a white woman—to carry animals in her own body!"

She blanched and shuddered.

"How did it happen that your mother allowed Consuela to be your maid?"

"Consuela's mammy was my mothah's maid, and when Mama was sick with me, the way I'm sick now, the very same way, my papa—well, a Creole gentleman has *needs!* And then Mama died of fevah and Consuela's mammy took ovah wet nursing me and her own suckah. So we were raised togethah, the way white and nigra children are. Latah, cousins took me into their home, and she became my servant."

"And your father never married again."

"He didn't live. They said he had consumption, but I know he pined away because no othah woman could take Mama's place." She pierced his eyes with hers. "You going to take up with some wench now? If you touch Consuela—"

He laughed, truly amused. "Of course not."

"And if I die? Could anothah woman take my place? If I die having youah son—could you replace me?"

He held her in his arms as she burst into tears and sobbed. "No one can take your place, no one." There was only one Carita. Only one red-haired, blue-eyed beauty. Only one pampered, headstrong Creole princess. Only one with such spirit that it could, he knew, change into pure evil. The knowledge that her passionate Spanish blood was tempered by the French gaiety gave him comfort.

Yet, though he was now to make the trip alone and could spend time freely with Olive, he was unable to leave at once. For Carita, having told how her mother had died after childbirth, now became convinced that she, too, would die. She wept so much and clung to him so strongly, that he dared not leave.

It took much devotion to gradually bring her into a state resembling calm. By the time Carita brightened, René was weary from the strain and concern for how things might be with Olive.

"I want my things from New Orleans," she announced at the table one noontime. She flashed a smiling glance, which touched each of the little girls, who instantly smiled back, Emelia, the four-year-old, giving a wriggle. "And on my list is a surprise for everyone. Even for youah grandfathah and Hippolyte," she added, giving René her most sparkling smile.

By this time he knew Carita well enough to sense a deeper meaning. "Have you added a surprise for yourself?" he teased.

"I know!" cried Elena. "Missy wants emeralds!"

"Or diamonds!" Eulalie said gaily.

The banter continued. René was happy over the atmosphere, relieved to have Carita sparkling. He had already determined to bring home the most beautiful emerald and diamond ring in New Orleans for her. He wondered if Olive would be pleased to have emeralds for her ears, one perfect stone on the dainty lobe of each ear.

Suddenly he could scarcely wait to leave.

It was during the ten days in New Orleans that René determined to establish Olive on Bayou Teche. Married to Carita, it was impossible for him to make trips to the city without her, which meant accounting for every moment of his time.

51

Careful planning, ingenuity, meticulous behavior—all these would make it possible to have Olive nearby. It would take months to provide and ready a suitable home, to present an acceptable explanation for her presence on the bayou, and to conceal their relationship. But first he would have to convince Olive that she could not deny him this as she had denied him marriage.

He engaged an agent, paid substantially to keep the name of Leblanc out of all negotiations and, with the agent acting for him, bought the five hundred acres he earlier told Carita he wanted to buy. This property, The Willows, was just below St. Martinville, a little over three miles from L'Acadie.

It was bought in the name of one Olive Rivard. The agents, both the one acting for René and the one for the estate of the deceased owner, were told that she was the wife of a sea captain who would quit the sea and live on the plantation, to be known, henceforth, as Rivard.

He next had his agent engage one John Bremer as overseer on behalf of Olive Rivard. For this service, which included orders to Bremer concerning the house, buildings and stocking the place, he paid extra, with a further bonus for keeping everything concerning René secret from the overseer.

Only when all this was accomplished, did he reveal his plan to Olive. Their reunion, this time, had been sweeter and deeper than in the past.

They had had supper and Nette had retired to her room when René blurted out to Olive what he had done. Her eyes looked greener than her emerald pendant when he had finished.

Slowly she shook her head.

"Yes," he insisted, "you're coming to live near me. No getting out of it. You own the property; your name is on the legal papers."

Again she shook her head. Her eyes softened, then became wistful. "It could never work, my darling. Here, on this street, the cottage well away from other houses, they've come to accept me, to accept that my husband is at sea. But in the bayou country—"

"Bremer is to let the word out—he's going down now to inspect for repairs—that the place has been bought by a sea captain named Rivard. They'll have months to get used to the idea, because it'll take time to repair and decorate and for Bremer to buy stock and tools and slaves. By the time he's putting in a crop, everybody'll take it for granted."

"But when only a woman moves in—"

"A woman with a seafaring husband. No. A widow—a new widow who has come to Rivard, which her late husband acquired, a lady who wishes to live quietly."

"No, my darling, no."

"You can deny me nothing but marriage," he reminded her. He was using Carita's tactics, but he was desperate.

At last she agreed.

"I've been cautious," he assured her. "Bremer has no knowledge of our situation. You'll pay all bills out of your own bank account, to which I have added a large deposit. He will consult you in all matters."

"But what do I know of a plantation?"

"You know how you want the house. Hold him responsible for the other buildings. Instruct him to buy full-blooded Negroes."

"And problems which arise—planting and such?"

"When he needs advice, which will be rarely, tell him you'll consider it. Then ask me and instruct him later."

She nodded, thoughtful. Then he took her into his arms and carried her to the bedchamber for love.

"Somehow," she smiled as he lowered her to the bed, "I feel like a man right now."

"You look all woman to me," he replied, folding back her garments, revealing her ever-entrancing body.

"I mean—I'm more anxious now, this moment, for us to love each other than I've ever been. This must be the way a man feels—that he simply—cannot—*wait!*"

"You vixen!" he whispered, springing into her eager, reaching arms.

There was talk, some weeks after René bought Olive's plantation, that The Willows had been sold. Old René knew that it was this land that René had gone to New Orleans to investigate.

"Did the agent tell you the name of the party who bought it?" he asked one noon at the table.

"No, he didn't, Grandfather."

"Hippolyte hears it's Rivard—something about a seafaring man. Or his widow."

René didn't question the source of Hippolyte's information. This would rouse his grandfather's curiosity. The slave grapevine, which covered the bayou, was known to be accurate.

"How can a seaman—or a widow—grow sugah cane?" demanded Carita.

"Hippolyte says he's—or the widow has—sent down an overseer. Married, with four sons. He's brought in a few blacks and has work underway on the house, is pruning trees, clearing ditches, getting cane in the ground, planting kitchen gardens. When it's working smoothly, the owner will move in."

"The overseer must be exceptional," René said cautiously.

"Bremer. Hippolyte says he knows his work but is closemouthed. Too much so for the Rivard blacks, to say nothing of those up and down the bayou. The Rivard slaves don't know anything yet about their new owner."

"I could find out," Carita said lightly. "Consuela sets up a bettah spy system than any nigra. She can find out whethah this Rivard man is alive and if he and his wife are old or young. Not that it mattahs."

René felt uneasy, and was relieved when the talk went to other subjects. Consuela could learn nothing that Olive's own slaves didn't know and never would. Further, when she discovered that Olive Rivard was young and lovely, though it would make her cross, it

54

was of no importance. His one concern was to keep his visits to Rivard secret.

What hell there would be to pay if Carita found out!

NINE

Carita was brought to bed the last day of April, a hot, steaming afternoon. She fainted with the first hard pain, and it took them all—Consuela, Myrtle, Eleanor Ramsey, kitchen servants, René—to bring her out of it. Apollo had gone at once for the doctor.

At two o'clock May 1, 1855, fourteen hours later, Carita delivered a fat, squalling, extremely red baby girl. The doctor handed the infant over to Myrtle and bent over Carita.

René pushed himself up from the chair into which he had slumped and approached the bed. Even in her exhausted state, after the labor she had made worse by fighting it, she was beautiful.

She looked at him, her eyes wild. "Is it—ovah?" she asked, her voice torn.

He nodded.

"You've got a fat little girl," the doctor said. "Ten pounds if she's an ounce."

"Not a boy? *René*—!"

"Not this time," he soothed.

"¡Oh Dios!" she screamed.

"Quiet, now," the doctor ordered. He stood back so Consuela could clear away the afterbirth. "Yes," he said, reading the wild question in Carita's eyes, "you had a pretty hard time. You found out what suffering is, but it's over."

"My own mama—she died! Not right away—two weeks—"

"We know a little more now than doctors did then,"

55

he said. "You'll be on your feet in two weeks, as healthy and beautiful as ever. That's a promise."

She was even more beautiful, slim and lively, within two months. She played with the baby as though she were a doll, gloried in the fact that she had red hair, worried that she was so fat, and demanded that her cot be draped, at all times, with mosquito netting.

"You keep all those nasty things out of her bed," she ordered Lura, the wet-nurse. "The way Consuela keeps our bed. I don't want those ugly bites on her delicate skin."

"I've never seen the mosquitoes worse," René admitted when she complained to him.

"Well, if a breeze would just come it'd blow them away! The othah girls have bites, and I've told their nurses to see to the nets. They'll ruin their looks, clawing and scratching."

Old René, though fond of his other great-granddaughters, was fascinated by the new one. Twice daily, with an equally fascinated Hippolyte, he made a visit to the nursery.

The little girls, Eliza who was now two, included, couldn't get enough of touching, patting, and marveling over the new sister who was so different, with her red hair and blue eyes, from them.

Carita took weeks to decide on a name, claiming the right because she was the one who had suffered. At last, well into summer, she announced that she had settled on the name, and everyone was assembled in her sitting room to hear what it was.

Old René was given an armchair, behind which stood Hippolyte, whom Carita had consented to invite. She herself sat in another chair, surrounded by the excited little girls, with René behind her. Consuela and the nurses of Emelia and Eliza stood along the wall.

Lura entered proudly, bearing the fat, thriving baby. After lowering the infant into Carita's arms, she stood by, moving a fan back and forth lest any wandering mosquito venture in.

The little girls hung over the baby, laughing quietly, as they had been taught to do. Even Eliza gave her gurgling chuckle and patted the baby's leg.

"I've thought seriously," Carita said, "so I can give my baby the nicest name there is. So. Dolores Victorie Leblanc, that's youah sistah's name, girls. That's youah new daughtah's name, René, darling. Dolores for her Spanish blood, Victorie for her French blood. We'll call her Dolores."

Euphemie and Eulalie, now thirteen, pleaded for turns holding Dolores, and Carita consented. As Eulalie cradled the infant, Elena touched the downy hair covering the round little head.

"Her hair's a little darker than yours, Missy," she said, and looked adoringly at her stepmother. "But it's *almost* like yours."

"Of course—what else? Red hair's in my papa's fam'ly!"

Emelia, now five, sidled closer, gazed into Carita's face, and patted her arm. Carita embraced her carelessly, but permitted her to remain within the circle of her arm.

René's attention was caught by the way Carita suddenly stiffened. Then she was feeling Emelia's face, her brow. "Consuela!" she cried.

The maid came hurrying.

"Feel this child! Lura! Has she got fevah?"

Both servants laid a palm on Emelia's skin. Lura felt her small ears. Their glances locked; their expressions went blank.

"Well?" demanded Carita. "*Has* she?"

"Yes, Missy," said Consuela, "she's got a high fevah."

Terror visibly swept Carita. "Eulalie, give Dolores to Lura!" she screamed.

When this was done, she pushed the clinging, now weeping Emelia away. "Take her to Old House," she ordered the child's nurse. "All of you go and stay until the doctah finds out what's wrong with this child!"

Emelia began to wail and fought to stay with Carita, but she held the little girl at arm's length until René picked her up. He felt the burning little brow and, alarmed, he tried to soothe her.

"All of you—*do* something!" Carita screamed. "Don't you re'lize Dolores has been exposed to what Emelia's got—and so have I? Take her away, get Dolores out of this room to her nursery where it hasn't been contaminated!"

René handed Emelia to her nurse, who hurried out. VeeVee carried Eliza, and Consuela shepherded the bewildered older girls out.

At the door, Euphemie paused. "We'll be all right, Papa," she said.

René gave her a brief smile. "I'll be over soon," he promised.

After she had gone, he told Consuela to send a servant in their fastest pirogue for the doctor. Almost before he finished speaking, she was gone, followed by a strangely silent grandfather and his grim-faced valet.

"Why did you send Consuela in the pirogue?" Carita demanded. "I want her to tell Lura to give Dolores a bath. I want her to fix me a bath, to get this room cleaned, to scrub away the sickness that child's got! Have the suckahs down in the Quarters got some animal disease you haven't told me about?"

"No, Carita."

"You *know* that Dolores isn't but a tiny baby! She'll sicken with anything, she'll *die*! I'll have nothing, nothing whatsoevah to show for all the months—"

"Now look," René cut in. "There's no reason for panic. Wait until the doctor comes. See what he says before you have Emelia mortally ill. Probably she ate something. Children do get fevers, and it turns out to be an upset stomach."

"And sometimes it turns out to be something else, something far worse—don't tell me!"

René held his tongue and headed for Old House.

This time Carita was right. Emelia had yellow fever, the scourge that came in hot weather, came unexpectedly and for no known reason, ravaging a plantation, an area, a countryside, killing black and white, rich and poor, not letting up, it seemed, until cold weather set in.

Emelia died the fourth day, died in René's arms. Even as she breathed her last, the other little girls were in the throes of the disease, and René went from bed to bed, helping and comforting, his hands tender.

One after another—Eliza, Elena, Eulalie—went the same path. First came the sudden fever, then chills, backache, nausea, and vomiting. The third day jaundice appeared; after that came death.

Only Euphemie survived, frail as a breath, sadder than grief. She and the weeping nurses remained at Old House, as did René, who now cherished for this eldest daughter a new tenderness.

But it wasn't over. The doctor and the priest were on continuous rounds—L'Acadie, Double Oaks, Hebert Plantation, over all the bayous. The little girls' nurses and their cook sickened and died.

Before the plague ended, scores had died. The population at St. Martinville was decimated. At Double Oaks, at Hebert Plantation—everywhere—planters, wives, children, and slaves died by the dozens. Slaves died as fast if not faster than did their masters. L'Acadie lost one-third of its slaves. Double Oaks lost one-fifth, Hebert Plantation more than that. Rivard, where, thank God, Olive was not yet in residence, lost one-forth of its slaves and Bremer lost two of his sons.

In L'Acadie, Carita moved restlessly between bed-chamber and sitting room throughout the epidemic. She banned René and Euphemie from the house; those already inside she forced to remain.

For René, time was a torment. The day when four small, new cypress tombs joined the others in L'Acadie's burial grounds, his heart seemed to split.

When the plague ended, when the deaths ceased and no one else fell ill, René and Euphemie moved back into L'Acadie. He ordered that every building and every house on the plantation be fumigated, scrubbed, sunned, and repainted.

The other survivors of the plague were doing the same. It was while they were in the midst of this, that a disastrous fire burned the entire business portion of St. Martinville. To complete the horror, fourteen persons perished in the flames.

At first, when René and Euphemie moved back, Carita remained locked in her suite. Then, after some days passed and there was no illness, she admitted René, alternating between white-faced terror and raging panic.

"Don't touch me!" she cried the first time he entered. "And don't go *neah* the nursery! Nobody but Consuela and Lura can be with Dolores."

"Euphemie and I are clean of illness, Carita. The doctor says it."

"What does he know? What does any doctah know? Dolores may *still* get the plague!"

"Euphemie's staying here with us, Carita. She can't be in Old House alone."

She frowned. "Well, we *can* send her off to school soon!"

Even knowing Carita so well, René was stunned. "Understand this," he said. "A man who has lost four daughters, almost lost a fifth one, to the plague won't be fool enough to endanger his one child not yet touched! It's safe. Hasn't it gotten through to you that we've been—bereaved?"

She went utterly white. He waited for her to swoon, but she didn't. Instead, tears flashed into her eyes. "Have you gone mad?" she whispered furiously. "Of course I re'lize, and I've cried ovah them! But it doesn't change this about my own baby. It wouldn't bring back the othahs if you go in there and—why, I don't go in, and I'm her mothah!"

"Are you sure you're not afraid of me yourself? I've been exposed more recently than Dolores."

She was speechless. There was bewilderment, quickly gone. "It's been more than a month, René Leblanc! Youah strong, and she's a baby. She can get the fevah by herself. And then we can get it from her!"

Abruptly he realized that, while he had been caught in the struggle of the plague, Carita had kept to her rooms and stayed away from Dolores, in terror for her own life. Seldom, throughout the nightmare, had he seriously feared for those in the big house. He was aware that those who were stricken with the fever fell ill within two or three days of the outbreak. Once this period had passed with those at L'Acadie well, he had scarcely thought of them.

His mind had gone to Olive, and he feared lest the plague flash across the bayou country to New Orleans. Blessedly, each time he inquired when boats touched at St. Martinville to quickly unload, the reply was that the fever had not spread beyond St. Martinville and the neighboring areas.

"We are not," he told Carita now, "going to live one more day in fear. The plague is over, the fire has burned itself out, and we are going to take up where we left off!"

She stared, her eyes wide. A pulse at her throat began to leap, and as it grew faster, the glitter left her eyes, and they became as soft as their brilliant color would permit. Her lips softened, almost smiled.

Desire, the first in all the weeks, touched him. He reached her in two strides, swept her into his arms, carried her into the other room, and dropped her onto the bed. Deftly he stripped her, then stripped himself.

"Contagion—" she murmured.

"Contagion be damned!" he growled. "Double damned!"

TEN

Carita was still too shaken to go with him when he said he had business in New Orleans. Thus, armed with a long list of things she wanted brought back, he was able, at last, to see Olive.

They made love daily and nightly. One evening, after making love, they lay entwined. "Damn," he muttered, "if only you could move into Rivard now."

"We're together. That's enough."

"For this moment," he agreed, gathering her to him. She stroked his brow. This was a new gesture, a wordless comforting for the loss of his daughters.

Moving his hand across her breasts, he felt the warmth of the emerald that nestled between them, then cupped one breast and tenderly fingered the nipple. He throbbed anew with need for her, though it had been moments only since he had possessed her.

"Are you—ready?" she whispered. "Again?"

"So help me, I am. But it hasn't been—"

Softly she touched his male part.

"That doesn't matter," she whispered, her breath hot on his cheek. "If only one moment has passed, it doesn't matter. The instant you—like this—" Again the touch. "Now, my darling, quickly—don't make me wait!"

He groaned and again poured into her all his passion, all his love.

Before dark he rose and dressed. He was staying, Apollo in attendance, at the hotel. Mornings he went to the slave market to buy for L'Acadie and to the shops for Carita. Afternoons and evenings he spent with Olive, filling himself with love.

He wrote to Carita daily, even though his letters would arrive in packets. He told her, truthfully, that he was awaiting arrival of a ship that was bringing not only French furniture but some fine new silks. It was also bringing the delicate lingerie she wore, and he promised to make selections in her blue-green.

She wrote enthusiastic replies, sending him a new list in each letter. She wrote that he was to bring everything with him, and he wasn't to return until he had gotten every item, along with whatever else he might think she would want.

In this manner, he was able to stretch his stay for five weeks, returning to L'Acadie the second week in November. He went then because otherwise he might rouse Carita's suspicion, also because harvest was now in progress and, in view of the shortage of slaves, he should at least be present.

He found Carita happily renovating L'Acadie, even permitting Euphemie to help and to play with Dolores. She was delighted with his purchases, complimented his taste, and admired the Spanish comb he had brought her. The single strand of pearls he had brought Euphemie won him the first spontaneous smile he had seen on her for months.

That first night Carita willingly, eagerly came into his arms. Afterward, she lay with her head on his arm, her hair spread out. She gave a little purr, for all the world like a cat.

"What's that for?" he asked lazily, knowing the purr to be special. He felt sated, quenched. Yet there was a stir in his groin.

"Men are funny, that's what! I vow, tonight you acted—hottah—than the first night!"

"We've been apart."

Two days ago, he had lain with Olive.

"Makes you appreciate me! Deny it?"

"No," he said, because he must, and with some truth, nevertheless. His intimacies with Carita were passionate, with a strong element of play to them. With Angeline he had assuaged his youthful, rampant passion. But the fulfillment Olive gave him surpassed all else.

To divert Carita, to avoid her quick mind fastening onto the idea that he might have someone in New Orleans, he spoke of the renovation that was underway. "How long will it take?" he asked. "Will we be able to have a Christmas house party—all the aunts and cousins and connections—Pierre and Serephina—everybody?"

"You mean have them stay for *weeks?*"

"L'Acadie's famous for that."

"Oh, you *men!*"

"The house should be finished, of course."

"Well, I should think so! Do you re'lize, when I came here, what I was faced with? Doing ovah this big house and Old House and Honeymoon House and *four* boys' houses! And youah children by anothah woman and devoting time to Aunt Hebert and youah grandfathah. Getting used to him in the mastah suite, scribbling in his journals, to say nothing of that Hippolyte and all the slaves! And meeting people, with goodness knows how many more yet to meet!"

"I understand. You needn't explain."

"But I am *going* to explain. And then you got me enceinte right away, didn't wait until I got things undah control. You *know* what an awful time I had, and you *know* I came near to dying from the pain. And right away, before I could get ready for this comp'ny you all of a sudden want, came the plague."

"Put it out of your mind."

"How can I—all those months? And now, the minute I'm making progress, you want to have this comp'ny! I want to go to New Orleans myself first! I want to have some pleasuah before I have to entertain, and I can't go until I've got all this renovating done. The soonest I can have a house party'll be next summah."

"That'll be splendid," he agreed.

Under Carita's direction, the main house took on beauty it had never possessed. She ordered minor remodeling and repairs, new paint, wallpaper, carpets, draperies, and furniture throughout, except for their own suite and for Old René's. She offered to redecorate his suite, but he gently declined.

Euphemie trailed after her, still frail, smiling when Carita became ecstatic over some color or texture. For the most part she was quiet and serious until she was permitted to take charge of Dolores, and then she came alive and laughed and was happy.

Daily Carita dragged René from room to room, pointing out each bit of finished work. "What do you think?" she would demand. "Do you like it?"

"Indeed I do," he would agree.

He didn't betray that he was bewildered by the many varied and vivid colors Carita had chosen. She was like some bold artist, the mansion her canvas.

Whatever effect L'Acadie might have on others, René approved it because it was like Carita herself—gay, restless, filled with surprise.

He thought of how Olive was decorating Rivard. "The woodwork is to be white," she had told him, "but muted in effect, and the walls papered in muted, simple patterns. I've chosen Persian carpets in jewel tones of red and blue. The furniture, like this in the cottage, which I'm taking along, is mahogany. It's polished, but softly, so that it gleams."

René had nodded. "Thank you, darling," he had said. "It will be a quiet and restful home."

The next trip he made to the city was in February. He found Olive enceinte, beautiful and glowing with health. Already, at three months, he condition was apparent; it was the first thing he noticed.

"No!" he groaned.

She laughed, the sound richer than he had ever heard it. "But yes! Three months, and not a sick moment, not a pain, not a twinge." She became gently solemn. "The doctor says this time I'm certain to bear a living child. Before there were—signs—and this time there aren't."

"Thank God," he said. "And thank God this time you'll be at Rivard, not across the whole damned bayou country. When—what month?"

"August, darling. Our son will be born in your bayou country and grow up in the house his father has provided!"

"You're mighty certain it'll be a boy," he growled, teasing. Inwardly, he was frantic, as well as furious that her sweet body was swelling—his doing—again. He held her with tenderness.

He wouldn't make love to her, wouldn't risk injuring her. Not once, during the entire fortnight, did he do more than hold, kiss, and caress her.

Before he left, he put the emerald earrings on her delicate earlobes. The earrings made her eyes even softer and lovelier than he had dreamed. He asked her to wear them the first time he made love to her at Rivard, after the child was born.

"Of course," she smiled. "Once you put a jewel on me, I never take it off." She touched the pendant, reminding him.

As an afterthought, he purchased a diamond brooch to take home to Carita and a thin gold chain with a small gold cross for Euphemie.

ELEVEN

When all was finished at L'Acadie, René took Carita to New Orleans for her fling. The house party was to be assembled at L'Acadie on their return, of which she approved. She was lovely and happy and excited, wanting to do everything in New Orleans at once.

They stayed at René's usual hotel, taking the largest suite. Carita and Serephina spent the days shopping and with dressmakers, and René saw to business matters. Each evening Carita, René, Serephina and Pierre made the rounds of the fine restaurants and took in all the music and dramatic presentations the city offered.

One evening, after they'd dined grandly and attended a concert, they had coffee in the Leblanc suite. Serephina and Carita discussed the coiffures, gowns, and jewels of the other ladies they had seen that evening, which eventually led to local gossip. Suddenly the name Rivard caught René's ear, and he began to listen. Carita was speaking casually.

"That's the place down from us that's been vacant so long," she was saying. We don't know the people, so I'll not invite them to anything at ouah house party. That's for old-time friends and Leblanc connections. We'll have scads of comp'ny when we get home, you'll see! I don't think you've met them, Serephina. Aunt Hebert's there now, being hostess until I arrive." She flung out her hands charmingly, her smile flashing.

"I know her," Pierre said.

"She likes to stay in Old House. Lots of the guests are kin, fam'ly connections, as I said. The Perraults, the Cloutiers, the Hanins, and the Heberts, naturally—and—oh, scads!"

"Not all staying at L'Acadie?" marveled Serephina.

"Oh, no, but lots are. That's why I simply stole away even though the guests will be arriving. They *are* fam'ly, they know what I've been through, and they urged me to do it this way. Aunt Hebert loves to be hostess, and the housekeepah runs the place anyway. We'll be there day aftah tomorrow, and no one's due until tomorrow."

"It's going to be wonderful!" exclaimed Serephina.

"I hope so! They'll just adore you. Oh, and I forgot! There's the Romeros—pure Spanish. Carla Romero is a real Spanish beauty. They're new. I'd hoped for more acceptable newcomahs by now, to trade dinnahs with, and the Romero's are perfect. But it doesn't look promising about Rivard, because a widow's moving in—Consuela told me."

"A *widow*! What a shame!"

"What's the shame?" Pierre asked, daring to grin.

"If that isn't just like a man! It's important to Carita that neighbors be acceptable. With a widow, there's the seating problem at the table, and no escort. It makes things awkward for Carita, mistress of a great place like L'Acadie, expected to set the *tone* of the entire area!"

René kept his face blank. He caught Pierre's amused glance, but could only look stonily back. He saw his friend's eyes become sober, then regard him sharply as the wives continued to discuss the widow.

"Where's she from?" Serephina asked.

"New Orleans, Consuela found out."

"Rivard," Serephina mused. "Is that the name of the plantation or the widow?"

"Both."

"H'm'm. No, I've nevah met any Rivards," Serephina mused on, "though the name seems familiar." She brightened. "Maybe René's grandfathah knows.

67

He's been around forever, you say. Or René—*you* know ev'rything."

"Sorry," René said.

"I imagine," Pierre commented with a sharp look at René, "that you'll deal with the problem of the widow, Carita."

She flashed him a smile. "Certainly! I'm not going to associate with any *young* widow who'd live alone on a plantation! And if she's an oldah woman—" She moved her shoulders.

Pierre laughed. "Ladies never cease to amaze me," he declared. "René, join me in the room across the corridor for a smoke—if the ladies will consent."

"Please do," Carita said, and Serephina nodded. "We've got things to discuss—what we'll do during the trip and the dinnah I'm giving the last night in Serephina's honah!"

"Don't spin it out, please," Pierre said as they left. "It's past midnight now, we've still got the drive home, and we must be ready, as well as have our son ready, to join our friends at the boat at noon."

The men crossed the corridor. René entered the room first, and Pierre closed the door, then turned, his face gaunt. "What, in God's name, are you up to?" he demanded.

"What, in God's name, are you talking about?" countered René. But he knew.

"It's Olive Rivard, isn't it?"

René stared at this friend who somehow knew, and had kept, his secret. He felt his body stiffen and the blood drain from his face. He closed his hands into fists.

"No fight," Pierre warned, his voice taut. "My God, ami, I know how you feel, I know what it's like, what you've gone through these years, imprisoned for months on end at L'Acadie, the hell you must have lived through to get time in New Orleans."

René loosened his fists. The hell with it. So Pierre had known.

"Did Angeline—?" Pierre asked.

"No. Thank God. No."

"I never forgot how smitten with Olive you were that night at the ball when I made my arrangements for Zoe. I saw enough—you didn't know I was alive. Later Zoe told me Olive was living in the Garden District, passing as the wife of a sea captain named Rivard. Now, suddenly, a 'widow' Rivard turns up near L'Acadie, and already Carita's talking about her. You'll never put it over, René!"

"There's no way for it to get out. The overseer knows nothing; the slaves were bought here in the city. The grapevine can't get hold of a thing."

"How are you going to visit her? How long do you think it'll be before one of those blacks at Rivard sees you slipping up—"

"I've got to have her there."

"Why, man—why? Here, in New Orleans, it's common practice. And I know your philosophy of life, which is to enjoy, to charm, to get what you want, yet to be kind. I've seen it since we were lads and am much like that myself."

"That's one reason we get on so well," René said thoughtfully. "I suppose, in my case, I'm the product of the rich, easy plantation environment, used to having what I want from birth on."

"But this, René! To take your mistress to St. Martinville, where everybody is blood kin or family connection! Why invite—why subject Olive to it?"

René told him bluntly. He told of the stillborn son, of the child soon to be born. On hearing this, Pierre dropped into a chair, then held his head. René slumped into another chair, deeply miserable.

Pierre looked up. "What do you think our ladies will do when they find out about the widow's baby? You'd better reconsider. Call it off. You're going headlong for tragedy, for ruin, you damned fool!"

"Olive's already at Rivard."

"Carita—"

"There's nothing," René heard himself say, "that Carita can do about it if she does find out."

"Nothing but make your life a hell on earth."

"Then," René said, getting to his feet. "I'll have to

make certain she doesn't find out!" He tried to smile at his friend, to smile with all the warmth and charm that had never failed to win him what he wanted. He failed; his heart twisted at the plight of Olive, of Carita, at the fact he might be ruining both their lives.

"René," Pierre said, low.

Still he couldn't smile. "Carita mustn't find out," he repeated, sick within. "For I shouldn't be happy in hell. Nor would Carita and Olive, mon ami."

When they were alone, Carita gaily demanded that René wait in the sitting room. "I want Consuela to brush my hair," she said. "I'm going to be more beautiful for you than I was this evening!"

As she danced away into the bedchamber, René loosened his shirt and sat down, suddenly weary. Soon he would go across the hall so Apollo could help him, but not yet. He knew what his mercurial wife was about; she was grooming herself for lovemaking. As always when she had been stimulated—in this case, the gay evening—she delighted in luring and conquering him. Not that he minded. On the contrary, he had never failed to find delight in the encounter.

Despite his talk with Pierre, he almost smiled to himself over her tricks. He couldn't think about the retaliation should she ferret out his secret. Barring everything but the pleasure to come, he went across-corridor to disrobe.

When at last he was admitted to Carita, he found her in a nightdress the exact red of her hair. Her diamond necklace glittered above the shimmering silk gown; her eyes were more wildly blue than ever. Twin bracelets burned their diamond beauty on her arms, and her green wedding band glowed as she spread her diaphanous skirt.

"Well. What do you think? You've nevah seen me in anything but aquamarine before. How do you like this on me, darling?"

He never knew what to expect from her. He had come to accept her heated statement that she would die, simply die, before she'd let herself be seen in any color other than blue-green, and now she had put on a garment that swirled and looked like fire, and he was bewitched.

"You're exquisite," he said, moving toward her.

She danced away. "I keep you guessing, don't I?"

"Yes, you witch, you—" He moved faster, his one need to get his hands on her.

She stayed just out of reach. "Would you want me any othah way?" she teased. "Any diff'rent than I was at the Circus—at the concert. Would you change me?"

"You're damned right, I'll change you, here and now!" he half shouted. He caught her and held her, vibrant and unstruggling, and with his free hand he stripped the fiery wisp of silk off her.

Dropping his own robe, René pulled her nude body against his and danced her about the room. She began to laugh, and the bright sound made a beat, as of music, and he stepped to the beat, feeling her vibrant breasts move against him. He pressed her closer; her laughter was low and melodious now, and he felt the brush of her thighs against his, the kiss of the hair between.

He threw her on the bed, and she held out her arms to him, laughing, and when he would have bestrode her, she slipped away and went dancing about the room alone, dipping and swaying, nude but for jewels and flying hair.

He stumbled after her; she eluded him.

Then, suddenly, she had him by the hand and was tugging him to the bed, onto it.

The next morning Carita sat up in bed so unexpectedly that she woke René, who started. She began to shriek with laughter, sitting back, her breasts quivering, her whole lovely body adorned with jewels. "You didn't know I was awake!" she cried. "I've been watching you, and I vow, youah the handsomest thing in the whole world!"

He gazed at her in puzzlement, then began to laugh. She gave him a keen look, but finding only indulgence in him, she pouted and began to fiddle with her bracelets, to hold out her wrists and admire.

He reached out for her, but she slid out of bed, stood impatiently and gazed helplessly about. "Wheah's that lazy wench?" she fretted. "I want my gown and robe!"

René, himself naked, rolled to the other side of the bed and lifted her nightdress from a stool. Taking it to her, he lowered it over her head, then held her robe so she could put her arms into the sleeves.

She belted it, pouting, tossing her hair back. Then she slid her hands under her mass of hair and flipped it from under the robe so it rippled and flamed down her back.

"Oh, for heaven's sake!" she cried. "Get youah clothes on! If theah's anything a lady hates, it's to see a man. . . . Put on youah robe and go find that wench. I vow, I'll have her whipped!"

"No whipping of L'Acadie blacks," he reminded her idly, shrugging into his robe. "I told Apollo not to disturb us, that we'd send for him, and he's told Consuela."

"Since when does my slave take ordahs from a buck? She *knows* I've got to have my coffee the instant I open my *eyes!*"

René looked at his watch. "I ordered the tray at nine if I didn't send before that. It's five minutes yet. Where do you want it, on this table, or in the sitting room?"

"In heah, silly!"

Consuela and Apollo arrived promptly, the small black valet bearing the tray. While he arranged the table at the windows, Consuela brushed her mistress's hair and tied it back with a flame-colored ribbon.

"You serve us," Carita ordered. "Apollo, you leave."

She permitted René to seat her. When he had taken his own chair, Consuela poured some of the steaming coffee into Carita's cup. Its rich, full aroma curled into the room.

Carita waved her hand before her face. "Whatevah's the mattah with the coffee?" she fretted.

"I didn't know somethin' was wrong, Missy," Consuela said, pot in hand. At René's nod, she poured his cup. He ladled cream into it and added sugar as Consuela anxiously did the same for her mistress. "Or do you want me to pour this out and fix anothah one, Missy?"

"Where did it come from—who made it?"

"Apollo, Missy. He went to the kitchen like he been doing. He made it himself, Missy."

"It smells *terrible*! Take it away. Get a new pot!"

René sipped cautiously. "Tastes fine to me," he said. "Tastes like it always does."

"Well, it's not the same! Anybody with a delicate nature could tell you that! It *smells*! So call that buck, Consuela, and take this cup away. Take the whole pot away unless the mastah wants it."

"Leave the pot," René said.

After Consuela had gone, René took an empty cup, poured it half full of coffee, ladled cream into it the way Carita liked it, added a generous amount of sugar, then stirred. He set it at her place, hoping that the cream would weaken whatever odor had assailed her sensitive nostrils.

"Try it," he urged. "You had a wearing day yesterday. It's not too strange that even coffee might be a bit offensive, but a few sips will bring you alive—they always do."

She pouted, but lifted the cup and sipped. She kept sipping. "I just hope it does work," she moaned. "It's so hot it's scalding my stomach, and it's got a taste it shouldn't have, you can't deceive me. Consuela'd bettah get me some decent coffee!"

Apollo came in at this point with a tray of food. He placed a shaved slice of ham on Carita's plate, a small serving of grits, a buttered biscuit, and some marmalade. When he reached for the gravy, she gestured impatiently, and he then offered each serving dish in turn to René, who helped himself generously.

After Apollo was dismissed, they began to eat, Carita taking very small bites. She was frowning slightly, as though she found the food distasteful. In fact, she looked so much like a spoiled child that René grinned.

"What you smirkin' about?" she demanded. "I vow,

let me feel tired, and ev'rything tastes like *slop!* And you sit and gorge youahself like a—"

She clapped a hand to her mouth, sprang up, and ran for the bathroom. He was at her heels, but even so she was hanging over the basin vomiting when he caught up to her.

My God, he thought, there *is* something wrong. Trust Carita with her fine sensibilities to spot bad food, to be stricken. Retching, she swayed, and he took her arms from behind to steady her. She retched again.

At last, trembling, she turned. Her face was white. "You beast—you animal!" she whispered. And then she fainted.

René carried Carita to the bed, then shouted for Apollo to fetch a doctor. Carita revived before the doctor arrived but lay in the bed, white as the linen.

After the doctor had spoken privately with René in the sitting room and departed, René ordered Apollo to finish packing. He returned to the bedchamber, sent Consuela out, and faced his stricken bride.

"I'll send word to Pierre," he told her. "They can go on ahead and take part of our luggage. We can go on a boat later, when you feel better."

"That doctah said I can go today. I'm going."

"Maybe tomorrow—"

"It'll be no diff'rent than today."

"It may be, Carita."

"Beast," she said, lying there so white, so weak. "Animal! I could kill you, that's what I should do, kill you dead! You just won't leave me alone, will you? You simply will not control youahself! I hope youah satisfied! This was to be ouah honeymoon, Dolores is only a year old, and now you've got me enceinte again!"

He didn't know whether to comfort or reassure her. That she believed that he should suffer guilt and remorse was evident. She was waiting for him to apologize, but he'd be damned if he'd do that. They had not discussed future children, and perhaps that had been a mistake, but she was his wife, mistress of L'Acadie, mother of Dolores, and she knew an heir was needed. Also, despite her tendency to swoon, she was basically strong. No, he wouldn't apologize.

She sensed what had gone through his mind. "This is the last time!" she cried in white-hot rage. "I'm no breeding wench! If this baby isn't a boy, if you don't get youah precious heir this time, you'll nevah have one! You can set youah mind to marryin' Dolores to a Creole and hyphenate Leblanc to *his* name!"

"You're not yourself, Carita. Once over the shock, you won't feel this way."

"Oh, yes I will! I won't face it ovah and ovah, being sick ev'ry morning, getting all swollen, wondering if I'll evah be the same again, I won't!"

"You'll be the same. You were after Dolores, just the same, only more beautiful. You'll be even more beautiful after this baby."

"I won't endure that pain and torture again! You sneaked up on me, didn't give me any time, none at all! Why, I hadn't even thought, hadn't considahed whethah I'd be willing, undah any circumstances—and now look at me! *Trapped!*"

He felt sorry for her, but didn't take her into his arms. She couldn't be allowed to continue this hysterical self-pity. Rage would be better, one of her genuine, fighting, physical rages.

Deliberately, he tried to provoke that rage. "You haven't exactly held me off," he said. "And, I'd say, you've been enjoying yourself, too. Take last night for example—that nightdress and the romp we had, a better, longer romp than usual!"

She flew out of bed, face contorted. "*Romp!*" she screamed. She whirled to the dresser, snatched the small jeweled dagger she used for everything from breaking the seal on a letter to cleaning her fingernails, and came at him. "I'll kill you! I'll cut youah heart out! I'll . . . !"

Quickly, but not before the point of the dagger had drawn blood at his shoulder, he caught her. He gave her arm a twist and the dagger fell.

She broke into a screaming storm of tears. It took moments before he was able to hold her close and comfort her.

TWELVE

By the time they left the hotel, Carita felt well. "Don't you tell Pierre, now," she warned.

"I wouldn't think of it, darling."

"I may tell Serephina when we get home, and I may not. I may not let anybody know, evah."

"That won't be easy to accomplish."

"Oh, hush! Consuela knows, she's got to. And you tell that buck that if it gets out at L'Acadie befoah I tell—if evah I do—if the nigras find out and it gets on the grapevine and people all ovah the bayou country go to *watching*, that silly rule about no whipping goes out, bang!"

René kept his face sober, but he was grinning inwardly as they joined Pierre and Serephina, along with their two-year-old son Pierre, his nurse, their maid and their valet, at the waterfront. Carita greeted Serephina as though it had been months since they had met. She kissed baby Pierre, who sat scowling in his nurse's arms and passed the servants as though they didn't exist.

Aboard the steamboat, Carita was the center of their party all afternoon and evening. René began to speculate as to whether the doctor had made a mistake and to wonder if her illness might actually have been the result of yesterday's bloody excitement.

The next morning banished such speculation. She woke early, sent Consuela for coffee, swallowed it down, then ran for the basin. She didn't faint—she was too outraged to do so, René thought—and she didn't vomit as long. But she was fully as ill, as white and weak.

"I'll stay in bed until noon," she quavered. "Serephina won't think anything of it. I told her I want to be at my best when we get home."

She ate noon dinner in their suite, and did not vomit again. If she still felt shaken, if there was lingering weakness, it wasn't evident, and René avoided inquiring. She hadn't turned on him again, and, once with their guests at L'Acadie, he trusted that her unhappiness would be eased.

After dinner, the four of them sat on deck watching the shore slide past as the vessel made her way along Bayou Teche. Other passengers were sitting, strolling, chatting, or standing at the rail, those who knew the Leblancs pausing to exchange a few words.

Viewing his homeland, aware of the muggy heat, then trying to see through the eyes of the exclaiming Serephina, René let the beauty of it come into him. Below New Iberia, which was some thirty miles from St. Martinville, the Teche was broader and deeper, the plantations larger, the houses finer, and there were fewer trees growing on its banks. Here were palatial residences, eclipsed only by his own L'Acadie.

The bayou followed a winding course the last five miles. Serephina exclaimed at its width, comparing it to some of the lower reaches.

"My God!" Pierre exclaimed as St. Martinville came into view. "I knew the fire did a great deal of harm, but—did everything burn?"

"The entire business district burned to the ground!" Carita cried. "It was right aftah that awful yellow fevah. It wasn't enough that we had to have the fevah. Then ev'ry shop in town was gone, and we couldn't buy a thing!"

"I see some new buildings," Pierre remarked.

"A few," René said. "It takes time to rebuild. Debris had to be cleared up, property changed hands because some shop owners died. Then there have been arrangements, building plans, money to assemble."

"It's just been one disastah aftah anothah!" Carita declared. Then she fell silent, in a near pout.

"That's two—fevah and fire," Serephina said. "There'll be anothah. They come in threes."

Carita's pout suddenly became the real thing.

René's party was greeted at the L'Acadie landing, which they reached by pirogue, by an assemblage of guests, calling out, waving, laughing. Children were racing about and shouting.

Old René, attended by Hippolyte, waited on the landing, surrounded with guests. To René, he appeared both frail and wiry strong in the evening light. René led Serephina and Pierre first to his grandfather, then waited while the old gentleman shook hands with Pierre, and Serephina and her son were presented. Then Carita held up her cheek for a kiss, and, as she lightly kissed Dolores, held by Lura, René, unexpectedly moved, embraced his grandfather.

"I must talk to you," Old René muttered.

René pressed the old man's shoulders in agreement, embraced Hippolyte, and the two old men turned and walked toward Old René's carriage. They waited while Aunt Hebert greeted the arrivals, after which she, too, got back into the carriage, which then moved away.

The guests closed in, the men shaking hands, slapping backs, and swearing mildly, the women squealing, kissing, and hugging. Serephina and Pierre were introduced to everyone.

Gill Hebert darted here and there, small, dark, wiry, marshaling his offspring. "My sons, René," he announced, pushing forward two small boys of perhaps six and eight, who resembled him. "Michel and Emil. You remember them, no?" Gill, though no blood kin, was looked upon as a cousin. René chuckled, then tousled the dark hair of the boys. He embraced Gill's fat American wife, who had been Frankie Griggs, knelt to hold the two little girls, Eda and Lillian, younger than the boys, fatter than their mother.

"This is your cousin René and your cousin Carita," Frankie said in her great, resounding voice.

Carita smiled, shook hands with the parents and

with the boys, then patted the little girls on the head. They stared up at her, their eyes like raisins. René observed that they, as his own daughters had done, were giving Carita instant, unsolicited adoration.

Watching them reminded him of Euphemie, and he looked for her. She was at the far edge of the crowd and came gracefully to him walking as Angeline had walked, and they embraced.

"Youah all settled?" Carita asked Frankie. Absently, she accepted Euphemie's kiss. "Did Mrs. Ramsey give you propah chambahs—and the children?"

"She sure did!" Frankie said heartily. "The girls are in Old House with their nurses, and the boys are in one of the boys' houses. It's a pleasure to see you, Cousin Carita. I've pitched in and helped Aunt Hebert and Mrs. Ramsey my best. Everybody's all sorted out."

Carita nodded, smiled, then turned to the next group. Admiring her untroubled manner and her faultless hospitality, René devoted himself to his duties as host.

He greeted Cesaire Hebert, Aunt Hebert's nephew, down from Baton Rouge and exchanged a cousinly kiss with Louise, Cesaire's childless wife. There were Charle Landry, his wife Claire, and their son; Charle's sister Nanetta and her husband, Justin Belacourt, their two small, loud sons, and their four daughters; Baptiste Robineaux and his wife Clothilde; Clotis Pere and his enceinte Felice; and Omar Bouard and his talkative Lydia, whom the other ladies accused laughingly of chattering to herself if she had no one else.

Justin Belacourt, his short, fat body rippling with laughter, shouted, "Well, René, we stole a march on you! Everybody's here and accounted for! We couldn't have surprised you more if we had conspired to arrive early to greet our host and hostess. It's a great pleasure."

"Indeed it is!" René laughed.

The entire party began moving up the long avenue between the moss-weeping rows of live oaks to L'Acadie, their voices loud, excited, laughing. The slaves, who had waited at a distance, took up the trunks, bags, and boxes and trudged along after them.

When they reached the gallery, Aunt Hebert drew Carita aside and offered to show the Le Fleurs to their suite. "They'll want to settle in," she said, "and you'll be held back by all the others."

Graciously Carita accepted the old lady's offer. At long last she bore René away to their own rooms, tore off her bonnet, and flung it at Consuela, who caught it and fled into the bedchamber.

"She knows!" Carita cried. "That old woman *knows* I'm enceinte!"

"Aunt Hebert—how could she know?"

"She took one look, and she knew! There's something about a woman's eyes who's enceinte—some silly look around the eyes! I nevah believed it, but I *saw* her, and I saw her *know!* She'll tell, and befoah tonight ev'rybody on this plantation'll know!"

"She won't say anything. She's discreet."

"Just the same! Well, if it shows so much, if she can tell just by looking at my eyes, she must know how to get rid of it! And she'd bettah tell me, 'cause this minute, this instant, I've made up my mind I'm not going through with it, I just am not!"

René stared at her. "You don't mean that, Carita."

"I'm a human being, a lady. My flesh hurts when it's torn. I have delicate sensibilities that make my pain keenah than the pain of ordinary women!"

"If you—it's murder."

"But not when you miscarry!"

"Just the same, you said—"

She began to weep. "How can you put a bad meaning on me? It's just that I'm so sick and upset!"

His impulse was to seize Carita and shake her, but instead he reminded her evenly, "You said that you want Aunt Hebert to tell you how to kill my child."

"Do you actually b'lieve I'd ask that old lady *anything?*" she wailed. "I wouldn't have to! Consuela—but I'll miscarry by myself, from my own delicate—oh, this awful heat!"

She whirled, and a high note entered her weeping.

"Consuela, get youah worthless self in heah! Go away, René. I've got to make myself beautiful, the way a hostess has got to be!"

The following morning, heat clamped over the bayou like a baking lid. Carita fainted, this time before breakfast.

René had just lowered Carita to the sofa and Consuela was trying to revive her when there was a soft knock on the door. René opened the door. It was Serephina and Frankie, who, when they saw their hostess unconscious, hurried to her.

Eventually, Carita revived, and spoke briefly to Serephina and Frankie. She tried to send them away, but they insisted upon staying to help her. After they left, Carita ate, vomited, and the doctor came and left, having verified the pregnancy, Then, René was told by his bride to leave their rooms. He was reluctant, yet eager to escape. Yet there was no real purpose to escape, for it would be madness to go to Olive at this time.

Still, although she had ordered him out, Carita detained him. "What are you frowning about?" she demanded.

After everybody's asleep tonight, he thought, after Carita's asleep. Then I can see Olive.

"Shouldn't you go back to bed?" he countered.

"Fiddlesticks! I'll be all right now until tomorrow morning! It's the same as befoah. Besides, you heard Serephina and that Frankie. They're coming back to sit with me."

"Along with others. Did you have to include others?"

"How could I keep from it? You just would call the doctah and that Frankie just would not leave, and she found out. Serephina'd nevah tell, but Frankie couldn't keep a secret if someone used a pistol on her. Oh, I know. There's not a mean bone in her body, she's honest and good, but she's so—American!"

René nodded, watching Carita. She did not look quite herself, but, kissing her lightly, he departed, stopping first at his grandfather's suite.

"You wanted to talk to me," he said, settling into the chair across the reading table from the old gentleman. "Sorry I didn't get to it last night."

"You had guests. This has to do with my journals."

René waited, as did Hippolyte, who was sitting at an open window.

"Certain information has reached me," Old René said, "which indicates that now is the time for you to read those journals."

"If you like," René agreed, puzzled.

"There's a bit I must add, then I'll put them into your hands."

"Whatever you say, Grandfather."

"You will read them? At once?"

"Of course," René promised, wondering how, with L'Acadie filled with guests, he was going to steal the time.

After René had gone, Carita kept Consuela on the run, fetching garments, changing the position of a chair, a vase, moving the glass-domed clock to a table, pushing back draperies so any breath of air could get into the muggy rooms.

Despite the unendurable heat, despite her own impossible condition, she became fiercely energetic, trying the sofa cushions this way and another, seeing to it that the roses were perfectly arranged. Then Consuela arrayed her in a new, sheer cotton dress of such a delicate aquamarine it was almost white. Because she was so hot, Carita stripped off the jewels in which she even slept, keeping on only her wedding ring.

She examined herself in the mirror, leaning close to make certain the pallor had left, that her skin showed its normal glow. Yes, it was fine. And her lips were as always, with no need for any of the salves she kept hidden at the back of a drawer. In no degree did she look less than herself. The pregnancy was no disadvantage on this occasion when first she was to enter onto more intimate terms with the elite of the bayou country.

Even so, her pulse raced as she received the chosen—Serephina, distant Leblanc cousins, wives of cousins, Aunt Hebert. It isn't different from holding court, she thought as they seated themselves in her room. She smiled, and her tone sparkled as she made them welcome, charmed and enchanted them, making a special effort with Aunt Hebert, who accepted the best chair.

Carita led the conversation along various paths. Then, before the women could give her secret, searching looks, Carita cried, "Yes, it's true, I'm enceinte. I'm goin' to give René his heir!"

She watched their delight and hated them for it. She listened to them gasp and give their graciously worded congratulations. She permitted a small and regal smile to touch her lips as they exuded admiration for her beauty, her daughter's beauty, that of L'Acadie, and for her exciting condition.

"You're like a princess!" exclaimed Nanetta.

Their adulation became her wine. If she were a princess, then these commoners—Frankie, Nanetta, Louise, Claire, Clothilde, Felice, Lydia—were her ladies-in-waiting. Serephina, Creole Serephina, was her favored lady-in-waiting. Even Aunt Hebert—well, she was a dowager at court, bleak eyes or no.

"Goodness!" Carita exclaimed. "That's enough about me! We've got to discuss the dinnah and ball, such as they've nevah seen in the bayou country. And that's in just two weeks. We must discuss clothes because we in this room have got to be the most beautiful theah!"

For an hour, the women excitedly discussed the upcoming affair. They decided on decorations, music, silks, satins, jewels, coiffures, food, and wines. They described other, similar events, and chattered about guests who were to be invited from plantations along the bayous. Their excitement mounted and their voices rose and blended like music in the airless, hot room.

"Where'll you put up all these guests from Bayou Lafourche and ev'rywhere?" cried the excitable Lydia Bouard. Her black hair had loosened and threatened to tumble down about her piquant Acadian face.

83

"You've got L'Acadie filled, and you're talking about maybe fifty more!"

"Some will stay at Hebert Plantation," Carita said. "Also, René's spoken for rooms at the hotel—we'll have the hotel filled. And then some families have kin we've invited, and will entertain them."

"Are you invitin' ev'rybody from all the plantations?" Lydia asked.

Carita gave her a keen glance. This one had a reputation as a chatterbox. Still, though she'd just met Lydia, Carita knew there was something behind her seemingly innocent question.

"Not ev'rybody," she said, "but almost."

"You invitin' that Rivard woman?"

For no reason, Carita felt a stitch in her heart. "I've not met her," she said, "and none of my friends have, so theah's no obligation. Anyhow, I believe this Rivard person is a widow. She might considah an invitation in bad taste."

"She's pregnant, too," Frankie said baldly.

"But so'm I," exclaimed Felice Pere. "And Carita!"

"You're a connection, silly!" chided Nanetta. "And Carita's the hostess. Diff'rent from a strange, enceinte widow!"

Carita realized that she didn't like the name Rivard and didn't like to hear it mentioned. She had been hearing it with peculiar frequency.

"She wouldn't want to come," Frankie said. "She's a new widow. My maid found that out from some L'Acadie servant. She wouldn't be interested in a dinner and ball."

"She might have more interest than anybody," said Claire Landry.

All turned questioningly to her.

"A young widow wants a new husband," she explained. "Which means no man is safe. Because a new widow has a *wicked* attraction for many a man. It behooves us all to be careful. Husbands do—get tempted."

For a moment, the other ladies stared, stunned, at Claire. Then Lydia suddenly stood. "I'm going to see what my Omar's doing!" she declared. "Not just today, but all the time! Forewarned, you know." She laughed and chatted on, but made her excuses and tripped purposefully out.

There was a general move for departure, led by Aunt Hebert. Each young woman tarried to congratulate Carita anew, to embrace her, but at last Carita was alone with Serephina. She dropped onto the sofa and gazed at her friend.

"You poor darling," murmured Serephina. Then, "I nevah dreamed—Dolores is only a year old! And you didn't have *her* deliberately."

"Indeed I didn't. Why, I waited for just the right husband, and when René—I thought I was going to really live! That's all I've evah wanted, to *live*, to hold life in my hands, the Creole way. Oh, I re'lized a man'd want a son, but I meant to have pleasuah at least a reasonable time, and then there was Dolores. She's a perfect doll, and I love her right to her toenails, but I didn't want anothah baby! Not yet, and maybe nevah!"

"Then why did it happen, darling? Why did you let René—?"

"You know what a man's like! You've had a baby!"

"I have, indeed. And I put a stop to it."

"How, Serephina, how? Just tell me. It'll look like a miscarriage, won't it?"

"No, oh no—that's dang'rous! You could die!"

"I'll die anyhow!"

"You didn't with Dolores. The second one comes easier than the first. Ev'rybody says so. Besides, I don't know any way—"

"But you *said!*"

"Fortunately, I had a son. So, I said to Pierre, told him before I was able to get out of my bed, 'Darling, I've given you an heir. I've hated, despised, and loathed ev'ry month of discomfort and agony it has cost me, beginning on ouah wedding night and lasting to this minute. I've done my duty. I will submit to you once in a great while, if you take the best precautions. Othahwise, I'll be a mothah to ouah son, I'll run

85

youah home, I'll be youah hostess, I'll bear youah name, but I'll not be youah bed wench!"

Carita's eyes widened. "What did he say—do?"

"Oh, he argued and cursed. He talked about husbandly rights. But I've been firm. Sometimes—maybe his birthday—but he has to be very careful. To me the choice was easier, because Pierre isn't Acadian with that silly idea of having twenty children. He's satisfied with one son."

"René wants a son."

"He kept Angeline enceinte constantly."

"I'm no Angeline!" Carita cried. She heard the ache in her tone, the sob behind it. "I feel no—distaste, but I can't have all those babies! I'd be dead, just walking around. Because, if I can't live the way I want to, what am I going to *do*?"

"Have this baby. Then tell René, as I told Pierre. He'll do the same thing, all men do. Then you can live like a lady."

"You mean Pierre's got—someone else?"

"A placée. Down on the Ramparts. He's had her at least since young Pierre was born." Her eyes narrowed. "But when I considah it, I come to the same conclusion—he had that wench before he ever met me! He'd been with her all along and used me to grace his home and get his heir. Now it's a relief that he does have her."

"Doesn't it—hurt—to know?"

Serephina had paled. She nodded. "But I've got intelligence darling. I have the best of ev'rything. I bear the name of Le Fleur, hold the highest social position in New Orleans, have the greatest wealth. I have the most beautiful clothes to be found and so much fine jewelry I have to *think* what to wear. I have a fine son and practically complete freedom from the ugly side of my husband. He's thoughtful of me, he's kind and good company, and with him keeping his—well—lust undah control, I've got all the advantages."

"René can't keep a placée, it's too far. He'd nevah go to a wench on L'Acadie or any othah plantation.

And the women on the bayou and in St. Martinville—
he'll just have to *suffah!*"

"He'll not suffah. He'll find a way."

Carita, eyes locked with Serephina's, saw the
thought rise in her friend as it rose in herself. That
widow, that Rivard woman. She pushed it aside.
René, as yet, had no excuse to go looking elsewhere.

With a touch of sadness, Serephina rose. "I'm going
to join Pierre," she said. "He invited me to stroll in the
rose gardens."

Carita went to the door with her. She watched her
friend vanish along the corridor, then shouted, "Consuela! Get in heah!"

Consuela appeared from the bedroom.

"You heard what she said?"

Consuela murmured an affirmative.

"Then," Carita said, speaking fast and low, "don't
forget that the spy system Hippolyte's got is the
sneakiest thing I evah knew, and you've got to be bettah than he is. You mustn't delay. Now, here is what
you have got to do. . . ."

THIRTEEN

Each day seemed hotter, more airless, more humid
than the one preceding. The men spoke often of hurricane weather. One morning, Carita was so drenched
with perspiration that she ordered Consuela to fill her
bath with cool water. She lay back in it weakly, head
throbbing.

"It's so hot—I'm so sick!" she wailed to René another
morning. Her nightdress was pasted to her body, her
hair damp and unruly.

"It's this hurricane weather," he said.

"The last thing I need is a hurricane!"

There was a storm raging within her, against the
intruder in her body. Must she endure, as well, the

shriek of wind, the slant of rain, uprooted trees, a dis-ordered world?

"It's the last thing I need, too," René said. "It'd flatten the cane, ruin the crop. It would kill some of the cattle and keep us all shut in."

"I'm afraid of hurricanes."

"You're safe enough if you stay inside. L'Acadie's built to withstand them."

"Just the same, if a hurricane comes, you've got to stay with me, ev'ry minute! Promise, René!"

"I can't," he said flatly. "I've got the place and all our stock and our people. The guests. I didn't say a hurricane will come, Carita. I said it's hurricane weather."

That night she again wore the sheer nightdress that flamed like her hair. She wore it to tempt the husband who hadn't turned to her since the night in the hotel.

She stood in the lamplight, her beautiful limbs showing through the thin gown. She half closed her eyes at him and smiled. Her heart was beating fast, her knees were weak, her skin burning. She longed for the raging delight they had known, and now there was no reason to do without it.

She saw his eyes flare and caught her breath as he roughly pulled her to him. She tipped her head back and laughed, low.

He thrust her away. "No, Carita, no."

"Darling!" she cried, in alarm.

"It won't do, it won't do at all."

"Is it because I said no more babies?"

"It's this baby. I don't want to risk it."

"Risk what, for heaven's sake? With Dolores—"

"It isn't that I don't want to," he said, buttoning his nightshirt. His desire was evident in his eyes. "My God, any man would want. . . . Afterward, Carita. After the baby is born."

"There won't be any aftah! *Now's* the only time!"

"I'll wait," he said. "You'll feel differently later."

Long after he slept, she lay awake. She was in a fury at everything—René, the child in her womb, the guests, L'Acadie, the slaves, and the very existence of men, with their relentless power over women. He'll find out, she raged, he'll be sorry!

The next morning, she remembered the mysterious widow. When Consuela had helped her into the pale dress and pinned up her hair, she moved into the sitting room.

"I'm going to sit by the front window where it's shady," she said. "Bring a chair and fan me. The iv'ry fan, not that sickenin' sandalwood!"

"I wouldn't use the sandalwood, Missy. I know it make my Missy sick."

"I'm so mis'rable, I'm so terribly mis'rable!"

"Yes, Missy. How that feel, Missy? That nice breeze!"

"It helps." She closed her eyes. The empty weakness filled her. Gradually, her trembling stopped, and she knew that soon, if she sat quietly and absorbed the cooling breezes from the fan, she would be back to herself.

"I've waited and waited," she said presently, "for you to report what you've found out concerning that certain mattah, and you haven't told me one thing!"

"Missy been so sick. And it's not easy. I've got to watch for them nigras of Hippolyte's. And it takes time to get them Rivard nigras to be sociable."

"I didn't want you to go to Rivard, you fool!"

"I wouldn't go there, Missy. But remembah, one of the L'Acadie slaves I find things out from is Gussie."

"Mrs. Ramsey's cook at her own house?"

"Well, Gussie's daughtah, Tallah, is hot for a stud at Rivard—Rafe."

"Nevah mind his *name!*"

"Tallah tells me things 'cause I give her ribbons and petticoats Missy lets me have. When she sneaks ovah to Rafe, she finds there's a mystery at Rivard. She finds out from Ursina that her and Nette, the widow's maid—"

"Who is *Ursina*, you infuratin' —"

"She the wench the widow bought to help her maid, Nette. They the only slaves at Rivard that the ovah-seah didn't buy, and she the only one in the big house with Nette and the widow. All the slaves at Rivard are new to each othah."

Carita sat with her eyes closed, and now impressions she had barely noticed due to her sickness, her panic over her condition, and her preoccupation with guests, came to her.

René's moments of abstraction, his uneasiness, the times, since they had returned, that she didn't know where he was; the inability of Apollo to locate his master; René's shrug when he did appear, his careless reply that he had ridden here or there to see to this or that; his lack of protest when she told him she would not bear more children; and the comparative ease with which he now resisted her in bed.

Suddenly and instinctively she knew there was a connection between René and the Rivard widow. For no provable reason she knew, beyond a doubt, that René had a mistress and that his mistress was to bear his child. A vast, still wariness filled her.

"When is that Rivard baby expected?" she demanded.

"Any day, Missy, any houah. They ready and watching. Ursina say her mistress lost one baby, say Doctah Gilbert waiting to be called."

So. He was going to have Doctor Gilbert there, who had brought Dolores into the world, who had labored over Angeline. He was ready to dishonor both his dead wife and his living wife by having their physician attend his mistress! No wonder he was distraught! He was beside himself over the hussy he had smuggled into decent bayou country, over his by-blow! He was scared to death that she, his Creole wife, would ferret out his sin. Little did he dream that she knew, that she was positive. There remained only the proof. And that she would get.

She opened her eyes. "Now, Consuela," she said, "you are to follow the master, no matter where he goes, or when."

"Oh, Missy!" wailed Consuela. "He'll catch me!"

Carita's teeth gritted. "I wouldn't," she said, her voice like the edge of a honed blade, "hesitate to use my daggah to cut youah face all to pieces, you stinkin' black baggage!"

Consuela moaned. "Yes, Missy. What Missy want af-tah that?"

"We're going to set a trap, Consuela! A fine, sure trap!"

FOURTEEN

René lived on the edge of fear. He attended his duties as host; he was loving toward Carita, carelessly affectionate with Euphemie and Dolores, but he waited for any moment in which he could steal away to check on Olive's welfare. The last time, as he rode the byway, he had reined in and waited in shadow because it seemed he heard someone following.

But there had been only the narrow, deserted lane stretching behind, and he had ridden on. Imagination, he reflected, was playing tricks on him.

The stop shortened his time with Olive. He sat with her only moments, tormented by her thinness, by the ethereal quality to her face, by the tremendous bulge.

She assured him that she was in good health. "The doctor was here this afternoon, darling. He calls twice a week. He says there's no reason for concern." Her eyes were green and glowing, the tiny smile on her lips tender.

"I've got to know when it starts," he insisted.

"We'd be risking everything, darling. The doctor will be here, and Nette and Ursina. Also, one of the women in the Quarters is a midwife."

"She's not to touch you. Send Bremer. Send him to Ramsey."

"And what can he say, darling, without—?"

"My God!" he cried. "Anything'll do. Some matter on which he wants an opinion. No, that won't serve. Ramsey knows as much as I do, more. I wouldn't know Bremer had come. I've got it! He's to ask Ramsey that I consult Grandfather on the breeding of two of your blacks. That's as devious as the slaves' own grapevine, but it'll serve."

"In the middle of the night, René?" She asked, her voice full of both love and teasing.

He stared at her, his mind still working.

"In any event, darling," she asked, "is it wise for the Rivard overseer to consult about breeding slaves when his employer is in the labor of childbirth?"

His impotent rage deepened.

"If it happens at night," she promised, "I'll send for the doctor immediately. Next day I'll have Mr. Bremer come to L'Acadie on some pretext, and then you'll know it's over."

"That'll take too long. And I want to be with you."

"You daren't be with me, my darling. But I'll keep you informed. I promise."

Forty-eight hours passed, and there was no word. He grew uneasy; the baby was almost a week overdue. He had to go over there tonight, as soon as the household drifted off to bed, or before that, if he could.

Rain had begun to gust in mid-afternoon and hadn't stopped. All the men were predicting a hard rainstorm if not an actual hurricane, and Ramsey ordered the slaves to drive in as much of the stock as the stables would hold and had them close the storm shutters on the various houses and cabins.

He ordered the boys in the boys' houses to move into L'Acadie, Old House and Honeymoon House after a strong wind sprang up. He suggested that those mothers who desired either join their children in Honeymoon House or bring them to their own rooms at Old House and L'Acadie.

There ensued much moving and arranging. The storm continued and increased. A hush fell upon all.

Husbands assured wives that it might be only a rain-storm. Now, in unspoken accord, families gathered in their separate and crowded quarters to wait out the storm.

Darkness fell early, rain blackening the dusk into night. At one point, René and Carita met at the foot of the great staircase. She was fretfully wielding her fan.

"I'm so *hot!*" she complained. "I vow, the minute it begins to rain and blow and we could be cool, you have ev'rything shuttered."

"This storm's got all the aspects of a hurricane, Carita. We daren't wait until winds of seventy-five or a hundred miles an hour blow before we batten down. In fact," he continued, seizing the opportunity, "I'm going to ride out and see to things."

"In the dark—in a hurricane?"

He nodded, watching. Her expression showed she considered this foolishness. Suspicion glinted in her eyes, and he wondered when and how and of what she may have become suspicious.

"I've got too much involved to neglect anything," he said, and this was true. It was also true all precautions had been taken already. "There's nothing I can do for the cane crop."

"I want you with me, in this house!" She suddenly felt very uneasy.

"As soon as possible," he said, meaning it. Abruptly, without speaking, she turned and went up the stairs, around the curve, and out of sight.

Gill Hebert came out of the library. "I heard what you told Carita," he said. "Let me go with you. It's been a while since I've experienced a hurricane, and I'd bet my best racing horse that's what we've got—hear that wind!"

The wind came, hitting the great house broadside, driving rain against the structure. But L'Acadie stood unshakable under blast after blast.

"I'd rather you take charge here while I'm out," René told Gill. "That is, if Frankie and the children are here."

"In our rooms on the third floor."

"Good. Then you'll take charge?"

"Anything, René, anything to help."

The wind and rain again hurled itself violently upon L'Acadie. Gill shook his head. "Take care, René. Get back inside before it hits full force."

René lost no time getting into oilskins and boots, for it was already nine o'clock. Pushed sideways by the pelting wind, he ran as best he could to the big stable, his lantern a yellow, jumping dot in the streaming blackness. He burst into the stable, shouting for the night boy, who jumped off his bed of straw, rubbing his eyes.

"Saddle Prince—fast!"

"Yas, suh," the boy mumbled.

René waited impatiently, listening to sounds of the storm. Once, at the far edge of lantern shadow, there was a flicker of movement. When it wasn't repeated, he reasoned it had been a cat.

He swung into the saddle, urged Prince into the howling night, and put him to a gallop. There was no danger of being heard over the storm. He leaned forward, urging Prince faster.

Olive could, at this moment, be in her agony, for it was past her time. The doctor might not be able to get to her, might be somewhere else, bringing some other baby into this hurricane-swept night.

He pushed on, rain covering his face, driving into his eyes, and running down his neck. He used the whip, and Prince sprang heavily on, but the speed gained was nothing, for the wind held them back.

Ahead, at last, he saw the house. The area around the house was deserted. He rode into the stable, fought the door shut, then wakened the stable boy. Then he fought with another, smaller door and went stumbling and diving toward the house.

He staggered across the back gallery and yanked open the kitchen door. The room was deserted, though an iron teakettle was steaming fiercely.

As he was stripping off his wet outer garments, Ursina came thumping in. She hastened to set down the bucket of slops she carried.

"Mastah," she said. Her plain face broke in a grin. "The mistress—?"

"She fine, mastah. Baby fine. Doctah bin an' went. Don' fret, none of us tell 'bout you an' Miss Olive . . ."

René raced from the kitchen, streaked through the lower floor, up the stairs, into Olive's chamber. Like a startled bird, Nette flew up from a chair, her finger to her lips.

Olive lay sleeping in obvious exhaustion. Her hair fanned across the pillow; the emeralds glimmered at her ears; the pendant moved with her breathing.

Some great hand clutched his throat, and there was thunder in his ears.

"Mastah," breathed Nette, "the mistress is safe. If mastah will come into the nursery?"

He followed into the room that Olive had prepared, a small and cozy chamber. Nette led him to the white-painted basket, and as he stopped beside it, Ursina entered and stood too, in a state of entrancement. Nette gestured, and Ursina hurried out.

René looked down at the new little face, so red against the linen. He looked at the swirl of hair, darker than Olive's, lighter than his own. He looked at the crumpled fists, red too, touched with dimples.

"A boy, mastah," Nette murmured.

The clutching in his throat swelled. His son and Olive's. Heir to Rivard.

"What did the doctor say?"

"He said Miss Olive is well and needs only rest. Her time came fast, at six o'clock. The doctah at seven, and the baby was born at ten minutes past eight."

She hadn't had time to send Bremer. If he hadn't been uneasy, if he hadn't come now, he wouldn't have known until after the hurricane.

He returned to Olive, sat beside her bed, and watched her sleep. The storm grew, rattling the shuttered windows. Ursina had stolen back to sit with the baby, her teeth chattering with fear of the storm, but so entranced that she pleaded with Nette not to send her to bed. Nette stayed in the nursery with her, stealing in, now and again, to check on her mistress.

When he left, reluctantly, René laid a note on Olive's bed table. Already, should Carita still be awake, he faced an inquisition as to why it had taken him so long. Though he wanted only to stay, he must leave to protect Olive.

It was past midnight when René reached home through the whirling deluge that drove bits of wood and tree branches through the darkness. The crackle and flash of lightning blazed from time to time. Trees bowed to the ground, pressing their sodden heads to the earth. Then released, they sprang up violently, only to be bowed again. The sugar cane lay flat, drowned by the thick downpour.

Prince went into the stable at a trot, and René dismounted. The night boy had been watching, waiting. A blast of wind struck; the boy winced as if he'd been hit.

"You're safe in here," René told him. "Dry Prince off, rub him down, feed him."

René fought through the storm and the flying debris to the house. He shed his oilskins in the kitchen, then made for the front hallway. The house was quiet, everyone closed away, sleeping or keeping watch according to their natures.

He was suddenly very tired, not convinced that Olive was as strong as Nette claimed, and uneasy lest Carita challenge him about his more than three-hour absence.

Which she did the instant he entered their suite.

She was in the sitting room, wearing a robe, and many jewels. Everything about her was glittering.

"Don't open youah mouth!" she cried. "I know where you've been! Consuela followed you to the stable and saw which way you rode—she's followed you befoah, all the distance—and I know why you went! I've got proof. You didn't go out in this hurricane to look ovah L'Acadie, not for three *houahs!*"

"Even you," he heard himself say brutally,

"wouldn't send Consuela out in this storm. Not even you would do that."

"Wouldn't I, though? She found out, and I found out. Oh, goodness, what I found out!" Her eyes were blue fire, her lips twitching. "You didn't stay with youah wife, mothah of youah daughtah, enceinte again. You didn't bothah to protect *me* from this hurricane."

"I'm here, Carita. The hurricane's still blowing, still building. It isn't half over yet, because the lull hasn't come."

"Don't try to change the subject!" she shrieked. "I know about that Rivard woman, what she is to you! I know she's havin' youah by-blow, youah—"

"Shut up!" he shouted.

"You beast! You perfidious, low-down creature! How dare you treat me, a Creole lady, in this mannah? Oh, I know enough, don't think I don't! Consuela found out. One of the Rivard nigras caught something that Ursina said to that Nette, and it gave the whole thing away. You've had this widow for a mistress I don't know how many yeahs. That I might ovahlook. Any lady might—her husband having a mistress befoah he married, but for him to keep her, a common, white-trash hussy aftah he's married a Creole, aftah she's brought him a fortune, is unspeakable! Then, for him to bring his hussy to within three miles and give her a plantation and fathah a by-blow and go running to her—oh, you should be challenged to a duel for what you've done to me! If only I had a brothah to call you out!"

Carita's tirade was interrupted by a subdued, persistent rapping at the door. Angrily, René opened it. Hippolyte was standing there in his old dressing gown, his lined face sad, every part of his twisted body apologetic.

"Mastah René," he said. "It's the old mastah. He requests that you come to him."

"Now? Is he ill?"

"He is as usual. It's—urgent, Mastah René."

Ignoring Carita's protest, René followed the old

slave to the master suite. There he found his grand-father at his desk, his journals stacked in front of him. He wore his tobacco-colored robe which, in the lamp-light, made his skin look sallow.

"So," the old gentleman said, "you got back." His tone implied he knew much. "As you know," he said, "Hippolyte has developed his own way of keeping me informed of everything connected with L'Acadie."

René nodded. Carita hadn't done badly herself. In her short time here, she had worked out a very effi-cient spy system through Consuela.

"If you prefer," Old René continued, "Hippolyte will give us privacy."

"Let him stay."

"Good. I know that the 'widow' Rivard is your mis-tress. This we learned after you brought her to Bayou Teche. Also, that she is to bear your child."

"Has borne, Grandfather. A son." Their eyes held.

The old man laid his hands on the journals. "I have finished them. Now you must read them. I read the beginning, the part my father wrote, when I was very young, and there was dire need. I've kept them up, entering each bit of Leblanc history, lore, shame. It wasn't needed that Gabe, who was my son and your father, read them. It wasn't needed that you read them when you married Angeline or even, it ap-peared, when you married Carita. But now—with Ol-ive Rivard—"

"Yes?"

"It is vital that you read them. They require a man of strength. No lad, such as I was when I read the first volume, could encompass their truths. Or no woman. Never a woman, René. Read them and go for-ward from them. Once it was my duty to rectify a wrong; now the duty falls to you."

René, silenced by his grandfather's seriousness, took the journals and went into the corridor. Behind him, the door closed.

The hurricane now was surging toward full strength. As he passed along the corridor, he could sense those behind the closed doors, some asleep, others, doubtless, praying.

Despite sleep, prayers, and fears, the killer hurricane grew. It wrenched whole branches off strong old trees, plastering them like feathers against whatever stood in their mad path. It uprooted trees, filling the night with flying bushes. It ripped a sturdy, moss-draped limb from somewhere and swung it in a mighty arc through the inky rain. The limb struck the belly of a cow astray in the pasture and slew the calf she was striving and laboring to drop. The hurricane battered the sugar cane, pounding it into the streaming earth from which it had sprung. It drowned the potatoes in the ground, devastated every plant, and still it raged, only beginning to near its full strength.

Carita was pacing the sitting room when René came in. Before she could do more than angrily cry his name, he strode into the bedchamber, with her at his heels. He opened his armoire, cleared a spot on the top shelf, stowed the journals, and slammed the doors.

"Those are youah grandfathah's journals," she said, surprised.

"Correct. I'm to read them."

She laughed, a bright, cutting sound. "Why?"

"Because he says they hold Leblanc truths that only a man can face."

He strode into the sitting room, toward the door.

"Where are you going?" she cried, running after him. There was honest fright in her voice. "Don't leave me, René! Don't you dare—I need you!"

She does need me, he thought as he closed the door, rushed along the hallway and down the stairs. But Olive's need was greater. She had no one but him; their son had no one else. Carita had a houseful of people.

Carita beat her fists against the door. She wrenched it open to pursue him, to hold him by force, and then she slammed it shut. He'd come back. Sooner or later, he would. She was the wife; she was the Creole; she would win.

99

She raced into the bedchamber and flung herself across the bed. She wept, crying René's name aloud, and in anger she screamed his name until her voice was hoarse and she was swallowing tears.

When Consuela ventured in and crept to her, Carita sat up and struck her across the face. "Get out of heah!" she shrieked. "It's youah fault! If you hadn't gone sneakin' and snoopin'. . . . Oh, you mis'rable black nigra wench, see what you've done! Get out and stay out! I don't want to see youah animal face evah."

"Missy," pleaded Consuela, "let me fix a nice bath, let me brush youah hair—"

Carita sprang off the bed, leapt to her dresser, snatched up her dagger, and with it chased Consuela out of the suite. Then she threw the dagger back onto the dresser, cast herself upon the bed once more, and wept, stormed, and screamed until she was trembling. And if any heard, it would seem that the hurricane had only added a new, high note.

Finally, she pushed herself up off the bed, and washed her face. Then she went to the armoire, stood on a chair, and lifted the journals, one by one, off the shelf, dropping them to the carpet.

When she had them all, she carried them into the sitting room and arranged them in consecutive order on the table at which she and René had so often eaten. She drew up a chair, and turned the lamp higher.

"Leblanc truths," René had said. Leblanc secrets, she thought.

With wind howling, thunder crashing, lightning blazing, with the hurricane reaching its wildest peak, with René certainly riding through it like a madman to be with his mistress, Carita Nuñez y Petain opened the first journal and began to read.

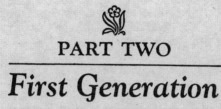

PART TWO

First Generation

1755–1773

ONE

That morning, Thursday, September 4, 1755, Gabriel overslept. Everybody else had risen at dawn to work three or four hours in the fields, then to return for eight o'clock breakfast, the second meal of the four each day. Now the sun was shining, and here he was, a sluggard.

The cursed clamor in his loins was worse. It had been bad last night as he and his parents sat with Georgette in the kitchen of her parents' house, but now it was a rage.

Then he had been in such need he hadn't given a damn about what they were discussing, though he heard. The two sets of parents spoke of the English boats anchored in Acadian waters; they were worried that the tents of the English soldiers were on the public square. They talked of how the soldiers paraded and the Acadians furnished them food. Gabriel scarcely heeded when they said that the English had turned the church into an arsenal and that the English Captain Winslow had established himself in the presbytery.

He had crossed his legs and not looked at his black-eyed, pert fiancée. Perversely she tried to catch Gabriel's eye, for well she knew his hunger and took pleasure in whetting it. She knew he would never molest her, never violate the celibacy that men in Grand Pré maintained until the banns were published and the priest joined the couple in marriage. She tormented him to keep him attentive, to show others that, despite being twenty-one, she was not to be a spinster.

Their wedding was four days away—if the priest arrived. The English had taken the priest away, and the families were anxiously awaiting his return. At the same time, they were harvesting their crops and making ready for the wedding celebration.

It was Gabriel's father who had instigated the marriage for his son, who had been too shy to act for himself. Pierre Leblanc had set a time for discussion among himself, his wife Aurore, and Georgette's parents, Marcel and Marie Babin. His proposition had been frank and dealt with the advantages of a union between Gabriel and Georgette, each being twenty-one years of age. The two had not been present, but were aware of the meeting and made no protest.

"As is the custom," Pierre had begun, "I have cut off a strip of my original farm and given it to each son when he married."

"Yes. As I will when my sons take wives. And I will build each a house, as it has been with you."

"Nineteen times I have done this. For each son, except Gabriel, the youngest, who has no fiancée."

"When you take off Gabriel's strip, you will have but a strip remaining, my friend."

"Yes. Gabriel, also, will have but a strip."

There was silence.

"I have spoken to Gabriel. I have made the offer some fathers make to a son. If he will bring his wife to live in my house, with the agreement that I run the land and Aurore the house until we die, Gabriel will then own not only the strip I would split off for him, but my own strip with all its good buildings, as well."

Marcel nodded. Marie's dark eyes brightened. She said nothing, but she clasped her hands in joy like a child.

"Why do you tell me this?" Marcel asked.

"Gabriel liked my offer. I asked if he'd chosen a girl and he admitted he had not. Aurore has told me that he is shy with girls and, if he liked my plan, it was my duty to suggest that he take a wife."

"You suggested, then?"

"Yes. It was he who spoke of Georgette."

"Georgette!" Marie cried, as if the thought of marriage for her daughter had never before come into her dark, alert head.

"Yes. No other."

"But why did he not—?"

"Eh!" Marcel chuckled. "The boy is shy. Georgette, on the other hand, has a quick tongue. It is no mystery that he did not make known his liking."

"You won't find him shy if Georgette likes this plan," Pierre said. "He'll want the banns published immediately. But there is the question of whether Georgette will agree to the terms."

"And if she won't wed Gabriel unless they have their own land?" Marie asked.

"Then it will be as they want it."

"Georgette is not a girl such as many," Marie said.

"Gabriel knows that; he said that though she is only eighty-nine pounds, she has strength and endurance and works harder than any girl, including the wives of his brothers."

"Eh!" Marcel chuckled. "He has been noticing."

"He said also that she has the quickest mind and, though her tongue is quick, her words are filled with sense. He likes the way she moves, the way she does all things, fast and well."

"Marie," Marcel asked, "what says the girl of Gabriel?"

"The pert things I said of you. But when you showed your intentions—eh!"

"We'll speak to her of Gabriel," Marcel said. "He can tell her your offer, and we shall see what comes."

What came was argument from Georgette because she didn't want to live in another woman's house under another woman's rule. But no, she didn't want a new, tiny house on a strip of land when the other way they would have twice as much and a bigger, better house.

Eventually she decided to live with his mother. Gabriel lost his shyness, impatient to be married. The most important part of last night's discussion had dealt with how to make certain the priest would return for the wedding.

"Now that Captain Winslow is established, we can seek an audience," Pierre had said. "We'll inform him that the banns have been published and the date set for Monday."

"Yes," Marcel agreed. "Otherwise, he has no reason to know the priest is needed."

"I can go to the captain alone," Pierre said, "though it might better impress him if you go with me."

"I will go."

"And I," Gabriel said.

The fathers shook their heads.

"The captain is not young," Pierre explained. "He has many duties and could easily be displeased by youth. It is better that only the fathers appear in this matter."

To Gabriel's dismay and Georgette's displeasure, Marcel agreed with Pierre, as did both mothers. This morning, then, the fathers were to see the captain. Gabriel willed the Englishman to agree to their request so the marriage could take place Monday.

It had to be. Otherwise Gabriel, who didn't know how he was going to wait even four days, would burst with the urge that every hour became stronger. It was rising in him again, that awful starvation. He must have gotten this punishment, this curse, from his father, who had sired twenty sons.

All Acadian girls were virgins, so he could get no relief from them. To make it worse, not even an Acadian widow would defile herself. The Indian girls, the Micmac, some of whom married Acadian, were taboo. The priest would frown on this indulgence, and besides, the Micmac lived too far away.

Until marriage, then, Acadian men must control themselves. How they did it Gabriel didn't know, for he hadn't discussed it, not even with François Hebert, his friend.

His part jerked. He almost gave it the tight, gripping comfort of his hand, and then he ground his teeth, willing the wildness to contain itself.

Once, when he was fourteen, his father had come into the room, had seen what he was doing, hauled him out of bed, and laid the belt to him for that. But his father, in later conversation, had made him understand that a man's part was as dear to him as virginity to a girl and that if he wasted himself he might not later experience the truest delight of a wife.

He suffered guilt for the wetness he sometimes found on his sheet, and knew that, with his mind asleep, the devil had gotten him. His mother made no comment, and in time he dared to hope that either she did not notice or, being pure and a mother, would not realize what it was.

He had kept away from girls, working until he fell senseless into bed. But now there was Georgette and Monday, and he was losing control.

He yanked off his nightshirt, then threw it onto its peg so hard it swung. Scowling, he put on his undergarments. He pulled on his yarn stockings, his trousers, which didn't reach below his ankle, his waistcoat, and the round, and short jacket that barely covered it. All of these garments were blue, dyed in the same pot by his mother, the same color all the women used. He put on his moccasins and went to the looking glass.

He had the build of his father—two inches under six feet, with broad, strong shoulders and big, strong, tireless hands. His body was muscled from working on the land and in the forest. His features were heavy and bold. He was smooth shaven, and his skin, like that of his parents, bore the olive tinge of the Latin, as did that of some other Acadians.

He ran a comb through his dark hair until it lay in a shallow wave on each side. Even in his discomfort, he didn't frown, but let his heavy brows lie in their straight line above his dark eyes.

Georgette said he was handsome, but he didn't see it. He considered himself a bit stocky, but there was no fat, not an ounce, just endless strength and energy. And that other, that curse. That part by which, without so much as glancing in its direction, Georgette was leading him around the way she wanted him to go.

Angrily he grabbed his round blue cap and put it on, then swiftly made his bed. With twenty sons, his mother had demanded from each this daily task, along with hanging up their clothes.

In four days, in this bed—! Just then his mother's voice rose up the narrow stairs. "Gabriel, are you dressed?"

"Yes," he called back.

Georgette said his voice was rich and firm and heavy. To him, it was just a voice.

"Come down, then! Someone's here—surprise!"

The unexpectedness of a visitor delivered him from his state of misery. Now he was simply irritated. The last thing he wanted was a surprise.

He stamped down the stair, mollified by the noise he made, even in moccasins. He thumped into the big, scrubbed-wood kitchen with the huge chimney piece, the open fire, and the flagstone hearth. Before he even looked, he knew who the visitor was.

It was Georgette, standing in the open doorway, sunlight behind her, a napkin-covered basket on one arm, a wooden bucket dangling from the other hand. His Georgette.

He stared.

Georgette's costume was new, that he saw. The waist was blue and reached to the hip, and the petticoat, which served as a skirt, was made of the same coarse cloth with perpendicular blue and white stripes. The handkerchief, thrown over her dark hair and tied under her sharp little chin was blue, as were her stockings. Her moccasins, also, were new.

Gabriel's throat filled with a great lump, and he couldn't speak.

"Can't you talk?" The way her eyes danced told him that she was teasing, though she didn't smile. She rarely smiled. At times she would give a sharp laugh, which she did now.

"I can talk," Gabriel managed. "It was that I was surprised. I had something to tell my father."

"They've gone," his mother said. "They may have to wait a long time to see Captain Winslow, and the earlier they arrive, the better their chances will be."

"Then—the harvest. I'll get to the hay."

"No!" Georgette contradicted. "This is special! Later, I'm to help with our hay, and so is Jean-Jacques. But we have been given the day until one o'clock, while we wait to hear from our fathers, as a gift of time. I have it planned. Your father is gone, so your mother does not need to cook the second breakfast. You will eat from my basket!"

Bewildered, Gabriel looked from Georgette to his mother.

"This is true, my son. It will fill your waiting time. But you'll work until dark and after, until you go to bed, as a result."

It was unheard of. What he had endured upstairs was as nothing. For his own mother to speak the word bed; for a girl's parents to let her go into the forest, even chaperoned by her brother, was unheard of.

"Fool!" chided Georgette. She gave her laugh. "We are young; the young set new ways! It has always been so. Jean-Jacques has gone ahead with buckets— we will gather wild apples. So come—hurry! We must find our chaperon."

Georgette darted north, past the houses of some of Gabriel's brothers. He had to run, to stretch his legs, and still he didn't overtake her, for she sped like an arrow from a bow.

Suddenly she came to a whirling stop. At first Gabriel thought she was looking at him, ready with one of her witty remarks, and then he saw that she was staring back at his parents' house and that she was frowning.

"What is it?" he asked.

She had seen the house every day since she had been born. What could she possibly be staring at now? He took a look himself and saw only what he expected.

"The barn's bigger than the house," she said in an amazed tone.

"Not really. It was, at first. It had to hold fodder to keep the stock six or seven months in winter, remember. It has the sloping roof to hold back the weight of the snow. Father says the ties had to be even stronger than in the house. The beams are eight inches apart and firmed with rivets and spikes. With all the stock in the barn all winter, the walls have to be thick and insulated."

"I know, I know a few things. I know that for people to be crowded, and stock—"

"They're just as crowded."

She tossed her chin.

"Besides, we won't be crowded, Georgette. Four of us in that big house."

"I'd rather have a stone house."

"We talked that out," he said, bewildered. "It's better to stay at the home place than to do as my brothers."

"As everybody! And get the house they want."

She turned, then walked along toward the forest.

"It's too late to change," he said. "With the papers signed."

"I know. It's only that I don't like to wait to set my plates on my own shelf."

"Do you think my mother will be hard to live with?"

"Don't be a fool."

"She welcomes you. She has said that you will want to make changes it is beyond a man to comprehend."

"She knows I want my own bedcovers."

"She might object? You fear this?"

"No. But I think it is her house, and if I get you to build an oven inside the kitchen, it must be with her permission. And she has said that she doesn't mind the oven outdoors, when everybody else has them inside."

"In the beginning, my father had to build everything. First the kitchen, then the barn. Later he built the oven in bitter cold, put it outside to avoid much opening of the door, which would have let in the winter on my mother who was enceinte with my first brother. She says that he built the oven with love, that he, my brothers, and I have stoked it and watched the baking for her when the snow is deep. She would not have it changed because of the love."

"That's what I mean. To give me love, Gabriel René Leblanc, you'll have to build me an indoor oven *now*, not after your mother is dead. If she does not herself suggest it, you must lead her to do it. Then I'll have my oven, and you'll have peace."

"How can I, Georgette? In the face of what she's said?"

"You find how! She and I are the women who love you, the only women in this village who love you."

She grabbed her skirt and raced up the path, speeding to the great pine and fir forest, which was as trackless as Acadia itself, where there were no roads, but only paths. He had to run to overtake her.

And then they ran together, free and fleet.

TWO

On they sped, past all the houses, Gabriel now carrying basket and bucket. Soon all the houses and farms were far behind them and they entered the deep forest of towering pine, fir, cedar, birch, and wild apple. Georgette stopped so suddenly that Gabriel almost bumped into her.

"What is it?" he asked.

Even though she was frowning, he became uncomfortably aware of her tiny figure and imagined, as he had so often done, how it was going to be for her to contain him, how tight so tiny a girl must be inside. He throbbed and turned half away, lest she see and be offended beyond forgiveness.

"Our fathers—and Captain Winslow," she said.

"They will persuade him that our priest must return

for Monday. Both are persuasive men. The English like them as men, not merely as Acadians."

"But if the captain says no, what then?"

"First we must hear that he says it, Georgette." He didn't know what else to say, or how she would receive it, but he wouldn't have to wait, for whatever troubled Georgette came out with the quickness of a knife.

"Have you changed your mind?" she demanded. "Is it that you don't want to marry me, that you wish to make the English an excuse?"

"Now who is the fool?" he asked, giving her a warm smile.

Her frown remained. "Maybe the captain will say that, with the English flag on the church, he can't permit out priest to marry us there."

"Our fathers will reply that the wedding can be at the home of the bride."

"He will not bring back the priest. I know it."

"How do you know?"

"He can say, 'Sign the oath of allegiance, and then you can be wed in the church that flies the English flag, wed in the English manner.'"

"But that would mean that we—our children—would from that time be English, not Acadian!"

"Yes. And we will do it if we must."

"We'll not marry the English way. Not by signing the oath."

"What does an oath mean? It is words only, a scratch on paper."

"You would do that? You'd feel one way, but proceed in another?"

"Yes. You are to be my husband. I do what I must!"

"But we'd not be truly wed."

"There'll be a priest sometime, and until there is, we won't have to wait. I can't wait, Gabriel. My dress is sewed and ironed, my linens are folded. If the captain does say no, we have got to take the oath."

"No, Georgette. No."

"I won't even mention a stone house or whitewashing your father's house. I won't mention anything but the inside oven, I promise. I'll do more. You've never seen the things I'll do."

She whirled again and went darting through the trees, deep into the forest. Garbriel followed.

His need had grown so that it was difficult for him to run. Lured by the flick of her skirt, by the glimpse of her ankles, his male part hardened, and everything was wiped from his mind. She fled on, and he could but stumble after her. Soon, any moment, he thought, they would come on Jean-Jacques and at that time, with the three of them together, he would be able to quiet himself.

He worked at it now by keeping his eyes off her. He put his mind on the conversation he would open with her brother the moment they caught up with him; he formed words and held them ready.

Georgette, he knew, would continue their argument, and Jean-Jacques would learn her impossible demands. Though the lad was only sixteen, he held Acadian beliefs and possessed a keen mind. He would be Gabriel's ally, for certain.

Suddenly she stopped running and whirled to face Gabriel. Her skin had never looked whiter, her eyes blacker, her lips redder. He stumbled, and the basket flew from one hand, the bucket from the other.

As he scrambled for them, she laughed. "Why are you so clumsy?" she taunted.

He said nothing, but picked up the bucket and basket, and headed toward the small clearing where she stood. It was as if she were in a little room carpeted with pine needles and walled with fir and pine, the sky its ceiling.

He came to her, then threw a look into the trees. "Jean-Jacques," he called. Then, turning to Georgette, "Where is he?"

"I sent him to the south forest, what else?" Again that sharp laugh. "You don't want a chaperon, do you?"

Wildly, he said, "We've got to have one."

"Why? In four days we'll be married."

113

"We shouldn't be alone, you know that. A man—can't be trusted. Does your mother know this?"

"But no! She thinks my brother is with us, as your mother thinks. So all are happy. Except my waiting brother."

Gabriel set down his burdens and stared at her.

"Why do you gape?" she demanded.

"You let them think a lie."

"I was only clever. I didn't lie. Perhaps I pointed south instead of north."

"We shouldn't be alone."

The black fire of her eyes melted, and they were like night sky. "Our banns have been published."

"We shouldn't be alone," he repeated.

"You don't want to be alone with your bride?" she chided, and for the first time in his memory, her tone was nearly soft and definitely slow, lingering on every syllable.

"My God!" he croaked on. "I want it more than my next breath! That's why—"

"Go on, say it. You're *afraid*!"

He was afraid, but not for the reason she thought. He was afraid that, should he fail to control his baseness, she might come out of the forest not virgin, but besmirched.

Her eyes bored into him. The blackness fled, and there was the flame. She smiled, the first real smile he could recall seeing on her face.

In only a few seconds, she had the blue waist open from collar to bottom, and it slid, along with her petticoat and inner garments, down her body and fell in a heap.

His breath sucked in, a hammer blow that seemed to drive through him.

Now she had her moccasins and stockings off, the blue kerchief gone from her head, and she was nude, white as a moonbeam. He tried to turn his back, tried to force his eyes away, but nothing would move. Nothing but that cursed part that had not, yet, the right to leap and reach. He had never before seen a woman's body.

He had known Georgette was tiny and well-formed, but not like this, never this. Her body was so white it was impossible to comprehend the whiteness. Her breasts were tiny but in absolute harmony with the rest of her body, and they were round and firm and tilted up. The tiny nipples were pink and, even as he stared, seemed to stiffen.

Her waist was so small that surely he could span it with one hand. Her hips swelled gently outward, forming a nest for her woman-place, which tilted upward with the pertness of the breasts. Her thighs were delicate, her lower limbs slim beyond belief, yet with a shapely curve.

"Don't just stand there," she said. "Say something."

And when he could not, she came to him. One soundless motion and she was there, hands on his clothes and that cursed, torturing rod leapt free.

Somehow, in the years to come, he could never figure out how it was accomplished—whether Georgette stripped him, whether he did it himself, or whether it was a joint effort—but he, too, was naked. He saw her blazing eyes, the quivering of her breasts; he was blinded by her white perfection, by her near-black hair, which had tumbled free or had been taken down and lay glistening on those delicate hips.

She cast herself onto the pine needles, a thickness of old, brown needles and new, pungent green needles, held up her arms to him and cried, "Now, Gabriel. Don't make me wait!"

And how could he have made her wait, when it was all he could do to himself to live until he drove that aching part into her, tearing through, scarcely hearing her cry out, before his seed poured. Even then, before he could pull away, he was plunging again, and the needles sighed under them and somewhere, in the sweet rhythm, a woodpecker was pounding his tree, and her tiny, strong body was moving, was joining the woodpecker beat, and again came the hot, joyous flood, and this time their cries rose into the air.

Then, after moments, he turned again to her. And

the third time was the best. It proved that this was the reason for man and woman, the curse and its assuagement.

Then, when she said, "Now, Gabriel Leblanc, I've got you where I want you!" he thought he was imagining it. But when she continued, her voice as sharp as any needle, "Now you'll have to take the oath!" he knew it was not his imagination.

A small wind pierced the trees and swept coldly across their forest room, raising bumps on Gabriel's sweating skin. Georgette had spoken just as he had leaned back on his haunches, hands out to lift her, cover her, apologize, plead for forgiveness.

But when he touched her, she jerked away, scrambled up and stood raking him with the hottest eyes in all Acadia. "Well?" she cried. "Well?"

"It won't come to that," he said.

He couldn't stop looking at her astounding body, stunned at the impossible thing that had happened. Even a married woman, he knew from overheard talk, would never let her husband see her naked. Even one of those girls in Paris exacted an unheard of price to show herself.

Yet here was Georgette, totally naked, telling him he had to marry her, forcing him to do the thing he most wanted. He met her burning eyes. He had known that she was different, that she wasn't like other girls, that she worked harder, planned deeper, and had stronger desires.

"You think I'm bad!" she accused.

He shook his head.

"You forced me! I had to do it to get us married."

"I'm going to marry you, Georgette."

"Yes. I was a virgin when we came here, and now you've *got* to marry me! I tempted you, yes, but you didn't have to take advantage."

He found he could barely whisper. "You didn't! You wouldn't have planned this!"

She laughed. He began to dress. She, however, stood angrily, rigidly.

"Put on your clothes, Georgette," he said.

She began snatching up her garments. "Fool—stubborn!"

He pulled on his stockings and moccasins, then buttoned his shirt.

"I had no right to take advantage."

"If I have to tell my father, he'll take his knife and cut your heart out. What do you say to that?"

"Now listen," he said, his jaw hard. "We have our course laid out."

"The oath—you'll take the oath?"

"First we find Jean-Jacques, then we eat. Then we gather apples as expected and go home at the hour set. No?"

Her sharp little nose jerked up; her lips narrowed. "Yes. And then?"

"If our fathers are not yet home, we go to the fields. We work until they bring word."

She sniffed, but she nodded.

"If Captain Winslow doesn't agree for the priest to come Monday—"

"If, if, if! What happens if he says to our fathers, 'Go home, don't come begging. We are in power until you take the oath.' What then?"

"That we face when it comes," Gabriel said firmly. And indeed, inside himself, he was firm in his allegiance, while at the same time he quivered like jelly at the thought of Georgette, of what she had been to him, what he had done with her, and how he wanted to do it again, endlessly.

"You want twenty sons of me?" she demanded.

He swallowed, then nodded.

"I will have twenty— more. I'll fill that house with children, so many you'll have to build rooms to hold them. Each year, while I'm making a new baby, I'll also work in the fields and in the house. The boards of your mother's kitchen will grow whiter than she has made them. And I'll ask for nothing—only the oath and the indoor oven."

She was dressed now, and he began to pick apples and put them into the bucket. "It's not a thing we can

117

settle right now, Georgette. We have a course and must follow it."

"Don't keep saying that!"

"Let's fill the bucket, then find Jean-Jacques—"

"I can take care of my brother."

"We must arrive home as expected. Otherwise—"

"Pah!"

"No more. You'll be Madame Gabriel Leblanc. That I promise with my blood."

Instantly, the argument was ended. True, the line of Georgette's lips was thinner than usual, but then she had lost her innocence, and that was a weighty matter. It troubled Gabriel, though perhaps to a lesser degree than it might, for he could not regret the joy he had known.

Even so, as they gathered apples, Georgette darting as she always did, Gabriel helping, a thread of pride wound into him. She wanted *him*, clumsy, big-handed Gabriel. This quick girl with the tiny bones, the firm and beautiful flesh, the hot inner secrets, really wanted him for her husband. She wanted him so much that she would show all, give all, risk all. She had threatened him with death at the hands of her father. She would even take the oath.

The bucket full, they went southward through the forest. Midway they met Jean-Jacques, who was frowning. He carried four empty buckets and called out sharply.

"You weren't where you said! I'm hungry. I didn't have the second breakfast!"

"Young fool!" Georgette scoffed. "I said north, and you went south."

He threw a lock of dark hair out of his blazing eyes. He might or might not believe Georgette, but his attention, now that he had found her, centered on the basket, which she was uncovering.

They sat on the ground and ate the thick, buttered slices of bread, the hard-cooked, salted eggs, and some of the apples they had picked.

Swiftly, then, they gathered more apples, filling their buckets, searching for trees, crying out with delight over one that bore especially fine fruit. The time slid past, and it was time to go.

Jean-Jacques picked up two of the heavy buckets and went on ahead. Gabriel carried two and Georgette one and the empty basket.

Jean-Jacques was out of hearing, but they didn't talk. Gabriel was relieved that Georgette hadn't mentioned signing the oath before her brother. As they walked, the only sounds were forest sounds and later, as they neared the farms, the swish of scythes through hay, the lowing of cows, the whinny of a horse.

The sun, now, was almost hot. The smell of cut hay rode the sun, and Gabriel breathed it. Unexpectedly, he was glad to have Georgette return to her home so that he could strip off his shirt and go into the field with his brothers. To swing the scythe, to hear the blade cut through, to see the hay fall in a rich carpet, and later to gather it into heaps, to tie and stack it, was a satisfaction always. He liked to do his work, bearing the sun on his back, breathing his sweat, feeling it run from armpit to inside his trousers. He half grinned at his own foolishness.

"Why are you laughing?" Georgette demanded. She never missed anything.

"A man feeling. Nothing to offend you."

"What feeling?"

"How good it is to work in the fields."

"A girl feels the same way."

Jean-Jacques was now out of sight. Georgette and Gabriel were just walking past his house because he was carrying the apples home for Georgette when Aurore came out and hailed them.

They went toward her and could see that she was weeping. Just then Pierre Leblanc came out. His heavy-featured face looked to be carved in despair.

"Tell them," Aurore sobbed.

"We waited at the presbytery all morning. We were the first ones there, and we asked for an audience with Captain Winslow. We were told to wait. The hours passed, the English soldiers drilled on the square. No one came to say we could approach the presbytery.

"We were prepared to wait until night. A short time ago one of the aides came to us. He said the captain is too busy today to grant an audience, that it will have to wait. For tomorrow, Friday, September 5, at three o'clock in the afternoon, all the men of Grand Pré and boys of ten years and older are to assemble in the church. This is by order of the English."

THREE

That night there was a large gathering at Antoine Landry's home and a still greater one at the home of René Le Blanc, notary. Pierre, Aurore and their married sons, wives and children, Gabriel and Georgette went in a body to Le Blanc's. The big, candlelit kitchen overflowed, people standing both inside and beyond the windows on the outside. The children were silent, the elders sober and quiet.

The old notary presided. Gabriel searched the lined face of the old man, who had always been full of confidence, in favor of the government and zealous in its service. Now the man's face was anxious and mournful.

Pierre Leblanc, who was no kin, was the first to speak. "Honored notary," he said. "We are troubled and confused. If you will guide what we say tonight, it will help our thinking."

There was a muted chorus of agreement. Someone called out for Pierre to start.

"Of course," he agreed. "Nova Scotia, as you know, is the first permanent settlement of North America, from Canada to the Gulf of Mexico."

Another man spoke. "And French fishermen, our ancestors, made the long voyage to fish here and take the catch home to sell."

"Yes," agreed Pierre. "Then they began to settle and called the land Acadia, from the Micmac Indian word meaning 'fertile land.' Acadia was the beginning of New France."

"It's birth," put in the old notary, "set off an English-French struggle for possession that lasted a hundred years."

"England won," squeaked a very old man. "She tried to get us who lived here, who had borne arms against no man, to sign an oath of allegiance."

"But we refused!" shrilled an old woman. "Because it had no word exempting us from taking arms against the French and their allies!"

"And they wouldn't grant us free exercise of our Catholic religion," piped another old woman.

The notary was nodding his head. "So it has gone. We give them allegiance, yet always they want us to take the oath."

"But we've held to our neutrality through all," said Pierre Leblanc.

Suddenly, his heart leaping, Gabriel heard himself speak up. "If England doesn't want us as neutrals, why won't she pay for our land and permit us to move to a French province?"

"The territory we occupy is the best. We are productive."

"Then, have the English used us? To develop the land for them?"

"It is probable," the old notary said. "For over forty years. It could be."

"On the third of July, honored notary," said Pierre Leblanc, "we were again asked to take the oath. Our delegation replied that they could not, without consulting all our people, take the oath."

"Yes," agreed the notary. "And on the tenth of August, our priests were taken away. Only this afternoon was I informed that our own priest, with the others, has been deported to England."

Gabriel felt Georgette, pushed against him by the crowd, stiffen. He took her hand; her fingers were rigid.

"On the thirtieth," the notary spoke on, "boats came to the mouth of our river. When Captain Winslow arrived, he asked for the keys of the presbytery and the church, and they were handed to him. There has been no opposition to him or his soldiers. He has asked for food for them all and has been given more than he needs. His orders have been obeyed with submission and respect."

There was a silence so deep that one person could not distinguish the breathing of his neighbor from his own. Their bloodstreams flowed in a single, throbbing river.

"Then why, in your judgment, honored notary," asked Pierre Leblanc, "are we ordered to the church?"

"It is reasonable to believe," the notary replied, "that they are going to demand that we sign the oath at once. Or be threatened with deportation."

Again silence.

"And our decision, sir?"

"Our stature as French neutrals, people of peace, is our one course. We must still consider ourselves loyal subjects of Great Britain; we must furnish all supplies for the British garrison, be subject to the whims of the English governors and permit our priests to be subject also. We must serve England faithfully and receive nothing in return but to remain on our land and to bear arms against no man."

It was late when the people moved toward their homes. Georgette held back so that she and Gabriel walked by themselves.

He looked at her in the moon-touched night, uneasy over what wild thing she might demand because there was no priest. He could see the thrust of her jaw, but she didn't speak until he suggested that they had fallen too far behind the others.

"What do you care, eh? What difference?"

"At a time like this, a family stays together."

"We're a family! Have we got to be under their noses?"

"You misunderstand, Georgette."

"I understand. You don't want to be alone with me."

"Why shouldn't I want to?" he retorted, angry. He had been alone with her when he never should have been.

"Because you think I'll make you take the oath even if the others are going to refuse."

"You can't make me do that."

"The oath's not the reason."

"There's no other—none."

"There is! Why don't you ask—why don't you care?"

"Then I ask. What is this senseless thing you keep talking about now, when—"

"The 'senseless thing' is what happened this morning."

"Mon Dieu. It was not my intent, and you know it. Come, things are bad enough. Must we quarrel between ourselves?"

"Over and over you did it to me. Not once, not twice, but three times. More! How is a virgin to count, to know? How many babies did you put into me? One—three?"

Her words were drowning him. He walked on, holding his pace to hers. She was right. Not once had he thought of anything, not once considered or even, until now, realized that he may have made her enceinte.

"So. You see!"

"I do."

"Don't say you're sorry, don't dare! If we were back there now, you'd do the same. Wouldn't you? Don't lie."

"I'd do the same."

"But you still won't take the oath."

"I won't take the oath."

"What, then, will you do?"

"Go to our parents."

"Never! Before God, I'll kill myself, rather than be known as. . . . No one will ever sneer at Georgette Babin or at her bastard!"

The catch in her voice convinced him that she half meant every word. "What we did—" he reasoned, "it doesn't mean for certain you're enceinte. Often it's years before a married woman has a baby."

"But you don't know it didn't happen to me. What will you do? Wait until the month passes and I put a knife through my heart? Is that the way you'll escape?"

It was then that a solution, wild but possible, hit him. That it would mean forfeiting his land bore no weight against the enormity of what he had done.

"There is a way we can marry, Georgette."

"Are you mad? You won't take the oath—and the priest is in England."

"We'll go to the Micmac."

"That's on the French side!"

"Yes. At Beausejour, a long distance."

"The English won't permit it."

"We'll run. We'll be safe with the Micmac."

"How does that marry us?"

"We'll marry the Micmac way."

"And live Micmac—not really married?"

"As married as the Protestant way. I'll build a small house for the time we stay, long enough for the English to forget us. Any baby will be a Leblanc. I'll trap and sell furs. In a year, we'll go to the French and be married by a priest."

"Why not go straight to the French?"

"Because of the English. We'll be missed from the rolls, and they'll search. Later, when we have money, we'll join the French, for the English should then be occupied with other affairs."

"Let's go now, tonight."

"The soldiers are watching now. We can't go before the meeting, when things will quiet down."

"No—now!"

But Gabriel would not agree. "We'll wait," he said. "What happens at the church may not be against us. But if it is, we'll slip away as the village sleeps."

FOUR

Captain John Winslow was impressed by the scene of peace and prosperity upon which he was gazing through the presbytery window. From this point he surveyed a wide expanse of the Acadian country, and wherever he looked, he saw serene homes and fields.

He had thought, upon being ordered here, to meet a restless and turbulent population, one ready to spring into revolt. Instead, he found that he and his soldiers could come and go among all in friendliness, and the eagerness with which they had given him the keys of the presbytery and church had rendered him thoroughly bewildered.

Squads of his soldiers had marched up and down the little country paths, and none of it had caused any stir. His every order had been obeyed with respect. And all the while, the Acadians had continued to harvest their golden fields. He had come with the attitude of a war-making general. He had been met by peaceable, reasonable men, by pleasant, hardworking women, and harmless children. The more he considered, the deeper his puzzlement grew.

Like a perplexed cat watching an unconcerned mouse, he sat scanning the paths. He glimpsed from afar clouds of dust made by people on foot, dressed in blue, slowly wending their way from distant farms. They all passed before the church, casting glances at the tent-covered square.

All were grave and nearly silent. They appeared to exchange a word now and then. But their minds, he knew, were busy with thoughts. Concern was on their faces; it showed in their eye and kept them from smiling. Men looked at the church and at the soldiers. They looked next at one another, and the captain knew there was a longing in them to have today's meeting over and done with.

Now it was three o'clock. The officers appeared at the front of the presbytery, and the waiting groups of Acadians moved, drawing toward the church. Eventually the men, and the boys of ten years or older, entered.

Winslow followed in full uniform, surrounded by officers. He took his place at the table he had ordered to be set at the head of the middle aisle.

The church was crowded. The silent Acadians were kneeling.

Gabriel, between his father and the old notary, dared a look at Winslow. He was past fifty, had a double chin, a smooth forehead and arched eyebrows. He wore a powdered wig, and his round, ruddy brow, from which the weight of this meeting had banished any look of satisfaction, still rose smooth and confident.

Gabriel swept a fast look at his compatriots, the men and boys of the Minas. Strong products of the soil, burnt by the sun, hardened under labor, they awaited the words of this English captain as they prayed in silence.

He could feel the wonder, bewilderment, and fear of the small boys. The demand of the English, he was certain, would be for them to take the oath, which they would refuse to do; for military orders to benefit the soldiers, which they would obey; for some undreamed of action or reprisal.

Into the silence, Winslow began to read a statement he had prepared. Only one portion of it did Gabriel comprehend, and that beat into him so that he was never to forget it.

"The peremptory orders of His Majesty are that all the French inhabitants of these districts be removed, and, through His Majesty's goodness, I am directed to allow you your money and as many of your household goods as you can take with you without overloading the vessels you go in. I shall do everything in my power to assure that all these goods be secured to you and that you not be molested in carrying them away and also that whole families shall go in the same vessel; so that this removal, which I am aware must give you a great deal of trouble, may be made as easy as His Majesty's services will admit; and I hope that in whatever part of the world your lot may fall, you may be faithful subjects and a peaceable and happy people.

"I must also inform you, that it is His Majesty's pleasure that you remain in security under the inspection and direction of the troops that I have the honor to command."

The captain's voice fell silent, and the words surged through each man. Even in the lads of ten was the understanding that their home was no more.

Even the wise old notary himself did not immediately comprehend that the extermination of the Acadians had now begun according to a long, hidden, wily plan. With the bold cloak of deception torn away, he still did not believe that their submission was to be rewarded with imprisonment, their loyalty to be thrown aside by an event which was to be called Le Grand Déportation.

Surely, the hope throughout the silent church was that the captain was pretending. But the speechless shock was soon followed by a wail of anger and sorrow. It grew louder until the soldiers on the square, and the waiting women, could hear it.

The shouts of the men joined into a tremendous bellow, and then they sprang from kneeling and moved as one body, rushing the doorway. But they found the doors closed, guarded by soldiers with bayonets, and when they rushed the windows, more bayonets appeared.

Imprecations rang through the church until the old notary held his hands aloft, as often their priest had done, and the men and boys stilled. They listened.

"There is no escape," he said. "It is our lot to await the will of God. Sit in the pews, stand along the walls, kneel. Hold to our neutrality. We have prospered under it; it cannot be destroyed in an hour."

127

Moved by his voice, the men regained their composure. They did not try again to storm doors or windows. There was nothing the soldiers need do, now, but stand with their bayonets. The captain and his officers departed.

Gabriel, stiff with shock, regarded the composure of the Acadians. He saw the hard-drawn face of his father, and those of his brothers. Suddenly a realization dawned on him, and he looked again. Only thirteen of his immediate family, himself and his father not included, were present. Some of his brothers and nephews were among the missing.

"They've gone to the forest," Gabriel whispered to his father, who was also making his silent search.

"They're going to the French," his father whispered back. "Jean came in the night to tell me. May the good God keep them!"

The English would pursue, and Gabriel's brothers, their wives and children could be killed as they fled.

Across the church his eye caught that of his friend, François Hebert. His friend's mustache formed a black line above his stern mouth, and his cheeks looked less ruddy than usual. He would be thinking of Elodie, his beloved.

Gabriel's mind went to Georgette. He knew the panic she would feel when she heard the ill tidings. She'll do nothing foolish, he told himself. Not until this thing is settled, for we can get on the same vessel. The English will permit that, for we are betrothed. And even if they didn't, he knew that never, under any circumstances would Georgette give up.

❀

Now, at L'Acadie this hurricane night, the tempest lashed and blasted its spreading course over the bayou country. It built steadily toward its peak; the winds seized the great oaks lining the drive, twisted off a mammoth limb, bore and hurled it through the rage of blackness, and slammed it against the house, high up, almost against the shutters of René and Carita's sitting room.

Carita bent over the journals and flicked her hand at the thundering crash as at a mosquito, her eyes skimming through the long-ago happenings on the pages, René, his mistress and, even his bastard forgotten. She was furious for the Acadians and at them—for them because they had been magnificent, then ruthlessly used, and at them because they had permitted, even endured, such usage.

Georgette Babin, now there was a girl with spirit, with wits in her head! If only this first Gabriel René Leblanc had been like her, quick to seize what would forward his own cause. Indeed, what *was* an oath, a silly oath—words only!

But perhaps Gabriel had taken the hated oath to get Georgette. Her eyes flew to the pages.

FIVE

The dire news spread over the village. At first it was not believed but later, when the men did not emerge from the church and the soldiers continually surrounded it, every wife felt herself to be a widow, her children orphans. The women wandered about sobbing, some wailing aloud, going from the home of one to the home of another. They gazed at one another, not knowing what had been said in the church or the extent of the evil that had fallen upon them.

"On those from afar as well!" cried a grandmother who had only one tooth. "On all Acadia this English evil has come!"

"But what is the evil?" cried an enceinte bride. "Our men are locked into the church, but is that evil? That they are in a holy place?"

"It is evil," declared the grandmother. "You will see!"

And when they did learn and know, their anguish was not to be borne. Georgette, who was one of the strongest, was the first to faint. But most women stood like stone, tears on their faces, women who knew the years of toil that had aged their men. They knew of the submission all had shown toward the British, the loyalty that they had rendered. These women knew but could not believe that their lands, houses, and cattle would be taken, that they all would be put onto ships, and taken into the unknown. Such a monstrous thing would not, could not, be visited upon them.

One of the women spoke. "It cannot be! There are many thousands of us—eighteen thousand—here! Only last month my husband said that at the Minas alone there are six thousand cattle and other stock. How can the English take care of so many, where will they learn?"

"Some know now," said another woman. "The English set their jaws. What they want to do, they do."

"At Grand Pré alone," said a woman with toddlers and a new baby, "my husband said we have more than a thousand bulls and more than half again as many cows."

Marie Babin spoke. "Marcel was saying only yesterday that all of English Acadia has over one hundred thousand head of stock!"

"They will take all," Aurore Leblanc said. "They hold our men in the church, and they are going to send us away, an officer told me, with only the money and household goods we can carry."

"Who has money?" cried someone. "I want my husband. My mother wants her last-born son who was ten only a week ago!"

The women's lamentation grew. And in the church, the men could hear.

Gabriel clenched his jaw. He eyed the windows, one by one. The soldiers remained there, as did the soldiers at the door. He wanted to get out of the cursed church, away from the false God who had shown himself to be an accomplice of the English. He wanted to find Georgette, with whom he should have fled last night, and leave this behind. All they needed was to get to each other, and they would go.

He looked at his father. His lips were moving. "Ave, ave," he was saying. He looked at other faces. Some were like that of his father, some were without expression, some were stricken, a few of the lads were weeping. Most faces were set in anger.

He gazed at François. He was solemn and, when their eyes met, Gabriel found in his friend a resistance and determination that matched his own. Yet for the moment, they could only wait.

Just before dark, upon the prisoners' request, Captain Winslow ordered women to bring a meager ration of food. This was left in the churchyard and from there handed in through the doorway. No man saw his wife, no mother her son.

The night passed. There were over four hundred captive in the church. The old men lay on the pews. Others lay on the floor between the pews, the kneeling benches cutting into them, others in the aisles. Many stood along the walls to wait their turn to lie or sit, for it was very crowded, and the soldiers remained, with their bayonets, filling a share of the space. There was little rest and less sleep, except among the boys. Even they sobbed, cried out, and woke themselves, then wept before they could sleep again. When morning dawned, every man was wearier than he had been.

That day a few prisoners were sent out, under guard, to warn Acadians who lived in remote sections and to find those who had hidden in the forest. "Tell them," Winslow ordered, "that if they don't surrender, they'll be shot."

Both Gabriel and François tried to be included in this party; both were rejected. The delegates chosen, men of experience, departed. The women, who would have pressed forward for a glimpse of their husbands were held back by a barricade of soldiers at such distance that none could be recognized.

It was later known that several of the messengers, after the village was behind, tried to escape. The soldiers shot one of them dead in the presence of his comrades, and this information was sent back to the village and reached those inside the church.

When the delegation returned, Acadians from remote sections were herded to Grand Pré and the men locked into the church. Of those who had fled into the forest, there had been no sign.

Five days now—one day beyond Gabriel's planned wedding—Winslow had kept the four hundred captive. For all five days, Gabriel listened for Georgette's cry and strained to look through the windows at the women who gathered at a distance and were held back by soldiers. But it was too great a distance for him to be able to single her out.

At first the prisoners did not discuss their situation, for the guards permitted no conversation. At the end of the five days, however, men were muttering together despite the guards. The guards, failing to stop the muttering, could interpret it only as the hatching of schemes for escape and fighting back at the English.

This, Gabriel and François agreed, would be reported to Winslow. "He'll weed out the young men first," Gabriel murmured.

"Yes," muttered François. "There were five ships at anchor when we came in here. I've counted the young men, and there are two hundred and fifty. Winslow may reason that by putting fifty of us on each ship, fewer if more vessels have arrived, we'll be kept in control, and without us the older men won't rebel."

And indeed that very day, toward dusk, when it was raining bleakly, all the Acadian men were drawn into a line outside the church, guarded by many soldiers as were their women at a far distance, and the order was given for one hundred and forty-one unmarried men to step forward. Until this moment, except for the initial outcry, the later rush to the door, and the recent muttering, these men had submitted without resistance. Now, knowing they were to be marched to the river to embark, they cried out as one and refused to obey.

Gabriel, who, like the others, had not stirred from where his feet were planted on the ground, shot a quick glance sidewise, to the rear. There, in the chill rain, still keeping their lookout, stood women, girls, and children. There were many more of them than there were of men, and somewhere in their midst was Georgette.

If Gabriel made one fast turn, one dash toward those women, Georgette would recognize him, and she would break from the women. Together they would escape the soldiers, flee through the forest to the Micmac, to earth's end. He whirled and was knocked to the ground with the butt of a musket.

"Try that again, and you get the bayonet through yer gut!" the soldier growled. "Get up. Do what yer told!"

"Step forward!" an officer shouted.

But the prisoners stood their ground and screamed their refusal, protesting that to tear father from son was the act of barbarians. But the soldiers proceeded, shoving, prodding, and threatening. They singled out the number of young men required, among them Gabriel and François, who pretended not to be acquainted so they might stay together.

The rest were drawn into columns six deep, along which were stationed soldiers. Fathers, brothers, sons, and grandfathers were parted.

"March!" came the order to Gabriel's group.

Not one man moved. Cries of anger rose, interlaced with pleading, with adamant refusal, and with the calling of son to father, of father to son.

Gabriel watched the soldiers. Rain was falling past their hard faces and over them, even as it fell over Gabriel and the others, though the faces of the Acadians streamed tears with rain.

"March!" came the order again.

The prisoners stood fast. Only when the soldiers turned their bayonets against them did the march begin. The wives, sisters, mothers, fiancées, grandmothers, and children huddled in the rain, held back by other soldiers. Their horror, terror, and disbelief reached the marching young men.

Gabriel became more alert with every step, watching for a chance to escape, but a soldier marched close on either side, and there was not yet the opportunity. Behind him came François.

Gabriel marched on. To be driven from country and family, he thought, Winslow's lying promises already broken, to be loaded onto ships like cattle and scattered in strange lands, to be torn from plenty and thrown to poverty—no, that I will not endure.

They reached the river where the ships were anchored. At the gangplank of a schooner, the *Esne*, the soldiers fell into single file so that there was a bayonet ready for the back of each Acadian in Gabriel's line.

His soldier prodded him. He hesitated, then began to move up the plank, but stepped no faster than he had done ashore.

Behind his soldier was François, behind him a soldier, and so through the line, prisoner and soldier alternating.

Slowly, on and up, they moved. They were nearing the deck when Gabriel turned his face into the rain and peered down, past the gangplank, through the rain, and saw how it blanketed the darkened surface of the river. Between one step and the next he was ready.

He took one long breath and held it. Then, like an arrow from a bow, he leapt. He fell with the rain, and plummeted with all his strength toward the water. He heard the shouts from above, the rage.

Water sang past his ears, and he stayed deep. Shouts, muted now, hung above. The water was stingingly cold, mercilessly dark, and he swam through it, stroking carefully, staying underwater as long as possible.

Instinct made him ration his breath and warned him to make a semicircle out and away. His mind flew ahead. It was necessary that he come ashore at a quiet spot, a field stacked with harvest.

There he could hide and rest. His mind could work; it would plan. Then he would go for Georgette, and they would escape.

His chest was bursting. On he stroked, more strongly, his lungs filling with pain and fire.

He had to surface. He must break water silently, take one instant to breathe deeply, and the next time swim deeper, faster, farther, longer.

He shot upward. Rain covered his face and streamed past his eyes, over his mouth and into it. Noisily he gulped air.

"There!" came a shout. "Between us and the sloop!"

He sucked in air, dove, and swam as he had never done, arrowing out from the ships, going ever deeper. He squeezed each drop of air until it no longer existed, and after that he waited until he could wait no longer, then waited still.

Next time, he would estimate how far he had come. When he dived then, he would know whether to start circling. Once on course, he would be lost to the English and could come up for air at will.

Only when his body threatened to explode did he shoot to the surface, the dark, raining surface, silent as a sea creature. As he broke through, all the lights of hell erupted in his face. He heard the voice of the devil, split into countless voices, shouting around and upon and encompassing him. There was the scrape of oars.

"That's the bastard. Drag him in. Faster—up with him—dump him now—hard!"

Waterlogged and streaming, he was yanked, dragged, lifted. He struggled, but the claws were as many as the voices, and he couldn't pull free. Above the struggle, the lights of hell, the many-splintered voice of the devil, he heard water running off him and felt rain pounding on him.

"Good that he jumped!" shouted a voice.

"Damn God, but 'tis!" another shouted back.

"Make 'im a example?"

"That's right!"

There was a chorus of ayes.

"Chains fer 'im!" screamed a man. And he laughed.

"Chains!" chanted the others. "And fer the other bastard, too!"

Then came the final order. "Dump 'im—*hard*!"

Gabriel felt himself strike the wooden seats of the boat. His head thumped, then bounced. The lights blacked out, and he lay still.

First there was his head, filled with pain. The pain extended from his head, through his body, to his ankles. Gabriel could feel that his wrists were chained behind his back; he traced a finger up the chain to an iron ring set in the wet wooden deck. Only then did he grow aware of movement that he recognized as the sway of an anchored vessel. He heard the lapping water, the sound of voices somewhere and knew he was on the *Esne*.

There was no need, yet, to open his eyes. The rain had stopped, and the sun was shining. He became aware that someone was beside him.

"Gabriel," said a familiar voice, "has your mind returned, my friend?"

François. He groaned, then gritted his teeth. Pain speared his head. "Are you chained, too?" he asked.

"Like you. We're an example. So they won't try what we tried."

"You, too?"

"Yes."

"Elodie—?"

"I think I saw her at a distance."

"Georgette—?"

"Like a wild thing. As we were driven up the plank, she broke through the guards screeching, 'Where Gabriel goes, I go!' "

"No! I'd have heard. I'd have—"

"You were in the river. I dared one look back, but I saw. It took three soldiers to subdue her, two to drag her away."

Gabriel scowled, which caused a shooting pain in

his neck. He struggled to sit, open his eyes, turned his pounding head, and stared at the blunt features of his friend.

"They beat you in the small boat, Gabriel, and again when they hauled you aboard. They almost beat you again, but the captain said not, that he wants you alive and aware."

"Did they beat you?"

"They punched me around and gave me a big lip. They grabbed my ankle when I tried to jump. I never made it."

"Damn God!" Gabriel cursed. "Damn him for being the devil!"

"Don't blame God, my friend."

"I blame. The Protestant god is the devil, and he has won. There is but the one God, he belongs to the English, and it is from him that they get their cruelty and their orders. But I, Gabriel Leblanc, will show them! I will marry Georgette, and our people will send the English devil back to the hell from which he has sprung!"

"Hold down your voice. There *is* le bon Dieu. The English are instruments of Satan and will be subdued. When time passes, when you are with Georgette and I with Elodie, your feelings will change."

"I'll not wait. I'll get away."

"Have you got a file in your clothes? So we may cut our chains?"

"I'll manage."

"It's the beatings. If you think you can escape, then your brains are ready to fry like eggs. Look around you—look well."

Burly, blonde-haired soldiers, all uniformed and armed, bayonets ready, were on deck. Pockmarked sailors moved everywhere. Men swabbed the deck, polished metal, coiled rope, mended canvas. One soldier caught them looking, took a step toward them, made as though to spit in Gabriel's face, then directed the spit overboard.

At a cry from above, Gabriel looked up and saw

that the great sea birds were circling, winging tire-
lessly.

"Where are the others who were brought aboard?"
he asked.

"Below."

"Women, too?"

"Not yet. And no children under ten."

"Any of your family or mine?"

"No."

"Do you know where we're bound when we sail?"

"No. Nor does anyone," François said.

In the days that followed, Gabriel and François
worked fruitlessly at their chains. Exposed to cold and
rain, they contracted and threw off chest colds. More
men were loaded onto the *Esne*, brought from the
church, but no kin to either of them. Forty-three
women and fourteen girls were loaded. Similar numbers were driven onto other ships. Never did Gabriel
and François see kin or fiancée.

Rarely were the prisoners brought up for a turn
around deck. The women who were ashore were allowed to bring food, which seldom reached the cap-
tives. Winslow, it was rumored, ordered the soldiers to
eat the food.

The prison boats remained in harbor. More arrived—at least two dozen vessels were eventually to
transport the Acadians to destinations in Maryland,
Virginia, Pennsylvania, Massachusetts, Connecticut,
and the Carolinas. The number of Acadians sent to
the American colonies was to be, during the last part
of the year, 1755. The length of the journeys enroute
varied from twenty-eight to forty-two days.

Daily the same scene was reenacted—people were
forced to walk to the ship, and the road became one
moving mass of despairing people who could hardly
proceed in their forced march because of crowding
and confusion. Old women with heavy burdens fell
and were forced up and on at the points of bayonets.

It was at the moment of embarkation that the most

heart-tearing scenes occurred. With bursts of prayer, the marchers reached the shore, only to see that the docks were cluttered with household goods others had been forced to leave. They knew, now, that the assurances that they could take their possessions were false and untrue.

But, at embarkation came the worst trial of all, for, despite Winslow's promises, families were separated. Small children shrieking, were torn by English hands from mothers. Women screamed and waited, and every Acadian sobbed and cursed. They were driven, grief-wracked, pell-mell onto the vessels that would carry them apart.

Hour after hour, day after day, the transports were loaded with Acadians. Each transport was to be guarded, on its voyage, by six non-commissioned officers and eighty privates.

Once, during an airing on deck, Piquet, a Minas farmer, said to Gabriel and François as he passed, "Be glad you're on deck. Let the rain be wet, the wind cold; let it sleet and snow. Below, though we have blankets, we have not room enough, but are crushed and cramped together."

"The women?" asked François.

"The same. But apart from us."

Not until after the weeks of anxiety, grief, cold weather and scant rations had become habitual, did the first fleet of vessels set sail. This was on October 27, 1755. They were under escort of three British vessels of war, the *Nightingale*, the *Halifax*, and the *Warren*.

At the moment of sailing, a fierce gale, which pierced to the bone, caused the five ships under escort to separate. Gabriel and François, in harbor though they were, had to hang onto the iron ring in the deck and even then were tossed and flung like flotsam as the gale blew itself into a raging storm, the worst either of them had experienced.

Wet to the skin, Gabriel shouted, "If we were below, we'd be dry!"

"But it's clean here!" François shouted back.

From that moment, they were so busy hanging to the ring, and the storm was so loud, it was impossible to speak or do anything but endure.

SIX

The next day, though the storm had ended, Gabriel's concern for the transports that had sailed into it troubled him. He was frowning as he helped François spread their coats to dry, as best they could. "Some of the ships must surely have been lost," he said.

The two pockmarked soldiers assigned to bring their rations had showed up empty-handed but full of talk. They heard Gabriel and guffawed.

"Fine if it did happen!" roared the broad one, whose name was Mott. He had unruly, fiery hair and blue eyes that rolled in every direction. "Then we're rid of that many lice!"

"Plus your own soldiers," Gabriel said.

"They take to the boats," snarled the other soldier, Cullen. He was taller than Mott, younger, and evil looking. He was hard-chinned, hard-eyed and had the blondest hair Gabriel had ever seen.

"You can't know they'd get to the boats," François said.

"Ye saying the English not the best?"

"Leave it!" growled Mott. "We got the girls, and we got privacy."

On December 1, 1755, the *Esne* finally set sail. The weather was bitter cold. There had been snow and sleet, and the deck was periodically coated with ice. Gabriel and François, chained so long in the open, never grew accustomed to the cold, though their chains permitted them to move a step or two and thus exercise.

Just before they sailed, Cullen and Mott swaggered up. "It's below with ye!" Cullen announced. "Too good fer ye up in the fresh air—yer to be with yer mateys!"

He opened the padlock and yanked the chain free from the irons on his ankle so roughly that Gabriel felt it cut into his skin.

"Stand—march!"

Unsteadily Gabriel got to his feet, as did François, numb from the cold, and started for the companionway, a few steps before his friend. The soldiers prodded them with bayonets and cursed.

Half stumbling, half falling, Gabriel was filled with hatred. He wanted to mangle, to knee them both and then, after crushing their maleness, to again dive overboard. Somehow, he held back. If he let fly, he knew François would also leap into the fray. Though they might vent their rage on these two, other soldiers would overpower them and they would accomplish nothing.

He stumbled down the companionway. What he and François had discussed was better. They would endure until the *Esne* reached port; they would land where they were doomed to land. After finding a way to live, they would begin to search for fiancées and families.

Cullen yanked open a door. "Yer quarters! The hold!"

The stench took Gabriel's breath away; continuous moaning that seemed to rise and fall with the movement of the ship filled his ears. And then he saw, and could not believe, the mass of human cargo.

Men wrapped in blankets covered the floor. Ranks of men stood against the walls, crushed together. The women and girls were elsewhere.

Gradually, in the flickering light of bracketed lanterns, he began to recognize individuals. There was Bisson on the floor. He looked feverish, his lips were puffed, and his face was covered with sores. Nearer

141

was L'Esperance, in much the same pitiful condition, and beyond him Merciers and Samson, bone-thin, his face one great running sore. There were many others he recognized.

Mott gave François a jolt, and he crashed into Gabriel so violently that both fell onto the nearest blanketed men, crushing them. They scrambled up and made their way, stumbling, to the nearest wall. The crowded, miserable men standing there pressed together to open a niche, into which Gabriel and his friend pushed.

Cullen guffawed from the doorway. "Now yer out of the weather! Ye'll get a turn to lay down and wrap up in a blanket—ev'ry one sent from Boston! Fer Acadian lice—a special Boston product!" He roared with laughter, then slammed the door shut.

Breathing the thick, putrid air, viewing the sickness, hearing the moans, Gabriel could, at first, only stare, appalled. He recognized many men, but only a few returned his look of recognition, so weakened and ill were they. He held his breath against the stench, then breathed because he must. It was the stench of the excrement, vomit, and disease of hundreds.

He studied the sore-filled faces, heard the moans, all but felt their great wave of fever. All the faces were thin and worn, and most were ill. Some looked feverish, others had a few sores, and several, eyes bright and unknowing, leaned against the ever-moving wall, held upright only by the press on either side. Occasionally one of them got his turn at a blanket, at a slot on the deck, and traded the anguish of standing for that of lying on the filthy bottom while the man he replaced took his tight, miserable space at the wall.

There was, mercifully, no Leblanc, no Hebert among them.

François stood at Gabriel's right, and Gabriel turned his head to the man jammed at his left. He couldn't see into the man's face, though he believed there were no sores and knew that he wasn't from Grand Pré.

"What's wrong with the sick?" Gabriel asked.

142

"Pox, my friend, smallpox. Some are dead, and the soldiers won't take them out until we're at sea."

"How did they get such a sickness?" asked François. "Acadians are strong. They—"

"The blankets, my son. It is from the blankets."

"This is not possible! To say that a blanket can—"

"Everything that has been touched by a person with smallpox must be burned," Gabriel said. "My father's mother sickened with it in France. She survived, but her bed, everything she touched, required burning. To protect the family."

"The English," said the thin man, "brought aboard blankets from Boston on which smallpox victims died."

"Only the mad would do that!" cried François.

"Yes. They mean to kill us so."

"To exterminate us!" Gabriel said, through his teeth.

"That way no man may point to the English and say, 'You murdered the Acadians.' With the pox, the English will reply, 'The Acadians were weak. When taken to a healthy life at sea, they died. Not even the ocean air could save them.'"

Gabriel leaned against the wall. He realized, from the motion of the wall, from the roll underfoot, that they had at last set sail.

"I am Gabriel Leblanc," he said to the man beside him. "This is François Hebert, we are both from Grand Pré."

"Martin Veco, from the Minas. Torn from wife and sixteen children. One of my sons was brought aboard, the English not knowing he belonged to me. He was the first to die. He lies now in the far corner. He was nine only."

François cursed.

"He—Marcel—is with God. It is merciful so, which is how I try to comfort my heart, and in prayer I ask if it is not so. But in me is guilt. A soldier gave us one blanket. He taunted, said it carried pox. I did not believe.

"At the end, a soldier tore his body from me and kicked me. He boasted that all soldiers who come into the hold have survived the pox and that we will not survive. I beg you, my sons, freeze if you must; do not accept a blanket. Freeze to the bone, for that is a clean death."

Time crept. The *Esne* climbed swells, dropped into the trough, climbed again, then glided on endless smoothness. The swells returned, and so it continued. There was seasickness, along with the pox. Each morning soldiers came, took away the dead which the Acadians, by order, had ranged near the companion-way, then returned to fling the blankets of the dead to the living.

Gabriel and François took their turns lying flat, then standing. Though they used no blanket, they ministered to the ill. Most of those who died breathed their last moan for priest, mother, wife. Veco and others warned that the pox victims were doomed and he who tried to help was likewise doomed.

Most of the ministering occurred when rations were brought, in the morning after the dead were removed. Gabriel and François, along with two or three others, crept over the blanketed figures trying to feed each one his portion.

The stale bread and rancid meat were impossible for the dying to chew, but Gabriel and his fellows persisted until they got something, if only water, down nearly every throat. When they failed to get food into the sufferer, eager hands reached out and carried it to other, starving mouths. Eventually, Gabriel ceased to warn that the food was contaminated by the stricken, for none would heed.

Gabriel himself was always hungry. After the English cut the rations in accordance with the number dead, he reckoned that each man, sick or not, was allotted a daily ration of five-sevenths of one pound of flour and one-seventh of a pound of pork, along with a portion of water.

One day Gabriel, whose time to lie down had ended, couldn't rouse François, lying beside him. He discovered that his friend had been stricken.

Veco helped tend him. Gabriel, now constantly trembling from hunger, protested, reminding the older man of his earlier feeling.

"I must live," Veco had said at that time. "I've got to find Marie and the children. A man's family is first, even when he is parted from it and others are in need."

"Your family," Gabriel warned now.

"Until this moment, my son, I would not admit that all on this ship are my family. You and François have become as sons. May God raise this one from the jaw of death. May He move, in this moment, someone else, on some other ship, to help one of my own sons."

They did what they could for François, who tossed without ceasing, disturbing the sufferers on either side. He mumbled incessantly, always the one word, the one name, "Elodie—Elodie—"

"His wife?" Veco asked.

"Fiancée."

"And you?"

"A fiancée."

"It tears a man, this. Marie is strong, she is quick in the wit, she has a hand for sixteen children and holds their love. She can endure. But still, it tears a man."

Veco roused guilt in Gabriel. Was something wrong with him that he didn't feel this being torn of which Veco spoke, which was ripping François, even in his delirium? Was something wrong with him that he felt Georgette would somehow look out for herself? That his greatest longing for her had come when he was manacled on deck and one night in particular, when stars shone, and that unruly malady of his loins recalled her body and yearned for it?

Well his body did not torment him now. Standing his hours, and adapting to the plunge, roll, and leap of the vessel, trying to stretch out on the hard, wooden floor that made his bones ache, he had no desire.

Hourly the well were stricken, the already-stricken died and were laid near the companionway. A few, slowly and almost reluctantly, bested the disease and

145

lived to look about in despair and wonder, scarred and pitted, some almost beyond recognition.

François fought to live. It was as if his mumbling "Elodie—Elodie—" was a lifeline to which he clung, by which he held himself from death. Imperceptibly, at first a thing sensed but not seen, he began to resist the disease. Then it became definite. François, despite the mortal illness, and the stinking, pest-filled hold, was making progress. Gabriel and Veco shared their rations with him, and eventually he began to get better.

Now he refused to take their food. Too soon, Veco predicted. And, his face pitted, he struggled to his feet too soon. But he endured. "The scars," he said. "Elodie won't mind."

A day later Veco fell into their arms, burning. He died faster than most, and Gabriel and François laid him with the most decency possible, with the other dead. When the soldiers came, the two friends stood with stiff jaws, and Gabriel heard François whisper an ave.

The dying went on; recovery of victims continued. The *Esne* plowed the seas; the lanterns swung on their hooks.

"How long has it been?" François asked.

"Thirty-five days since sailing. We've not dropped anchor yet."

"Because they've tried to kill us with the pox!"

"They'll have to drop anchor sometime," Gabriel said.

Later, Cullen threw open the companionway door. Mott's hair flamed behind him.

"We're givin' ye a show, a entertainment!" Cullen bellowed. "Never knowned ye'd see that on the *Esne*, did ye, mateys?"

He waited, taking the silence as his due.

"Not that ye deserve it!" he bellowed on. "And not fer all of ye, only a se-lect number! Young mateys, the strongest, 'cause they's the ones to 'preciate what

they'll see! You!" He pointed at a tall young man.
"And you—and you—"

By the time he finished, he had singled out twelve
prisoners, among them Gabriel and François. Mott
leading, Cullen bringing up the rear, they were hus-
tled up the companionway and onto the deck.

The sun, after weeks below, struck Gabriel's eyes
mercilessly, though it was winter sun. The air cut his
lungs like an icy knife, hurting as no air had ever
done. But he drew it in again and again, and soon it
had driven the stench of the hold out of him.

There were some twenty soldiers, including Cullen
and Mott, on deck. These now proceeded to bind the
prisoners in a line along one ship's rail, hands lashed
behind them, the ropes gouging their wrists.

When this had been done, Cullen stood in the middle of the deck. Gabriel had never seen more bristle to
his blonde hair, more hard sparkle to his eyes, more
evil to his face.

Mott stood a pace behind, his fiery hair wild in the
breeze, his blue eyes rolling delightedly. He was grinning.

"We been ordered to give ye fresh air," Cullen told
them at a shout. "We're not to drop anchor with a
cargo of all dead! While yer takin' air, we're goin' to
let ye see more than sun and water. Yer goin' to see a
show, as promised, the ruddiest show ever, 'cause we
been practicin' the whole voyage."

He wheeled toward the companionway. "Here they
come!" he yelled. "Here come the wimmin! Now, grab
yer balls, ye lice, and hold on—no mess on deck. This's
all fer soldiers, none but soldiers! No sailors can take
part!"

The women were herded onto deck. There were
five of them, none of whom Gabriel knew, all under
twenty and comely despite the sufferings of imprisonment and scant rations. Their faces were expressionless,
none pockmarked, but the set of their jaws betrayed
terror as did the sudden quiver of a lip, the flight of
dark eyes to avoid the stares of the men.

Cullen gave the orders. Mott served as his aide,

making certain the orders were carried out. Five of the soldiers bound the girls to the ship's rail opposite the bound men, leaving a space of several feet between each girl.

Every soldier had to struggle with his girl, to wrestle her into place, for she twisted, kicked, cried out, and tried to break free. It became necessary for a second soldier to hold the resisting girl while the first one lashed her, hands behind, to the rail. After that, he spread her feet wide, ran a rope from each ankle to the rail, and tied it securely.

"Ready?" bawled Cullen.

A cheer rose from the soldiers. The girls cried out in protest, fear, anger, and despair.

The hairs on Gabriel's neck stiffened, and he clenched his fists. The ropes sawed into his wrists.

"Stand back!" Cullen bellowed, though no soldier had moved.

Fighting down his own instinct to harden, his own damnable maleness, Gabriel forced himself to look carefully at the girls. He knew none of them. They all had the Acadian beauty, the soft dark hair and eyes, the smooth features, the enticing lips, now terrified, the shapely form.

They wore their everyday skirts and blouses, disheveled, torn, and dirty from the long weeks. To a girl, their eyes were on Cullen and they were panic-stricken as they stared at him.

This really isn't the first time, Gabriel thought. They've been here before.

The soldiers stood in their line, their breeches a betrayal. They watched as Cullen began a slow, deliberate strut along the line of girls, raking his eyes over the first one, hard, slow, evaluating. He shook his head.

"I had this 'un yesterday!" he yelled. "And this 'un—" he jerked a thumb at the third girl—"the day before, and her between them twice." He strutted on, considering, rejecting, his breeches bulging.

By the time he reached the last girl, a tall, lissome beauty, he had fumbled at his clothing and his great organ was exposed, jerking and dancing, fiery on the tip, bigger than any Gabriel had ever seen. It was the size of an apple at the end, thick as a man's wrist where it anchored at the belly.

The girl hadn't seen it yet, hadn't moved her frantic gaze from Cullen's face. He grasped the organ and thrust it at her.

"Look at it, wench!" he shouted. "Ye'll not see one to match it. Look what yer goin' to get!"

The girl seemed not to breathe. Her eyes never moved.

"*Look!*" Cullen roared. "Look, or ye'll take me hand acrost yer mouth!"

"Stop it!" cried the girl next to her. "She's not—never before! She doesn't know—she's only fifteen!"

His look burned. "Who're you, her ma'am?"

"She's my sister. She—"

His roaring laughter covered her voice. "She's still a virgin! Why ye think I been savin' 'er? Fer the end of the voyage, that's what! To finish off with a bit of somethin' new, somethin' with juice!"

"Leave it, man," Gabriel shouted. The ropes were cutting his wrists. "She's a baby!"

"He's right!" François yelled, and the other Acadians joined the protest. "Show mercy, man. Think if you had a sister!"

Laughing, Cullen tore the skirt from the shrinking girl and flung it over the rail, into the sea. With one ruthless thrust of hand he pawed her black-furred virginity, and in the same movement went into a half crouch and rammed his pulsing organ upward.

She screamed, the sound cutting like the thinnest, keenest blade, and it was borne away on the wind, into nothing. The soldiers shouted, laughed, and leaned forward, their lust growing.

Cullen pumped, bored, and grunted. The girl moaned, half fainting, tears running down her cheeks, her lips drawn back in a grimace, the muscles of her neck standing out.

Gabriel strained at his bonds, relaxed, then lunged,

but they held, cutting ever deeper. He strained again, as did François and the other men.

Not once did Cullen miss a powerful thrust. Not once did his face change. On it went, Cullen holding back longer than Gabriel had believed a man could hold back, tearing, rampaging, ravishing. The girl was whiter than snow; her body went slack; she had fainted.

"He'll stop now, the bastard," Gabriel muttered.

But Cullen kept going. The fainting only whetted his appetite, and his knees bent lower, his thrusts slowed, deepened, and struck harder. Then they quickened, and it seemed that the friction must surely strike sparks of fire. Suddenly, his howl, a howl that should have come from a beast only, filled the wind. His howling continued until he had shot his seed. Only then did he back away from the unconscious girl.

At his signal, five soldiers sprang forward, breeches open. They tore away the girls' skirts and, grunting and cursing, thrust into the girls—one into the unconscious girl. When this group pulled back, Cullen shouldered through the next, grabbed the girl who had tried to protect her sister, swatted her on the cheek when she tried to bite him, then rutted like a blonde bull, outdoing all the others.

Mott, who had held back until the second group finished, laughed all the way through his own encounter, screaming like a jungle brute as he sprayed into his girl. The other soldiers were fully as loud. The girls cried out, wept, and pleaded.

The virgin remained unconscious, and Cullen took her for the third time. Had she not been lashed in place, her body would have crumpled to the deck.

The Acadians watched in horror, some cursing, others praying. The air was filled with sobs, shouts, and curses of delight from the soldiers.

Gabriel thought this noise must carry below, that the commanding officer would put a stop to this. Then he reminded himself that the commanding officer could have his choice of girls in his cabin. The ravaging continued until every one of the girls had been used by twenty soldiers.

"Merci, merci," François muttered. "Merci, that Elodie isn't on this ship. The spirit would leave her body!"

As for Gabriel, he thanked no one for anything, even when the virgin was discovered to be dead and Cullen ordered her body tossed overboard. There was no prayer in Gabriel Leblanc, not even for the dead virgin.

SEVEN

The *Esne* dropped anchor at Annapolis, Maryland on January 10, 1756, some forty days after setting sail. The surviving Acadians, wan and emaciated, were herded ashore. Three hundred and twenty-three had embarked on the journey; less than two hundred set foot on Maryland soil. They were eager to land, to be reunited with their families, not knowing that almost all the ships had been sent to different ports.

As they disembarked, they eagerly scanned the crowds on the landing, looking for loved ones. François craned his neck, seeking for Elodie, and Gabriel looked for Georgette, for any member of his family. He saw face after face; there was not one he knew. Disappointment surged through him.

"Elodie's *got* to be here," François said. He was staring at every face, walking as fast as he could, even stumbling.

Before the full impact of disappointment hit them, they were met by a group of unhappy, puzzled officials and townspeople, whose lot it was to deal with still another penniless horde dumped on them by England. They were taken to a bleak, unheated meeting room with rows of benches. Gabriel and François sat side by side, their determination to remain together even stronger now that they had, at last, reached some destination.

One official stood at the front of the room. He was a tall, broad-shouldered man in good black wool, with a gray beard and gray hair. His light eyes, his firm mouth, and general air were those of a gentleman.

"I am William Piepmeier," he said, "citizen, proprietor of Piepmeier's General Store, and farmer. I speak for my fellow citizens who are as unhappy over your situation as you are. Though yours is not an enviable lot," he continued slowly, "I can state that the least unhappy of the exiles from Nova Scotia are those sent to Maryland. Here we have Catholics of English origin, so we do not look at you with hatred.

"There is much to tell you. You have been long at sea and know nothing of what has happened to your countrymen. First, let me assure you that we, in Maryland, have a true sense of friendliness toward you. The Acadians now with us are admired and respected, due to their sincere and simple manner and their ways of thrift and industry. They have already helped in the cutting of wood and stand ready, as soon as weather permits, to cultivate our fields. They want to earn their way. At the same time, the wound in their hearts is so deep that any word of the homes they have lost brings a flood of tears."

He waited, for many of those to whom he was speaking had begun to weep.

"Half the city of Baltimore is now populated by Acadians, so rapidly have the English put them upon us. Torn from their country, left in a new, strange world with no means of support, their living quarters are, unfortunately, poorly built and the English government keeps them from locating in the better parts of the city.

"They cling to their mother tongue and are strongly attached to all that has to do with Nova Scotia. Yet, despite their closeness to us, they do not mean to remain in Maryland, but wish to find an even more hospitable country."

"Sir," spoke Gabriel, standing up, "do any other colonies feel kindly toward us?"

"No, they don't. They dislike, even hate and fear you. They have no intention of permitting a Catholic population to take over their communities. They resent having thousands of penniless exiles landed in their midst. They see no way to provide employment for the exiles."

"What treatment, sir," Gabriel asked, "do the other colonies give us?"

"My brother in Georgia," Piepmeier replied, "writes that he personally felt shame as the exiles went down those shores—men who had known abundance are now pointed at, derided, ridiculed, and repulsed as vagabonds and reduced to charity."

"And colonies other than Georgia, sir?"

"Virginia is, to use a kind word, inhospitable. One transport was refused, over one thousand French neutrals turned away. The very prospect of harboring them caused great discontent among the people. Further, some aboard had contracted smallpox. Not one soul was permitted to land; all were shipped to England."

Gabriel sat down. The silence of fear gripped the room.

Piepmeier's face grew more serious. "Some Acadians are being enslaved in the Southern colonies, especially those Virginia has been forced to accept. They're doing the labor of slaves, living in cabins with Negroes. The South isn't making them welcome, nor is the North."

Gabriel stood again. "Sir, are we being enslaved by the North, also?"

"It's not that bad. However, the treatment isn't gentle. Only recently in Pennsylvania, for instance, your countrymen were forced to remain weeks on their vessels before landing. They were put ashore in the proximity of the hospital of the pestiferous. Death had already taken a large number. There, as here, the wives and children were scattered like leaves of autumn and some men, who once were productive, respected citizens, are now insane."

Again gripping silence and tears.

"Please. My intent in speaking thus is not to torment but to inform. You are people of stamina. To deal with the future, you need truth."

He produced a document, which he unfolded. "This is a copy of a petition to the king from exiles in Philadelphia." He read aloud.

" 'We were transported into the English colonies, and this was done with so much haste and with so little regard to our necessities and sensibilities, that from the most sociable enjoyments and affluent circumstances, many found themselves destitute of the necessities of life. Parents were separated from children and husbands from wives, many of whom have not met to this day; and we were so crowded in the transport vessels that we did not have room even for all our bodies to lay down at once.' "

Piepmeier folded the paper. "It is reported that Papists are so hated among the Puritans that they're not permitted to assemble in prayer except in small groups. Without priests, the sacrifice of the Mass is substituted by *la masse blanche*, conducted by the most venerable man present. The young must marry without religious ceremonies."

Again Gabriel rose to his feet. "Sir, we hope, by advertising in newspapers, to locate our families. Have there been such advertisements here?"

"Many advertise," Piepmeier replied. "What the results are, we don't yet know."

A man at the back of the room rose and spoke. "You said, sir, that some of us mean to find an even more hospitable country than this. Should they wish to go northward, seeking their families, what would be their reception?"

"Not good, my friend. But don't despair. In time, some families or portions of families will surely be reunited. It is still early; transports are still arriving at destinations. As for you here, today, we will first see that you have shelter, food, and clothing. This we did for those preceding you. The citizens present will take you to quarters—the best we're able to provide—and at once, so that you may rest from the ordeal of your voyage."

There was a general, slow movement to the doors.

"I'm not going," François muttered, "not yet. I want to know more."

Gabriel, in accord with his friend, sat on the bench with him as the hall emptied. Soon William Piepmeier approached them.

"You have further questions," he said kindly.

"If we're unwelcome and hated in every place, sir," François asked, "if we can't move about, and if the newspaper advertisements don't help, how are we to find our loved ones?"

"Many lines of inquiry are reaching out from Baltimore, monsieur—"

"Your pardon, sir," Gabriel said, and proceeded to introduce himself and François, saying that they had lost their families.

"It is very sad," said Piepmeier. "Some, even though they don't speak English as you do, go from village to village, farmhouse to farmhouse, asking, 'Have you seen my Henry—my Marie?' It pains the heart."

"I'll do that for Élodie," François muttered.

"Those who do, have little success, my son. You can, however, move about Maryland. In most colonies, your people are prohibited by law from going from one village to another without a permit. He who violates this law is put for three hours into the stocks or is given ten strokes of the whip for the first offense."

The silence throbbed with bitterness.

"How can I help you further?" Piepmeier asked.

"By telling us where to get work," Gabriel replied.

The older man gave them a searching look. "I live on a farm outside town with my wife," he said. "My hired man died some months back of locked jaw, and since my son married after harvest and went to land of his own, we've had various Acadians come to do our milking until such time as they could find something better. Presently we have no one.

"We've agreed to offer two Acadians the job of planting and harvesting our crops this year. If the two of you want to do this, there's a bedroom for you to share, and you will eat at our table. You'd move in immediately—today—and help with chores and repairs until planting time."

The offer stunned Gabriel. This was the first act of kindness they had known, except from their fellow countrymen, since the afternoon they had gone to the church in Grand Pré.

"We accept with gratitude," Gabriel said. "Thank you, sir, thank you deeply."

"I'm offering no charity. I have one hundred acres, six horses, four cows, fifty hens, ten pigs, and a few geese. We butcher and cure our own meat. You'll earn your keep, some warm clothes, and stout shoes and, after harvest, a bit of gold. If, at that time, you decide to move on, I'll help outfit you and give you a start on your travels."

Smiling, they shook hands with him. They considered themselves unbelievably fortunate.

Months slid past. Gabriel and François did their work, and they pressed their search, placing advertisements, as well as carefully reading newspapers for advertisements. They visited their countrymen, some from the *Esne*, others from earlier transports. When Piepmeier gave them a week off, they spent it in Baltimore, searching. They stayed with an elderly Acadian, Jean-Pierre Fortel, who subsisted on the kindness of two Baltimore families. It was Fortel who gave them the first word they had had about their loved ones.

"Georgette was forced onto a vessel," he said. "I don't know the name of the ship or where it went. But I saw. It required three English soldiers to hold her."

"And Elodie?" François asked. "Was she taken, too?"

"I am sorry. I never knew your Elodie."

François' face showed his disappointment. He spoke of advertising for families.

"Results may come of that," Fortel said. "Jean-

Batiste Bourgeous, who disembarked when I did, advertises. He also writes letters of enquiry. Now he is walking north from city to city, village to village, asking, 'Have you seen my wife? Her name is Julie.' I have letters from him. He is still walking."

Before they left Baltimore, they wrote down the names of their fiancées and families and gave them to Fortel.

"I'll send these to Bourgeous at the next town where he is to ask for mail," he promised. "He'll search also for your loved ones and send news of them to me, which I will give you. If you move on, tell me where to write."

One day, shortly after they had returned to the farm, Gabriel was considering what Fortel had told him about various sections of the country. Suddenly he said, "Louisiana! We'll go to Louisiana."

"Now you're really mad!" cried François. We may go south, yes! We've spoken of that plan, but Louisiana—no!"

"It's French. Fortel said the French feel kindly toward us."

"No! Elodie would never go so far."

"Consider. Calm yourself. We'll not jump across the colonies between here and there. We'll be searching, questioning, and advertising. We'll see other, different newspapers. We'll have a destination, a place to be where the people are French."

"Without Elodie?"

"You don't know. She may be there now."

"How would that happen, eh? How would she get there?"

"The same as all—walk, ride a horse, go on a boat. It's no secret the French are friendly toward us or Fortel wouldn't have heard. He thinks others are there now; you heard him."

"He thought it a far chance."

"Anything we do is a far chance. Suppose we talk to Mr. Piepmeier, see what he thinks?"

"Agreed. Tonight."

The farmer was enthusiastic over the plan. "It's being said the French are giving out grants of land to settlers," he said. "Whether this is true or not, there's a wealth of land down there. If I were young, I'd be tempted myself."

"Then it's Louisiana," François agreed, "and land of our own. I want the biggest grant they give. If they're giving."

"When will you start?"

"That's your decision, sir," Gabriel said. "When we've done sufficient work for you here."

"The harvest is in. Go when you want."

"At dawn, then," François said and smiled.

"Not so fast!" laughed Piepmeier. "That's wild country you'll cross. You need a guide. I can guarantee you an excellent Indian. But it'll take a few days to make arrangements. I'll outfit you."

"Thank you, sir, but do you think," Gabriel asked, "that we should make up a party and travel in numbers?"

"Two of you, with the guide, will stand a better chance. Put yourselves completely in the hands of the Indian."

EIGHT

Years later Gabriel wrote of the trip:

Our journey was tedious, fraught with toil, dangerous. Our Indian guide was skillful and fearless, leading us through the wilderness as though we were not earthly men but silent, drifting leaves.

A thousand obstacles barred our progress, though we were strong and agile. We came upon deep and rapid streams that we could not cross for want of a boat. We traveled through mountain defiles, where the pathway, if it could so be considered, was narrow and full of peril, winding over craggy steeps, where one bad step would hurl us into the awful chasm below. We suffered from storms and driving rains, and at night we had only the light canvas we shaped into tents to shelter us.

But we were spurred on and lured by the hope that far, far south in Louisiana, we could find our kin. This hope lit our way; it was the beacon on which we kept our eyes, and it bore up our hearts.

When we reached the wild and mountain-bearing country of Carolina, it required a stubborn heart not to give up our plans when we saw the impossible wilderness that stretched endlessly before us. But we forced our hearts to be stout and thus, encouraging each other, refused to abandon the goal.

For weeks we moved slowly through never-ending forests, cutting our way through undergrowth so thick we could scarcely wield the ax, through brushwood where an enemy might lie hidden to murder us, for we were now in the deep of Indian country, and our guide told us that savages followed us, silently, day and night. We could glimpse them, at rare moments, with tattooed faces and head feathers, lurking through the trees. We were always ready for them, expecting an attack at any moment.

Our nights were sleepless. By day, worried and half starved, we moved ever southward. The devil had handed us a new hell in this venture, but we struggled on until, after two weary months, we reached the Tennessee River where it curves around the base of a mountain.

At dawn we took up our march again, and the country became more level. After five days, we camped on a hill by the river where a small creek runs into the stream. There we met a rough but friendly party of hunters and trappers who gave us provisions and told us that the easiest way to reach Louisiana was to float down the Tennessee and Mississippi Rivers.

With their help, we felled trees and built a raft, or flatboat, erecting our canvas at one end for shelter. With many expressions of gratitude, we parted from the hunters.

No dangers threatened us after this. During the day we floated, and at night moored safely and encamped on the banks of the river. Our guide brought in more game, now that we were out of the Indian-infested forest, and we caught many fish. Settlers along the river gave us meals, but no news of fiancées or families, though we never failed to enquire at every cabin and settlement.

After interminable twistings and turnings, we launched, at last, on the waters of the Mississippi and floated down as far as Bayou Plaquemines, in Louisiana, where we moored. How great was our joy to be once more treading French soil, free from English dominion!

Here our guide left us to return to Maryland, and a powerful blacksmith by the name of Pete Atcheson, who had been visiting here, came aboard to man a sweep, help us steer the boat that way and make his trip home to New Orleans. We had cause to be glad we had taken him with us, for he pointed us at our future and gave us much information.

He spoke in the manner peculiar to Americans. "You fellers had this kind of craft afore?" he asked, his voice low, yet booming out from the midst of his wild black beard.

"No," François said. "We were farmers in Acadia, and that's what we want to be in Louisiana."

Atcheson had pale eyes that stared from under bushy brows. He raked one powerful hand through his brush of hair. "Them damned English," he growled, "think they own the world. We know what they done to you'uns, and don't like it a damn. Last I heard, plans was bein' made in New Orleans to help you folks get a new start. If ye want, I'll take ye to the right places so's ye can be helped."

We agreed and floated on. Though François and I searched for our lost ones every mile, we learned nothing. It was as though they had vanished.

We saw, as we floated downstream, that a plain ran southward along the river in a broad belt that Atcheson said was fifty miles wide. The variations in this consisted of a series of ridges, which he called natural levees. The arable land of the high elevation that sloped away from the river he called frontier lands, and the area between these and the bordering swamps, back lands.

There were swamps, some filled with a variety of hardwoods, others with cypress and black gum trees. We saw Spanish moss draping cypresses, oaks, and even pecans and elms.

One day Atcheson said, "Effen you take up land, go to the bayou country. There you kin jest about have things yer own way. There's wild cane—grows thick, reaches ten to twelve feet. That dirt'll grow anything a man sticks into it and make him rich. Grows rice and indigo and tobaccer. Anything."

"What about the trapping?" François asked.

"Out in the marshes, muskrats thick as ants in a hill. Man can't do better, to commence with, then drain and cultivate his land, and then trap muskrat. Best market right in New Orleans, and it's a heavy breeder, three to five litters a year. Then there's the 'gator. It's found in all the lowland streams and inland waters, too. There's good trade in 'gator hide."

"What if we can't go into the bayou country?" I asked.

"Talk is that's what they want to open up. Anybody wants to go, kin. They's all kinds of space, not many folks."

"What else, if we go there?" François asked.

"Deer's found in wooded swamps. They's bayous windin' till they make a man dizzy. Some black bear. They's raccoon and mink, swamp rabbit and gray squirrel, beaver, otter, even wild hog."

"It sounds like the Garden of Eden," François said.

Atcheson didn't miss the skeptical note. "Case ye think I'm a big mouth, tain't so. They's fish, too—redfish, croaker, sheepshead, mackerel, crabs, shrimp, oysters. And in season ducks and blue geese." He grinned; his teeth were big and yellow in the sun.

"Only spot fer you'uns," he declared. "In New Orleans they'll outfit ye with a flatboat apiece an' men to help pole 'em. Ye'll git a start of stock an' seed—what's needful fer ye to settle and put yer land to work. An' they're bein' gen-'rous with the land, too. The trip in along the bayous'll take weeks, but it's purty—trees galore, all kinds of flowers, streams all over, and birds."

"What about dangers?" I asked, not forgetting the skulking redskins we had seen in company with our guide.

"They's snakes, mostly harmless. Water moccasin's the only killer you'll commonly find. Most dangerous, come to think of it, is the cane rattler. Puts a risk to workin' wild cane or plantin' yer own."

Silence fell on us then, and we watched the river, putting in at every landing to ask whether those for whom we searched had been seen. But at the first glimpse of New Orleans in the distance, our search slipped temporarily from our minds. It seemed that we were, after all our turmoil and effort, approaching an earthly paradise.

NINE

It was January 15, 1757, that first day Gabriel woke on his own land, a full league of land, over seven and a half square miles of lush soil, winding, fish-filled streams, huge swamp trees, animals to trap, and fowl to shoot. Almost two miles of his grant bordered the Bayou Teche, which lay far to the west, at least a hundred and fifty miles, from New Orleans.

He crawled out from his makeshift tent. His three horses, a black stallion and two mares, and his two cows were safely tethered, grazing. His two sows and the boar, along with those belonging to François, were grunting and rooting in the pen he and his friend had put together last night from crates after the government raft had pushed off downstream. His farm implements, seeds and food supplies, also government gifts, were safely covered by an extra canvas.

A feeling of pride coursed through him. This was his land, his own. It was his, this richness; it belonged to Gabriel Leblanc, and it was so far removed from the English, so deep in the strange, southern wilderness that not even one road yet crossed, that he was free.

He surveyed what he could see of his domain. In his pocket was a map marking his boundaries, but, knowing the vast extent of his holdings, it was a certainty that, from where he stood, he would see nothing but his own land, and he knew there was more yet that he couldn't see.

The gentle slope from the bayou down to the swamps provided some natural drainage of the fertile soil. He studied the slope as far as he could see, his view blocked by moss-weeping hickory and oak. The land lay smooth, sweet, and green, though laden with brush.

He yearned to ride his boundaries, to criss-cross his land, become familiar with every tree, bush, flower, and bird. But there was work to be done. He had to drain and plant some land; he had to build a dwelling, build a shelter for the stock, and put up fences.

He looked across the Teche, the water dark in new light. François had taken the league directly opposite this one, and he, too, was awake. When he saw Gabriel he lifted a hand, shouted, then jumped into his pirogue and began to row across the bayou to the spot where Gabriel stood.

He let the boat, which was also government granted, nose the bank, then threw the rope. Gabriel tied it to a sapling. François leapt ashore, smiling broadly.

"It's good that our cows haven't calved yet!" he laughed. "We need the time it takes to milk to do other things. I've been looking over the waterfront, and I mean to build Elodie's house facing the Teche but back from it a distance, so there'll be a large stretch of green. She can sit on her front porch and look out over it all. How do you like that, eh?"

"Very much. But we can't build houses until—"

"I know. Still we can plan. Our land is so much alike, do you think Georgette will want her house back from the water too—or in a grove of oak?"

"I don't know. But since we are the only settlers here, the sensible thing is to build facing each other."

"Good! Then if there's trouble we can signal across."

Nodding agreement, François helped Gabriel tend to his stock, then got out his flint and began to make their first fire so they could have coffee and cornbread. Gabriel watched him impatiently.

While his friend nursed the fire, Gabriel filled the coffee pot, mixed as much cornbread as his iron pot and skillet would hold, and set them to bake. "Waste of time," he grumbled.

"Yes, also no. This bread will last the day. And we've got to start somewhere. We'll eat well and then work hard."

They were drinking a second cup of coffee when a shout from the bayou sent them running.

"Burdell, Amos Burdell," shouted the newcomer. He tied up his pirogue, then came toward them. "I run the trading post at Attakapas!"

They shook hands, Gabriel and François introducing themselves.

"I know you seen the post when you come upstream," Burdell said. "The patroon, the man who captains the boat, stopped in on the way back, said you was in a rush to get to your land."

"That's right, sir," Gabriel said. "We were anxious to unload before dark. And the patroon—"

Burdell grinned, held up his hand understandingly, and Gabriel knew he liked him. The trader was tall, wiry, strong, over forty. Lines cut into his leathery, clean-shaven face. When he grinned, his pale blue eyes shone, and his deep voice somehow belonged to the wilderness.

"The patroon wants to get back to New Orleans," he grinned. "He left before day. With him and his men gone, I shut up the post and came upstream to get acquainted."

They insisted that Burdell eat breakfast. He accepted, and sat cross-legged, eating with relish. When he was on his second cup of coffee, the talk resumed.

"I know you're from Nova Scotia," he said. "We've heard how them damned English treated you people. Even way out here, tradin' boats bring news and newspapers. I said 'we.' The only other one's Morphy, runs the inn, says there'll be call for it sooner or later. Nobody but Father Charles and sometimes a patroon puts up there now. It's not far from the post."

Gabriel nodded. "We saw it."

"Morphy's a kind fellow. Good innkeeper."

"What about settlers?" François asked. "A church?"

"You're the first settlers, but likely only the start. No church. Father Charles, he comes a couple of

165

times a year, does missionary work with the Attaka-pas. But we'll get ever'thing—people, church, school. This Attakapas country is big, awful big. There's room for lots of Acadians."

"The French are extremely generous," Gabriel said. "A league of land, cattle, farming implements, seed, supplies. Surely this is the kindest treatment exiles have ever known."

"Yes," agreed François. "We're set up in life."

"W-ell," Burdell said, "the government's got a selfish reason, too. This is an enormous country—there's not only the Attakapas, but all the rest of the bayou country. It's all pioneer land, a wilderness. It's got to be cleared, not only of wild brush but drained and tamed. The government wants all this done and the whole land put to good use. I'd say they look on you and as many more of your kind who come as God's blessin'."

"It's a fair and honest trade," Gabriel said thoughtfully.

"That's my feeling," François agreed.

"You'll repay them ten-thousandfold," Burdell declared. "They know, for I've read it in the newspaper, how you developed Acadia, and that you'll do the same here. Only us, not being English, won't kick you out."

François asked. "Indians. What about them, sir?"

"The Attakapas. This whole district is named for them. Once they reached far and was very powerful. The other tribes was scared to death of them because they had the reputation of eatin' their prisoners of war. Attakapas means man-eater."

"Are they still dangerous?" Gabriel asked.

"Not at all. Three other tribes formed a league against them and made war. The Attakapas was bested in a hellfire battle on the hills about three miles west of here. Some went in with the winnin' tribes, some was let stay near the head of the Teche. They trap, trade, hunt. Trade at the post. You won't have no trouble."

"What became of their territory?" François asked.

Gabriel felt uneasy. Did the French, on the one hand, consider themselves owners of the wilderness with the right to parcel it out, while the conquering tribes, on the other hand, believed themselves to be the owners? If there would be no trouble from the Attakapas, how about the other, winning tribes?

"Nothin' a-tall," Burdell said in answer to that question. "They all got big chunks of territory. And the whole big Attakapas region is reserved by the confederated tribes, under mutual agreement, as huntin' grounds. If settlers let 'em trap and hunt—they don't never take too much—there'll be no quarrel."

François said, "The French own this country, and now we own some of it because they gave it to us. But the tribes fought and won it, and they haven't given it to us."

"The government controls the Indians. There's room for all. You got people coming—family?"

This set François to talking of Elodie. "We left letters at the governor's office in New Orleans," he concluded, "telling where we'll be. That way, if only one of them gets to New Orleans, it can lead to us all being together again."

Gabriel was relieved that François didn't mention Georgette. He preferred to do his waiting unknown to others. He was beginning to believe that she had been transported to England and that he would never see her again.

As Burdell and François talked, Gabriel gazed down along the gentle sweep to the bayou, then back and forth across it. There was one natural site to the south that would be unparalled on which to build one of those tall-columned white houses he had seen from the Mississippi. He would, as soon as more pressing work permitted, mark off a wide driveway leading from it to the bayou and line it, on each side, with a double row of young oaks. By the time he had his fine house, the trees would have grown and would make a moss-draped aisle from the front porch to the landing.

The first house, the one he needed now, he would build at the north, on an even line with the future mansion, and he would use cypress for the wood. It, too, would have its oak-lined driveway.

Once he wondered if Georgette would approve. What he dreamed of was so different from Acadia. The mansion was a queen of a house. But he would have this house, Georgette or not. The spacious site, the backsweep from the Teche, the majesty of the wilderness, all these cried out for the white pillared house, the house it must have. And will have, he vowed. One day.

Gabriel and François worked without ceasing, seven days a week, from dark to dark. They tended their stock, cooked, cleared brush; they plowed, planted, and went at the brush again. Their bodies, always powerful, strengthened. Their work capacity increased with their stamina. They alternated days—one on Gabriel's land, one on François' land. When they dropped to their blankets, they were instantly asleep; while they slept, their aching bodies recovered.

As they worked, talk of Elodie spilled out of François. "That missionary priest could marry us," he said once. "It being different here, maybe he can hurry our banns. But he could marry you and Georgette fast, because your banns are posted."

"It's no sure thing, François. Don't hurt yourself."

"What's no sure thing—hurt myself how?"

"That they'll find us. If you build hope so high and it gets knocked down—"

"That'll not happen because I'll never give up and she'll never give up. And Georgette. She's as stubborn as a girl can be. I mean no offense, Gabriel."

Despite the uncertainty, Gabriel had to swallow a grin. Georgette was indeed obstinate; she would not give up.

Two Attakapas turned up one wet afternoon just after Gabriel and François had dressed a deer on François' land. They were strongly built, wore breechcloths and moccasins and their bodies glistened with the warm rain. Their copper colored skin was hairless and tattooed, heads shaved except for a tuft from which hung one long black lock down the back. One wore a short necklace of shells, the other an armlet. Each carried a bow and arrows and a sharp hunting knife.

For a moment no one spoke. Dark Acadian eyes searched dark Attakapas eyes. Despite Burdell's assurances that the Indians were peaceful, both Gabriel and François felt wary.

"Friend," Gabriel said, pointing to himself.

"Friend," François repeated, with the same gesture.

One Indian touched his smooth chest. "Attakapas," he said, and his voice seemed to come from the great, raining wilderness.

Gabriel and François nodded. "Friends," they said.

The Indians looked at François' sodden, makeshift tent.

"Teepee," one said.

"His teepee," Gabriel responded, indicating François. He gestured to where his own tent could be seen, pointed to himself. "My teepee." He then pointed to François' ax and pantomimed chopping. "Teepee. Like post, like inn. Teepee here—teepee there."

The Attakapas gazed. Then Gabriel noticed one of the Indians eyeing the deer meat. "Gift," he said. He lifted a hindquarter of the deer, and François a forequarter, and they held them out to the visitors.

Each Indian took his quarter, expressionless. "White man teepee," said one. "Friends."

They turned and moved toward the wet and dripping forest. Suddenly they vanished.

François wiped his brow. "They walked off with half our meat," he said, "but they didn't scalp us. What do you think they'll do next?"

"Nothing," Gabriel predicted. "Burdell said they don't go in for thievery, though maybe it was different before their war. Now they probably just want to be left alone."

"And get gifts," François said, grinning.

Gabriel grinned, too. "Even the Micmacs liked a gift," he reminded François. "Just courtesy, that's what it means to them."

They labored on, barechested, sweating under the Louisiana sun. They cultivated their crops; they felled trees and built fences to confine their stock; they hewed boards and built stables. It seemed to Gabriel, as they whittled out pegs by the light of cook fire and lantern, that he had never been anything but exhausted. At the same time, he knew he had never been stronger.

François agreed "It's Elodie and Georgette. Because it's for them."

Gabriel felt a stir in his loins, the first real one in weeks.

They tossed a stone, Gabriel won, and they built his house first. They felled cypress, hewed boards and shingles, and whittled pegs. When they formed and fired the brick, they made enough for both houses.

Gabriel's dwelling was erected on the site he had chosen that first morning. The main house held a sitting room with a fireplace and a bedroom. There were four slender posts across the front of the porch, and a stairway from it leading to the attic. Behind the house was a separate building, a kitchen-dining room.

The day came when every shingle was on, shutters in place, floors rubbed to a glow. "It wants but one thing," François said. "Glass windows, and those we'll get. I'm going to build Elodie's house like this if you have no objection."

"I'm honored."

They built the other house. The endless work continued, the felling, hewing, whittling. They hoed their crops, tended stock, supplied themselves with game and fish. They dried moss, got credit against future trapping, bought stout cloth at the post and made themselves mattresses. They set the double rows of oaks to mark the driveways—two for Gabriel, one for François, who wanted no fine mansion.

When François' house was finished, Gabriel began to labor on a new, more immediate dream. North of the kitchen house, so there would be a full view of the Teche, he set posts into the ground in the shape of a room. He made a door opening and a window opening on each of the four sides, and laid roof poles. Once the framework was done, he found grapevines, dug them up, and planted them all around the skeleton he thought of as his grape house. He would train the vines so that, when they reached maturity, the vines, with their green, glistening leaves, and dewy bunches of purple grapes would form the walls and the roof. He would make chairs later, and this grape house would be a highlight of his plantation, a creation of beauty.

François' cow dropped a fine bull calf. François went about singing over that as they cleared ditches, never missing a stroke of the hoe. "I've named the cow Daisy," he announced. "And now I've got two bulls— that will put fresh blood into our stock. I'm calling the calf Prince and the old bull King, because he's the oldest bull on the Teche."

Gabriel laughed, accusing his friend of foolishness. But when his mare foaled he named her Lola and her wobbly-legged colt Belle.

"Belle!" scoffed François, laughing. "What's so fine about that knob-kneed filly?"

"She'll be a perfect red. With my other mare due, I may decide to breed fine horses right along with growing indigo."

"Sugar cane."

"That, too."

"You breed horses, my friend, and I'll breed cows." Gabriel nodded.

Though he bantered with François about naming a cow, he had long since given the name of Noir to his black and beautiful stallion.

He thought of his house, of the grape house, up the sides of which his vines were now creeping, of the great white dream mansion to come. He thought of his league of land, and he realized that it, too, must have a name.

L'Acadie, he thought, L'Acadie.

TEN

It wasn't until September that François and Gabriel stopped work for two days to explore their grants at last. Though they had ridden over much of their lands while working on the roads, felling trees, and hunting, they had been too busy working to either evaluate or appreciate their lands. They agreed to take turns. One would explore, while the other would tend both home-sites and all stock, and the next day they would reverse the procedure.

"I mean to see every inch of my land," François proclaimed happily from Noir's back that first day. "From one end of both bayous to the other, and everything between. I'll know my land, how it lays, where I'll plant every crop, where I'll pasture every cow. I'll know every bird, every mosquito."

Gabriel spent the morning working on his vines, thinning and transplanting. He rowed across the bayou, found things as they should be, and returned to L'Acadie. He walked through the empty sitting room and into the bedroom, where he stretched out on his mattress on the floor.

Suddenly such a need took him that his male part sprang erect. Why, he wondered miserably, after all this time of working himself numb should he be cursed the first time he lay down during the day to rest? He wondered, not for the first time, whether François suffered the same torture.

He groaned, cursed, and turned on his lonely mattress. Without Georgette, there was nothing he could do about it. Even if he were so disposed, there wasn't another women, other than Attakapas women, between here and New Orleans. He wished Georgette would find her way to him damned soon.

It wasn't only that he wanted to bed her, he told himself. It didn't mean a man didn't think fondly of a girl because he had a desperate need to push into her body. That was a part of loving.

Yet, at this moment, is his state, he knew love was the last thing troubling him. If Georgette came through the door now and even if she berated him for seducing her, for permitting the English to separate them, he would grab her, and tear off her skirt. He would be into her in a breath; he would assuage this agony, this damned curse as he had back in Acadia, amid the trees.

He wasn't aware of falling asleep, much less did he remember any dream. But when he woke, his clothing was soiled, and so was the mattress. He had never felt so hopeless since first he had become a prisoner and was taken from his native land. For if a man couldn't be master of his desire, of what could he be master?

He had just had time to clean up and turn the mattress over when he heard François shout from the bayou. He went onto the porch and watched as his friend permitted Noir, still full of meanness even though he had been out all day and had swum the Teche twice, to go at a full run for the stable.

Gabriel smiled over the spirited creature trapped in the wilderness with four mares, all unavailable to him for some time to come. He determined to work Noir harder, ride him faster, to help him by tiring him.

François halted at the steps, shaking his head. "Never did I ride such a one. What colts he'll give! And Gabriel, mon Dieu, such land, such wealth as is mine. My own bayou! It's small beside the Teche, but on the league that I, François Hebert, own, my own bayou begins and winds, so crooked you would not believe, and also ends, all on my own land. Elodie, I'm calling it, Bayou Elodie. My land, Gabriel, is wonderful. Tomorrow, you will find that we have come to heaven on earth."

That night, happy for his friend, anticipating his own day of exploration, Gabriel slept untortured and dreamlessly.

Noir was in wild spirits the next morning when Gabriel slid the bridle on him. He fought the bit, reared, and pawed the ground. Gabriel, keeping a hard hand, his rifle slung by a strap at his shoulder, led the prancing stallion through the gate.

With Noir sidestepping and trying to rear, Gabriel watched his chance and vaulted astride the sleek back. Instantly Noir began to buck, and then he went into a full run, and Gabriel stuck to him, his knees dug in, never letting full up on the reins.

The stallion plunged on so fast that Gabriel could see nothing. Gradually Noir dropped speed and was as manageable as ever he was, and Gabriel could look out upon his land in the early light. My farm, he thought, and instantly corrected himself. Plantation, L'Acadie was a plantation. A farm, even a big one, could be seen with one long look, but this seemed to reach from one side of the sky to the other.

All morning he rode his land. He rode where it lay smooth, gently sloping, ready for the plow. He rode past brush, through scrub that would take back-breaking labor to clear, and smiled. The brush was his own at least, and he would deal with it, for what lay beneath it was his, also.

He rode through his trees and listened to his birds. As he viewed what he owned, excitement and awe rose in him, and he understood his friend's elation the night before.

It was afternoon before he neared his own small bayou along his eastern area, and he made for it because he himself was thirsty and knew that the horse was in need of a long drink and a rest. He staked Noir, who began to drink and eat grass. Gabriel lounged beside the stream, eating cornbread and venison that he had packed. Graceful magnolias followed the bayou here. Downstream, he glimpsed cypress trees, their great knobs in water that looked almost black. The timber was deep on each side so, when he set out again, he led the stallion.

He discovered the spot at which his bayou rose from swamp to begin meandering, widening as it wound through the fresh-water marshes. Walking through the thick forest of cypress trees, he was struck anew by the solidity of this tree, and determined to build his mansion of it.

Leading the head-tossing Noir, he followed the bayou to where it dwindled into swamp. He estimated the inlet ran six or seven miles.

It was almost dusk as he rounded what he thought to be the last bend. Noir was coming along behind, with only an occasional jerk of his head. Here were more, huge cypress trees, which seemed, in the dark light, to be kneeling in black water, the long moss like the hair of women trapped, unable to lift their rooted feet. He snorted at his own foolishness, wondering if a man could go crazy because of his own hungers. Like yesterday on his new mattress, thinking of Georgette. Now even cypresses were turning into women.

Tomorrow, he thought, turning his mind to other matters, he would harvest. After the crops were in, he would cut winter wood, clear ditches, cut trees and start building furniture.

Ahead, one of the cypresses moved its knees. He stopped. Noir snorted and yanked his head. The tree moved again. Gabriel's hand went for his rifle. Again there was movement, then a sliding sound.

"Who is it?" he called. "Answer, or I'll shoot!"

The words were foolish; they wouldn't impress an Indian. But it was no Indian, for a redskin would have sent his arrow by now.

There was a splash, then a moan. "M'sieu—" said a voice, filled with pleading. It was a soft voice, a woman's voice, and it was rich, with a hint of secret, hidden music.

"Where are you?" he asked, peering.

"M'sieu—ahead—at the big cypress—"

He moved toward the voice, not breathing, lest he lose her. Silently he cursed Noir for the sounds he made.

He reached the biggest cypress, and now he could see a face, white against the dusk. Only a face, for otherwise she was submerged.

He tied Noir, slid into the water, and made his way to her. Putting his arms around her, he lifted her and, water streaming from them, he climbed ashore with her. It wasn't until he laid her on the ground that he realized she was naked.

Gabriel saw a slender, perfect body that was scratched, cut, and bruised from high-boned cheek to feet. He saw a golden girl—golden skin, and long hair darkened by water, which, dry, would be a deeper gold. Her eyes were closed, lashes upcurled. Around her neck, on a cord, was a small leather pouch that hung below her collarbone. In the well of her throat a pulse leapt so hard he knew she was both conscious and terrified.

"Why were you in the water?" he asked.

Slowly, she opened her eyes. They were so dark a gold they hinted at amber. She stared up in fright and wariness.

"I was frightened, m'sieu," she whispered. "Hiding."

"Who were you hiding from?"

"—them—"

"Who are they? What are they?"

Her eyelids fluttered shut. He waited, then realized she was unconscious. He put his head between her small but full breasts and listened. A tiny golden nipple touched his cheek like a flower. Her heart was beating.

He sat back and regarded her in dismay. He had no idea what to do, how to rouse her. He stared at this girl who had materialized with the suddenness of a storm at sea. He had never seen a girl so beautiful. She looked as if she had been dipped in honey, in pale, melted gold. He had not known breasts could be so lovely, beckoning, delectable. The gentle insweep of her small waist, her flat stomach, the curve of her hips made him catch his breath, as did the lustrous, darkly golden thatch, which was like a jewel.

He was aware of his male part throbbing, but there was a difference now. The yearning was combined with tenderness and the wish to protect.

He had, somehow, to awaken her, so he put his hands on her shoulders and shook her gently. "Mademoiselle," he said quietly. But though he shook her again, repeating the word, there was no response.

Looking at her body, he saw every scratch, cut, and bruise and knew he had to get her to shelter. He tried once more to rouse her, but could not. She had reached the end of her endurance. Whoever she had been hiding from had terrified her into running, and it had to have been for her life.

The hair on his neck lifted. Who could be after her? Would they attack him, should they appear at this moment? He listened into the swamp, but there were only wilderness sounds—the song of frogs, the buzz of mosquitoes, the swishing of water.

He lifted the girl. Even as he turned to Noir, her body in his arms, he felt the delicate bones and knew that she was half starved.

"Whoa!" he muttered to Noir, "whoa, damn you!"

The stallion moved nervously, switching his tail. Quickly, before Noir could react, Gabriel dropped the girl face down over the horse's sleek back.

Holding the girl with one hand, he grabbed the reins with the other. "Stand, you devil, stand!" Noir snorted and tried to toss his head; Gabriel took his hand off the girl, gripped the reins close to the stallion's mouth and bore down on the bit; with his other hand, he untied the end of the reins from the tree.

Giving them a tug, he moved away from the bayou, exerting downward pressure to keep Noir from rearing. Somehow, the stallion followed. Gabriel pulled cruelly on the bit, cursing and commanding, wondering how much the animal would tolerate without fighting loose, bucking off his unwanted burden, and galloping away.

At the head of the bayou, Gabriel turned west for the house. He walked as fast as he could, and Noir followed, giving no trouble, probably, Gabriel thought, because he wanted some grain. It was getting very late.

The girl must be half starved. If she had been fleeing through the swamp, she would have had nothing to eat but wild cane and a few berries.

When the house showed under starlight, Noir wanted to trot, and Gabriel had to hold him in. As they drew near, he saw the glow of a fire outside—he was keeping the kitchen house new as was François for Elodie—and knew his friend had supper waiting.

Instinct told Gabriel to bring Noir up on the north side of the house, carry the girl inside, and try to keep her presence a secret. But there was no reason for that, he told himself. If it had been François who had found her, he would be bringing her home. No man would leave a girl unconscious in the wilderness, no matter who was chasing her or why.

So he called out. "I'm here! I've got someone who needs help."

François came running. Gabriel shoved the reins at him. "Hold this devil steady while I get her off, will you? Then turn him into the pasture and bring the lantern."

François asked no question.

Gabriel strode through the dark sitting room, carrying the girl, and into the bedroom, where he laid her on the mattress. He was in the sitting room lighting a candle when François hurried in with the lantern.

"Who is it—what's wrong?" he demanded.

With a candle, Gabriel went again to the bedroom, François at his heels. "You going to tell me or not?"

"I found her. She's in serious trouble. She fainted and hasn't come out of it."

"She's not dead?"

"She was breathing when I carried her in."

They were at the mattress. They knelt, one on each side, shining their lights. Light touched the hollow of her throat. Her pulse was beating, but not violently, as before. Light flickered across her lovely breasts, which were rising and falling unevenly and too fast.

"Mon Dieu!" whispered François. "She's naked—in the swamps, naked!"

Gabriel sprang to the wall pegs, took down his other shirt, and covered the girl.

François lifted the lantern higher to reveal the lovely face, the high cheekbones, the even features, the shapely lips. "Mon Dieu," he whispered, "but she is beautiful! She is without doubt the most beautiful girl I have seen."

"She's young," Gabriel whispered.

"Yes."

"Is she going to—do you think—?"

"She'll be all right. A girl who faints comes back to herself. Have you no idea what happened?"

"I found her in my back bayou, up to her neck in the water. She said she was hiding. I got her onto the bank and asked who she was hiding from. All she said was 'them.'"

Just then she moaned, and François held the lantern close, studying her face. She moaned again but her eyes remained closed. Light showered the golden skin of her face.

"Mon Dieu!" breathed François.

"We must do something," said Gabriel. "Put water on her face, rub her hands—"

"She is waking. And it is not of the beauty I said, 'Mon Dieu.'"

Slowly the girl opened her eyes. Her eyes were lustrous, and she gazed at Gabriel with trust, then closed her eyes once more.

François tugged at Gabriel and drew him away to the sitting room.

"What is it?" Gabriel whispered. "We've got to—"

"We will. But there is a thing you have not realized."

"What thing? What's so important it must be said now?"

"It's the way you look at her, my friend, your tenderness. She is in deep trouble indeed, and I have in me the sureness that this has come upon her because she is—different. She's not like Elodie or Georgette."

179

"Of course she's not like them! She's not Acadian. Her French is different, softer, what I heard of it. But something very bad happened to her, or she wouldn't be in the swamp!"

"Yes. What has happened to her is what I lie awake fearing has happened to Elodie, and I'll help with this girl and pray someone else will help Elodie. But before we tend this one, my friend, before we touch her, there is a fact you must know."

"What's so damned important for me to know? When she's in there—"

"That which was on your face when you looked at her is impossible, Gabriel, friend. You are Acadian, seeking a new life in a new land of Southern people. You have a fiancée, and for her you have built a house—"

"So?"

"This beautiful girl is not for you, my friend. Even if you had no Georgette, it would be thus. Because the girl in your bedroom is not white."

ELEVEN

"You're mad!" Gabriel exclaimed. "She's as white as we are! Whiter! We've got an olive cast, and now we're as brown as any Attakapa!"

"Olive from Latin blood, brown from the sun. This one—her skin is gold, her cheekbones high and a little thick. Her lips—I've seen such lips on the streets in New Orleans. I thought you saw them too, that you'd know—pah! It's not a thing to quarrel, friend. She is what she is, and we are what we are."

Silently denying any truth in what François said, Gabriel went back into the bedroom.

"I'll bring coffee," François called.

She was sitting up. She had put on his shirt and buttoned it. It was so large it hung in folds and the sleeves more than covered her wrists, though she had turned them back. Her hair, which was drying, curled about her face. Trust shone from her. "M'sieu, merci."

There really was a dark richness to her light voice. He crouched beside the mattress.

"It is your home you have brought me to, m'sieu?"

"Yes. I've just built it. I'm from Acadia," he continued, casting about for a way in which to assure her that she was safe, that she could, in turn, speak of herself.

"My papa knew of the Acadians, of how unjust the English were. He had sympathy for you." She hesitated. "You also, m'sieu, were pursued. And your friend?"

"We were taken—driven."

"And now you hide, like Tonton?"

"That's your name—Tonton?"

"Oui, m'sieu."

"And what else?"

"Just Tonton, m'sieu."

"We're not hiding," he said. "The French in New Orleans gave us land grants, and we've each built a house, drained land, and grown crops. This land here is mine. Across the bayou, the land belongs to my friend. His name is François Hebert, mine is Gabriel Leblanc."

"Papa spoke of grants. It was your land, where you found me?"

"Yes."

"You have much land, m'sieu. I knew when you put me on the horse, sometimes I knew I was being taken a distance, other times I think I slept."

"You fainted."

"You saved me. Merci, m'sieu."

"Who was chasing you—why?"

She was silent for a moment. "You I must tell, m'sieu," she said. "For, because of me, you risk yourself."

"Who was it?"

"Men who hunt slaves who escape, m'sieu—white

men. It is their business to track down such as Tonton. There is a reward."

At first he couldn't accept what she had said. And then he would not accept it. It wasn't true. François was wrong, she herself was mistaken. The whole thing was a mistake—the chase, the need for the chase.

She sensed this. "But it is so, m'sieu."

"Who set them on you?" he demanded, words clogging his throat.

"My master, m'sieu. My new master, who bought me in New Orleans. He paid five thousand dollars."

He stared.

"Oui, m'sieu. I'm a danger to you."

"There's more to it than that, there has to be!"

"Oui, m'sieu. My papa was white, a Creole, with blonde hair from his Spanish mother and fair skin from both her and his French father. I'm so much like him, so little like my mother, who was his. . . . He was getting me freedom papers, but before—he died from his heart."

Gabriel was speechless.

François had returned. He extended a cup of coffee to Tonton.

She held the cup in both hands, and, though they trembled, lifted it, and sipped. Her eyes, over the rim, never left Gabriel.

François departed to bring supper. Gabriel stared at her.

"M'sieu—"

"You say you're a slave, but your speech, your manner—"

"Papa, m'sieu. He was of intellect—mathematics, poetry, history, languages. He kept a tutor for his white children and a governess to teach his daughters many graces. I was included in this, for it was his intention for me to go far away and live as white."

"The man who bought you. What is he like, what is his name?"

"The name doesn't matter, m'sieu. Not in the swamps. He is old, older than Papa."

But he hadn't treated her as had her father, or she

182

wouldn't now be sitting on a moss mattress in a raw, new Acadian house. She wouldn't be holding a wooden cup against his rough shirt, the material of which must be painful against her battered body.

"What did this man—do to you?" he asked, unable to keep hoarseness from his tone. When she didn't reply, but dropped her gaze, he gripped her shoulders, feeling her cringe.

"Tell."

She met his eyes fully. "He is evil, m'sieu."

"Did he—touch you?"

"No, m'sieu. Never."

"How did you avoid—? You're so young!"

"Seventeen, m'sieu. A woman. Papa told me many things. He didn't wish to frighten me, but it was through him, he said, that my life would not be like that of his white daughters. He explained what a woman like myself can expect. He told me the name of his good friend in Mexico City, a white man who would see me settled as white, and he gave me gold. " She touched the spot where the pouch at her neck lay. "This a kind slave girl hid for me while I was naked on the block, then managed to give it back when she was sold and tied beside me. Papa made a plan of escape to follow should he die. The moment I could, I followed the plan, m'sieu. And, until now, have failed."

François had returned and now gave her a bowl of stew. "Eat while it's hot," he said.

She ate hungrily. When the bowl was empty, she set it on the floor with the cup.

"We must tend your injuries," François said.

"I can do it if you'll give me water, m'sieu. And ointment or whatever you have."

They moved to fetch things, but she stopped them with a gesture. "It is your right to hear all, both of you. To decide if you can keep me, even tonight."

"Do your telling," Gabriel said. "But I'll not put you out, exhausted and hurt."

She whispered, "Merci, m'sieu," then looked questioningly at François.

"I know you've been running," he said. "I heard."

"Oui, m'sieu. My father said that, should things go badly and I was sold, and if my master should mistreat me, I was to take my gold and go to the nearest city, taking with me also the blackest wench I could trust.

"I was, by this plan, to dress as a lady, let it be known that the woman was my slave, and take passage to Mexico City."

"You said your master didn't—" Gabriel stated.

"No. But I could tell, from the fine chamber I was given and the clothing being made, what my lot was to be. And Hazelette, the wench given me, told me that the master, who is handsome and courtly, would never make use of one such as myself until everything was of perfection."

"And you didn't wait for that?"

"No, m'sieu. Hazelette quickly let me know how she hated the master. She told of things he had done to many others. He has knives and whips. He burns the skin—does other acts I don't even know. She had been a maid to these wenches and said she'd like to kill him with her own hands because once he had used her the same way. She showed me the scars."

Stunned, the men waited for her to continue.

"I acted on Papa's advice. I had fine clothes, gold, a servant who hated the master and wanted to escape with me. Still, I was cautious before letting her know. I led her in talk until it was she who mentioned running. We worked fast. We boarded a ship, but never sailed. Hazelette betrayed me—the master had used her to test me."

"How did you get off the ship?" Gabriel asked.

"I saw her watching, m'sieu. She kept glancing at the cabin door. I sensed that she would betray me, so, as calmly as I could, I told her to unpack, that I was going on deck. This disturbed her, but she couldn't prevent me from going. On deck, I saw officers come aboard, and I slipped down the gangplank and away. Knowing they would search every ship, I engaged a man to bring me in his small boat to the bayous, hoping they would search upriver.

"But we were pursued. My boatman quickly decided that I was running and said unless I would . . . he'd turn back to New Orleans and collect the reward. I offered him gold, and he tore my dress. He—"

"Did he handle you, touch you?" demanded Gabriel.

"His hand—he grabbed my—bosom. He pinched."

"Bastard!" Gabriel muttered.

"He—knocked me backward in the boat and took hold of my dress again, and I tore loose, leaving most of it. The rest tore away as I fled, and I was without—as I was in the bayou."

"How long ago was this?" Gabriel asked.

"Days, m'sieu. Three—six. There was always pursuit, even dogs. I spent most of one day and all of a night sitting to my neck in bayous."

"Did you eat?"

"Wild cane, m'sieu, some nuts. Once I caught a fish with my hands and ate it raw."

"See any Indians?" asked François.

"None, m'sieu. After a very long time, I heard no one pursuing me. I kept going, bearing in the general direction of Mexico. I was following another little bayou, and—" She spread her hands expressively.

"That's where I found you," Gabriel said.

"Oui, m'sieu. I heard movement, and thinking it was trackers, though I heard no dogs, I slipped into the water again. It was then the weakness took me, and when I thought I would drown, that is when I made the sound that brought you to me."

"That's right. You moaned."

"I hold deep gratitude to you both. I shan't stay long enough to put you under suspicion."

After they had supplied her with what she needed for her scratches and cuts, Gabriel and François squatted at the cook fire. Gabriel listened into the night. "Nobody headed this way," he said.

"She's right, you know. She can't stay."

"We've got to let her rest, feed her."

"Not for long."

"What else can we do, throw her back into the bayou? The way the English threw our dead overboard?"

"Don't be a fool! We're harboring a runaway slave, breaking the law of the land that's giving us so much."

"A land where they sell humans like cattle!"

"That wench belongs to the man in New Orleans."

"Don't call her a wench. Her name is Tonton."

"So. It's 'Tonton' now! All right. Forty-eight hours we'll give her. And every one of them a risk. Then, if she isn't gone, we've got to tell about her at the post. We've got to report to somebody."

"The way colonists report Acadians when they're worked as slaves?"

"I'm not going to break the laws of this country."

"It is I who am harboring her, François. On my land, in my house. Besides, who would know she is a slave?"

"I knew. She is beautiful, and in countries where there are no black people, she would be as others. But here, in slave country, they will look hard and they will see. As I did. Do not risk it. You will lose everything."

Gabriel set his jaw, poured coffee, and thrust a cup at his friend. They watched the candle glow of the bedroom. When it went black, Gabriel set his cup down.

"In the morning," he said, "I'll give her that shirt and this pair of trousers. A packet of food and Lola—the colt can get along. She'll have a chance, riding, to reach Mexico."

"She won't get across Texas. A girl, alone."

"She'll have to have her chance."

François stood. "I'll make no report," he said, "but I'll not be back until she's off L'Acadie and gone."

"That'll be at dawn," Gabriel said. "She'll be on her way at dawn."

TWELVE

But even after dawn, Tonton hadn't left.

Gabriel, who had sat the night beside the fire, listening for her pursuers or for any stir she made, had heard only the usual swamp chorus. After the chores, there was still no sign of her, so he stole into the house and listened. The bedroom was silent. The thought that she had somehow slipped away sent him through the door and into the chamber.

She lay as though dead, arms outstretched, her cuts and scratches clotted with blood. Going to her, Gabriel put his ear to her heart. It was beating fast. She was burning hot, and her lips were parched.

"Tonton," he said, though he knew it was useless.

This was no swoon. She was ill and unconscious and when she did stir would probably be delirious, and he didn't have the least idea what to do. At least it wasn't smallpox; she didn't look like those on the *Esne*. He touched her again, and her skin was like fire. He had a flashing thought of the snow, the ice, back in Acadia. And then he thought of water.

He rushed to the bayou and came back with water in a cup. Lifting her, he put the cup to her lips, pressing them open with the rim. Some water trickled into her mouth, though most of it ran down her chin. He tried again, and this time he knew that water did go into her mouth, for she swallowed. He kept it up until he had gotten a small amount into her.

When he lowered her to the mattress, she moved her head from side to side, her hair curling around her flushed, golden-skinned face. She murmured, in great distress, and he tried to rouse her, assuring her that she was safe, that she was with him, but she murmured on.

He bathed her face, laying the dripping cloth first

one one cheek, then on the other. Moved by instinct, he pulled the shirt off her, wet the cloth, and wiped water across her chest, her breasts. He rubbed her wet skin with the palms of his hands until it was dry. He repeated the process, working downward over her body, wetting and rubbing, frightened by her hotness, awed by her beauty, and aware of a tender ache in his loins, a new hunger, that held both longing and reserve.

He went to the bayou for colder water. Glancing across for a sign of François, he heard the sound of an ax on wood, and knew that his friend was working on his granary. He went back to the house.

Tonton seemed to have grown hotter. He resumed the wetting and rubbing, turning her over so he could bathe her from the shoulders down.

As the hours passed, the fever began to drop. Her skin didn't burn against his palms, though it was still warm; the murmuring and tossing lessened; her lashes fluttered. Aware that she was nearing consciousness, he covered her with the shirt.

Her eyes opened and looked directly into his. She stared, puzzled, then aware. "I must go," she said, trying to sit up.

He pressed against her shoulder, and she was so weak that she fell back.

"Not now, not yet. You've had fever, may have had it all night. It's afternoon now."

"But I'm never ill, m'sieu. I can swim, ride, work—"

"You may be strong, but you've been on the run, in and out of water, with nothing to eat. You took a fever from it. You've got to rest, build some strength."

"There isn't time, m'sieu. They'll find me."

"They're not as liable to look into a settler's window as they are to comb the bayous."

"Your, friend, m'sieu. He doesn't want me here."

There was no way for her to know that. It was at the cook fire that François had spoken. Yet somehow she knew.

She was watching him. He couldn't lie to her. "No. He doesn't want to break the laws."

"M'sieu? You quarreled over a slave?"

"We didn't agree, but we didn't quarrel. He won't report this."

"But m'sieu, did he not so promise because he thinks I'll leave?"

Reluctantly, he nodded. Again she tried to sit, and again the merest touch pushed her down. "He didn't know about the fever. You've no need to worry. The last thing he said was that he'd not come here until you've gone."

"If you'll help me to stand, m'sieu."

"No," he said. Then he told her his plan. After she gained strength, he would outfit her, and she could ride for Mexico on her own horse.

"I'll pay, m'sieu."

He made a chopping motion. "I've got my land. You'll need your gold and more."

Because she must, she agreed, her eyes filled with trust. Even so, there was a listening about her, as if she were straining to hear the baying of a hound in the distance.

Her fear, along with the thought of that forest beyond his eastern boundary and a particular spot where a tremendous oak with a hollow trunk stood, put the idea of hiding her into his mind. What François said about trackers not giving up held truth not to be ignored. He would hide her, then, so that no tracker would find her.

By the time he returned, she had put on the shirt. He said nothing yet about his plan, but brought stew and milk, urging her to take all she could.

After she ate, he lowered her to the mattress and marveled when she fell instantly asleep. After a night's rest, sleeping like this, he thought, she'd be all right, and might even be able to press on and not risk hiding in the forest.

Gabriel worked on his own half-built granary, looking in on Tonton now and again. She slept the rest of the day. Just after dark, he took in a bowl of stew, and found her still asleep. He laid his palm on her brow to waken her, and once more she was burning hot.

He took off the shirt and began tenderly bathing her again. No other girl had such delicacy, he thought. Her purity flowed into him, through his gazing eyes, through the stroke of his hands. He knew that this bruised and burning girl was worth far more than five thousand dollars, that this body was beyond price.

As night wore on, the fever went down and flared again, but now Tonton was conscious. Gabriel apologized for removing the shirt. "It's the only way I can give this treatment, such as it is. I mean no disrespect."

"M'sieu," she whispered, "I've been seen so before. No master will pay money for a wench unless—"

"Hush," he muttered.

"Merci, m'sieu. This treatment is what the women in the quarters use when a baby has a high fever."

By dawn, she was still warm but eager to leave.

"No. That fever the babies had, how did it act? Did it come and go?"

"Oui, m'sieu. I've had it two days now?"

"About." He frowned. "I'm not going to trust it. Even without fever, there's weakness. You can't ride yet."

"I'll not stay here longer, m'sieu."

He stared. There was the gentle beauty of her scratched face, and there was the quiet of her nature. But beneath the gentleness and the quiet, he had come upon steel.

He told her about the hollow oak. "It's on government land, not an inch belongs to L'Acadie, so you'll be off my plantation. I'll make you a shelter today and take you there tonight. That way, nobody will be 'harboring' you, and you'll be reasonably safe while you mend. Even if they come through with dogs, they won't get your scent because you'll go there on horseback."

"You'll take me, even with fever, m'sieu?"

He hesitated, nodded.

"Merci, m'sieu. Then I will go."

"And stay until I agree you can ride?"

Now she hesitated, and he frowned.

Then she said, "Oui, m'sieu," and smiled. "Always, I am saying oui."

He grinned. "Except when you're saying no."

Her smile faded. "You don't treat me as a slave, m'sieu."

"As far as I'm concerned, you're not one," he said grimly.

She had no Negro features. He knew Acadian girls with heavier features, with skin darker than her golden skin. The only difference he could see, which resulted in making her lovelier, was the slight broadness of her cheekbones and the fullness of her lips.

"But I am a slave, m'sieu," she said.

The words were a blow across his heart. "I'll bring food and a bucket of water," he said abruptly. "Then I'll go and build your place."

He made up a tool kit, bridled Noir, gave a tug to let the stallion understand there would be no foolishness, and then gave him his head. They raced, speeding to the start of the small bayou, then crossed the swampy prairie strip, and cautiously entered government forest.

He watched for that hidden space he had found during his exploration. He almost couldn't find it, but when he did, he was well pleased; it was as he remembered it.

There was a tiny clearing, room for the shelter and a small cook fire, nothing more. Beside it was the big hollow oak, surrounded by larger trees.

He fell to work, scraping dry leaves and rubble from inside the hollow of the oak, then went deeper into the forest, cutting enough saplings to make a pole framework.

He used the inside of the oak for the rear wall and set his poles to form an area about eight feet square. He pegged roof poles, and left a door opening.

He went again into far growth and cut palmetto fronds, which he wove between the poles, making walls, and then he made a thick roof the same way. Last he gathered old, dry Spanish moss and piled it at the back of the wilderness room for a bed. He covered the moss with his own blanket.

When all was finished, he studied it from every direction. The shelter melted into the forest. Even he, who had built it, discovered it not easy to find. If anyone else spied it, it would be through sheer accident.

The job had taken longer than he thought. It would be dark soon, and he wanted to get back to L'Acadie before then. He had his outside work yet to do, and Tonton and various supplies to transport afterwards. Now he not only gave Noir his head, but urged him faster, and the stallion ran with abandon.

He rushed into the house. The bedroom was dark. He couldn't even make out the shape of the mattress. "Tonton—are you—?"

There was a small sound. Kneeling, he felt her brow. It was hot, but it was wet; she had been using the water.

"It isn't so bad now," she said. "Do we go at once, m'sieu?"

"As soon as I do the chores. Then we'll eat and go. Can you ride bareback?"

"All my life, m'sieu—bareback, saddle, anything. Mares, stallions, any mount."

He took all three horses because he wouldn't risk trying to get Noir to carry double. He loaded Trixie, the mare yet to foal, with a blanket for the door opening and other necessities.

He helped Tonton, wearing his trousers and shirt, mount Lola, and they started single file, slowly, Gabriel first on Noir, holding him in, leading Trixie. Tonton rode Lola, reins in hand. She tried to conceal her weakness, but when Gabriel had lifted her onto the horse, he had felt her trembling.

Clouds hid the stars. Neither of them spoke, but Gabriel looked back frequently to make sure she was still on the mare. At the bayou, Gabriel filled the water bucket, remounted, and held it with care, dealing with Noir with one hand.

They rode into forest and on. Here the darkness

thickened into impenetrable blackness, and Gabriel had to trust Noir to lead, avoiding growth until, gradually, his eyes began to adjust. It took awhile to locate the shelter, but at last he reined up near it. He tied Noir and hurried to Tonton, leaving Trixie's reins hanging.

"We're here," he said as he reached for her.

As he carried her into the shelter and laid her on the blanketed moss, he could feel the wild fever through his shirt. She murmured something, and he leaned over her, speaking her name, but there was no response.

Once again he bathed and rubbed her. In darkness he battled the fever. Eventually it ebbed, and the moment came when she was again merely warm and again aware.

"M'sieu—we have arrived?"

"Yes. There's no way to make a light." He spread the shirt over her, and she knew at once.

"How long did it last, m'sieu?"

"Long enough."

"As long as before, m'sieu?"

"Not that long."

"It may not come again, m'sieu."

But it did return on each of the following days. Gabriel laid out a routine, racing Noir the short way of four miles, which took forty-five minutes, between forest and L'Acadie, timing his visits so they would coincide with Tonton's rise of temperature. When the fever lessened, he rushed home, tended his stock, and cooked for himself and Tonton, taking her the food the next day. She ate obediently but never enough. The need to harvest was on his mind, but the need of the girl helpless in the forest was greater.

Once the fever leveled off, he managed one noon to cross the Teche to François, who was about to harvest. He hastened through stubble to where his friend had stopped working and stood waiting.

He called, "She is gone, then?"

"She's gone," Gabriel called back.

Guilt shot through him. Then he thought of that awful fever, of her helplessness, and knew he must contain the guilt.

"I'll ask no questions," François said. "The less I know, the better. I never wanted to harm her, you know."

"Yes, my friend. I do know."

Acadian or runaway slave, he ached to say, there wasn't any difference between them. The Acadian wasn't allowed freedom in Nova Scotia or some of the colonies; the Negro wasn't allowed freedom in the South, not even here, in the wilderness.

They fell silent. They were, basically, in accord. Yet Gabriel knew that, underneath their friendship, the clash they had had over Tonton would remain.

"You started your harvest," Gabriel said, changing the subject.

"It's all right. I didn't expect you. Not with—you've had enough to deal with first."

"The truth is," Gabriel confessed, troubled over the deceit, "I can't help today, either."

"Don't worry," François said, an uneasy note in his tone, almost as though he knew that the trouble had not yet really ended. "Take the time you need, my friend."

Gabriel had returned to his property when he saw a pirogue rounding the bend. He waited, unable as yet to make out the two men in the boat. For no reason, he felt alarmed. Don't be a fool, he tried to reassure himself. It's Burdell and that man Morphy from the inn.

But, as the craft drew nearer, he could see that neither of its passengers was Burdell. The possibility remained that one was Morphy, whom he hadn't yet seen, and some trader. The men were dressed in rough clothes and were lean, weathered, and hard faced. They were also hard eyed.

Wary, yet offering common hospitality, Gabriel called out, "There's a good spot to tie up yonder, just before you reach my boat." He pointed.

One of the men gave a chop of his hand to indicate understanding. They veered to shore and, though their manner wasn't exactly threatening, neither was it friendly. The hair on Gabriel's neck stirred, and his throat was so dry he couldn't swallow, but he forced himself to maintain a relaxed stance as they walked to him.

"Gabriel Leblanc," he said. "This is my plantation."

"Simpson," said the first man. He was tall, gaunt, and brown. "Winters there," he said, jerking his head at the other man, who was only a shade less gaunt. "Feller at the tradin' post told us there's a couple settlers here."

Simpson shot a look at the house and beyond. Gabriel broke out in a sweat. He didn't need to hear what Simpson said next, he already knew.

"We're trackin' a wench," he announced. "Property of Monsieur Crozat, New Orleans. She was run into the swamps. Our dogs lost her scent, and the handlers took 'em back. Give up. Me'n Winters ain't the givin' up kind. Been all along the Teche, the other bayous, one back of you, and back of the place across-bayou. Even in the forest and Injun villages. Nothin'."

"And now you want to search my house, my buildings. And those of my friend."

"That's right."

"To see if we hide runners."

"No sech thing! The nigra's tricky, Mr. Leblanc. You wouldn't know they was anywheres near, and they'd be hid, listenin'."

"There's not much room here to hide in. You can see that."

"They're tricky, awful tricky."

"Which means you want to look for yourselves."

"With yer permission."

Knowing nothing of any law in the matter, Gabriel was of the opinion that these men could not, without a legal paper, step foot on L'Acadie to search. Simpson's next words seemed to verify this.

"If ye don't give leave, we'll keep watch. And if the wench is on either plantation, we'll git her."

"Go ahead," Gabriel told them. "Look."

They tramped roughly through the main house and through the kitchen house, where they opened the oven, looked inside, then slammed it shut. They went through the stable. They even tramped around the unfinished granary and the pigpen. They examined the Grape House, and finally went into the fields.

Gabriel went part of the way, then waited where they could see him while they literally beat his fields. He stood hardly breathing lest they go further, to the little bayou and on again, into the forest. But at the end of the fields they turned and came back. By this time Gabriel was drenched with sweat.

"If she ain't across-bayou," Winters said, after he had drunk his fill of water, "we got no choice but to head fer Texas."

"What's for a runner in Texas?" Gabriel asked.

"Space. She ain't in the bayous. She can't go back to New Orleans or upriver. We know she headed this direction. There ain't nothin' left *but* Texas. And we're goin' to git her, wherever she runs."

Gabriel kept his face blank but surged with inner relief that Tonton hadn't been well enough to ride, not with these two at her heels. He walked with them to their pirogue and waited as they pushed off.

After they left, he sat on his porch. Then, lest they notice that he was idling and become suspicious and return, he went to his granary and began to work.

François would let them search, but he would not mention Tonton. He'd not betray, even by the twitch of an eyebrow, that she was supposedly, at this moment, on her way to Texas. It would take them fully as long to search François' place as it had taken here. He kept doggedly on at the granary.

It was quite late in the afternoon by the time Gabriel saw the trackers clamber into their pirogue and start back downstream. They glanced back at L'Acadie as they rowed, and once he thought they were going to return, but they did not.

François resumed his reaping without a glance

across-bayou, and Gabriel returned to his granary, but a few minutes after the pirogue had rounded the bend, he was hurrying to the stable lot. In record time, he was astride Noir, streaking for the forest.

THIRTEEN

Tonton was sitting on her moss bed, wearing the shirt. The wooden bowl was at hand, the cloth in the water. "I'm better, m'sieu," she said, but there was weakness in her tone that she couldn't hide. "By morning it is certain I can leave."

"You can't go tomorrow." Before she could protest, Gabriel recounted the trackers' visit.

"But now I *must* go, m'sieu! These men never give up, and if they come again to the little bayou—"

It was then he had to tell her: "They're heading for Texas."

"Oh, m'sieu!" Her eyes became so luminous he knew she was holding back tears.

"I'd guess they'll ride out first thing tomorrow. Your only chance is to stay here."

"M'sieu, it's too dangerous!"

"Your only hope is to give them time. They'll turn back, have to, because they'll not find a trace. They'll go back to New Orleans. Your trail will be dead." He didn't believe his last statement. No devil in New Orleans who had paid five thousand dollars for such beauty would give up. The reward would be raised, and fresh trackers would enter the hunt. However, the longer she could remain hidden, the fainter her trail would be. Then, with luck, after Simpson and Winters gave up, she could get across Texas and into Mexico.

"How long must I wait, m'sieu? Weeks, months?"

"Something like that."

Her expression was sad, and she was even more beautiful to him.

197

"I could leave sooner, m'sieu. I'd be traveling behind them, days behind."

"It would be impossible to avoid meeting someone they had questioned. Someone who had seen you would claim the reward."

"I'll avoid people, m'sieu. Until San Antonio, where I'll outfit myself as a lady. None will suspect."

"That's a wild, crazy chance."

"So Papa said, m'sieu. But it is the only chance."

"Not before you're strong enough."

"That will be soon, m'sieu. I am most grateful."

He seized the opportunity for which he had been waiting. "Then," he said, "you'll make me a promise."

"Anything, m'sieu."

"Unless someone finds this place and you're forced to run, you won't leave until I agree."

She waited, her eyes sinking into his. "I promise, m'sieu. Unless I'm forced to run. This I owe to you for your kindness."

"Promise that you'll come to L'Acadie. If you can."

"That as well, m'sieu."

"Even if the fever burns. It sounds wild, but set your mind on it. Promise. To remember, even with the fever."

"Oui, m'sieu. I promise."

When he returned later, she was burning with fever. Gratefully, she let him bathe her, and he worked in darkness, only the palms of his hands knowing her beauty. Rubbing, he caressed that beauty, his hands moving gently, and when they came onto the softly firm breasts, the flowerlike nipples, he was drawn to her with marvelous hunger.

She was cooler. He worked on, his yearning growing. He stroked slowly across her breast; the nipple hardened, and he trembled.

Lifting her hand, she laid it along his cheek. "M'sieu," she whispered, and the manner in which she shaped the word, the tenderness, made him tremble. Her other hand came to his other cheek, and she whispered, "Oui, m'sieu. Please—oh, please—!"

No thought of Georgette entered him, no memory of banns or of what had happened in that forest far to the north. No anger at being torn from Acadia existed; the voyage, smallpox, searching for lost ones, letters waiting in New Orleans, all vanished, had never been.

The identity of the whispering girl under his hands was forgotten. Her desperate flight did not exist. Even her illness was gone. There was only the feel of her, the whispering tenderness; there were only his glowing loins, the true and honest need to join himself to her who offered.

Swiftly he was naked, was pressing that throb where it must go, his breath a tremendous knot. Something kept him from reaching her core, and he recognized that she was a virgin.

He drew back, then thrust vigorously, heard her breath catch, and was enveloped by her tight, hot depths. Even as he began to move, somehow holding himself under control, he felt her inner walls close and grip, hold and bathe. He moved faster because he couldn't do otherwise. The voice of night sighed outside; a salt-laden breeze rattled the palmetto walls. His breath shuddered, and he plunged now, not too fast, giving her time, his arms quivering as he held his weight off her.

Ever so slightly, she began to move under him. Within those sweet depths, he felt himself moving helplessly faster. Her movement grew stronger and spurred him beyond endurance, and he burst within her, and the bursting sent sparks and a flood of blazing fire through his veins, along his spine to his head. It lasted, bursting on, the sparks and the blaze, but never once, caught in ecstasy, did he forget the source, the lovely, priceless girl he had miraculously found.

He lay joined to her, and again they moved together, a new music of the bayou country. The glory that contained him, the arms that held him, the gasping, "M'sieu, oh, m'sieu . . ." led him to burst anew, murmuring truth, "I love you, Tonton, I love you!"

"M'sieu—"

The thought of her illness struck him, and he rolled aside, holding her. She was gasping, her breath shallow, her body damp.

"Have I hurt you?" he asked, alarmed.

"M'sieu," she murmured, "it has done no harm! I've been in a dreadful nightmare, and you—have taken it away and given me beauty. It has broken the fever. Please—feel."

Her damp body was cool. His breath unknotted, but his blood was still pounding. He lay as one stricken, both from what he had taken from a girl so ill and from wonder.

He was driven to speak. "I love you," he repeated. "Do you—is it possible—?"

"But oui, m'sieu! I wouldn't offer myself without love." Her fingers touched his chest. "It is a miracle, such love, m'sieu."

"Gabriel," he corrected. "It's not 'm'sieu' now."

"M'sieu, she insisted. "It is as I was taught. White gentlemen are addressed so. That is what I called Papa himself."

"A husband is different."

"You're not my husband, m'sieu."

"I will be."

"It is not allowed, m'sieu, that a white man make a Negro his wife."

"You're no Negro!"

"I have the blood, m'sieu. I am mulatto."

"It doesn't matter, and it doesn't show."

"People can see it, m'sieu. Here they can, and here it does matter, and here is where you live."

"This bayou country is so big, with so few people, and if those who come are Acadian—"

"Your friend is Acadian. He knew."

"If we say you're from Mexico—"

"Possibly, m'sieu. Only my master—we'd live in danger of his finding me and prosecuting you for stealing his property."

"I'll buy you from the devil!"

"M'sieu, m'sieu!"

He would never be able to raise five thousand dollars. He couldn't borrow on a land grant, couldn't sell it to any penniless settler who himself would apply for a grant.

He brooded. Tonton grew heavier against him, and he knew that she slept. He moved his head so he could feel her breath on his cheek. She was his beloved; she needed him. She was his life; there was no other. He wanted to protect, cherish, and work for her. He wanted to take her to L'Acadie now, this moment and build for her that great, pillared mansion.

Georgette, he thought suddenly. With her, it had been that rod of lust. Even in the forest, there had been no tenderness, and now he knew there had never been love. Georgette had wanted a husband; he had wanted a wife to bed, tend his house, bear his children. Holding his beloved, he wished Georgette well, wherever she might be, and believed with certainty that she would get for herself the husband she wanted.

Now, though Tonton needed sleep, he put his lips on her softly parted lips and kissed them long and lightly. She stirred, her arms entwined him, and she kissed him tenderly in return.

"M'sieu-love," she whispered. "That's what I'll call you. M'sieu-love."

Before he could reply that it was the most beautiful name in existence, she had fallen asleep. He lay holding her, not daring to stir, knowing that his future would be ruined if he couldn't keep her.

FOURTEEN

Gabriel waited for Tonton's strength to build. When she was well again, they would discuss marriage.

While he waited, he taught her how to keep a small, smokeless fire. He cut wood and hid it nearby. He brought candles, which she could use with the blanket covering the door opening, brought pen and paper from the post when she confessed, shyly, that she, like her papa, enjoyed writing verse. He brought foodstuffs at night and water from the bayou so she could remain in her hidden spot.

She showed him a squirrel she had tamed that would sit on her shoulder and accept a nut from her fingers. All day—for he came to her now after dark and left before dawn—he feared lest some prowling wildcat find her or some wandering Attakapas. As time passed and she saw nothing more dangerous than the tamed squirrel and birds, they both came to feel a degree of ease.

"Especially, M'sieu-love," she said one night as she lay naked beside him, "as you're always with me when it's dark."

"And this?" he teased, making a path of kisses between her breasts.

"This most of all, M'sieu-love," she murmured as she turned to him.

With his days free, Gabriel threw himself into work. He and François helped each other harvest; they finished their granaries and filled them.

Each night Gabriel rushed to Tonton, and she came into his arms. He had never thought, would not have believed, that there could be such intimacy. He told her so one night, after they had made long and lingering love. "I didn't know," he said, "that such a thing could be."

"I did, M'sieu-love," she whispered. "But not that I'd ever find it."

He could hardly bear to be away from her. Days became torture. Occasionally, as he worked with François, he saw his friend give him a sober look. At last François asked, "Is something wrong, friend?"

The question startled him, but he kept fitting the kitchen-house shelf to the wall at what he judged would be the proper height for Tonton. He took a few seconds to consider his reply. Not yet, he decided. Not until he had worked out a plan so sound that François would neither feel obliged to report Tonton nor forced to struggle with his conscience.

"What could be wrong, eh?" he countered.

"You never quit working now. Sometimes, at night, we used to sit together on our porches. Now we speak only of work; that is the only time we're together."

He had thought François assumed he went to bed at dark. Now he wondered if his friend had been putting things together and might arrive at the truth.

"You're right," he said honestly. "We need our talks. Come for supper tomorrow."

François nodded acceptance.

Despite his rage to be with Tonton, Gabriel found it was good to sit again with his friend. They discussed the breeding of their stock, the future of planting sugar cane, and estimated how much they could add to their roads each year and the amount of extra ditching and planting they could do.

"When L'Acadie starts to pay," Gabriel said, "I'm going to buy more land. Another league—two."

"I'm satisfied. I thought you were."

"No. I'm going to make L'Acadie the biggest and the finest."

François chuckled. "You've got a fancy name for it. I've decided on Hebert's Plantation for mine." There was silence. Then François said, "If you're going to be so big, you'll have to use slaves."

"I've thought about that."

He knew that one man, with the sometime help of one lone friend could not develop even one league, much less additional land. With no money to pay wages, in an area where white men didn't hire out to do field work, he would have to bring in slaves. He would buy one or two, then more, as he got the money. They, like the cattle, would breed and increase.

"You'll need them, too," he told François. "You can't work a league by yourself."

"I don't know how Elodie'll feel about them. She

may think it's wrong to buy and sell human beings."

"It is wrong, damned wrong!"

"They're not like that Tonton wench, Gabriel. We can get pure blacks and keep them black through breeding. We need strong field hands, carpenters, blacksmiths, and strong wenches for work and breeding."

"You've been thinking about it."

"Yes. We've got to use them. If you don't accept that, you can't build the—dynasty you want."

There was a lengthy silence.

"I'll use them," Gabriel said, "but I'll treat them well. They'll be housed, fed, clothed, and cared for when they're sick. They'll be married, and no slave bought for L'Acadie or born here will be sold. Grandmothers will know the children of their sons. And all will be black—one hundred percent black."

Shortly after this conversation with his friend, Gabriel realized that Tonton was now strong and glowing with health. She was more beautiful than ever.

Gabriel spoke of marriage.

"It isn't possible, M'sieu-love."

"I've got a solution for us."

"What solution could there be, M'sieu-love?"

"It'll take time, until the priest comes. The weather's colder, so I'll make this shelter into a little house. When the priest comes, we'll be married."

"Without banns, M'sieu-love? Even if he did not see me for what I am?"

"He stays a few weeks. We can publish banns. He'll not know you're a runaway."

"Because of my blood, M'sieu-love, he will refuse."

"He may not. He's married the Attakapas."

"And what of my master, M'sieu-love?"

"The wilderness is in our favor. Even if that devil should trace you, he can't take a man's legal wife."

"It wouldn't be legal, M'sieu-love. Ask your friend."

"My friend will say nothing," he told her.

"The Elodie he was parted from, M'sieu-love. Would he keep a secret from her?"

"He won't even tell her. All he asks is to be with her again, the way any man—"

She looked at him searchingly. His heart pounding, he waited for her to ask whether he, too, had a fiancée in Acadia, but she didn't. He broke into a sweat. There was trouble enough without Tonton's knowing that he'd been all but married to Georgette, toward whom he now felt small guilt because she, like anything else before Tonton, assumed the properties of a half-forgotten dream.

Tonton hadn't moved her eyes from his. "M'sieu-love, it's not possible."

"It's not possible for you to go to Mexico, either."

"Because we have met—because we—?"

"Exactly. I won't give you up."

"I'm grateful, M'sieu-love, for what we've had."

"You talk like you mean to leave."

"Only when you agree, M'sieu-love, or if I must. As I promised."

"I won't agree."

She gazed at him quietly.

"You still mean to go."

She nodded.

"Then I go with you. We'll make our life in Mexico."

"No, M'sieu-love," she said with firmness. "Don't ask it again."

But he did ask and argue and quarrel. The best he could get from her was an extension of her promise: that she would remain until there was no longer danger of her meeting the trackers on their way back to New Orleans. But he determined to keep her for himself in spite of any obstacle. He would never agree that the time was safe.

They made love through the night. Never had their passion flamed with such purity, burned more steadfastly, sweetened their blood more deliciously. It was this night on which Gabriel discovered a new and wonderful fact. With the candle flickering its soft light over Tonton's exquisite beauty, Gabriel took pause, sat back on his heels and studied her, inch by inch.

She smiled up at him, her golden eyes studying him in return. He drew one hand along her shoulder, down her arm, past her fingers. Her flesh was live, throbbing.

She reached up, and with one finger copied his gesture from shoulder past his hand. "So strong," she murmured, "M'sieu-love."

Gazing at the trusting, smiling beauty of her face, even with the memory of their lovemaking, he thought, how innocent she is, how pure.

He stroked her face again, barely touching it, faintly tracing one eyebrow then the other. He outlined the curve of her lips. Even as he did this, as though he were making a portrait of her, she repeated each action on him, one after the other, and made her own portrait.

He moved his lips toward her as slowly as they would go, and she lay to receive them. They came to her lightly, and he kissed her reverently, with all the love in him. And when he had kissed, then she kissed him in the same manner, murmuring softly in her throat, which led to their kissing together, at the same instant, and with the same gentleness.

Worshipfully, he placed one hand so that it held a beloved breast. He lowered his head and kissed the nipple as he had kissed her lips. Slowly, he took the other breast and caressed it.

He trailed kisses from that wondrous spot between her breasts along her silken stomach, down to the golden, curling nest of hair that he so loved, and all the while her hand rested on his head, her fingers wound into his hair.

The kisses traveled her thigh, along the curve of her leg, the slim ankle and to each and every toe, from the small one to the largest. And then they traveled upward, beginning with the toes on the other foot, that soft moaning in her throat constant and beautiful, her hand in his hair, until his kisses arrived, once more, at the haven in which he reveled.

"M'sieu-love—love!" She was sobbing now, without

tears, the tremor of love itself a sob. "Do not wait, M'sieu-love. Oh, please—!"

Still with slowness, with control that was by now all but beyond him, he entered. Afterward they lay, breaths mingled, bodies absolutely quiet.

It was she who moved first. "M'sieu-love," she said again, in that soft moan of hers and he stirred and could not resist.

Still, his one motion was slow, savoring. Straining to keep it thus, the wonder flashed in him that love was an art. He had never before known this long, deep probe, this pulsing wait, this slow, partial withdrawal, the eager wait, the next slow probe.

The time came when their motion quickened. But it did so gradually until, at the moment in which they burst into singing flame, they were both moaning aloud. The flame and the moaning went on and on, and when it did end, they lay, replete.

"M'sieu-love, oh, M'sieu-love," she breathed.

"That's the way it's meant to be," he whispered.

"Oui, M'sieu-love, oh, oui!"

"I have never loved before," he murmured.

"Nor I, M'sieu-love."

"Nor have we loved like this," he said.

"It can be so again, M'sieu-love? The way it was now?"

"Better. For we will make it so."

"M'sieu-love!"

"Always. Forever. Like now."

"As long as we can, M'sieu-love."

"All our lives."

She made no response.

He knew that she was strong-willed despite her soft grace and that she still meant to flee to Mexico. He didn't speak, but lay holding her, his treasure. It seemed impossible that a mere six or seven weeks could have changed his life so deeply.

Later, they again made love. And this time, when at last they flamed together, it was as if they had died and been reborn.

When it was time to leave, he held her nude body

and kissed her tenderly. She shivered, and he released her so that she could get back onto the mattress and cover herself.

It struck him, as he rode, that she must have clothing. While the weather held, she could launder what he had given her and put it back on. He frowned. It was out of the question for him to go to the post for dress goods.

His solution was to go hunting. François went with him. Afterwards, Gabriel dressed his share of hides, making sure there was enough for a dress, moccasins, and coat. He took the skins as well as sewing equipment from his government kit to a delighted Tonton.

He and François cut hay, got in their potatoes, tended their pumpkins; they chopped and stacked wood along the sides of their kitchen houses and did some more work on the ditches.

When François was busy building a sitting room table, Gabriel went into the government forest, cut trees at remote and scattered spots, hid the trimmings, hewed boards, and moved them near Tonton's shelter, hiding them nearby.

The ditch digging continued, and Gabriel threw himself into it, knowing that he couldn't build Tonton's house until after they had finished the ditch. François, too, poured himself into the digging. They both wanted to meet the schedule they had set up.

We're working for the same reason, Gabriel thought, for a girl. François wanted everything ready, even to a cat in the stable, on that long awaited for day he believed Elodie would arrive. Gabriel, on the other hand, wanted only to build that tiny wooden house for Tonton to use until he could establish her at L'Acadie.

One night when he suggested that she brew coffee, Tonton went about it so obediently that he realized she had spoken hardly a word since he had arrived and that they had embraced, long and with unusual tenderness.

"What is it?" he asked. "Is something wrong? Are

you worried about the smell of coffee tonight? That there is someone around?"

"No, M'sieu-love. There's been no sign of danger."

It was then, watching her brewing the coffee, that the enormity of her situation flooded Gabriel. She had been sired, reared, educated, and loved by a white father, a gentleman. She had spent hours in a great plantation house with her father's white children, she had been taught many graces. When she did go to the Quarters, it was to a whitewashed, weather-tight, clean cabin where she was the only—and beloved—child.

Now she had a price on her head. Though, other than the trackers, no soul had been near, she could still be discovered any day. And she had fallen in love with him, dearly in love. He had given her only a thatched shelter in which to live, deerskin to wear. Her future was precarious and unknown, and he had had the temerity to ask if anything was wrong!

"Tomorrow," he said, "François is going to the post and spend the day waiting for the trading boat, if it comes. I'll build your house while he's gone."

She said nothing.

"I could just take you to L'Acadie," he said angrily.

"M'sieu-love, please! We agreed."

"I know what we agreed. That we'd let time pass. That you stay until all the trackers—stay until I. . . . If that's what you're getting at, put it out of your mind. I won't have it. Right now you may think I'm ruining your chances. But later—"

She held up her hand for silence, and he gave it.

She rose from the fire and turned to face him, but when he would have taken her into his arms, she held him back with another lift of her hand. The light from the fire revealed her solemn, troubled face.

"M'sieu-love," she said, "I understand. Your intentions are the highest, but the law . . . If I ask you to release me from the promise, will you do it, out of love?"

"Why?" he asked hoarsely. "Why would you ask this thing? Because you don't trust me, because you think

I can't. . . . We have a—difficulty—but it's the same as before. Nothing has changed!"

"There is a change, M'sieu-love, in my body, my breasts, and it increases the difficulty."

"What change? I see no change!"

"It is, M'sieu-love," she said softly, her voice scarcely audible, "that I am with child."

FIFTEEN

He grabbed her shoulders, then instantly eased his grip. His chest, his ears, his whole body was pounding. "You're enceinte?" he cried, the sound flying above the trees, going he cared not where. "You're going to bear my son?"

"M'sieu-love, when you shout—if someone—"

"Who's to hear?" he demanded, but lowered his voice.

"M'sieu, my love. The baby is impossible here, don't you see? He'll be a quadroon, and in Louisiana—" She was quivering in his arms, and her voice was quivering, but she pressed on. "That is why I ask for release. So that I may reach Mexico now, while I can ride, so the baby will be born free."

"You don't mean it—to take him—you can't!"

"Oui, M'sieu-love, I mean it."

"Why would you take my son—our son—away from me?"

"Did you not hear me, M'sieu-love? It is that the baby has no right here, nor have I. If he is not to be a slave, he must be born where his mother is not a slave. It is best for us, best for you."

"How in hell is it best for me?"

He had never been truly angry at her before, but now he wanted to shake her. Instead, he sank with her to the ground, and she did not try to pull away.

"It is that you will not be father to a slave, M'sieu-love. But to a free child in another country."

"If you get to the other country! It is mad for you to ride such distance. If it were safe, we'd ride there now, be married, and ride back. But you might lose the baby. And there's still danger from the trackers."

"M'sieu-love, I do not want my baby born a slave!"

"He'll marry white."

"In Mexico, M'sieu-love, he will."

"I won't give you up, I won't give up our baby. I'll work it out, but I'll not free you from the promise, and you'll not break it—will you?"

A long, fire-whispering moment passed.

"I can never defy you, M'sieu-love," she said.

He longed to gather her close, to fill her with his love. Instead, because all of life was at stake, he held her and spoke.

"You are my wife. Church aside, laws aside, that devil-master of yours in New Orleans aside, you are mine. The baby is my son. He is a Leblanc. L'Acadie is our home, this child is my heir. He is the second Gabriel René Leblanc. No one, not even his mother, has the right to rob him of his heritage. The accident that put some black blood into him, the accident that you were sold as a slave, we will overcome."

He built her a tiny house. He hunted, softened skins, then gave them to Tonton, and from them she sewed small garments. She was happy with him but thoughtful, and he knew she was still disturbed that her baby might be captured as a slave.

The enormity of this, should it happen, grew in him. But determination to prevent it, to have the son as his own, to have him a Leblanc, overrode his apprehension. He would make Tonton his wife; their son would be legitimate. First, though, she must remain safely hidden until after the birth of the baby.

During this period, on rainy days, when François was inside building furniture, Gabriel rode to her and built a cradle. She helped polish it and made a deerskin-covered mattress to fit. He also made a small table for her, a straight chair and an armchair.

He got her newspapers at the post, a journal, a supply of candles. "Just keep the shutters closed," he warned.

"Merci, M'sieu-love. I do like to sit by candlelight. My mother wouldn't allow me to read books Papa gave me longer than half an hour by candle."

Books. If she had books.

"How do you fill your time, being prisoner?" he asked.

"Not prisoner, M'sieu-love! In New Orleans would have been the prison. Here I have the wilderness, my house. I have breakfast and supper to cook. I have my squirrel, and others getting tame. I have sewing, my journal, paper and pen. And every night I have you. Also, every moment, there is our baby within me, so that I am never alone."

He opened another subject, which had worried him along with the chance she might, even yet, be discovered here. "When your time comes," he asked, "how can we manage without a woman to see you through the accouchement?"

"We will, M'sieu-love. I've helped my mother with the wenches. You've helped mares, cows—no?"

"Yes, but you—"

"M'sieu-love, I have also read in books that when Indians are on the move to a hunting ground, a squaw who must give birth stops, alone, delivers her own baby, then overtakes the tribe with it in her arms. We have nothing to worry us!"

Winter passed. Gabriel and François worked on their roads and ditches; they trapped, hunted, and fished, taking furs and hides to the post to add to their growing credit. François grew restless and made extra trips to the post in the hope a trading boat had come, that there might be news of Elodie. Gabriel went with him, hoping for news of the priest's next visit. They saw Attakapas men at the post, trading furs for rifles and cloth, and they talked frequently with Morphy, the innkeeper.

Morphy was a small, balding man with a pot-belly. When he smiled, his face broke into wrinkles far in advance of his age, which couldn't have been past the mid-forties.

"When the priest comes," Gabriel once asked casually, "is it by trading boat?"

"Father Charles? He's got a pirogue, goes up and down all the bayous." Morphy looked sober. "He's getting old, and he's sick. Last time he came was just before you two. Said he was going to take a long rest in New Orleans before his next trip."

By June the crops were shooting up. Father Charles had sent word by trading boat that he was starting another trek. By this time, Tonton was so big with child that Gabriel marveled how her once-slim body could have expanded so much. She glowed with beauty, peace, and contentment.

On a steaming, humid July day, thick with mosquitoes, when Gabriel saw François head downstream, he decided to make a quick trip to see Tonton. He was wildly anxious to get to her, for she was due any day, any hour. This morning when he had left her, he had caught a drawn look on her face. He had asked if it was the baby.

"Am I screaming, M'sieu-love?" she teased. "Am I clinging to your hands?"

"You'll do none of that," he'd replied.

"A woman doesn't know what she'll do, M'sieu-love. I wish to be quiet, not to betray this safety."

"I'm coming back as soon as I can," he had said.

"M'sieu-love, it doesn't happen so fast! It takes hours, even after the first small pain. It takes six hours—twelve."

He had held her and groaned. He had known, of course, for he had heard snatches of talk in Grand Pré. Suddenly he remembered Adrienne Marceau, who had died and been buried with the dead baby in her arms.

Tonton, sensing his mood, had stroked her palm along his face. "I'll be safe, M'sieu-love. You'll see. I'm young, my bones are supple, it will be easy."

Now, riding to her, he still wasn't confident. What did she know, actually? It was one thing to help deliver a slave wench, another to deliver your own child with only the help of a clumsy, inexperienced man.

What would he do if things went wrong?

Because of his lust, he had put Tonton into this situation. It seemed that everything he did was provoked and colored by it. Tonton who could, but for him, have now been safely in Mexico, was trapped by him and his seed. He kicked Noir's flanks.

She didn't come flying to meet him. He tied up Noir and rushed to the house. If someone had found her, if she had had to run through the forest, if—

He rushed inside and found her on the mattress, clutching the blanket, her body arched, her lips tight. His chest pounding, he dropped to his knees.

"I'm here," he croaked. If only he could remember what one did for a horse, a cow!

As the pain eased, her body relaxed. "Water's heating—"

He had no idea what to do with hot water. He remembered dousing an animal, afterward, to clean her. But with cold water. He didn't know much . . . .

"The knife, M'sieu-love—scald it. To cut the cord."

But there was no baby yet. No cord.

"How long have you been—when—?"

"M'sieu-love, your hands. If I can pull—"

Her body arched again, her hands gripped his like traps, and he felt such strength in her that he was terrified that, pulling so, she might rip herself. He had to call upon his own strength to meet her pulling, to swallow the bellow of rage that swelled in him.

It lasted beyond lasting. Then her hands dropped away, and her body hit the mattress. "Now—M'sieu-love—water—"

214

His knees buckling, he hurried and brought the kettle. He set it on the table, the knife beside it.

She gasped. He leapt closer, gripping her reaching hands. Her nails cut through his flesh. He felt through his own body the tremendous, relentless pulsing that coursed through her. In that moment he knew the struggle of women, he knew the battle of the unborn, forced to ram, batter, and tear out of a torturing passage too tight, too narrow.

The struggle raged. He tasted salt from his sweat. At times it stung his eyes, so that he couldn't see.

He felt a breeze spring up; it was evening. Wind rustled through the leaves of the forest and from out there, unheard until now, was a birdsong, both sounds—breeze and bird—louder than her slow breathing. The sunlight was at a slant across the door when the child came shooting out, red and slick, and with the child blood. Gabriel clumsily caught the baby and saw that it was a boy.

Gabriel crouched, holding his bloody son in his hands. Tonton whispered, "Please—hold it up, M'sieu-love—by the heels. It must cry—breathe."

He did as she said, and his slippery baby wailed.

"M'sieu-love—is it a boy?"

"Of course he's a boy!" His voice was shaking, and he didn't give a damn. He had delivered his own son.

When all was finished, they looked the baby over for any signs of his black heritage. There was not one trace. Even Tonton admitted it.

"Merci, merci!" she wept, smiling.

"He weighs at least eight pounds," Gabriel boasted.

"He has your build, M'sieu-love—not the heavy bones, he'll be slimmer, taller, but he shows he's your son."

Bursting with pride and determination to see to the future, he made certain his wife, for so he thought of her, and his son were well and then went home to tend his stock. He was at the bayou, carrying water for the pigs, when François' pirogue appeared around the bend and made for L'Acadie.

"Father Charles is here!" François shouted. "I had a talk with him about Elodie and marrying us when she comes!"

SIXTEEN

Puzzled, the robed priest waited at L'Acadie while Gabriel rode to the forest house and back, bringing the deerskin-wrapped baby on his arm. Father Charles was sitting, the candlelight flickering on his hair, which was snowy white. When he got to his feet it was slowly and with effort. He had a tiny, pale cadaverous face, but both the stamp of illness and the age it bore were softened by an aura of complete peace.

He gave a hacking cough. His pale eyes touched the bundle Gabriel held. "It is a baby you have?" he asked.

"Yes, father. His mother wishes him to be christened."

"He is your baby?"

"My firstborn."

"And where is the mother?"

"At a distance, father. She gave birth only this afternoon." He folded back the deerskin so the priest might see the small round head, its soft dark hair, the turn of new red cheek.

"The mother has no need to sacrifice herself so, my son. I'll be at the post some weeks. She can see her infant blessed."

At first Gabriel had no reply. He could not, before his son was blessed, tell this priest, this great man who innocently served the devil, what had passed between himself and Tonton not two hours ago.

"I'm going to have the priest marry us," he had said to her.

"But the banns, M'sieu-love!" she had cried. "My blood!"

"He can find a way, a priest can always find a way. He can marry us here, tonight."

"M'sieu-love, why would you bring an old, sick priest into the forest at night?"

"Not knowing your origin, with only candlelight—"

"You'd deceive a priest, M'sieu-love? You think he can't. . . . Oh, M'sieu-love, he would know!"

"He might not. It's trickery, yes. But if he'll marry us for the sake of the baby—"

"Marriage is a sacrament, M'sieu-love," she had said. "I cannot receive a sacrament through trickery."

"What other way is there? Besides, you're not Catholic!"

"But once you were, M'sieu-love. You can make a confession, and then you can beg of the priest to christen the baby. And you can intercede with him whether he knows how to make it possible to marry us."

He would not confess.

"Monsieur Leblanc," the priest said now. "Will you have the mother present?"

"No. You are prepared?"

"Oui, my son. I am prepared." His eyes rested on the head of the infant; a smile touched his lips. "The name of the mother?"

"Tonton."

The priest took the baby into his arms. "His name?" he asked, and Gabriel told him. Murmuring, touching the child with holy water, the name came full and clear. "I christen thee Gabriel René Leblanc."

It was done. Gabriel took back the baby from the priest.

Father Charles said, "I confess to surprise. Also to neglecting my duty. Until now, it was my belief that there were, as yet, other than Attakapas in the bayous, no married couples, except for a few Spanish far from here. I spoke with Monsieur Hebert this afternoon, and—"

"He mentioned I'm not married."

"No, my son. He spoke of his fiancée."

"You have christened my son, father. Now I want you to marry me to his mother."

The priest began to cough.

"And his mother? Again, to my knowledge, there are no women on the Teche. Is it that she is Attakapas, Houma—"

"No, father."

"What, then? Do you wish to make a confession?"

Gabriel shook his head. He couldn't go through the charade; but neither could he further trick his saintly priest.

Thus, standing with René asleep in his arms, he told everything, confessing what had happened from the moment he had found Tonton.

As the priest listened, he seemed to grow smaller. There was a stillness in him, an aura of compassion when Gabriel finished.

He said, with regret, "I can't marry you, my son." He held up a hand to stem Gabriel's flood of argument. "You've heard of the Black Code?"

"No."

"There's no way around it. It's a decree that came to us from France in the 1600's. It forbids cohabitation and intermarriage between white and black subjects."

"She isn't black! She's—"

"Over thirty years ago, the French king promulgated the decree for the colony of Louisiana. Under it, any child born of an illicit union is called a bastard. Any freeman who has such child by a slave is subject to a penalty of two thousand pounds of sugar.

"If a master has such child by one of his own slaves, the slave and the child are confined to a house of correction unless the master was unmarried at the time of the concubinage and chooses to marry the slave in accordance with ecclesiastical rules. In that case the slave and the child become free and legitimate."

"I'll marry Tonton under any rules at all!"

"I'm not finished, my son. Many of the articles of this decree were complemented by provisions found earlier in the Black Code, and note of this was made at the end of the decree.

"Marriage between white and black is forbidden, and members of the clergy are forbidden to celebrate such marriages. Whites and blacks born free or freed, are forbidden to live in concubinage with a slave."

"It's insane!" cried Gabriel. "It contradicts itself!"

"It is the law. Even so, you'd have to buy your Tonton first, for she has a master, and she ran away. Lawfully, both the mother and this baby are the property of the man in New Orleans."

"No law is going to take away my son," said Gabriel, his teeth clenched. "And I will marry Tonton."

The priest lapsed into a prolonged attack of coughing. It occurred to Gabriel that his future lay partly in this frail priest's hands.

"You won't—priests don't—"

"No. I'll not speak of your baby or of your Tonton, my son."

SEVENTEEN

Tonton refused to live at L'Acadie as Gabriel's wife. There was no way he could explain her, she pointed out, and both she and René would be in jeopardy should trackers come again.

He had another plan, but it must wait until the harvest was in, until Tonton was truly strong and René beyond first infancy.

The summer lagged, though it was crammed with labor. It seemed that harvest would never come, that he could never leave.

By October, when they were harvesting, René was three months old, his dark eyes alert on Tonton, on Gabriel, on everything. He was such a handsome baby that there were times when Gabriel's impulse was to bring François here and say, "My friend. Tonton is my wife. René is our son. Help me bring them to L'Acadie." But it was his problem and he kept it to himself.

One evening he arrived at the tiny house before dark. He picked up the kicking, gurgling infant, stared at him and exclaimed, "I'll be damned! He's got a face!"

"He's always had one, M'sieu-love."

"It's changed." He studied his son, who smiled and chortled. The baby's skin had lost all redness and was of the same olive cast as his own. The child had Tonton's slim nose, along with a slight uptilt at the corners of the eyes. "He looks like you, Tonton—and like your father, I imagine."

"Oui, M'sieu-love. And he has your hair and cheekbones. And lips."

"We've improved the breed, Tonton. We've made the most handsome Leblanc yet!"

It was that night, after their slow, artful love, that he told her of the trip to New Orleans.

The next morning he went across-bayou and asked François to look after L'Acadie and the stock for seven weeks while he went to New Orleans.

François was astounded. "Why go? It's a mean trip, and we've got trading boats! You could be extending your road, your ditches!"

"I have—well, it's private."

"The only private matter here, ever, was that wench. She was to leave, you were to give her Lola to ride to Texas. Only Lola's still here—and so is Tonton. Isn't she, Gabriel?"

Gabriel stood speechless.

"There've been signs. Our evening talks ended, less time working together, you riding in at dawn from the east. You'd damn well better tell the truth, my friend, or I don't look after the stock and you can't go!"

There was nothing to do but to tell the truth. He hated to add to his friend's already burdened conscience, but Gabriel told him everything.

"You—with her?"

"I came to feel for her as you feel for Elodie."

"You put Georgette out of your mind, eh?"

"I suppose I did. You knew Georgette. She's probably married by now."

"But you don't know."

"Hundreds of us will never know, François."

"This trip, it's for Tonton?"

"And our son."

"You'll go to the governor's office and see if there's a letter from Elodie waiting there?"

"The moment I step ashore and again, before shoving off."

"And Georgette?"

"I'll ask about her. And all the others who may have left their names or messages." He'd have to ask about Georgette, have to help her, should she have arrived. But he felt she wasn't there and would never be.

"You can't make people accept Tonton," François said.

"When she's at L'Acadie as Madame Leblanc, our neighbors, who will be Acadian, won't be looking for such things. And no eyes, not even yours, can see it in René."

"It would become known."

"Not through you, my friend."

"Not through me."

"It will be bred out."

François shook his head. "What will this trip accomplish?"

"To learn if wanted bills are still out on Tonton, to learn if there is a search."

"You know there will be. Even a rich man doesn't easily lose a property for which he paid five thousand dollars."

"I'll learn whether trackers are searching for her or whether they're after runners more easily taken."

"And then?"

"We'll risk the ride across Texas into Mexico and be married there. When we return, we'll say we met in

Maryland when she was visiting, that she came to New Orleans with me, and I'm bringing her from her family home, where she has since gone, with our son."

"There are dates. The age of the baby."

"Who on the Teche will count on the fingers, eh? Burdell and Morphy? They'll shrug. It'll be forgotten."

"Why not go to Mexico now? Forget the trip to New Orleans."

"It is for the safety of Tonton and René, who will be slaves if captured. Think, my friend, of what it would mean for them to be slaves, bought and sold. I cannot sleep at night from the horror of it. No. First I must determine whether there are now trackers in Texas."

François sighed. "I'll bring your stock here. But your—what of them?"

"I'm leaving her food for nine weeks, longer than needed. Wood is cut and hidden. She will go to the bayou for water only at night, when René is asleep."

"If you wish I'll take—them—fresh game and milk, see that all is well."

"Merci, but no. Tonton is accustomed to the forest. She knows the normal sounds and can sense danger. She is not afraid."

"But seven weeks!"

"It is long, yes. But this way, if trackers come again, you'll have nothing to lie about. You've seen no wench; you don't know where she is."

"If she senses danger, what then?"

"She will come to you for Lola. She will run for Mexico."

François was silent.

Gabriel asked, "You do not want her to come here?"

"Not that. It is that it is all so savage."

"No more than Le Grande Déportation."

"No. The wildness then was families torn apart. Yours is to form a forbidden family."

"What happened before," Gabriel said, "was a tearing up. This is building."

"Perhaps, my friend. When do you leave?"

"At dawn—even before."

There was news at the governor's office. Ten Acadians had arrived in New Orleans and were even now enroute to grants far down Bayou Lafourche. The letters Gabriel and François had left had not been called for. The aide showed Gabriel the list of newcomers, but there was not one name he recognized.

There was no wanted bill in all New Orleans for Tonton. The day before Gabriel was to return to L'Acadie, he bought a gold wedding band, a dress length of tawny gold cotton, and thread to match. He bought a start of chickens and feed, then, with a part of the money he had left, purchased a fine gold chain for Tonton. He could see in his mind how it would look around her neck, glowing delicately.

At journey's end, he eyed his house as he pulled upstream. It was more beautiful to him now than those fine New Orleans houses. It was beginning to weather just the way he wanted it to. One day, when he had doubled its size, he would paint it white. And when he built the mansion for Tonton, that would be a dazzling white.

He was drawing nearer. Here, on the east side of the bayou, out of the current, rowing was easier. When he was so close to his own landing that all he need do was nose east, he heard a shout. He looked, and there was François, coming at a run, towards the bayou, carrying an ax.

"Over here!" he yelled. "Here first!"

"I am—I am!" Gabriel yelled back.

As he swung the pirogue, he glanced again at L'Acadie. A curl of smoke was coming out of the kitchen house chimney. His gut leapt. Instinctively he began to swing the boat for home.

"Not there—here!" François screamed. "There's news!"

Gabriel sent the pirogue scuttling for Hebert landing. He strained, bending to the oars in inexplicable desperation.

François was standing in the edge of the water. He

223

caught the rope that Gabriel tossed, then tied it. "Some Acadians came in!" he called.

"I heard, in New Orleans. No one we know, François. They went to Lafourche."

"All but one, friend, all but one! She came on the trading boat!" François' pockmarks showed up against his suddenly pale face. "Gabriel," he cried, "it's Georgette! She's the one! She's at L'Acadie now!"

EIGHTEEN

Georgette stood on the porch, arms akimbo. Gabriel saw that she was thinner, sharper, tauter. A slow, awful pulse coursed through him, but he moved steadfastly on, stopping at the bottom step.

Her eyes threw black fire at him. Her forehead was furrowed; her chin looked sharper than he remembered. Her skin was white, pallor underlying it. Her lips were narrower, the once-familiar sensual dip of the lower one lost. Her hair, pinned atop her head, gave her a harsh appearance; the bones at her neck stood out.

"Well," she said, "have you swallowed your tongue?"

He managed to shake his head.

"Haven't you anything to say—after what I've been through?"

He had much to say, but not now, like this. But it was her way to speak out. So he responded with the only thing he could think of, feeling as if he were someone else, a stranger to this tiny, bird-quick woman.

"What happened, back in Acadia?"

"What do you think, stupid? I was thrown onto a ship. I knew what ship you were on, but not where it went. I was—abused—and thrown off in that awful colony, the worst one!"

"What colony, Georgette?"

"Virginia! They treated me like a beast on the ship *and* on the land. I was put into slavery—me, Georgette Babin! I worked in the fields with those stinking Negroes, and at night I was locked into a cabin with them."

He couldn't speak. There was no acceptable sympathy, no possible comfort.

"Have you nothing to say, Gabriel Leblanc?"

"What can I say? I would have saved you if I could." He didn't tell her that he had tried.

"I had to sleep in a place not twelve feet square. Four of us. I slept on a dirt floor with big, black wenches. And I had to work all day in the cotton fields, had to go to the fields when—" she stopped. "Where were you then, eh?"

"Were you the only Acadian?"

"There were others, you know it! Where were you and that precious François put ashore?"

"Didn't he tell you?"

"He won't talk. He said Maryland, and that's all he'll say. And don't think I don't know why!"

His heart knotted. Did she, somehow, know of Tonton? "And why is that?" he asked carefully.

"Because I got here, not his Elodie!"

His relief was enormous. He tried to speak, but surprise and shock gripped him. Tonton, his blood beat, Tonton!

"You don't talk any more than he does. *You* didn't have to sleep with stinking blacks."

"No. We didn't. We worked on a farm, were helped on our way when we started for Louisiana."

"Eh! If they were so good, why didn't they let you come for me? Or didn't you want to? Were you glad to be rid of me after what you did in the forest?"

"I searched for you. I put advertisements in newspapers, asked everywhere."

"I never saw them!"

"I inquired in Baltimore, arranged with a man who was walking north to look for you. He would then write to another man in Baltimore—"

"Pah! You can't let another do your work! You've got to do it yourself, as I did."

He felt sorry for her tribulations. Even so, he recognized that his instinct had been right. She had, indeed, looked out for herself, and here she was, she had come to him through whatever hell. And now there were Tonton and René.

"Aren't you going to ask how I did it, eh?"

"Yes. How *did* you do it?"

"There were ten Acadians as slaves, and we'd talk. I did much thinking, looked at all I saw. It took much time, but I got the plan, and the others liked it, and no newspapers, nothing!"

"What was your plan?"

"I had heard on the ship that Louisiana was French, and I thought, 'The English have got Nova Scotia, but they haven't got Louisiana.' And I'd think, 'The ship is taking me south, toward Louisiana. No matter what they intend, it's carrying me nearer to French land every hour.' That was as far as I thought then. On the plantation, I waited. For you to find me."

He started to speak, but she gestured. "Yes, foolish. So I thought of Louisiana being French, that you'd know, that you'd come, and I had but to follow. It was as if I had a map."

He stared. Her acumen, her unrelenting determination, were overwhelming. "And you spoke to the others of this and planned an escape," he said

"But yes!"

"How did you escape?"

"One Acadian fixed the outside bolts on his cabin. When the trusty locked us in, he didn't notice. So, all Anton had to do was push, and the bolt fell. It never woke the stupid slaves. Anton came to our cabins and lifted the bolts."

"No dogs?"

"Two, but chained. The wind was in our favor. They never barked."

"You were lucky."

"That was the last of our luck. We had to go in what we wore, without shoes, without food. They put out

226

'wanted' bills on us because we'd worked so well and they didn't want to lose us. We had to hide and run at the same time, live off the land, steal onions, raw potatoes, corn. We milked cows in pastures, one doing the milking, another holding the cow's mouth shut."

"You headed straight for Louisiana?"

"And got here. The others are on Bayou Lafourche. They got land grants."

"Why didn't you ask for the letter? I left you one at the governor's office. I'm just back from New Orleans, and it hadn't been asked for, and your name wasn't on the list of arrivals."

"I didn't want a letter. I wanted to surprise you. I kept my name off the list. I knew where you were because the aide said two Acadians had settled here, and he told your names."

"Didn't your companions say anything when you didn't claim your letter?"

"No. They understood about the surprise."

Tonton . . . Tonton.

"Eh! What have you to say, you?"

He seized on a triviality, anything to divert her. He knew it was safe. François had betrayed nothing. Otherwise, accusations would long since have come spilling across those thin lips.

So he asked, "François brought you here?"

"He didn't want to. He said I could stay at the inn, that you'd pay. But I wouldn't do that, not when he admitted that I had a house, standing and ready. He clamped his lips, which I didn't mind because when he didn't scowl, those ugly marks—"

"He had smallpox on the *Esne*."

"Eh. We didn't have that, but we. . . . François brought me here three days ago and hasn't come back, only to leave milk at the landing. I never see him, only the milk."

"He knows there's a good supply of food. The milk's from one of my cows. You found what you need?"

"There's no lack of food. But something else is missing."

Wariness flooded him, and with it the conviction

that whatever he said now would be wrong. So he waited.

"There's no welcome!" she cried angrily. "I plan to surprise you, and you're not here. And when you do come, you stand there on the ground, like a stranger!"

There was no rebuttal.

"*Why*—eh?"

"I'd—given up. Then, finding you here—"

"You act like it's a shock! You'd think a man who lost his fiancée and has been searching for her, building a house with an inside oven, would have been up those steps, grabbing her into his arms!"

He couldn't move. His ears were beating.

"What's wrong with you?"

He felt truth burst out. "I am—shocked."

He paused, hearing a wailing sound. Where was it coming from? And then he realized it was inside the house. Georgette went flying inside. He climbed the steps, the noise inside rising. Who, in the name of the devil, has she got here? he wondered. Abruptly, the wailing stopped.

Suddenly she was in the doorway. In her arms she held a young male child, with hair like flax and eyes as black as her own. His skin was very white, with rosy cheeks, dirty from tears.

"Baby," crooned Georgette in a tone he would not have believed to exist in her. "S'h'h. It is Papa, baby's own papa!"

Her gaze on the child was tender, but when she turned on Gabriel, there was no tenderness in her eyes. "You see what I have endured? Crawling rows of cotton, pulling the towsack, my belly so big I almost put my knee into it each time I moved!"

His throat was completely dry. He couldn't swallow. He stared at the flaxen-haired baby.

"You can't—he can't—"

"But he is, Gabriel Leblanc! He's what you did to me. This is your son, he was christened as we ran, Gabriel René Leblanc. The moment we can get to a priest, you have got to marry me, but secretly, so I'll

not be ashamed and my son will not be called bastard!"

"H-how old is he?"

"Count your fingers!"

He studied the boy. He wouldn't question, not
Georgette, her pride was too desperate.

❀

Reading these words, safe in the mansion at L'Acadie, held in a very nest of hurricane, alarm leapt in
Carita. She bit her lower lip as her eyes sped down the
ink-written lines and her hand turned the pages of the
journal without pause, swiftly and anxiously.

❀

"You couldn't wait four days, there in Acadie!"
Georgette accused. "No, you had to make me enceinte, so I'd be forced to carry this baby through all
the abuse!"

He couldn't tear his eyes from the child's flaxen
locks.

"Why do you look at Gabby's hair?"

"It's—different."

"My father's own mother in France had such hair.
But lighter—from Sweden—and Gabby is the same."

Gabriel nodded. Nature did have odd ways. He had
poured white blood into René, and he had come into
the world white.

"You've got much to make up for, Gabriel Leblanc.
And keep that François from telling we weren't married in Acadia!"

"He won't talk. There's nothing to worry about, not
there."

"Then what is to be worried about?" she demanded
keenly.

This was not the moment to tell of Tonton and another son.

"The priest," Georgette urged. "We'll go tonight."

"There is no priest. Only a missionary at times. He was here only five months ago."

"I told my companions I'm married, I told the priest who blessed Gabby that I'd lost my marriage paper. You've got to find a way, after all I've done to keep the name bastard off your son."

"I know why you did it, Georgette." He felt the trap about to close.

"We'll wait for the missionary. But you'll not touch me until I'm your wife. I give you no rights until you are my husband."

He nodded because he must. He couldn't rely on his voice. She would be quick to hear the relief her ultimatum gave, and demand the reason.

"We'll be known as Monsieur and Madame Leblanc. Gabby and I will sleep in the house, and you in the stable. You can eat with us. Gabby's a good eater, now that there's food. The things I've suffered! After my milk went, your son cried with hunger. When we caught fish and game, he got his share. Anton Branche, who's on the Lafourche, did the dividing, and he gave us ours first."

"That was kind of him."

Her eyes blazed. "Go tell François that you'll be living in the stable. Now—this moment!"

He seized the chance. "It'll take awhile."

"Eat with him. I've only got enough for Gabby and me. When you do get back, go to the stable and don't come near the house until breakfast. And make certain your friend understands we'll live clean."

"All right," Gabriel agreed, keeping the excitement, the joy of escape, from his tone.

After talking briefly with François, Gabriel brought Noir and Lola home, put the mare into the stable, then led Noir to where he couldn't be seen from the house. He opened the fence, led Noir through, and replaced the poles. He rode at a walk, going through concealing growth. Only when he was out of hearing did he put Noir to the run.

Night was falling with tropic speed.

NINETEEN

Gabriel held Noir quiet as they entered the forest.
Tonton's wedding band and her golden chain burned
in his pocket, his heart was afire. Now, this close, all
the fears about the dangers that may have touched his
beloved rushed over and consumed him.

There was the tiny house. He slid to the ground,
tied Noir, then went toward the house, a shadow in
early night. He made their private signal. The door
opened to candlelight, he stepped inside and closed it,
and she was in his arms.

"M'sieu-love!" she breathed. "I felt you coming."

He put his lips on hers and drank love. Gone was
any other thought. She had never been softer,
stronger, more precious. Her palms, on the sides of his
face, were more tender than in the past.

He held her so that each curve of her body followed
the angles of his own, so that her mound of love cush-
ioned the seeking, starving part of him that she had, in
innocence, by herself come to fondle and kiss so many
times.

She drew him to the mattress. She was naked first
and helped him undress, crying out softly when he
sprang free. In accord, they held back their hungry
eagerness and took a long time, a very long time, caressing.

Now Tonton took his male part into her hand and
placed his body within her own. Deep in that inner
clasp, it was as always—their movements beginning
slowly, then increasing until they found ecstasy. In all
creation there was only this girl, this Tonton.

Soon she whispered, "M'sieu-love—again—please?"

He was ready. Her voice made him ready, the ca-
resses, the inner grip, the slow rhythm. It was even

slower this time, better, more tender than tenderness, more delightful than delight.

They lay quietly, nude in the candlelight, her head on his shoulder, her hair soft on his face. Though it was cold in the little hut, they were warm.

"M'sieu-love?" she whispered.

"Yes," he breathed, ready again.

"Did you learn what you hoped in New Orleans, M'sieu-love?"

Her question brought crashing back the reality of Georgette. Whispering, Georgette's presence like a curse on him, he told of his trip to New Orleans, of the fact that the search for her was not as intensive now.

"We can go to Mexico then, M'sieu-love?"

"Yes," he replied. "We are going."

Excited and not yet sensing anything amiss, she tugged at him to get up. "Our son, M'sieu-love. You'll not know him, you have been away such a long time, and he has been so busy growing! Come—see!"

Naked, they went to the cradle. The soft light showed a curve of cheek, dark, tousled hair, one baby fist. Warmth for this, his son, welled in Gabriel, filling him with tenderness, which, though it was as deep as the tenderness he held for Tonton, was yet different. This child of his loins, this helpless one, it was his privilege to protect and shape.

It was then, standing nude beside his love, the two of them embracing and gazing at that which together they had created, that the reality of Georgette, which threatened now more than Tonton's white master, hit Gabriel. He drew Tonton to the mattress and covered her with the blanket.

He said, "Tonton. Tonton-love. There is a thing I have got to tell you." She nestled closer.

"In Nova Scotia," he said, "there was a girl. Georgette Babin. Our banns had been published. We were to be married in four days. And then the English came."

"And you were parted, M'sieu-love."

"I should have told you."

"It wasn't needed, M'sieu-love. I knew there must

232

have been a girl for one like you, who is so much man, who must share love."

"I didn't—wait."

"Even that, M'sieu-love."

"I intended to marry her."

"Of course, M'sieu-love."

"I searched for her. I left a letter in New Orleans. Then I found you."

Her palm came to his cheek.

"This trip, at the governor's office, my letter still hadn't been called for. But ten Acadians had arrived to settle on Lafourche."

He felt the tremor of her palm and heard her catch her breath.

"One Acadian came here. Georgette."

He felt a wisp of a sigh in her.

"She means nothing to me."

"She's your betrothed, M'sieu-love. She has endured much, no?"

"So she says. And she's got a child, a boy, she says is mine. He was christened for me. They're in my house."

"Oh—M'sieu-love!"

She stirred, but he held her. Only gently did he hold, for there was no resistance. "It doesn't matter, Tonton. René's christening remains. He is my son. I know him to be my blood. The other—"

"M'sieu-love, she was a virgin, she was to marry you! The child is of the proper age?"

"She says he is. I haven't seen papers."

"A mother wouldn't—"

"If she lies to a priest and says she is married, the baby's age is a small matter. She decides what she wants, then goes after it. Like moving into L'Acadie, taking possession, dictating that I sleep in the stable until we can be married!"

"How is that, M'sieu-love?"

He told her of Georgette's plan that they marry secretly. Tonton moved against him. Her lips brushed his cheek.

"I'm not going to do it," he said. "I'm taking you to Mexico, getting married, and coming home."

"We can't, M'sieu-love."

"Why the hell not?"

"There's a similarity between you and her, M'sieu-love."

"We're nothing alike!"

"You both decide what you want, M'sieu-love. You both go after it and will allow nothing to stop you."

"I am going to marry you."

"What will you do about her, M'sieu-love?"

"Get her out of L'Acadie, get her a room at the inn, find her a husband. Burdell hasn't got a wife."

"This would shame her, M'sieu-love. And this she does not deserve. It would shame the child, who is as blameless as our own baby."

Gabriel felt as if he were afire. He held Tonton close, no longer tenderly, but fiercely. "Stop it!" he shouted, his voice traveling into the forest. "This obstacle, that obstacle, another one! I don't know how I'm going to solve it—a pretended divorce, maybe. That's it! I'll let it be known we're divorced. The boy can have my name. He may even be my get, I'm not saying he isn't. Let there be two Gabriel René Leblancs, one with his hair, the other with your blood, what the hell do I care? You're mine!"

"M'sieu-love, you could be heard." For her he quieted. "When you bring this to pass, M'sieu-love, when you persuade her to announce a divorce, when she and the boy are settled—"

"You'll be my wife."

"And two sons by two wives—so fast?"

"No one will be here to challenge."

"Not challenge, M'sieu-love. But they'll look closely at your new wife, compare her to the other. And they will compare the babies."

"So?"

"Georgette has fair skin, M'sieu-love?"

"Very. And mine is olive and yours is golden. If they wonder, let them damn well wonder."

Her breath caught. He touched her face and felt

her tears. This was the first time he had known her to cry. Her tears sent a slow, sweet longing, such as he had not yet known, through him. He felt himself grow firm with that slow delight, that warm and gentle ache, which he had not known, until Tonton, could exist.

His moan joined her tears, and this time they did not linger. He entered with eagerness but also with reverence, and they moved together, bestowing a comfort and a joy that was entwined with sadness.

Before dawn, he fastened the golden chain around her neck. She touched it wonderingly, and a smile curved her lips. The chain was even more beautiful on her than he had thought it would be.

"M'sieu-love. It is my first jewel."

He told her of the golden cloth. Her eyes glistened, and her lips formed her name for him soundlessly.

"I'll be here after dark," he said, leaving.

"Tonight, M'sieu-love?"

"Every night. Until we leave."

He kissed her again, took a last look into the cradle, and left.

TWENTY

At dawn Gabriel pushed open the door of the kitchen house and entered. Georgette, wearing a clean blue dress, was stirring in an iron pot at the fireplace. Gabby, who had been pushing around a chair, took one look at Gabriel and fled to his mother.

"Aren't you ashamed?" she snapped. "For your son to be afraid of you!"

There was only one answer. It was her due; reluctantly, he said the words. "It's because I'm strange to him."

"And whose fault is that, eh? If you'd been searching for me, as I was searching, it would be different!"

"You couldn't do much searching," he pointed out.

"But I was thinking! I never did stop."

"Yes. You've always been sharp."

"That's good, or I might have run off to the forest, off to the Micmac, like your family."

"So. They did go to the Micmac, as I felt they must have done. I thought you might do that. It was our plan."

"Not with you on a ship, I wouldn't!"

Gabriel stood under a wave of angry guilt. This was a fine predicament he had gotten two women caught up in and, if Georgette spoke the truth, his own two sons. Four living souls in a dilemma through him. Tonton, fleeing a devil, giving him love and René; Georgette, seeking him out against insurmountable obstacles, bringing him Gabby.

"Well," she snapped, "I'm here, and it's over."

He opened his mouth to tell her it wasn't over, that it was just beginning, but she started giving orders about breakfast. She was thumping wooden bowls of porridge onto the table, and Gabby, running after her, sat down unexpectedly on the floor, scrambled up, his face puckering.

Georgette glared at Gabriel. "Aren't you going to hold him? Put an end to being a stranger? You don't want to touch him. Let's eat and get it done. Then you can talk to him, call him Gabby, get him to hold your thumb."

After they had eaten, she set Gabby down, gave him a big wooden spoon with which he began to beat the floor, then turned her attention to Gabriel. "Well, are you going to pick him up?"

"Not at the moment."

"He needs a chair on tall legs so he can sit at the table," she said, exasperated. "How long will it take you to build him one?"

"There's a thing I've got to tell you," he said. "There's something I'm going to do. You're not going to like it. All the blame is mine."

For the first time ever, he saw her eyes go blank.

236

But for an instant only. Then she was the alert Georgette she had always been. "What is it, then?"

"I didn't have your faith, though I searched. On the *Esne*, François and I talked of you and Elodie, and always he was certain, as he is now, that some day he would find her."

"But you weren't certain?"

He told her now, of how he had jumped overboard. "I did it because I wanted you, Georgette," he finished.

She stared at him warily. "When did you give up?"

"It wasn't so much giving up as coming to understand how slight our chances were."

"Not if you fight! If Elodie does get here, François won't give her the reception you're giving me—and Gabby!"

"There's a reason, Georgette. There's another woman."

Again the blankness, followed by a lash of fury. "Another woman!" she screamed. "You're married to me, and you marry another woman, and now you're a bigamist!"

"I didn't marry you, Georgette."

"Same as married. The banns—the forest. Your son, and he bears your name. You're *not* married to that woman."

"Not yet."

"Why not? No—I know why! You can't do without a woman, nobody knows that better than Georgette Babin!" He stood mute. "So you took a slut!"

"No."

"Then why didn't you marry her?"

"It hasn't been possible, yet."

"And why not? She's got a husband?"

"No husband."

"Who is she, this hussy?"

"It doesn't matter."

"And where is she? There are no women in this country, except those who went down the Lafourche!"

"There are a few Spanish, at a distance."

"She is Spanish, then?"

237

"It has no bearing."

"If you don't tell me, I'll go to François—"

"He doesn't know where she is."

She smacked her hands onto her hips, tossed her head, her eyes flashing. "I got here in time. You're not married to this one, and now you'll never be married to her because I'm here."

"No. I have a feeling for this woman. I'll not let her go."

"You had a feeling for me in the forest!"

"It puts me to shame. It was—bestial."

"I don't know what you mean!" she screamed. Gabby's head jerked, he stared at his mother, then he, too, began to scream. She swept him to her and stood rocking back and forth. " 'Feeling!' There's only one feeling a man knows, the one you ruined me with! Thank God I got here in time!"

"But you didn't, Georgette. My course is laid."

"Do people know of her, this woman?"

"No."

"So?"

"It makes no difference. I'm sorry."

"Sorry! And what about me, the shame? What about Gabby? How can you explain to people who know, because I told them, that you and I are husband and wife!"

"Divorce," he said, recognizing the cruelty, but saying it, even so. "We can say we're divorced."

"Divorce!" she shrieked.

Gabby, who had almost quieted, screamed anew.

"It would protect your honor. It would account for him."

She tried to scream above the child's shrieks but first had to soothe him. Eventually, his nose wiped, he let himself be put on the floor and accepted his spoon.

"Don't shout," she said fiercely. "Even if you do want to throw your son, your namesake, out of the house and with him me, his mother."

"I'll see that you want for nothing."

"But you'll throw me out. Why? That's what I want

to know. What's the difference between her, who has no rights, and me, who has every right?"

"Love, Georgette."

"Pah! A word for babies."

"There never was love between us."

"What, then?"

"Passion. My damned lust."

"And the Acadian way, to marry, to live on the land, have a family?"

"Yes, that."

"Here it is different? Where there is so much land, so much work? Here you must have love, as well?"

"You'll marry, Georgette, someone better than me, maybe find love yourself."

"I found a better man than you! He was on that plantation, and he took a tenderness for me. He used that word love, but he never opened his trousers to me. He spoke of many things, like the way I can work, how quick I am, and he had admiration that I never give up. He said all those things.

"He didn't have anyone, and he asked me, thinking I was married, knowing I was searching, if I'd marry him. He said I might never find you and asked me to promise that, if you weren't in Louisiana, I'd go with him before the authorities and ask to have my marriage set aside."

"He's on Lafourche, this man?"

"Anton Branche, that's who he is! Yes, he's on Lafourche, and he asked my promise that, if things were wrong with you on the Teche or if you weren't here, I'd come to him!"

"Did you promise?"

"That I'd remember it, only."

Gabriel started to speak, but she motioned with her hand.

"Don't think," she hissed, "that because you want this slut and Anton wants me, that it will be so. Don't think I'll pretend to have a marriage set aside."

"Tell him the truth."

"Then he'd know that Gabby—never."

"You've got a place to go, a husband waiting," Gabriel said. Shame as deep as a man could feel ran through his veins while in them also beat one thought, Tonton—Tonton.

"I'm not going. I've got the rights here, not her. Send *her* away, marry *her* to another man, drown her in the bayou, get rid of her!"

The knot in his chest all but stopped his breath.

"I'll have no arranged marriage," she cried.

"When our parents spoke together in Acadia," he said, "that was an arranged marriage. Branche has spoken for himself, so where is the arrangement?"

"Pah!"

"Am I a better man? Bigger, stronger, more handsome? Have I got more land?"

"He excels you in all things! If I'd known him in Grand Pré, I would never have let happen what I did in the forest."

"Then why not marry him?"

"Because here there are no complications for me, things are my way. There is only the one trouble, for you!"

"Which I'm solving. That trading boat you came on—it goes to Lafourche before it heads for New Orleans."

"So?"

"You and Gabby will be on it. It'll push off tomorrow, so you've got today for some clear thinking. I'm sure," he pressed on, feeling ashamed, "that when you've considered, you'll see that Anton Branche, who loves and wants you, is the man you'll take."

She was sputtering furiously when he strode out. At the stableyard he bridled Lola and swam her across bayou.

François had been cleaning his stable; he held the fork in both hands, the tines piercing the earth. He waited for Gabriel to come within speaking distance.

"When does the trading boat push off?" Gabriel asked.

"Tomorrow at dawn. What's so important?"

Gabriel told him everything.

"You have considered well, my friend?" François asked Gabriel when he had finished.

"As well as I know. Because I started wrong, I won't go through life wrong, causing others to live wrong because, when I was in another world, I acted the beast."

"Is it because the boy has hair like that devil Cullen, that you don't think he is your son?"

"The hair is nothing. It's Tonton and René."

"When Georgette is gone, then you will start for Mexico?"

"As the trading boat goes in one direction, we will ride in another," Gabriel replied.

At noon he ate with a silent, frozen Georgette, a staring Gabby. Not one word was uttered until Gabriel was at the door, on his way out.

"Be ready well before dawn," he said. "I'll take you to the boat."

Her eyes blazed hotly. "I'm not going!" she cried, all of hell in her tone. "I'm here, and here I stay!"

TWENTY-ONE

Not finding Noir grazing with Lola, he went to the stable, but the stallion wasn't there, either. He eyed the fence; the horse must have jumped it, or else Georgette, angry, had deliberately let Noir out.

Knowing that Noir would return when he got ready, he decided against searching. So he mounted Lola, circled the pasture, and, at a spot beyond the stable, rode into the woods. Georgette, even though she spied him riding off, had no mount.

He trotted Lola, anticipating Tonton's joy when she learned they would leave the next day. As he walked the mare into the clearing, he noticed the total lack of sound other than that of the birds and breeze. Of necessity Tonton kept a quiet house, but even so he felt the hair on his neck stir. The silence was too deep.

He tied Lola amid concealing trees, then turned. His eyes went to the cook fire. It had died to winking ashes.

The door and shutters were closed. His pulse stepped up. At this hour, even in cold weather, one shutter was kept open for light, the baby kept warm in his deerskin.

That knot sprang into his chest. She had had to run. Just when things were about to come right for them, some tracker had spotted her and she had had to take their son and go running through the forest.

No! his mind cried. She's inside, waiting!

One last stride, and he had his hand on the door and opened it. Their mattress was made up, the blanket neat. The baby was in his cradle, asleep, his thick hair making one big ringlet at the brow, his thumb in his mouth.

Of course. She had slipped away for firewood!

And then he saw, on the table, a sheet of paper with writing on it. He strode to the table and picked up the paper. It was her handwriting, the same bright, delicate script he had seen before.

M'sieu-love, I must do this terrible act. All through the night, when you slept, my blood told what must be.

Even when I kissed you this morning, this had been decided by my heart. But I could not tell you, for I knew you would not listen, and I knew that, in your arms, I would not be strong enough to deny you the new promise you would demand—that we drive Georgette, who has suffered so much and come so far, out of the house you built for her.

M'sieu-love, in accordance with my promise, I flee because I must. Not from trackers, but to save us from hurting the innocent.

I leave René with you, his father. I believe that you will persuade Georgette to remain

242

*with you, that he will grow up with her son,
grow up white, and only you will know of his
blood. If I take him and am captured, he will,
as you know, become a slave.*

*He will be safe in his cradle, for I shall feed
him, then tie him into it. He may cry, and he
will be very wet and very hungry if it is long
before you come.*

*Do not try to find me, M'sieu-love. I'll not go to
Mexico. I have a clear and workable plan. Forgive me for taking Noir. My chances with his
speed, my new plan, and the gold are as sound as
possible.*

*As to our son, M'sieu-love, I wish him not to
know of the blood. However, if it should at
some time be your judgment that he must learn
the truth, know that I am willing for you to reveal it.*

*Do not grieve, M'sieu-love. Do not fear for
me.*

Tonton

He read the letter a second time. Folding the sheet,
he put it into his pocket. Swiftly, he untied René from
the cradle, which woke him and set him to crying. He
was indeed wet and undoubtedly hungry.

He found a small, clean garment and changed him.
As he did so, he saw something glinting at the baby's
neck. It was the delicate, cobweb chain.

He piled the extra baby things on the blanket,
folded it into a bundle, hung it from his shoulder, his
rifle over it. Then he picked up the howling René,
again tied him into the cradle, mounted a skittish
Lola, and set out for L'Acadie.

When Gabriel opened the door, Georgette was mixing something in the wooden bowl and Gabby was
staggering about like a little drunkard, holding his
spoon. Georgette didn't glance up.

"I've done the thinking," she snapped, "and it's the

243

same. You're my husband, the banns say it, Gabby says it. No matter what hussy—" She turned, arms akimbo. Her eyes went first to the bundle on Gabriel's shoulder, next to the cradle in his arms. "What's happening?" she shrilled.

Gabby, startled, looked at his mother. He puckered his face and turned red.

"What are you doing with that cradle? Whose baby is that?"

He set the cradle near the hearth, then lowered the bundle to the floor. He looked at Gabby, who was staring at this small newcomer.

"This," Gabriel said evenly, "is my son."

"By that hussy, that—?"

"By a lady. He was christened Gabriel René."

"That's Gabby's name! There can't be two Gabriel Leblancs!"

"There are three of us now. I didn't know about Gabby when René was christened."

"Why is he here?" she screamed. "Why do you bring your bastard into my house?"

"His mother has left, and I am going to look for her. You're the only one to care for him while I'm gone."

He heard her hot intake of breath. Quickly, before she could shriek, again, he shouted, "Look for me when you see me!" Then he plunged out of the kitchen house, grabbed necessities as he raced for Lola, sprang astride, and put her to the gallop.

❀

The mammoth hurricane stood yet on the land. In her sitting room, Carita Nuñez y Petain felt benumbed, her mind a hurricane of suspicion. Crouching over the journal, she muttered to herself as she read, holding the pages open with the heels of her hands. "She's right. One man—two sons—one name—!"

She read on, faster, seeking to find that things had worked out the right way, the only way. . . .

TWENTY-TWO

He had been gone twelve days when, at noon, he rode back to the kitchen house and dismounted. He dropped the head reins in front of Lola and entered.

Georgette was setting the table. She stared at him, her eyes flaming. Gabby was standing at a chair, beating his spoon on it. The cradle was near the hearth, and René was sitting up in it, tied with the deerskin strip. His hair was brushed, the big curl in front. He looked as if he had grown. He stared at Gabriel with his upslanted brown eyes, and then he broke into a smile, gurgling and flailing his small hands.

In one move Gabriel was kneeling at the cradle, his insides feeling like melted butter. He caught one of the tiny hands, laid it carefully against his bristly cheek, and smiled. René bounced, and Gabriel was on the point of taking him up when Georgette spoke.

"No! He's clean and fed and quiet." The edge to her voice sharpened. "Why do you go to him first? There's your true son." She indicated Gabby, who set his face into an instant pucker. "But you go to your bastard."

"They're both bastards," he said.

Her gasp was so shrill it was like a scream. She opened her mouth to speak, but no sound came; all she could do was stare at him with blazing eyes.

He had known, from the moment he spoke, how unjust he had been to both her and Tonton and to their babies. He told her that. "I'll not say it again," he promised.

"You'd better not!" she shrilled, her voice recovered. René looked startled and Gabby screeched, tears pouring down his face. She snatched him up, rocked him, talking still, but hissing now, and the child quieted.

"You really went after her—and dumped her bastard on me. You've been gone twelve days, do you know that? With me forced to take care of your by-blow!"

He had searched so keenly, so fruitlessly. He had lost Tonton in the trackless reaches. He knew that she had gone out of love for him and René, perhaps he would never know her fate. But would try to find out.

"I was trying to find her, Georgette," he said quietly.

"Where is she? She's to take him out of my house!"

"She's gone. She'll not be back."

"Then all we've got to do is get rid of—"

"Quiet! What do you suggest I do with my son? Throw him into the swamp?"

"Give him to her family."

"There is no family."

"Everybody's got family!"

He would never let her know of the mixed blood. Never. "Not her," he said. "Not René. Not Acadians, either."

She gestured. "Get rid of him. Then we marry, with no reminder of your slut!"

Each time she called Tonton that name, Gabriel longed to smash her face, but he kept his control. Georgette was vicious, but he had given her cause.

"I'll marry you, Georgette, when the priest gets here."

"Secretly."

"Yes."

She gave a sharp sigh.

"On one condition."

She waited, cradling her son, her eyes alert.

"René. He stays."

"I won't have him!"

"You have a choice. Take Gabby to Anton Branche."

"And how will you explain the baby?"

He stared at her unblinkingly.

"I've got the right to stay!"

"If you come to terms."

"What—terms?" she blazed.

"You claim René as full brother to Gabby."

"Insane!"

"And you'll never let him know he wasn't born of you."

She clutched Gabby. "If I do this, how will you explain two Gabriel René Leblancs? Eh? And one when we were parted. What about those things?"

"You have a sharp mind and a quick tongue. It is wilderness here, new people will never know. Those here now won't notice or, if they do, will forget. François will never tell."

He would say no more. Any idea must be her own, or she would not help.

Her eyes slitted. "If I choose, yes, if I choose!"

He waited, but she stood mute. She wanted a response. Well, it was her due. So he asked, "And what is the explanation—if you choose?"

"That I so loved my lost Gabriel that I named both sons for him. Who is to know we didn't find each other, not here, but in New Orleans, that you left me there, without telling anyone, until my house was built? Who can prove that I had not one, but two babies, when I arrived?"

"I knew you could think of something."

"If I do it, Gabriel Leblanc, if I do it!"

The lump in his chest thickened. Through all the shame, for what he had done to Tonton, through the concessions he now demanded of Georgette, hope rose. Perhaps, in this manner, René would have a mother.

"You've solved every problem," he said.

"Oui. You owe me, Gabriel Leblanc!"

He met her flaming eyes.

"The torture I went through, bearing your son, searching—now this! You'll marry me if I claim 'her' bastard as my own clean and lawful flesh! You've got the effrontery to do that."

"Yes. I have."

"You admit it!"

"And know it for what it is. Further, you'll play no favorites between the boys, nor will I. They are equal, Leblanc both, Acadians."

"Beast!" she hissed, the fires of hell in her eyes. "I'll marry you on those terms. And I'll keep to them."

"I know you will," he said, a sudden, consuming weariness in every bone. "You're a schemer, you're a fighter, you're a hard worker. You'll be a good and watchful mother. You'll be mistress of L'Acadie. I will be true to our vows."

"I've got other rights!" she spat. "I want no talk of 'her.'"

"I'll not speak of her again."

Her eyes bored into him.

"I won't doubt Gabby, either. He is my son."

"Are you hiding something else?"

"No. I'm laying our foundation. In Grand Pré we were to have a different life, living with others, seeing others, because we had a civilization. Here we'll live with babies and, except for three other white men and some Indians, have only the wilderness around us for now. Each life, the Grand Pré and this, was to have been and now is to be a family. If our parents and brothers find the Teche, we will help them settle."

"If I stay."

"If you do."

She frowned and set Gabby on the floor. "It is settled. I'll be the best wife in Louisiana. You can hold your head in pride, I promise. But I promise more, Gabriel Leblanc. I'll never forgive you for what you've done! And, whenever the feeling takes me, I'll make you pay. I'll make your life a living hell—when I please—until the day I die!"

He had deliberately to block out the thought of Tonton—his love for her, the heartbreaking search. He didn't, at that time, know there wouldn't be a week, a month, a year, in which he would cease wondering about his lost love. He didn't know, either, that there would be no time, ever, when he would hear of her or that the sweet ache in his loins for her would never cease.

TWENTY-THREE

After dinner Gabriel swam Lola across-bayou to report to François about where he had been, what had happened, his upcoming marriage and its conditions. They sat on the edge of the porch, feet dangling.

François shook his head. "Georgette hasn't changed."

"She's stronger, quicker, fiercer."

"There's much deceit."

"As little as possible. I have no excuses. I let myself be pushed by circumstances, but I don't regret loving Tonton, only losing her, and I don't regret René. But after Georgette came, things got to the same point as when you and I were dumped off the *Esne* and had to do what came to hand. I do regret treating her as I've done. She knows about Tonton, but not about her blood or René's blood. She is never to know. She has agreed to claim René as her own."

"I'll hold my tongue, ami. Another life begins for you now, almost the one you first planned."

Gabriel squeezed François' shoulders clumsily. Then he jumped off the porch and stood. "Why do we chatter like women?" he demanded. "I need to get my stock and my pirogue across-bayou. Will you help me, my friend?"

By the time the stock transfer had been made, leaving the cat that Gabriel had brought from New Orleans and its kittens with François, it was time to milk. Gabriel plunged into this work after spreading fresh straw in the stalls, planning to bring one of the kittens to live in the stable when it was weaned. This would both keep it from under Georgette's feet and keep the stable free of rodents.

Georgette had the wooden bowls on the work shelf when he brought in the milk. Briskly, as though she had been doing it from the beginning, she took the bucket from him and strained the milk through a cloth.

The rich smell of ham frying suddenly made Gabriel aware he was hungry. The table was set for two.

"Where are René and Gabby?" he asked.

"Asleep. In the main house, in the bedroom. The— he's in the cradle, and Gabby's on a moss mattress I made. We need beds built."

"I'll see to it. One for us, too. And a couple of long-legged chairs so they can sit up to the table."

"The—he'll need arms to his chair."

"Gabby, too. He's not all that big he won't fall."

A flash of what, in Grand Pré, might have been tenderness crossed Georgette's face.

"Gabby said Papa today," she told him. "And the—"

"Don't avoid his name. Say it right out. René. Get used to it."

"René—he looked at the door, watched."

"He waits for me," Gabriel said. Then, seeing her quick frown, he continued, "The past is gone, except for the boys. We've got to speak freely of them, to tell what happened in their first days. That's part of being a family."

"Just like nothing ever happened?"

"Yes, Georgette." He smiled deliberately, at first to show friendliness, but the smile grew as he recognized, in that flashing retort, the Georgette he had known in Acadia.

She put ham, cabbage, potatoes, and bread on the table, and they ate. Once she went to the main house to look at the boys, and returned, reporting they were asleep. She remembered that he liked to drink coffee after his meal and brought a cup to him.

"What are you going to raise on this land, you and François?" she asked.

"Food, feed, hay. Indigo. Later on, sugar cane."

"You're mad! The boatmen said it freezes sometimes in December. And frosts. They said sugar cane can't stand the cold, that it's a tropical crop and the bayou country is only sort of semi-tropical. Whatever that means."

He was relieved to be speaking together as they had done long ago. It was good to talk. "It means it's tropical to a degree, but not as warm as the real tropics."

"Why do you want to raise a crop that'll be ruined? Indigo is the thing here, the boatmen said."

"There are troubles with indigo. The more we hear about sugar cane—well, we're going to try it. In spite of freezes and the difficulty of getting it to a sugarhouse until we build our own—"

"You wouldn't be such fools!"

"We'll not start for a couple of years."

"I'm against it."

"You run the house, Georgette, and raise the boys. I'll run L'Acadie."

"Ah oui, and I can bear the babies, no? I can suffer, and you say, 'We will raise the sugar cane,' and I, who run the house, bear the babies and endure pain—do not forget the pain—I will be in the fields also, with the sugar cane, which will freeze. You are mad, mad mad!"

For the first time in days he grinned. Georgette, in this moment, was so much the Grand Pré girl that it was no small task to overcome the grin. However, it would only irritate her, and she would accuse him of making fun of her. Beyond that, it seemed, coming so soon, to be disloyal to Tonton.

Forcibly he put Tonton out of his thoughts. He accepted the offer of more coffee and sat watching Georgette clear the table and get her dishwater ready. She set the wooden pan on the end of the table, the things to be washed neatly stacked to her left.

As she worked, something approaching peace shaped her features into their old attractiveness, or almost so. He noted that her bosom had rounded out, but otherwise, she was thinner, honed. Well, here, with exile and slavery behind her, once they were married and she had settled in, she would fill out.

His attention returned to her bosom. The old lust rose and that part, which for Tonton, had been an instrument of art and love, became again an angry rod straining at his trousers. He cursed inwardly. He *was* a beast, an animal! Two weeks only—less—since he had lain, in love, with Tonton. Yet now—

"Smoke if you want to," Georgette said.

He shot a look at her. She disliked tobacco. "You mean here, in the house?"

"That's what I said."

"You don't have to offer. There's no need to go to extremes."

"I made the offer. Do as you will."

"I'll smoke later, outside."

"At the stable, around that hay? What do you want, a fire?"

The talking had helped. He could now safely stand. "No, not in the stable," he said. "Well—goodnight. Call if you need me, if the children—"

"Gabriel Leblanc, don't you go, don't you leave me!"

"What do you mean?"

"You're not sleeping in any stable."

He stared.

"You'll sleep on our own mattress in our own room."

His part bulged instantly. She saw. Shame flared from his scalp to the soles of his feet, but the bulge grew.

"Well?" she demanded.

"We don't know how long it will be before the priest—"

"Pah! We'll be married when he comes!"

He was like a log of wood there, like iron, and now he had an actual, stabbing pain. He didn't know how long he could manage. The Gabriel in Grand Pré would have had her on the bare floor by now, her skirts pulled up. But now he wouldn't take advantage; now he would make sure. Even then, beyond that, was Tonton.

"We'd be living in sin," he said. "There could be a new baby before the priest gets here."

"I know it. Thanks to you, I know! But if it's learned that you sleep in the stable, not in the house, that's a scandal I won't have."

He was free to ease his torment, freed by her own beliefs, freed by Tonton, who had taken love away so that he could establish this family in this house. He groaned.

"Are you going to be stubborn?" Georgette asked.

"You finished out here?" he countered.

"I am."

"Then get into the house. Fast."

She led, running, he all but stepping on her heels. He carried the lantern, and as they came into the bedroom, they glanced at the children and saw they were asleep.

"Put out the light!" she hissed. "If you think I'm going to let you watch—blow it out!"

He did it in one puff, then pulled off his trousers. He heard her skirts rustle and the mattress give.

He came onto it, bestrode her, one hand braced on either side, quivering.

"Don't hurt me—don't tear me!"

It was in the back of his mind that she had said nothing of hurt that day in the forest. But those English devils. If she'd been raped like the girls on the *Esne*. . . . Then all thought vanished, and there was only now. He plunged into her, straight and swift. She moaned, but in acceptance.

Beside himself, he began to pump, and she rose and sank, meeting his rhythm. At first her depths were less tight than he wanted, but as her response grew, there came a rewarding tightness.

He was rutting, and he knew he was rutting, and he went at it faster, more greedily, frantically, yet wanting to make it last, to hold off that final, bursting instant. She was so strong. She was so tiny, but she met his every onslaught with her own, all but bucking him off.

Each time he slammed into her, she responded in kind. He was panting, sweating, and could hear her gasping, but not one stroke did she miss, and whether this utter fierceness, which she had not displayed the other time, was one that nature had since bestowed

253

or whether it had been learned, did not now, nor would in the future, matter.

He hammered full strength; it seemed he would grind her into the mattress. She hammered back; it seemed she might hurl him to the ceiling. He was grunting now, streaming sweat. He was beyond endurance; she was crying out, beating him with her fists. At last, unable to endure, his passion broke, hot and scalding. When it was over, when the last twitch had gone, he rolled away.

She sprang up instantly, and there was rustling. What was she doing after such exertion, how could she do anything but lie drained and seeking closeness, murmured words, sleep?

So he asked.

"Cleaning myself, what do you think?" she retorted. "Getting ready for bed. The way you'd better do if we're to get any work done tomorrow."

He sat up, took off his shirt, put it on the floor beside the mattress, and lay back. Busy with her own preparations, Georgette, even in the darkness, was aware of his lack of activity.

"Put on your nightrobe."

"I haven't got one."

"You sleep—naked?" She whispered the last word.

"I sure don't sleep in my clothes," he said.

He lay breathing evenly. He had eased his desire, and he couldn't truthfully say that he hadn't enjoyed every second of what went on—until it was over, until there was no soft form nestled in his arm, no soft breath against his cheek.

It was then he realized that he was eased only, that he wasn't satisfied.

Georgette laid down on the mattress, keeping to the far side. "You've got to go to the post tomorrow," she said, "and buy some lengths of white and white thread. You can trade for it, can't you?"

"I've got credit ahead. They've got the white; I've seen it. René needs some clothes, and François keeps talking about how Elodie'll want to make window curtains. I can get you some cloth for that, too."

"Your nightrobe comes first!" Georgette snapped. Then, when he turned over, "Keep to your own side. I'm not going to touch a naked man, now or ever!"

TWENTY-FOUR

He made the trip to the post alone. When he asked Georgette if she wanted to select her own goods, she snapped a refusal.

"Let that Burdell see René in deerskin? When he's dressed right, then I'll go!"

He admired her pride. She would keep the family dressed, fill the table with good food, teach the children according to her beliefs, and work unceasingly. And he knew that she would turn her venom on him when she chose. He would tolerate a certain amount of it, but beyond that he would require that she hold her tongue.

They settled into a routine. Days passed, and he and François added to their roads; they ditched; they cleared the endless brush to ready more land for planting. Georgette usually helped with this work on both plantations, bringing the children with her.

Never did Gabriel see her favor one boy over the other. She divided her attention between them equally, calling herself mama to both, holding René in her arms as often as she held Gabby. She spanked Gabby for hitting René with the spoon; she slapped René's hands when he dug them into his porridge. In a day Gabby had his spoon back and, though he glowered at René, he did not again strike him; René ceased putting his hands into his porridge. She found and gave René a smooth scrap of wood that became both a toy and teething device.

Time flowed. They labored, and the boys grew. René lunged to his feet and stood, holding to a chair.

Georgette abruptly said one night, "I should be enceinte, and I'm not!"

"What's wrong with that?"

"Night after night—six weeks—more!"

"Sometimes a woman goes three years without a baby."

"It took only the one time with Gabby!"

"That doesn't mean—"

"Doesn't it, Gabriel Leblanc! I had Gabby, and you had René, and nothing since. And there are diseases a man gets from a bad woman and gives to his wife, and she can never be enceinte."

Rage at the implication that Tonton, pure and innocent Tonton, was the cause of Georgette's failure to conceive, flamed in him. He thought of the soldiers who might have harmed her the way Cullen and the others did on the *Esne*, and he said, his teeth clenched, "That's not the reason here."

"Then why?" There was desperation in her voice. "I want to have twenty babies, more!"

He had never seen her like this and, seeing, felt compassion. He wondered if girls who were raped were rendered barren.

"It's what you've undergone," he said. "Your body isn't ready. When it is, we'll have to double the size of the house, and later I'll build a fine plantation house, the best in the region!"

"I don't want the house. I want the babies."

A few more Acadians made their way to New Orleans and, from there, into bayou country. The trading boat brought word that they were settling along the Mississippi and Bayon Lafourche. Two couples had received grants on the Atchafalaya River.

Gabriel and François were breaking a new field at Hebert Plantation the morning a pirogue nosed in at the landing and a stocky, thick-shouldered man leapt ashore. François pulled his mare up, dropped the plow and began to run for the bayou.

"Le bon Dieu!" he screamed. "It's Louis—my brother Louis!"

Gabriel abandoned his own plow and ran after his friend. When he reached them, the brothers were locked in a fierce embrace, tears pouring down their faces. François' mustache was wet from tears, his pock marks more visible than ever.

Gabriel, tears flowing, embraced Louis, too. The three of them stood embracing, weeping, overwhelmed by this miraculous reunion.

"How did you do it?" François asked. "How did you find me?"

"Newspapers, little brother. Then, in New Orleans, they knew where you'd gone."

"Elodie. Did she see the advertisements? Is she with you?"

Louis's expression fell sober. "She didn't know as soon as I did, my brother. Not until I met her and a party from the Minas—"

"Then she came with you? Where is she? I'll go after her. Louis, is something wrong? Is she ill, did some devil—I'll kill—"

Louis dropped his strong hands onto his brother's shoulders. Gabriel saw them tighten, and the gesture both gladdened his own heart and caused him to hope, briefly, that he too might one day thus greet one of his own brothers.

"She asked me to tell you," Louis said. "But I couldn't. So she wrote the letter."

"She isn't—here?"

Louis shook his head and handed François the letter.

François took it, and with deliberation, broke the seal and unfolded the sheets. Though his face remained blank, his eyes quickly scanned the written lines. Gabriel was helpless to look away from his friend and saw the olive-tinged skin drain to an incredible pallor.

When he had finished, François passed the letter to Gabriel. "Read," he said.

Gabriel drew his eyes reluctantly along the fine black script. There was no heading, no date.

I watched when the Esne *sailed, taking you away from me. Two days later I was on another ship, sailing in the same direction. The voyage was bad, as yours must have been. The English soldiers had no respect for Acadian women, and we were used in a way of which I can't write. I was fortunate, for I neither bore a bastard nor became victim of any disease.*

We were put ashore in Virginia, where we worked with Negro slaves. Among us was Joseph Belmerre from the Minas. His wife Marie went mad when they put her four sons on another ship, and she drove a knife into her heart.

It was Joseph who managed our escape from Virginia. He helped me search for you. Once he managed to get a newspaper for the advertisements, but there was nothing.

It was Joseph who said we should go to New Orleans. He said maybe you would do the same, but to me it seemed the farther from Grand Pré we got, the farther I was from you. I pleaded with him to lead us—we were fourteen in all—back to Nova Scotia. He wouldn't agree, nor would the others, and now I know they were right.

You know the way we had to travel, for you did the same. We had frightening escapes from Indians. One night, just at dark, one man was killed by an Indian, and the men buried him and left a cross at his grave.

I was mad with fear. I crept into the trees, away from the others, to hide. It was Joseph who found me. I wouldn't go back to our camp, where the grave was, so he lay beside me and held me, and that was the first time, the first instant I had felt a touch of safety since the English came. I crept closer to him. Our bodies warmed each other, and our hearts.

He took me there, in the darkness, in wilderness danger, and I was safe. And while it was happening, I forgot that somewhere you might be alive. He whispered that he had grown to love me and that, because of what we had shared, he considered me wife and asked that I consider him husband. He was my safety, my world. I promised. That night, in that manner, I promised.

We traveled on, eventually drifting into the Mississippi. There we tied up along the bank near another raft. Louis was with that party, and he had knowledge of you. And I knew that, as certainly as I was enceinte, you were building a home for me, waiting.

I told Louis how it was between Joseph and myself. I told Joseph about finding you. When I saw the hurt on him, my heart broke and splintered into my bones because of the situation I had brought to pass.

My love for you is the same love. But I am enceinte with Joseph's baby and hold deep affection for him. Could you, François, accept the woman I have become? And the baby. Could you accept it? Could I give it up, even to Joseph, who prays nightly that it will be a son?

He spoke once on the matter. He said that my first commitment was to you, and if I decided to honor it, he would release me. He asked only that I leave the baby with him. I put these matters to Louis, your brother. He said they were not for him to answer, that he had not the wisdom.

I was never a girl to spend many hours on my knees. But, by the time our rafts, which now traveled together, tied up at New Orleans, my knees were red.

Joseph wants to settle below New Orleans. As in a dream, in which another Elodie spoke, I told him to have our banns published along with those of your brother and Yvonne Granger, who had discovered love. Joseph and I are married now. As are Louis and Yvonne. I can't ask you to forgive. The act is done. The heart

*of Elodie will always belong to François, but
the life of Elodie belongs to Joseph.*

There was no signature.

Carefully, so the paper did not so much as whisper,
Gabriel handed the letter back to his friend. He, in
turn, offered it to his brother, who shook his head.

His lips clamped tightly together, François folded the
sheets once, then tore them in half. He folded them
again and tore again. Methodically he folded and tore,
and when the paper was nothing but small, square bits,
he stepped to the bayou and dropped them into the
water.

The three men watched the scraps inch into the current and begin the slow downstream drift. The silence
grew so loud that Gabriel's ears began to beat—a silence so filled with pain that it covered the lapping of
water, the flicker of a bird's wing, and the deep-
throated sounds of some nearby bullfrog.

"It's bad, my brother," Louis said finally.

"We live on," François replied stonily. "Time heals.
But only if a man does something about it, only if he
fights."

"She's his wife, my brother. He's a good man. She
has his baby. You can't go rushing through the wilderness and—"

"Who said I'd go after another man's wife?"

"Nobody, nobody."

"These others," François asked, "did some of them
come up the Teche? Or did every damned one of them
go to the Mississippi?"

"All but Joseph and Elodie came to the Teche. I've
taken the grant north of yours. Yvonne's father—"

"Your wife's father?"

"Oui. He's taken a grant down-bayou. Her grandfather will live with them."

"Eh."

"There's the possibility that we may find our
brother Étienne. I got an address and posted a letter.
Le bon Dieu willing, there'll be three Hebert brothers
on this bayou."

"Good. The others in your party, where are they?"

"Alexandre Landry's grant is on the Teche next to the Perraults', which makes their daughter Jacqueline toss her head."

"Landry. He's married?"

"Not yet."

"Is he after the girl?"

"Jacqueline?" Louis smiled. "She's eighteen, beautiful, and willful. She won't look at Landry. I heard her tell him he looks as if his feet smell. Up until then, he'd hung around her, but not so much since. At one time, both being free and coming into the wilderness—" He spread his hands and shrugged.

Only now did Gabriel permit himself to ask his own pressing question. "Did a priest, Father Charles, show up?"

He pretended not to see the look François gave him, but noted that his friend's stone-faced expression had gone.

"Oui," Louis replied. "He tied his pirogue to one of our rafts. He means to stay six weeks. So it would be possible yet for that pair to marry."

"Where are they at this moment, all of them?" François demanded.

"At the post."

"Come on. We're going down there."

"Before I see your house? Before we take a look at my grant, my brother?"

"You can see them any time. I want to see that girl, Jacqueline. Before they take her downstream."

Gabriel and Louis stared. "Are you insane?" Louis exclaimed. "One moment you learn—the next you're after—"

"The only girl on the Teche."

"You can't just walk up to a girl and—"

"Why not?"

"But Jacqueline—she's—"

"Willful. Straight talking. So am I."

"Meet her, friend," Gabriel reasoned. "Yes. But the other, so soon—no."

"The two of you can stay here and welcome. I've got no time to lose!" He started for his pirogue.

"You know damned well we're coming!" Gabriel said, hurrying, Louis beside him. And even as he spoke, underlying his concern for François, ran the thought that tonight, if Father Charles would agree, his promise to Georgette would be fulfilled.

TWENTY-FIVE

Before they reached the post, they could see it was full of activity. Tied at the landing were two big, flat-built boats like the ones that had brought Gabriel and François. Louis said that the other boats, loaded with stock and implements, were on the way. There were some pirogues; the area outside the post itself seemed to swarm with people.

As François' pirogue nosed in, two Attakapas came out of the building and went for their pirogue. Three others stood back from the unusual activity and watched.

Gabriel leapt ashore, tied up, then swept a look over the newcomers, whose voices and laughter made a pleasant sound he had not heard before on the bayou.

Shyly, a girl came toward Gabriel and his companions. She was a bit tall, a bit too slim, but she bore a look of strength, and she was unusually beautiful. Her thick, wavy auburn hair was drawn up in a swirl at the top of her head. Her eyes were large and dark, with a hint of auburn.

Her skin, by nature, would be very fair, but was now a light golden from the sun. Her features were smooth and even. She's really a beauty, Gabriel thought. If this is Jacqueline—

But Louis said, drawing the girl to him. "This, my brother, is Yvonne. This is my wife."

262

She placed a hand on Louis's arm and they exchanged a tender look. And in the look was the love Gabriel had once known, that François had felt for Elodie. Here it was again, in these two, in this wilderness.

Gabriel saw the warmth with which she greeted François, the spontaneous liking his friend had for her, even with his mind on another girl. Gabriel, in his turn, took her firm hand and smiled when he was introduced.

Louis guided them to the group Yvonne had left, putting one square hand on the arm of a hale, broad man with white hair and tanned skin. The man's face was lined, and there lurked a hint of humor at the corners of his mouth. His dark eyes met those of all the men.

"Our eldest citizen," Louis introduced him. "Monsieur Battistes Commo, farmer of the Minas, now of Bayou Teche. He is Yvonne's grandfather and will live with her family. Monsieur, my brother François, and our friend Gabriel Leblanc, of whom I have spoken."

As they greeted one another, Louis brought forward another man, who appeared to be well into his forties. He, too, had steady eyes and a firm mouth. Next to him stood a plump, sad-eyed woman.

"Monsieur Alexis Granger and his wife—Yvonne's parents." Gabriel smiled at the woman and knew, from her sadness, that she had been separated from other children.

A tall, broad young man with light brown hair and dark eyes stepped up to them, his hand outstretched. "Alexandre Landry," he said. "My grant's next to the Perraults', down-bayou."

He shook hands vigorously with Gabriel, who thought that, with his vigor and size, he would be one to get his land under control faster than most. He now turned to François.

Gabriel glanced at his friend, who was blank faced, though he did respond with his name and a brief handshake for his rival. Well, Gabriel thought, he may not fancy this girl when he sees her.

"Louis, chérie," Yvonne reminded. "You haven't yet presented them to the Perraults and Jacqueline."

"He's saving me for last," said a voice so bright it dazzled. "Does that mean I'm best—or worst? Speak truth, Louis—Yvonne won't be jealous, will you chérie?"

Laughing, Yvonne moved to her and put her arm around the other girl's slender shoulders. "This," she declared, "is Jacqueline Perrault, the girl I love above all girls, because of our travels together. She is strong, and she is so honest it hurts, and she works so hard it tires me to watch. She talks back, but she is so happy and beautiful no one minds. Chérie—François Hebert, brother to my Louis, and Gabriel Leblanc, their friend."

Gabriel observed the deep look François gave the girl and saw it pierce to the bone. He's going to scare her off, he thought.

She was almost as tall as Yvonne, her skin as golden. Her hair was dark brown, worn in a heavy braid wound around her head, and her eyes brown-black and they looked frankly and steadily into François' probing eyes. Intelligence, spirit, and vitality sparkled from her. She was even a bit like Elodie, but her extreme loveliness which just missed true beauty, transcended that of Elodie.

François' expression grew bemused. He hadn't expected this, Gabriel knew. No man could expect this. She stood erect and continued to return François' look, letting him search her. In turn she did her own searching. Neither had acknowledged the introduction.

None of the passerbys, including Landry, who had wandered off, noticed the little tableau. Louis, Yvonne, Gabriel, François, and Jacqueline formed an island apart. Now François put his hand under the girl's arm and turned her toward the other two men.

"I've got a thing to say to you," he told her. "It's what a man says to a girl in private, but I want my brother and my friend to hear so they can correct me if the words come out wrong. Your parents, also. I know this isn't ordinary, but I hope you have no objection."

"The times aren't ordinary," she said. "Let them hear."

She turned, motioning to a couple who stood nearby. They approached the group, their faces open and friendly. Looking at the man, who was tall, broad, and handsome, it was obvious that he was Jacqueline's father.

After Jacqueline introduced her parents, she said, "François has something to say. He wants us all to hear."

François was prompt, blunt, and definite. "I was to marry a girl in Nova Scotia, but we were parted by the English. I looked for her, I advertised. My brother brought me a letter from her today. She has married another man."

"Did you love this girl?" Jacqueline demanded.

"Oui."

"And now," said Dominic Perrault, scowling, "you've seen my daughter."

"Papa! He hasn't finished!"

"I've got a league of land," François continued, looking at Jacqueline only. "I've got fields and crops. I've got stock, chickens, even cats. I've got a new main house, a kitchen house, a stable, a granary. I've got a road started and drainage ditches. I need a wife. I need her now, as fast as the banns can be published, not some time off in the future, after more settlers, other girls, come to the Teche."

"So," growled Perrault, "your brother told you of my daughter, and you came running. No thought of courtship, of affection, but as if you were buying a cow!"

"Papa, it is my right to hear what this man has to say, what he's honest enough to speak before others."

Perrault's brows knotted, and he muttered. Jacqueline's mother gazed at her with an expression beyond sadness. "My daughter," she murmured, "you could leave us so soon—"

"Mama, you've lost three sons, and I've lost three

brothers. But you have Papa, you have a husband. Surely it is right that I, too, have a husband? This is a new country, and this man pleases me as no man has ever done."

Tears veiled Louise Perrault's eyes but, slowly, she nodded. Jacqueline's father glowered.

"Go on," Jacqueline told François, "say it all."

"I offer you life on this bayou. Work. I offer prosperity, a family, respect, and kindness. Meeting you, seeing such a woman as I hadn't dared to hope for—I offer the challenge to build your life with mine."

They exchanged a silent, deep look.

"This is my first offer," she said at last. "One word is missing. But that is no fault of yours."

"My daughter," whispered the mother, "to marry a man if you do not love—"

"There hasn't been time, Mama. Love grows. This you have told me, and this I have accepted."

"It's out of the question!" Perrault exploded. "Before I'll see my—"

"Papa! This is my marriage, not yours!" she cried, her eyes on François. "I'll be proud to be your wife," she said. "The priest will be here long enough, which is good."

François swallowed audibly. "We'll see him at once."

"He's at the inn," Perrault said angrily. "He needs to sleep. Go on. Disturb him. It may irritate him enough that he'll refuse banns such as these—insane—unheard of!"

Jacqueline demanded of François, "What's the custom in this wilderness?"

"Courtship's the custom anywhere," Perrault cut in. "We need to find out if you're good enough for our daughter."

"He's good enough, monsieur," Louis said. "He's a Hebert of Grand Pré."

"I'll come down-bayou, courting, three times a week while the banns are being published. That will have to be enough, monsieur."

Perrault spoke heatedly; Jacqueline's mother wept and implored. Jacqueline would have it no other way than that she become Madame François Hebert. It was only when she threatened, hotly, never to see her parents again if they refused consent, saying she would stay at the inn during the banns, that they gave in.

Now Gabriel escaped the party and went inside the post, where he arranged to use Burdell's pirogue, having left his own at François' landing. He slipped into the craft and away unnoticed, and set himself against the current to reach Georgette in all possible haste.

He had not seen her so like her old self, excited and dancing about, since Grand Pré. He had scarcely told her that Father Charles was at the inn before she wanted to start dressing herself and the boys, and when he explained that the old priest was exhausted and resting, she still wanted to go.

"We can sit and wait until he wakes up," she insisted.

"It won't do, Georgette. We'll go after dark, so we won't be seen. Besides, I have to do chores, get my pirogue and tow Burdell's back to the post, then come home again."

"What are you doing with Burdell's pirogue?"

She listened avidly as he told her the whole story.

"Eh!" she exclaimed when he had finished. "The priest came at a good time. We'll be the first married couple on the Teche."

"Louis and Yvonne are married. And the Grangers and Perraults."

"But they have no house yet."

"Which means—?"

"That we'll be the leading family. You say we'll have a dynasty and the biggest house in the region. I say we'll be the most important, that we'll entertain. We'll have people to be with."

"I didn't realize the wilderness bothered you."

"It doesn't, I've been too busy. I'll always be busy, but now we begin a settlement, and that is good."

He had never seen her more nearly beautiful. It was sad that he hadn't given her what she had expected—

just this bit now, after all she had endured at his hands, as well as those of the English.

He hoped she would conceive soon and complete her joy. He had no way of knowing that never again would she bear a child.

At the inn, Morphy admitted them. He put them in his parlor, a square chamber furnished with a hand-made table, two chairs with arms and two without. Drapes hung over the windows and a candelabrum in the center of the mantel held seven burning candles.

He left to inform the priest of their arrival, and they waited. René, seven months old, wearing one of his new dresses, slept in Georgette's arms. Once she moved the curl off his brow and arranged it carefully. Gabby trotted around the room, staring at everything, touching nothing.

When Father Charles entered, he looked older and frailer than before. The hem of his black habit scarcely swung as he moved. The kindliness of his face was the same, deeper perhaps, and sweeter.

"My son," he said, holding both hands to Gabriel, acknowledging Georgette with a smile. "How can I serve you?" His eyes touched Georgette, René, Gabby.

"Father, when you christened my son, I didn't tell you that my banns had been called in Nova Scotia. This is my fiancée," he went on, indicating Georgette, "Georgette Babin. We were to be married in four days, but the English—that's when they came."

"I understand, my son."

"I sinned against her, father. After we were separated, in terror, and hiding the shame by saying she was married, she bore a son, that one with the blond hair. He was christened with the name you later gave the baby there, against whose mother I also sinned. My fiancée has papers of our banns. She has agreed to take the second baby for her own."

"And the mother of the baby?"

"She has gone. Permanently."

The priest bowed his head. He lifted it and looked

at Gabriel. "You and Georgette wish to marry, my son?"

"Yes. Now."

"And you, my daughter. With your heart you wish to marry this man, father to these children?"

"Oui," she whispered, drawing forth her paper announcing their banns.

They waited while the priest examined it. "I deem this authentic," he said. "We'll need witnesses. Perhaps Monsieur Morphy will bring Monsieur Burdell."

"No witnesses, father," Georgette said.

"You want the marriage secret, my daughter?"

"It is because of the sinning, the children, Father," Gabriel explained. "I have continued to sin, for when my fiancée arrived, I told everyone that she was my wife, and we have lived together for nearly two months."

"You suggest, my son, that a priest deceive?"

"It isn't meant so, father. The way I see it, Georgette has suffered more now than she should. She's entitled to the marriage others assume she had long ago. If witnesses are brought in—"

"Rather than that," Georgette said, "I'll wait."

"Wait, my daughter?"

"I'll live as his wife, live in sin until we can go to New Orleans, whenever that may be, and marry among strangers. But such sin is not what I want, father."

A shiver flashed through Gabriel. He had never known anyone to blackmail a priest. Yet there Georgette sat, René in her arms, her voice respectful, but her words like a blade.

The priest sighed. "You've already lived in sin too long, my children. If you will stand before me, please."

Thus they were wed, René asleep in Georgette's arms, the bride wearing the dress she had made from the cloth Gabriel had bought for Tonton, the cobweb chain Tonton had left around René's neck glowing against it. And at the end Gabriel put Tonton's gold wedding ring on Georgette's finger. He felt a deep sadness that they had prevailed on this kind old priest to bless their union without witnesses, to save them from sinning longer in the wilderness.

François and Jacqueline were married three weeks later in the same room because the old priest had suffered a hard cold, which prevented his making the trip down-bayou. Jacqueline declared she preferred the inn because the first part of the Perrault house was only begun and they were sleeping in tents, as were the other newcomers.

It was Georgette's idea to give a wedding party. When François returned from down-bayou with Jacqueline's enthusiastic acceptance, Georgette went into a flurry of activity, cleaning her new and spotless house every day and all day. She prevailed upon Gabriel to go to the post and buy curtain cloth, red for the kitchen house, blue for the main house, and when she wasn't tending the children, cooking, washing, or cleaning, Georgette was stitching and hanging curtains.

She was too busy to attend the wedding itself. "I can't go, not with all these people coming!" she cried. "The women will understand why."

On the wedding night, after she put the children to bed, she was everywhere—out of the main house and into the kitchen, brewing coffee, slicing the turkey she had roasted, recklessly skimming the thickest cream, putting out her entire supply of butter, making certain the cake she had managed to make out of their remaining flour was in the exact center of the table. Checking the faultlessly set table, she suddenly began to bemoan the fact that she had no table linen.

"That's one of the next things I want!" she declared. "White goods for a tablecloth. If Burdell hasn't got linen, then the heaviest white goods he carries. Nothing sets off a table like white."

"I'll take you to the post," Gabriel promised. "You can choose what you want."

She stepped back from the table and, hearing a

small sound from outside, went flying to the main house, through the sitting room and onto the porch.

Pirogues were tying up at the landing. There was talk and laughter. Gabriel went racing down to meet Jacqueline, François and the wedding guests and walk back with them, while Georgette waited on the porch to greet them.

There was much merriment as the guests greeted first Gabriel, then Georgette. Georgette kissed Jacqueline and shook François' hand then led the way inside. The guests were laughing and talking when Georgette's voice rose above all, "Welcome, welcome to L'Acadie. You women, come see the babies."

She took a candle and led the suddenly hushed, tiptoeing women away from the men and into the bedchamber. Gabriel and the other men followed to the door.

As the women hovered over the sleeping children, Gabriel heard Georgette, her whisper keen and reaching, say, "This is Gabby, short for Gabriel, our firstborn son. And this," she continued, leading the women to the cradle, "is René, my second son."

Thus she laid public claim to René, invested him with her blood. Now not even the devil, Gabriel thought with heavy relief, could make her deny it.

TWENTY-SIX

From the journal of Gabriel Leblanc:

Georgette has proven herself. She makes my life a living hell. Never, since the night the priest married us and she stood in the dress she had made from the cloth bought for Tonton, with Tonton's gold chain at her neck, Tonton's wedding ring on her finger, has a day come without a flick from the tongue of hell.

If there is a worse thing than a fiercely "good" woman, I have yet to find it. Georgette has, however, held the Leblanc head proud on the Teche. And she has treated both René and Gabby well, not favoring one over the other.

She is a true neighbor. When François fell on his scythe and it went to the bone, she left her ironing, sent word to me in the field, and rowed across-bayou in response to Jacqueline's first scream. She helped Jacqueline tend the injury, nursing François day and night. And when he died, raving from the most excruciating pain a man can suffer, his jaws locked, she saved Jacqueline from losing her unborn baby.

Then, as soon as it was decently possible, Georgette arranged that Jacqueline, who was enceinte, become the wife of Étienne Hebert, a younger brother of François', who had just arrived. She swore to them it would be a good marriage. And so it is, blessed with three children—Catherine, daughter of François, and Claude and Clophus, sons of Étienne. All, Georgette declares, Heberts. They are a family, complete and whole.

Georgette and I argued many times over the purchasing of slaves. She finally gave in when I pointed out to her that if L'Acadie was to grow and increase, we must have help, much help.

The first slaves I purchased were Sam, Manda, and their six-year-old child, Hippolyte, a bright child who was badly deformed from spine fever. They were installed in a new cabin in a location called the Quarters.

Georgette was the one to decide where the slaves would live. "The Quarters must be where I can't smell them," she said. "But not so far that I have to ride a horse if one of the creatures is ill."

Gradually I bought more slaves, Velie, Horatio, and their two children, Lutie and Hinry, younger than René, as well as another couple, Kidi and Ovid. Since Hippolyte and René are the same age, at age seven I gave Hippolyte to René as his body servant. I offered Gabby Hinry, but Gabby refused, saying he didn't want "no nigra with his black paws on my stuff."

As more slaves have been acquired, the Quarters seems to be almost a little town by itself.

Georgette is humane toward the slaves, though she still hates them. Despite her feelings, she doses them when they are ill, clothes them well, and inspects their cabins to see that they are clean. She works as long and as hard as she orders any slave to work.

She is driven by ambition that equals my own. We have toiled and worked our stock, including the slaves, to the edge of exhaustion. We have drained our land and are growing sugar cane with success. Étienne and I built our own sugarhouse at Hebert Plantation so we can process our cane and that of others. Georgette and I have bought more land, doubled the original size of the house, and built matching garçonnières at either side of the house for Gabby and René.

My aim is to buy more land, as often and as much as I can afford. The country is filling up. There is a settlement at the post; there is a church. The bayous seem flooded with Acadians, and there are Spanish and Americans as well. These are only part of those who now inhabit this once deserted but fertile land and tame it to their dreams.

At this point in my journal, I feel it necessary to address you, René, directly, as you will, one day, possess these journals. Our dynasty moves forward. When in the future, René, it becomes needed that you hold these pages to read, you will have in your hands the past. At that time,

I commission you to write in the journals to be given to your own son if and when it is needed.

Georgette has been a good mother to you. I ask that you never let her know that it was an escaped slave who bore you. It would kill her.

L'Acadie will one day be equally yours and Gabby's. You have an instinct for land and will enlarge the plantation. Gabby wants a fine house, white and with many pillars, sketches for which I have made, but which your mama does not wish to live in. Between you and Gabby, L'Acadie will reach its zenith.

He hates being called Gabby. He covets to be called René. If he does take that name, it changes nothing and isn't worth bad blood between you. You share the identical name. It has ever been so and will so continue. Fortune go with you, René, son of Tonton.

PART THREE

Second and Third Generations

1773–1856

ONE

Carita opened the next journal, ignored the raging storm, read what the sixteen-year-old boy, René, had written.

❀

From the journal of René Leblanc:

> When first I read Papa's journals, my impulse was to burn them, to destroy words that could destroy lives. But this I did not do for love of Papa, for the labor he devoted to them and because I realized that, at sixteen, I had not arrived at mature judgment.
>
> I am bedeviled. Why must I be of two bloods? Why must this so affect my life? I feel only myself, as I've always been, simply René, and feel that is all I can ever be.

He couldn't remember a time when he and Gabby had liked each other. His most vivid memory was of a day, when he was seven, when his mother sent him to bring Gabby back from the Quarters, where they liked to play with the slave children. "Play, play. That's all you boys think about," she fumed.

He ran for the Quarters but was told by Kidi, who had a new baby that the children had gone to the stable. When he got to the stable, René could hear them in the loft. He also heard a tiny mewing that was quickly cut off, and a sudden intake of breath.

"That'll show you!" he heard Gabby cry.

He scrambled up the ladder and through the opening. Gabby and four slave children, one of them Hippolyte, were huddled over something at the big, high door through which hay was loaded.

They were staring at a water-filled bucket into which Gabby's arm was plunged. The mother cat, a soft, spotted, purring creature, was mewing anxiously. A step away, two of her kittens, eyes not yet open, were mewing in tiny, uncertain voices, heads turning from side to side.

"What are you doing?" René cried. "What have you got in that bucket?"

"Quiet!" Gabby blazed.

René looked at Hippolyte, who lifted his horror-filled eyes and looked at him. One big tear rose from each eye and crept down his cheeks. Lutie, Hinry, and Jasper, stared wide-eyed at the bucket. They were scarcely breathing. Gabby glared at René.

"Gabby—"

"I told you to shut up!"

"I don't have to!"

"You do! I'm the eldest, I'm the hair, Mama said it!"

"What's a hair?"

"It's the one gets to be boss of L'Acadie."

"Because your hair is yellow!"

"Prob'ly." He scowled into the bucket. "I expect that's long enough," he said, and pulled his hand out. He was clutching a dripping, spotted kitten.

"What'd you do to it?" René cried, knowing.

"I drownded it!"

"Why—what for?"

"Because it's a cat. And cats are dirty. Mama says it, you know that even if you are only a baby!"

Crying and in a rage, René snatched the dead kitten, laid it gently with the others, and urged the mother to it. She mewed, smelling it over. Not once did she purr, not even when René stroked her, and from that he knew that even she could not bring it back alive.

"Give me the black one, Hippolyte," Gabby ordered.

Hippolyte put his hands behind him. "Please, Massa

278

Gabby! Hippolyte can't hand no black kitten to be drownded!"

"You got to or Mama'll have Sam whip you."

Hippolyte stood shaking his head, cheeks wet.

"He doesn't have to!" René shouted.

"I'm the eldest, I'm the hair!"

"Papa gave Hippolyte to me. He's mine, and he doesn't have to do what you tell him!"

Without warning, Gabby lowered his head and rushed. He crashed into René, and they both went sprawling on the hay. Hippolyte watched in petrified silence. The other children screamed.

René scrambled up, dived toward the kittens and held his body over them. Gabby flung Lutie and Hinry aside and was plunging at René when Georgette shrilled at them, her head rising through the loft opening.

"What's going on here?" she screamed.

Both boys had sprawled in the hay again; both struggled to their feet.

"It's René!" Gabby shouted. "Sneakin' up, pokin' in!"

Georgette came up into the loft, and then she saw the dead kitten, the mother cat, and the mewing, sightless kittens.

"René, speak up!"

"Gabby drowned the kitten."

"Is that true, Gabby?"

"I done it for you. Because they're dirty."

René knew his mother hated cats. He didn't know whether she also hated little rabbits that Gabby killed by twisting their necks, or if she hated baby birds that Gabby took out of the nest and threw into the water.

"Why were you fighting with your brother, Gabby?"

"Because."

"*Tell* me!"

"I told Hippolyte to give me the black kitten. He wouldn't do it."

Georgette cuffed Hippolyte alongside the head. "Why didn't you obey, boy?" she shrilled.

"It was me, Mama. I told him not to."

"So. Now you're master of L'Acadie, eh?"

"I'm master of Hippolyte. Papa said it."

Her eyes narrowed. "Oui. You he gave a servant!"

"Mama," René said, trying to keep his voice from shaking, "do the kittens *have* to be drowned?"

"No. Papa wants them. To keep down vermin."

"But you *said*—!" wailed Gabby.

She boxed his ears, hard.

"I said they're filthy, and I hate them! I said they're to be kept in the stables. To work. We do not kill that which works."

"You going to whip me?" Gabby sobbed.

"I boxed your ears. It is enough."

"You goin' to hit Hippolyte for not obeyin' me?"

"I boxed his ears, too. We don't whip slaves."

"Will you tell Papa?"

"No."

"He'd whip me. He whipped me about the snake."

"A paddling only. It was just a water snake. Your Papa didn't understand that a boy might not know the difference—"

"Papa says not to kill," René said.

"It depends on what you kill. Papa shoots deer; he catches fish. He traps for furs. He does it so we can have food to eat and furs to sell to buy what we need. He doesn't kill from hate. But now that you've—take it to the back bayou, all of you, and throw it into the water. And run every step, so you'll be back before Papa comes from Double Oaks. I have dealt with this. And the first one of you—suckers, too—that says a word to him, I'll crack your heads! Understand?"

They all nodded. Then Gabby scooped up the dead kitten, and they scrambled down the ladder and out of the stable. Then they began to run.

TWO

Not only did Gabriel bring everything on Georgette's list when he came home from New Orleans, but Jean Dupiers, a very young tutor, as well. He brought books, a ball for Gabby, and two blank journals like the ones he himself wrote in—one for René and one for Hippolyte—which delighted them. René loved Hippolyte better than anyone but his father and he wanted the black boy, who was his friend, to share with him in all things.

Gabriel also, to Georgette's disapproval, brought a new family of slaves. These were Zach and Glade and their daughter, Didi, who was nine years old.

René listened to his parents argue the night before lessons were to start. The family was sitting in the Grape House, and M. Dupiers was unpacking in his bedroom.

"Classes will be in the sitting room of René's garçonnière," Gabriel said, "until the schoolhouse is built."

"What do you mean—schoolhouse?" Georgette demanded.

"I've ordered a one-room building. Work starts tomorrow."

"Are you mad? To build it for two boys?"

"It won't be just two. Before we know it, Catherine and Sibille—all the Hebert children—and even another family or so along the bayou, will have scholars for us."

"And who will pay?"

"We will, now. Later, the others will help."

"Pah!"

"If L'Acadie is the leading plantation, it has to take the lead, Georgette. Am I wrong?"

"No," she admitted.

There was silence. Then René said, "I promised Hippolyte he can go to school with me, Papa."

"*What?*" cried Georgette. "Do you hear, Gabriel Leblanc? That's what comes of being soft with him—"

"I don't play favorites," Gabriel said, angry.

Georgette was blazing. "That bandy-legged little nigra'll not sit in the school with my boys!"

"Hippolyte sleeps in the room with René. He is to learn with him. And any time Gabby wants—"

"Don't want no stinkin', black, whinin'—"

"Hippolyte doesn't whine!" yelled René and made for his brother, only to be caught into his father's strong arm.

"Bed. Both of you. And get this in your minds. When the school is built, the slave children will attend."

"Insane! That's what you are, Gabriel Leblanc."

"L'Acadie slaves will read and write and do sums."

"Insane—insane! I shouldn't have said get a tutor. I should have taught them myself, the way my mother taught me, and your mother taught you!"

"I had already considered a tutor."

"M. Jean Dupiers will never agree to teach slaves."

"I'll offer him more wages. I think he'll agree."

He did agree, and the next day René and Gabby met with him—Hippolyte barred because of Georgette's argument that it was unfair to let him commence before the other slave children—and things went smoothly.

M. Dupiers smiled, not only with his lips, but with his dark eyes behind thick lashes, and Gabby and René soon learned that he was nineteen and in love with a girl named Madelaine, whose wealthy father forbade her to marry a penniless tutor. This heartless man decreed they must wait six years. If, at the end of that period, they were still in love and M. Dupiers had put aside savings, then and then only would he be granted permission to marry Madelaine.

The schoolhouse, when finished, smelled new and had glass windows. There were benches and desks, as well as a high desk and a chair for M. Dupiers.

Both René and Hippolyte learned quickly. Hippolyte paced René in reading and spelling, wrote as well, and did sums slightly better.

As for Gabby, who preferred anything to confinement, he learned well enough, but only subjects he liked. Sums fascinated him, and he became a competent reader so he could comprehend the enticing problems laid out to solve. His grammar didn't improve much, though he had heard both English and French since birth. He spoke in his own manner.

Lutie and Hinry, forced to attend, rolled their eyes and swung their legs but still learned a little. They managed to write their names and could read a few words of English, but none of French, claiming that the accent marks would bite them.

Each year more children attended. The Étienne Hebert youngsters—Catherine, daughter of François, and her half-brothers, Claude and Clophus—also the Louis Hebert children, Sibille, Conrad, and Maurice. Other children came, mostly from American families.

It was Catherine Hebert whom René liked best in all the world except his father and Hippolyte. She always wore white dresses, and had long, auburn curls, and very white skin.

She was always happy, as was her beautiful cousin, Sibille. The two were always together, but often they invited René to join in some special game from which they excluded their brothers.

Another of René's strongest memories was something that happened when he was thirteen.

René had begun noticing girls, and about the same time had noticed that Gabby had started going off through the sugar cane. Once or twice René saw Lutie wander in the same direction, and he thought that she had better not tag after Gabby, who hated her worse than any black except Hippolyte, and slapped her around. She wasn't skinny now, and she giggled. At school, Gabby ignored her and hung around Sibille, who was maturing quickly and who flagrantly cast flirtatious looks at him.

One night Gabriel told René and Gabby he wanted them in the Grape House. René was on his feet instantly. In the quiet, fragrant Grape House, his father could be persuaded to tell stories of Grand Pré before Le Grande Déportation. These René meant to write in his still untouched journal and keep forever, so he could read them over whenever he liked.

It was August, the night was hot, and there was no breeze. Mosquitoes were biting, and fireflies were moving slowly, turning their lanterns on and off.

"Your mother thinks I should talk to you," Gabriel began. "She's right, it is time. And it had better not, by the horns of the devil," he continued, swinging his whole body toward Gabby, "be too late!"

"I ain't done—"

"Stop that ignorant talk! Say it right!"

"I haven't done noth—anything!"

"Now. You both know how to raise sugar cane, you know my land and slave and cattle buying. Should I live my allotted years, and there are still only the two of you to inherit, you'll be wealthy—men of importance." He paused. "Questions?"

"No," René whispered.

Gabby said nothing.

"You know a great deal for boys of fourteen and thirteen, even about the sugarhouse. You, Gabby, have a fine grasp of the figures involved."

"Yes. I watch those figures."

"There's another thing to watch. Slaves."

"We're to do as you do, Papa," René said.

"Family units, black only. But more, never mix your blood with them."

"How would we do that, Papa?" asked René, bewildered.

Gabby snickered.

"Enough!" Gabriel said through his teeth.

"He's stupid. Why shouldn't I laugh?"

René was burning in shame. He had been stupid.

"He understands now," Gabriel said. "Make sure *you* do."

"On other plantations," Gabby said, "boys get their own bed wench. This is the biggest plantation in the bayou country. Why can't I have what other boys got?"

"Devil take it!"

"Why not?"

"Because you get a baby that's not white, not Negro."

"You can sell that kind for good money."

"Speak that way again, and I'll boot you until you can't crawl!"

"What's a boy to do?"

"That settles it! I'm packing you off to college next week. I'd thought to send you at fifteen, but now off you go with a letter to my attorney instructing him to enter you in college."

"How'll that help me?"

"You'll get your education. And New Orleans is filled with women who—white women, damn you! Relieve yourself with them, keep your hands off the Negro women! You'll have an allowance that'll cover your needs if you're not too greedy!"

René listened to this bizarre talk. It must mean Gabby had gone off into the cane with Lutie to. . . . It must be like that feeling he himself sometimes—*sometimes?*

He had thought something was wrong with him when he looked at Catherine and. . . . His face began to burn.

"While we're on girls," Gabriel said in a hard tone, "the next thing both of you must soon consider is wives. Americans are coming into the bayous, and I'd prefer not to mix our blood with American, but keep it French. There are enough girls here now for you to find wives, if not on the Teche, then on Lafourche or Boeulf or Macon."

"I don't want to get married, Papa!" René protested.

"You're some years from it. First, college."

"Not without Hippolyte?"

285

"Colleges permit a body servant, I believe."

Relief filled René.

"I'll marry," Gabby said. "As soon as I can! That Sibille, now. I'll look at the girls in New Orleans, those you would approve, Papa, and on the bayous. But Sibille—she's got a wild eye, and it's for me. Unless I find a greater beauty, she's the one."

René was astounded. He had seen Gabby and Sibille talk, but never a sensible word. Then, right on the heels of that, Gabby would chase off through the cane at about the same time the giggling Lutie did. Besides, Sibille was only eleven, though she had an older girl's figure, and Lutie was only twelve.

"I'll speak to Louis and Yvonne," Gabriel said. "I don't see what they'd have against it. At the proper time. And your mother must want it."

"Mama gave me the idea. To have the biggest house, the greatest beauty for my wife."

"Your mother thinks of family. If the time comes, you'll have to ask Sibille yourself."

"If I decide on her. Mama says no girl would refuse a Leblanc. She wants Catherine for René. She says if I marry into the Hebert family, and René does—us marryin' girls that are cousins to each other, it'll tie up the three most important families in the bayou."

René felt hair stir on his neck. He'd have no one choose for him.

Gabriel was chuckling. "So your mother spoke of this. I should have known." He turned to René.

"If in the future, René, you find Catherine attractive and you want her and she wants you, it shall be as you wish. That's what has meaning. To want."

René thought resentfully that he would never want any girl, even Catherine. She was fun, true, and he liked her best. He supposed, if Papa ordered him, if he had to chase after some girl. . . . Disgusted, he pushed the whole thing out of his mind.

He had no idea that in three years, when he was sixteen and to enter college in September, he was going to find out that Rose existed.

THREE

The three years passed quickly. M. Dupiers had returned to New Orleans to marry his Madelaine. One of the Hebert male slaves was now teaching the plantation children along with the younger Hebert boys, at the L'Acadie schoolhouse. Catherine was going to Miss Merriweather's College for Girls in Vicksburg after Sibille's wedding. She was going to be turned into a polished young lady.

Gabby, eighteen, his education finished, was coming home on the same boat with Gabriel, who had gone to New Orleans on business matters. Gabby was to marry Sibille in November on her fourteenth birthday. There had been much debate on this point, but the parents' objections had been overridden by the young couple. Gabby was man-sized, man-trained. Sibille was mature, nearer to eighteen than fourteen in every respect.

Thus consent had been given, and even now a four-room dwelling, Honeymoon House, was being erected by the L'Acadie carpenter, Ruben, on acreage Gabriel had bought to the north of the Grape House. Here the newlyweds would live until Gabriel built the big house, Georgette permitting. When it was completed, Gabby and Sibille would take the old house.

The pirogues arrived from the post. Gabriel jumped ashore, followed by Gabby. He was taller, broader than before, and coarse featured. His hair was like molten sunlight. He grinned as he hugged his mother.

Off the second pirogue, moving sedately, came the inevitable new slave family. The man was in the lead, one of the blackest ever, maybe thirty-five, about the size of Gabby, but developed more. His wife was thin, her head not quite to his shoulder. Last came their daughter.

René stared, his breath gone. There was that feeling in his loins. She was, René thought, his age, maybe somewhat younger.

She was taller than her mother, shorter than her father, blacker than either of them. Her skin glistened like black satin. She walked as if to music, her up-tilted breasts pushing against the washed cotton of her dress, her legs curved to shatter a boy's control, her buttocks an invitation.

Wearing a scarlet tignon, she carried her head high. Her nose was straight, with a hint of broadness to the nostrils. Her lips were wide, very thick, shapely. Under their darkness was a whisper of red.

She glanced up, then down so swiftly it might be doubted those black lids had moved. But René glimpsed great black eyes, their luminosity, the sweet mischief. He stared and knew, with the lids swiftly lowered notwithstanding, that she had seen him, all of him.

He knew that she had seen, and liked, his features, which were less heavy than his father's but more handsome according to his mother.

He felt that awful rising in him. He dared not let anyone, especially the wench, see. Chances were, she knew exactly what a man did to a girl and would laugh to herself.

He responded to Gabby's offhand greeting. To hide his condition, he picked up his father's satchel and held it in front of him; to fight down that wildness, he forced his mind to other things.

Slaves were toting baggage and bundles to the house and to Gabby's garçonnière. Other slaves were coming at a run down the lane to help, as two additional pirogues laden with purchases arrived.

René could not look at the girl. Gabby, who ordinarily would have been gone on a run, was rooting around in one of the pirogues for a gift he had brought Sibille. Enduring his misery, René thought of Gabby disappearing in the cane with Lutie and knew why he was going to marry Sibille the moment he could. No wonder, he thought, no wonder.

Sibille, who believed she was marrying an exciting

man, the only one on the bayou with blond hair, might be ignoring the way Gabby's face often puckered, she might not know of that streak of cruelty—she hadn't been there when he drowned the kitten, or the other times; but she had a wildness for Gabby. Fourteen or not, she could hold her own.

"Georgette, René," Gabriel said, indicating the three slaves, "these are our new people. Hercules is a blacksmith, Ilene a seamstress. She can help Sibille decorate Honeymoon House. Rose is their daughter. She's learning to be a seamstress, too."

René made some kind of grunt, Georgette sniffed and said there were rules and that Manda would take them to their cabin. At last the family started for the house, and René could work at getting himself back to normal. He wondered how Gabby would deal with this problem before the wedding. Gabriel had long since sold Lutie, with her parents' consent, to Monsieur Louis to marry one of his slaves, so there would be no access to her. And all the L'Acadie wenches had husbands.

Back at the house, Gabby wanted to see Honeymoon House immediately. He glanced to where Hippolyte waited and shrugged. "You can come, too. I understand you're going to be a carpenter."

"Yes suh, in a mannah," he said softly.

"What you mean, boy? Either you're a carpenter or not!"

"I'm learning woodwork mostly, suh."

"Finishing work," René explained, because Hippolyte dared not. "Fine stuff. He's got a knack for it."

Shrugging, Gabby led out for the building site. When he saw it, he was furious. "Damn that Ruben! Why is he so slow? I've got to have this finished and done!"

"He and the other men have until November," René pointed out.

"That's four *months*! I want it to be decorated and all by September!" Gabby roared. It was obvious that Gabby wanted the marriage to occur sooner. Forbidden to lay a hand on any wench, not daring to look for some willing girl lest Sibille find out, he had four months of misery ahead.

But at the end of the four months, thought René, Gabby would have Sibille, while he. . . . Well, he thought, my college entrance is arranged. I can wait.

Georgette's eyes were angry and her lips tight as she sat at the noon meal. Impatiently, she waited for Manda and Cara to finish serving. After they had retired to the kitchen, she let fly. "Why'd you do it, Gabriel Leblanc?"

"Do what, Georgette?"

"Buy those blacks!"

"Hercules? You know I've been needing a blacksmith, and you've wanted a seamstress. I found them."

"It's the wench, that Rose."

"What's wrong with her?" Gabby asked, and grinned. "I'd say Papa got a real breeder."

Unexplained alarm flashed through René.

"Gabby!" Georgette snapped. "I hope you're not going to use such language to Sibille!"

"Sibille can manage. I ain't pretended to be a fine, perfect gentleman with her. I ain't had the first complaint, either. From her or any girl."

"Gabby, you stop that talk!"

For a moment it was silent. What his brother had said about Rose had caused René's blood to surge, and he concentrated on quieting it. He wished he weren't so quick to. . . . He wondered if he were quicker than other boys, if he were obsessed. There was Gabby, of course. Maybe it was a Leblanc weakness.

"Who you marryin' this wench to?" Gabby asked. "She'll need a strong buck, and I don't recall one not married already and pumpin' out suckers."

"That's enough!" exclaimed Gabriel. "Before your mother!"

If Georgette noticed Gabriel speaking up for her, she gave no sign. "You're mad," she said. "Manda told me. She's as angry about it as I am."

"When did you begin to permit a slave to voice an opinion, Georgette?"

"Black or not, she's right. We're both against it."

"Against what, for God's sake?" Gabby asked.

"That wench, everything about her! The way she's built, the way she moves, the look in her eyes, she's a bad one."

"She's virgin. I had her examined."

"Bad, just the same. Manda says it. She knows another black."

"Why is Manda in this?" Gabby pressed.

"Because your father bought that wench to marry Hippolyte. And Manda doesn't want her in their family!"

If his mother had driven her fist into him, René's breath couldn't have been lost faster. At first he thought he was going to suffocate, and after that what felt like a knife sliced through him, in and out, when he breathed. Hippolyte couldn't get married, he simply couldn't!

"I'm sorry Manda feels that way," Gabriel said. "Sam has no objections. He's like me, thinks it'll be a good thing."

"In what way?" Georgette cried. "Name just one!"

"Breeding."

"*Breeding!* You want to breed that strong—to that—"

"Sam and Manda are strong stock. Hippolyte was too, until he took spine fever. He's got fine intelligence."

"You'd not breed a swaybacked mare to any stallion, no matter how smart. But when it's the highest kind of stock, when it's *blacks*, you want to take the worst one—"

"Mama!" René cried. "Hippolyte's the best! He's got *brains!* He can *discuss* things—he could *run* things, with training!"

Georgette gave him an angry look.

"That's enough, René," Gabriel said. He turned to Georgette. "Hippolyte's got the right seed in him. Doctor Cline and a doctor in New Orleans both say the spine fever'll have no effect on the babies. So, to doubly insure good stock, I've been watching for the ideal wench for him. Rose is the one."

"Suppose they don't want it? You've made it a rule for wenches and studs to want it! How anxious do you think the wench'll be, Gabriel Leblanc? When she's told to marry a bandy—"

"Hercules and Ilene know. When I explained, they agreed."

"Who are they to agree?"

"They're Rose's parents. There'll be harmony."

"Not if the wench has the buck forced on her!"

"It won't take force. She's to eat breakfast in the kitchen house with Manda, Sam, and Hippolyte every morning in order to become acquainted. She's not to be given work yet, but to remain free to talk with him as he moves about. There'll be marriage in the air— Gabby and Sibille, Honeymoon House. She'll tire of being the only wench without a husband. I predict that at the end of two months, with a new cabin promised, she'll decide on Hippolyte of her own accord."

"But he's to go to college with me!" René cried.

"He'll go. He can marry before you leave, then have summers here. It'll give Rose some importance, her husband traveling to the city, bringing back gifts. You're not going to lose Hippolyte, my son, but every man needs a wife."

"But Papa, he's not a man, he's only sixteen!"

"Rose is fifteen. It's better for a man to marry young than to—"

"Stop it!" Georgette cried.

"Mama," Gabby said, "it's just getting interesting." He wasn't teasing, for Gabby never teased. "Suppose the wench balks?" he asked. "Or the buck? What becomes of harmony then?"

"That's not your worry!" Gabriel retorted.

"It is Papa! I'm to help run things now. This summer I'm to build onto the sugarhouse, get it in condition for the cane. Right?"

"It is, as you damned well know!"

"Then I need to know how you'd handle Rose. So I

can consider and decide, if the problem somehow fell on me, how to deal with it."

Gabriel drew a deep, angry breath, then replied, "In the unlikely event you suggest, Gabby—that contention over this marriage should threaten harmony— I'd inquire of the Heberts, of the Grangers and others, whether one of them has a buck needing a wife. Then, a buck located and the master willing to buy Rose, I'd put it to her parents—how she'd be better off and that they'd be free to visit back and forth. I'd never sell her without their consent."

"But if they don't give consent?"

"Hercules and Ilene aren't troublemakers. They'd prefer that to being sold again as a family."

"You see what that wench has done already!" Georgette cried. "She's just stepped foot on this place, and she's got you talking change. I say ask the Heberts tomorrow and get rid of her. She's nothing but trouble."

FOUR

René dared not tell Hippolyte what Gabriel had in mind and, since the boy didn't mention it, he concluded he hadn't yet been informed. He waited in near frenzy to know what Hippolyte's reaction would be and what Rose would say.

Early the next morning they joined the crew at Honeymoon House. They were working with cut, seasoned oak that Gabriel had ordered used instead of cypress because he was hoarding and adding to his supply of cypress for the great plantation house he meant, one day, to build.

René might have kept Rose off his mind if she hadn't followed them to the construction site. It was wrong; he knew it was wrong. All his life he had heard his mother's biting remarks about the slaves, whom she hated for no reason that he could see except that their skin was black. "Never touch a wench!" she would tell René and Gabby. "They're dirty. They're not much better than horses and cows. Stay away from them." She spoke of the bucks in almost as vicious a manner, making it known that, except for the fact that they were essential to running the cane fields, she would get rid of every one.

Despite this, René had never felt anything but liking for the slaves, and for Hippolyte, whom he loved as a dear friend. There was nothing dirty about Rose that he could see. She was beauty itself; her blackness added to the beauty. His loins clamored for her. A sweetly devilish glance from her would do it. Her thick-lipped smile, slow and filled with tenderness, would set him afire. Her voice, deep velvet, did it with two words: "Mastah René."

Even when he wasn't near her, he couldn't forget her. Rose, the name whispered in him. Rose, Rose. And she was a rose. A black, fresh, dew-kissed rose. He lay in his bed, staring into the darkness, with Hippolyte, his other self, Rose's husband-to-be, on his pallet nearby, and ached for her. There was nothing in all the world but Rose.

Hippolyte finally brought up the subject one night. "I don't want to marry that Rose, Mastah René. She doesn't want to marry me. My papa told me, and her mama told her."

"How do you know she doesn't want to?"

"The way she acts. The way her eyes do. We're to have the summah to get used to the idea."

"Did you say you don't want to marry her?"

"No, Mastah René. My papa and mama think it's good, and I respect them. Rose says she'd rathah not get married at all then. . . . Nobody could blame her. It's nothing against her. We talked aftah suppah, this being the only night she'll eat with us, coming for breakfast only, eating the othah meals with her parents—so she'll be chaperoned. It was friendly talk. But I wouldn't want Rose, even if she wanted me."

294

"Why not?" It seemed incredible that any boy, given the opportunity would turn Rose down.

"She's not for me, Mastah René. She's a beauty, and she can get the finest buck. And she's got some mischief in her. She—likes you. Today, she followed us, not to get acquainted with me, but because it's you she's aftah."

It was then, when his personal slave, his dearest friend, spoke so honestly that René realized the truth. He loved Rose. He, René Leblanc, raised by his mother to hate slaves, loved Rose, beautiful, mischief-eyed Rose, not Catherine Hebert, not some girl as yet unmet, but this magnificent creature who possessed and needed no name but Rose.

"Mastah René. Don't. I've watched how she looks into your face, long looks, and meets your eyes full on. That's no respect for a white mastah, only wanting to be your bed wench."

"She couldn't be that," René said, his heart roaring. "That's not allowed, you know it. That's why Papa's letting Gabby marry now, with both him and Sibille so young."

"Things are good at L'Acadie. White folks white and slaves black."

"You warning me to let Rose alone?"

"I suppose so, Mastah René."

René's misery grew. The thought of Rose, the allure, remained.

The next afternoon Gabby returned early from the sugarhouse and glowered at the progress on Honeymoon House, which according to him was maddeningly slow. Rose was there, trailing René and Hippolyte as they placed floorboards and pegged.

After Gabby had criticized, he started to eye Rose. She flashed him a look, but she did not flirt with him. He reached out and smacked her on those tantalizing buttocks, and she laughed, but her eyes slid to René.

Gabby laughed, then strutted away. If it weren't for his upcoming wedding, René thought, Gabby would have Rose bedded fast. Even now he would try, except that he worked all day at the sugarhouse, Rose was chaperoned by the presence of the carpenters by day, by Sam and Manda at breakfast, and by her parents from supper on.

Gabby must be in miserable condition, René thought. It became obvious that the days, for Gabby, were creeping, each torturing him more than the last. The more pent-up his feelings were, the snappier he became, the readier to quarrel.

René, because of his own miserable state, became convinced that his brother was watching for any opportunity to plunge into Rose or even Sibille, that he would grab the one he could get.

As for Rose, she continued to follow René. Though he ignored her to the point of cruelty, refusing to return her "Good mornin', Mastah René," striding on as though she didn't exist, she was not to be discouraged. She followed Hippolyte and him to Honeymoon House, stayed until noon dinner, then came back in the afternoon. At suppertime she followed them to the house then was obliged to proceed to the Quarters.

All day she smiled with those thick, beautiful lips, sometimes uttering velvet murmurs over René's peg setting. And always there were the high breasts moving under the cotton dress that clung and moved with her.

The carpenters watched her secretly, but she ignored them, except for an occasional swing of hip. All her velvet words, every sweet devil-filled glance was for René.

"Why has she got to hang around?" he muttered to Hippolyte.

"So we can get acquainted, Mastah René. Ordahs."

"Why don't you tell my father that you don't want it?"

"It's not my place, Mastah René—or yours. We must wait until the mastah brings it up. Then I can tell him how I feel. Only, I don't expect I'll need to."

"Why not?"

"He'll speak to Rose first. She'll say she doesn't want such as me."

For the first time, René felt resentment toward Rose. "You've got no reason to take it for granted. You might assume she'll see you for what you are."

"Maybe I should, Mastah René," Hippolyte said, with that stubbornness he occasionally displayed. "But I can't. She—shrinks—if we accidentally touch."

Watching, René saw this for himself. He wished Rose would stay as far from him as she did from Hippolyte. Instead, at any opportunity, she would brush a hip or a breast against him, under the pretext of holding a board in place or searching for a misplaced peg.

His only relief was after supper, when, tired from the day's work, he and Hippolyte devoted themselves to reading. They spent hours discussing what they studied, each helping the other to fully understand the subject at hand.

Gabby looked in on them one night a week after his return home. He had just returned from visiting Sibille; the front of his trousers bulged.

"Either one of you know a white woman I can get?" he demanded.

"You know the Teche as well as we do," René told him.

"The hell I do! I've been gone. People have been moving in. Every summer I had a little freckle-faced girl down-bayou, a poor-mouth, but she's married and gone."

René shrugged, then glanced at Hippolyte, who shook his head.

"We don't know anybody, Gabby. Really."

Gabby cursed. That God-damned Papa—him and his bed-wench rule! What the hell did he do before he got married?"

"Waited, I expect."

"Well, I ain't one to wait! And there's one wench not hooked up to any stud!" He turned his face from René to Hippolyte. "I'm goin' for that Rose, and if you even hint to Papa, there'll be hell to pay, and I'll see you get your share!"

Hippolyte said nothing, his face was expressionless.

"Understand, you?"

"Yes, Mastah Gabby. I won't talk."

He swung to René. "And you?"

Rene's blood sizzled, and his ears roared, but he forced his voice to come out evenly.

"Why should I tell?"

"Where's Rose now?"

"In their cabin."

"With her people! Damn to hell and back! Wipe that look off your face, I know the slut's been runnin' after you! She's hot for a white master, and with me off working, it's left nobody but you. Well, tomorrow's going to be different. I'll get her in the morning. I'll pin her to the ground; after that she'll slip out nights after I leave Sibille."

René could hardly breathe. "Why tell us?" he demanded. "Seems you'd want to keep it quiet."

"And have you get there first? I'm not only telling you—the two of you—but I'm warnin' you off. I'm the eldest, I've got hard balls, Rose is here, and it's my right!" He turned and left.

René and Hippolyte closed their books and retired, René to his bed, the body servant to his pallet. They lay in summer darkness, listening to the lapping of the Teche. They didn't talk.

What had been said earlier, what was going to happen to Rose, beloved Rose, was too filthy for discussion. If their father knew—René shuddered. He might throw Gabby off L'Acadie, stop his marriage, and disinherit him.

"Hippolyte," he said at last.

"Yes, Mastah René?"

"I can't go to papa."

"No, Mastah René."

But I've got to stop him, René thought. I can't let it happen.

FIVE

It was pitch-dark when René got up. He dressed in the darkness, telling Hippolyte to stay in bed until the wake-up bell.

"What are you going to do, Mastah René?"

"Get to Rose first. Warn her."

"She doesn't want to be warned, Mastah René."

"I've got to do it."

"One way might save her, Mastah René. If you can—"

"I mean to deal with her only."

"Yes, Mastah René. Sort of—lead her on."

"That's insane!" René cried. The idea of deceiving Rose, leading her to think he was going to—outraged him.

"Considah, Mastah René. If you warn her about Mastah Gabby, she'll be flattered, and he'll get her. But if you let her think that all the hip wiggle—"

"I'd be—"

"You'd save her, Mastah René. You'd be keeping her clean."

"But even if it worked at first—*November!* She'd never be able to hold him off." He couldn't mention that he, himself, could scarcely endure this torture or that at this moment he was fully as badly off as Gabby—worse. Gabby had had girls, while he, René, was a virgin as was Rose herself.

"Please considah, Mastah René." From Hippolyte's tone of voice, René realized that Hippolyte knew how he felt about Rose, the love, the hunger, the torment, and knew that René could not permit Gabby to violate his love.

His mind flashed through Rose's daily program. The only time Gabby could get to her was when she walked from her cabin to the kitchen house for break-

299

fast. Swiftly he explained this. "All I have to do," he finished, "is walk with her every morning."

"He'll find out. He'll just go earlier."

"Then I'll go earlier than he does. Don't worry."

He ran silently down the steps, across the dewy grass, past the still-dark kitchen house, and on down the street of the Quarters. It was dark here too, except for a few pale stars.

Her cabin was at the end of the street. René stopped under a big tree. His heart was thundering as he peered and listened. There was no sign of Gabby, who was sluggish about waking.

He had gotten there just in time, for now the cabin door opened softly, and a figure drifted noiselessly across the small porch, down the step, and onto the ground. René came out from under the tree, and Rose started, drew back.

"S'h'h, it's René," he warned. "I came to walk with you."

"What foah?" she whispered.

They began to walk, their movement as silent as the stars. He realized that this was the first time they had been alone.

Her whisper was a velvet wisp. She spoke decently, not in the manner of the field hand. Hercules and Ilene had raised her well.

"So you won't have to walk alone," he whispered.

"I been walkin' alone."

"Not any more."

"Why not, Mastah René?"

By accident—or female design—her step drifted, and for an instant she touched her body along his side. He felt her hip, her leg. When he grasped her arm to steady her, it was like holding lightning.

"Why not, Mastah René?" she persisted.

"It's not safe."

"Theah's nothin' to hurt me, Mastah René."

"Yes, there is."

"You mean Mastah Gabby."

She was as smart as she was beautiful. "How did you know?"

"He looks at me, Mastah René. He's got till Novembah. He's bound to look."

"He'll do more than look." He said it straight out. Now she was warned. Maybe Hippolyte was correct, and she wouldn't heed. But she would be safe today.

"You think he'll jump out and grab me, Mastah René?"

He was so miserable, so hard and aching, it was all he could do to match her free-swinging stride. His throat was hurting as much as the other part, and altogether he wished he had never come here, but at the same time he'd be damned if he'd let Gabby lay a hand on this delicious, wonderful ebony Rose.

"He'll talk first, then grab," he said.

She laughed, a velvet murmur. "You can save me, Mastah René."

"That's what I'm doing! That's why—"

Her fingers were on his wrist; they felt like fiery iron, and she was pulling him between two cabins and beyond, into the sugar cane, and he could not resist. There was, in the world, only the field, their own private, rustling place; only darkness with paling stars, and a moment that could be theirs.

Above all, there was that aching hardness that at last found hot, fluid release. There had never been such glory. He lay trembling atop her, lingering in what had been. Her hands were in his hair; her breath was striking his face.

"Mastah—dahlin'—René!"

"Rose," he murmured, his lips against hers. "I love you!"

The wake-up bell rang from the kitchen house.

"We've got to go!" she whispered.

She gave one strong heave and was out from under him, on her feet. "If I'm late," she whispered, "Manda'll tell my mama, and then I'll have to lie, and my mama, she always knows if I lie."

"Didn't you hear?" he whispered, scrambling up, walking fast to keep pace with her. "I love you!"

"Well, I love you, René, else I wouldn't be taggin' aftah you. But if they find out . . . . The big mastah told us he don't allow wenching, and now we've wenched, and I've got to get to the kitchen house befoah anybody gets suspicious."

"Gabby. We'll have to go a roundabout way or run into him."

"That's fine with me. Any time I can, I'll stay away from him!"

She left the path and went through trees. René speeded up. "Rose," he said miserably, "wait. Don't leave me like nothing happened!"

"I got to. That Manda—"

"We have to talk, to—"

A sudden streak of dawn touched the sky. Seeing it, Rose ran swiftly through the dawn-tipped night and disappeared. Instinct sent René into the growth of trees south of the kitchen house. He walked silently, a part of the waning darkness.

Over at the Quarters, hurrying along the street, was a figure. It was going toward the far end, where Rose's cabin stood. René breathed in relief. It was bound to be Gabby. There was no way he could find out what had happened. He would think Rose had walked alone to the kitchen house.

René was first, that morning, to enter the dining room. Next, Gabriel and Georgette came in. Manda brought the food, but they all waited. Before anyone could mention Gabby he came in, looking angry. As Manda served, he slid into his chair and gave René a black look. René's blood jumped. Could Gabby tell, just by looking? Could he recognize René's now fullstirred lust?

"Didn't you hear the bell, Gabby?" his father asked.

"I heard it," Gabby said, pointing out to Manda which four eggs to serve him.

"Then why were you late?"

"Slow dressing."

"Stop that!" Georgette said. "Gabby's got things on his mind—the sugarhouse, Honeymoon House and his wedding! If he's a minute slow dressing, the time's

302

due him. He's thinking about Sibille and being a husband, with all the responsibility!"

Gabriel gave Georgette a keen look. His mouth tightened. The thought struck René that his father knew what was wrong with Gabby. He might even suspect that Gabby was after Rose and was keeping him working at the sugarhouse on purpose.

René shivered when he thought of the risk he had taken this morning. But he would do it again, whenever he could. He would never be able to get enough of Rose.

The next morning, René got up an hour earlier. He refused to heed Hippolyte's fervent efforts to dissuade him.

"What if Mastah Gabby get there first, Mastah René?"

"Then we'll both walk her to the kitchen house."

"You know it isn't that easy, mastah!"

"How, then?"

"He'll fight you, then tell the mastah he was protecting Rose from you."

"Then I've just got to get there first every day. I'll take my chances. It's something I *have* to do, Hippolyte!" He wished he could tell of the new and wonderful love he and Rose had discovered. But he couldn't put the burden of that knowledge on Hippolyte, who, though a friend, was also a slave and would be punished if ever such knowledge was found to be his. It was René's job, and his alone, to shield both slaves. Now he heard sounds from Hippolyte's pallet. "What're you doing?" he demanded.

"Dressing, Mastah René. If I'm with you, and Mastah Gabby comes, it's only Hippolyte walking his wench, and his mastah along to see that he behaves. No fight, no trouble. He can't even get your papa to forbid me to walk Rose."

"No! It'll make it harder for you and Rose not to marry!"

"It doesn't mattah, Mastah René."

"I forbid it!"

"Mastah René—*suh!*"

"I order you to stay here. I order you to go to breakfast at the usual time."

There was silence, and René felt their mutual shock. Never in their ten-year association had he spoken so to Hippolyte. He had never forbidden him, never given him a cold, definite order.

"Is that clear?" he demanded, his voice stiff.

"Yes, Mastah René," Hippolyte said, his own voice sounding as though it had died. "Be careful—" The words followed as René sped down the steps.

He streaked for Rose's cabin where he stood under the darkest part of the oak. He was earlier than yesterday, so it was darker. He stood in the dark, breathing hard. So now Hippolyte knew about Rose and him, for there could be only one reason why he would order Hippolyte to stay behind. He felt shame, but he was helpless against the love.

Unable to endure, waiting, he made the low call of an owl, then made it again at intervals. Rose appeared less than five minutes after his first owl hoot. Hand in hand, they sped to the same field, the very spot, to greater, more heart-bursting glory.

If only there was time for a second taste. Still, there were moments to lie entwined, to whisper.

"You made the owl hoot?" she asked.

"Yes. It's our signal."

She giggled quietly. "I'll nevah love a buck, Mastah René. Just you—only you."

"Call me René, the way you did yesterday."

"René. Rose's René."

"You are a rose. That's what I thought the first day I saw you. You're a living rose."

"I saw you. How handsome, what a gentleman."

"I'm not handsome. You're the one—beautiful."

"You are, too, handsome! You say youah not one moah time, and I won't call you René!"

She was incredible. Now that they loved, had known each other in love, she was like the girls he had always known, like Sibille, like Catherine. Well, not quite, for, even with her new sauciness, there was that black reserve. But she was as good as the others.

He told her that Hippolyte knew about them and that he would not betray them. She accepted what he said. They planned ways to evade Gabby.

Finally she stood. "Breakfast."

"Just one more minute!" he pleaded.

"Huh-uh. I was almost late yesterday. It's bettah if I'm early."

He went to the garçonnière to wait. Relieved to find Hippolyte gone, he sat in a chair the necessary time, for, just as it was unwise for Rose to be late, it would rouse comment if he suddenly began appearing in the dining room early.

Today Gabby ate very quickly and had nothing to say. Once he sent a look at René, who managed to return it calmly.

René woke earlier each morning, then slipped to the Quarters, always by a different path to evade Gabby, who continued to be sullen and looked even sleepier than René felt. Daily, on the alert for his tenacious brother, René led Rose from one place to another, always a different one. He took her to other fields, to the bayou, in back of the new stable, into the loft, and once behind the kitchen house into the far trees. Their times of joy, followed by whisperings of love, of Rose describing to him his handsomeness, and his describing to Rose how like the flower she was, lengthened because of the very early rising.

That Gabby was permanently swollen-eyed, that he grew very angry when Gabriel attributed this to the late hours he courted, that he glared at René, was small worry compared to René's rapture. Nevertheless, René devised still other places to take Rose, never relaxing his watchfulness until they were safe in the morning's nest, and even then he was alert.

When Honeymoon House was finished late in August, Gabby wanted to furnish it, have the wedding, and move in. Sibille refused to set the day forward by an hour. She must decorate each room; her dress must be changed a bit; and there was the wedding to plan, the decorations, the music. Also, she would be married on her birthday or not at all.

In early morning one day René and Rose lay whispering, kissing, deep in a cane field. Their love making had been better, slower, more lasting than ever. Rose had sobbed with it. Now her hand stroked his arm so wonderfully the touch could be thought of only as velvet.

"René," she whispered. "Dahlin'. I have somethin' to tell you. Only, maybe I shouldn't."

"You can tell me anything," he whispered, happier than in any of his sixteen years. "Tell me Rose, my beautiful Rose." This was the way he loved to speak, in the way a poet might speak to his beloved.

"René," she murmured. "I'm—what do the white ladies call it? I have got youah baby in my belly."

SIX

Benumbed, he lay holding her.

Occasionally this possibility had crossed his mind, but it hadn't happened, and there had been so much else—the need to evade Gabby, the rapture of which he dreamed all day—that he had avoided thinking of it. Morning had been the one thing in life.

And now this. He didn't know what to say, do.

"René?" she breathed, and then she burst into tears. He held her to him, feeling the awful wrenching of tears along the length of his body.

"You don't b-b'lieve me!"

"I do, Rose, I believe."

Her sobs eased.

"How do you know?" he asked. "How can you be sure?"

"I m-missed my time, and my nipples changed. And

306

my titties are biggah, you talked about that! You l-liked it!"

He felt as if he had been hit on the head.

Raising himself up on one elbow, he kept his other hand on her. "But is that enough to be sure?"

"You don't b'lieve me, you do-on't!"

"Yes, I do, Rose. I believe you think—but we've got to be sure, because if it's so, then we've got to—I've got to—"

He'd do something. He wouldn't abandon Rose, couldn't give her up, couldn't let anybody know. But he couldn't think of a thing he could do.

"Rose, Rose, love, s'h'h. Is there more?"

"I been pukin' my breakfast for a week. Manda caught me at it yesterday. I ran behind the kitchen house, thought she wouldn't notice."

"She knows—Manda *knows*?"

"She knows I'm that way, she don't know *who*! I'll not tell her, I'll not tell anybody!"

"What did she say? What's she going to do?"

"She said she noticin' I'm early to breakfast. Noticin' my titties, and how fast I leave the table. So she caught me pukin' and asked if I was that way. I told her no, but she didn't believe it, I know she didn't! I begged her, on my knees, not to tell my mama. I said the pukin' wasn't but somethin' that didn't set with my insides."

"Maybe that's right."

"No, it's a baby. It's ouah little baby. I ain't goin' to breakfast, I ain't goin' to eat! If I don't eat, I can't puke."

"You've got to go, or Manda'll know she's right."

"If I go and not eat, she'll know. And if I eat and puke she'll know. And she'll have to tell. Any othah plantation—but heah, wheah the mastah don't allow bright suckahs—"

René's mind whirled. He couldn't think at all.

Rose's whisper seeped into him. "I undahstand 'bout the mastah—Mama told me how careful he is matchin' up slaves."

What have I done? he thought wildly.

"What you want me to do, René?"

"Does your mother—?"

"Not yet. She don't know 'bout my missin'."

"Go to breakfast. Eat some. If you feel like you're going to vomit, swallow it back somehow. I can't think yet. I've got to have time. The important thing is to keep Manda from telling. Your father—would he beat you?"

"He nevah has, but the mastah—"

"None of the L'Acadie people have ever been whipped."

"I know. But this—"

"I'm the one he'd whip, the one he should whip."

"They'll find out!" Rose quavered. "But not *who*."

"It won't take my mother long to decide. The way you've been chaperoned, all the bucks married and with their wives, it has to be Gabby or me or Hippolyte."

"That's it!" she whispered, suddenly sitting erect. "I been thinkin', but then I'd think no, but it's got to be. I'll marry Hippolyte the way I was bought. Nobody'll say much if it's Hippolyte!"

"What about when it's born?"

"It'll be just anothah suckah."

"No it won't. It may be bright."

"They ain't, always! Sometimes they're like the mama. Besides, it's a long time yet. And nobody'll know it ain't Hippolyte's if it's dark enough."

"Hippolyte'd know."

"Youah his mastah. He's got to do what you say. If you say, 'Marry Rose,' will he say, 'No, I won't marry Rose'? Will he?"

"Not that way. But he'd argue. He doesn't want to marry you any more than you want to marry him. He's tried to keep me from meeting you. We quarreled about it."

"But he had to hush, didn't he? Because youah the mastah."

Her question drove the numbness from his brain, leaving it a throbbing torment of agony, despair, and determination to never, under any circumstances, give up his love, his Rose. Or their child.

By hurrying, though they took a new path to confuse Gabby, they got to the south stand of oaks as Manda was opening the kitchen house. René waited there, Rose quivering beside him, until they decided she should go inside while he had time to see Hippolyte at the garçonnière. He kissed her, she squeezed his hand, then went running. Leaving the trees, he ran silently to the garçonnière, climbing the steps three at a time.

Hippolyte had a candle lit. He was dressed, had made René's bed, and rolled up his own pallet.

"Thank God you're still here!" René panted.

"What's wrong, Mastah René?" Hippolyte asked, concerned.

"The worst thing of all!"

"Mastah Gabby got to Rose?"

"Not that. She's going to have a baby!"

Hippolyte was silent.

René waited as long as he could. "Well, haven't you got anything to say? Rose is going to have a baby!"

"Wenches do that, Mastah René." His tone was quiet.

"But this is *my* baby!"

"It could hardly be anyone else's, Mastah René."

"You know the rule, no bed wench!"

"Yes, Mastah René," he said sadly.

The sadness was a reminder of how Hippolyte had tried to persuade René not to meet Rose. Seizing on that, René glared. "Don't 'Yes, Mastah René' me! I remember your arguments! But I couldn't leave her alone, can you understand that?"

"Yes."

He scarcely noticed that his body servant had stopped calling him master.

"Rose is a temptress," Hippolyte said. "Even if she doesn't mean to be."

"Has it occurred to you that I love her and she loves me? I can't marry her because she's black, because she's a slave; I can't take her openly as my wench because of my father's *rule*; I can't claim my own child!"

Hippolyte gazed at René. He swept the back of one hand across his eyes. When he spoke, it was with warmth. "I should have known. I apologize."

"The thing is, it's happened. We're in awful trouble."

"Serious trouble."

"My father's not to know. There's only one way. I'll tell you honestly so you can get used to it. I'm not the one who thought of it. Rose did."

Hippolyte waited.

"She could stay here. With luck, there'd be no trouble."

Hippolyte waited on.

"Damn it, Hippolyte! You know what I mean!"

"You want me to marry Rose."

"Yes, damn it, yes!"

"You want me to claim the baby."

"So he can grow up at L'Acadie! So we can educate him!"

"He may be a bright color. I'm black. Rose is blackah. How can we explain a bright suckah?"

"What can anybody do about it?"

"Your father. He can sell us away."

"He can't sell *you!* You're legally mine. And he won't sell Rose and the baby away from you, because he won't split a family."

Hippolyte was shaking his head.

"Will you—will you marry her?"

"If I say no, will you ordah me to do it?"

René's instinct was to cry, "Yes, I order!" But a deeper instinct recalled the shame and regret he had suffered when he had ordered Hippolyte to remain behind so that he, René, could be alone with Rose.

"No. It's a request, friend to friend." The insides of his bones seemed to shake, and he stiffened his jaw so it wouldn't tremble. They stared at each other.

Hippolyte spoke, finally. "We're only sixteen years old. We're scared. How can we have the wisdom to deal with this?"

"We've got to deal with it."

"If I marry Rose—I wouldn't want husband's rights."

"I don't want you to take them. I'll never give her up, never marry. I'll—as long as my father lives—when I'm master—"

"Then?"

"I'll build her a place. And you'll live with me again."

"You mate a black wench and a white man, you get a mulatto baby. Most of the time it looks mulatto"

"But not always! And Rose is so *very* black!"

Hippolyte frowned.

René knew it was all wrong, but he was half mad. He couldn't do anything but this. "Will you?" he insisted. "Will you do it?"

"Give me the day to think. I need time to considah. And now I've got to get to breakfast. If I'm late, my mama'll have plenty to say."

René nodded and Hippolyte departed. René stood, trembling with relief. In all their lives, Hippolyte, faithful, dependable Hippolyte, had never failed him.

SEVEN

At breakfast, Gabriel told René he wanted him to go to the Hebert plantation that day with Gabby. "I want you familiar with the changes at the sugarhouse before you go off to college," he explained.

"Yes, sir," René murmured, unwilling.

Gabby gave him a look of hatred. "You'll find out what work is over there," he gloated.

"I've worked there before."

"Not this year. It'll take me all day to pound into your head how things are."

René's head was already pounding. This meant he wouldn't see Rose until the following morning.

"Papa," he said, "Ruben's starting that new cabin. Maybe I can help on that, then use the afternoon to study."

"Haven't you been studying?" Georgette demanded.

"He ain't been," said Gabbby. "Look at his face!"

Gabriel demanded, "Why haven't you been studying?"

"I have, some. I've been so tired I've gone to sleep over the books." It was the truth. Faithfully, he and Hippolyte had settled to their books, but in no time at all the pages blurred, and René could only sleep. Working all day, napping a few hours, getting up so early, then pouring himself into Rose, had exhausted him.

Papa frowned. "Sugarhouse. But not to work, Gabby. Just to get things in his mind."

Thus, after breakfast the brothers went to the landing, got into one of the pirogues, and began to row. Gabby was so full of suspicions and hatred, jabbing his oar into the water, that René, himself brooding, felt no sympathy whatsoever for his brother's unhappy physical state. What he felt was anger that Gabby still meant to get at Rose.

At Hebert Plantation, they went toward the sugarhouse, walking abreast, but apart, as though the other were not alive. They passed slaves coming and going about their tasks, some, like themselves, bound for the sugarhouse.

Here, where Étienne had a force of blacks finishing the new part and another force going over the rest of the building and equipment, there was little talk. René inspected on his own, understanding without the explanations that Gabby withheld.

Gabby snapped out orders. He required slaves to do some simple task over so it would meet the perfect standards required, but spoke not one word to René.

The procedure of sugar production was familiar to both René and Gabby. Since childhood, they had worked in the fields with the slaves, planting the sugar cane, cultivating, and clearing the drainage ditches. When harvest began in November, followed by the intense period of sugar making, working to beat the first frost, they had been excused from school until the sweet brown sugar was in kegs and on the way to market, which sometimes ran through Christmas.

Today they ate dinner at the big house. There were only four at the table, Étienne, Jacqueline, René and Gabby.

"Where's Catherine?" Gabby asked, ignoring the absence of her brothers.

"She and the boys are spending the day at Double Oaks," Jacqueline replied. "Catherine wants to see every piece of linen, every dress in Sibille's new wardrobe, every day!" She laughed. "Those two, Gabby, may wear everything out just looking, and you'll have to buy more of everything for your wife soon."

"Sibille can have whatever she wants," Gabby grinned. "She tells me about the dresses Catherine's taking to the girl's school in Vicksburg." His grin widened. "How do you know she ain't up there for other reasons? The Alin boys go there on all kinds of excuses, either Sibille or Catherine, I'd guess. Only Sibille's spoke for."

"Catherine's too young for marriage," Étienne said.

"Remember how Sibille came to L'Acadie that day? And went home with my big pearl on her finger? 'She was too young,' you said."

"I remember what it stirred up with Louis. Sibille wasn't much past twelve."

"Thirteen," Jacqueline corrected. "And Louis told her she was too young to know what she wanted."

"And she went into a six-hour tantrum!" Gabby laughed. "And nearly had another one when they said we'd have to be engaged only. Now, with Honeymoon House ready, she's holding out to marry on her birthday, no matter how I beg."

"Girls can be contrary," Étienne said. He glanced at his wife. "So can women."

"Suppose," Gabby prodded, "it'd been Catherine I wanted?"

René noted the blank, polite expressions on the faces of Catherine's parents. He wondered how they would look if they knew it was Gabby's boast that he had had every girl he wanted in New Orleans. Probably he had. In his way, he was handsome. With his height and wide shoulders and blond hair, most girls noticed him because he was different. Catherine, however, never seemed to be impressed. She was polite, but nothing more.

"She's leaving right after the wedding for college," Jacqueline said. "It'll be somewhat late, but she wants to see Sibille married."

"Why doesn't she go to the convent in New Orleans?" Gabby asked.

"She's been to New Orleans," Étienne put in. "She didn't seem—we feel she didn't care for it."

René did not reveal what Catherine had told him. "I hate New Orleans!" she had declared. "There are too many carriages, too many people, and it's noisy and rough. I'm just glad to get home."

"I think it's interesting there," René had said.

"Not for me, but I can't tell Mama and Papa. They take me there for pleasure, and the whole time all I want is to get back to the Teche."

"Speaking of weddings," Étienne said now, "when is Gabriel going to marry off that wench? Before harvest, or after?"

Horror flashed in René. He didn't miss Gabby's venomous look or the grin with which he sunned it away. "Lord—excuse me, madame—that's a problem. If it happens, it'll be before harvest, because Hippolyte's going to college to be René's valet." Then malice entered his tone. "Seems they ain't crazy to marry, though."

The talk went on, about Gabriel's idea of breeding Hippolyte and Rose. René listened in misery, forcing himself to eat. When it was over, it was with tremendous relief that he returned to the sugarhouse.

The afternoon dragged, but the time did, eventually, come when they started home. Gabby jumped into the pirogue first, mostly to annoy René by forcing him to shove off and risk stepping on a cottonmouth. René gave the craft a running shove, jumped in, and grabbed his oar.

"You in a hurry?" Gabby gibed.

But René noted that Gabby worked his own oar quickly. He was in a rush to get to Sibille.

The pirogue bumped the landing, and they tied up, then went racing up the driveway between the double lines of oaks. Before they reached the house, they knew that all hell had broken loose.

EIGHT

Gabriel burst out onto the long porch. He came to a standstill between the twin flights of stairs leading to the upper bedrooms. Georgette darted out and stood beside him, her eyes blazing. The two of them, one an angry flame, and the other cold as an iceberg, waited.

René's heart began to pound. They couldn't know! Hippolyte would die before he'd tell.

Gabby stared. "What's wrong with you-two?" he demanded.

"Don't speak to your mother so!" Gabriel said through clenched teeth.

"Gabby hasn't done anything," Georgette hissed. "Ask René. Grind your teeth at him!"

"If somebody," Gabby said, "would tell—"

"You two," Gabriel ordered, giving them a hard look, "walk onto this porch, march through the house and into the kitchen."

It was going to come out, René thought. It was. He went up the steps ahead of Gabby, who was muttering, low enough that their father couldn't hear, every curse word he knew.

"I'd have you understand, sir," he said, raising his voice, "that I resent being ordered about like a child."

"Shut up," Gabriel said. "We'll talk in the kitchen house."

His tone, the way he carried himself, the frozen rage, was stunning. He was someone René had never seen before. His stride was that of a stranger, hammering, fast, furious.

Mama followed him in burning silence. René followed her, a petrified, walking object, with Gabby at his heels, still whispering profanities. The procession moved into the kitchen where Manda, Hercules, and Ilene stood. There was anger on Hercules's face, and Ilene's face was stark. Rose was not present.

In the fireside nook stood Hippolyte. He was holding himself as erect as his crooked spine and legs would permit. His face was blank, his great eyes shouting to René that he had told nothing.

Gabriel wasted no time. "Now, Manda. Talk."

Manda, her plump arms folded, made a gulping swallow. "I don't know nothin' new, mastah, suh."

"Repeat."

She told of the breakfast times, of Rose's vomiting.

"Go on. About Rose and Hippolyte."

"Yas, suh. Rose been havin' breakfast with us, like you say, so they get acquainted. They was po-lite to each othah, but nevah made no eyes."

"Tell about today."

Manda looked at Ilene, who had begun to weep, then at Hercules, whose jaw was as rigid as an anvil. "At breakfast, she look awful sick, but she didn't run out and puke. It was her eyes."

"The way a girl looks when she's enceinte," Ilene murmured.

"I could tell the chile was awful sick. Finally she did run out an' I follow. She was pukin' so hard it look like her insides come out. And she was cryin' so the tears got into the puke, and she like to choke. Befoah the Lawd God, mastah, you almost had a dead wench!"

"No wench dies from being enceinte."

"She nevah say she was, mastah."

"Suh," Ilene offered, her voice as thin as the cheeks down which tears flowed, "she told me, told her mama. Aftah Manda brought her to the cabin. Manda wanted to stay, but Rose was hysteric crying, wanting Manda to go, so she did."

316

Gabriel gestured, a brief, angry chop.

René felt as though his petrified lungs were getting scarcely enough air to continue life.

"Aftah Manda left," Ilene wept, "Rose threw herself into my arms, and she told. That she's goin' to have a suckah, and when I asked when she evah—she said it was early in the mornings. Aftah she quieted down, I hurried to tell her papa, and he came home and—" Tears overcame her; she covered her face with her little hands and swayed.

"I took charge," Hercules rumbled. "I was working, but I dropped a red-hot iron on the anvil, mastah, ran to the cabin, and grabbed Rose out of bed. Foahgot she's always been a good wench. She was sick—it was in her look, her weakness. But I shook Rose so hard her head flapped and ordered her to tell the name of the one she been—" He shook his head. "No use. I grabbed my razor strap, ripped her bare—me, who nevah befoah laid a stroke on one of his children that was sold off—but now Rose, the one I think of as my flowah. Today I put the strap to my only remaining chile, and it cut her flesh, mastah, and the blood showed. I flung the strap away. I couldn't—the blood. It took that one strip of blood to bring me out of wildness, to make me know I couldn't bleed the truth out of my Rose."

He stared, now, at his boots. "It took her mama to comfort Rose. 'We go to the mastah,' she told Rose, 'and tell him youah ready to marry Hippolyte. If youah suckah comes soonah, no mattah.'

"Rose was cryin'. 'I'll marry Hippolyte,' she said, 'but what's goin' to happen if the suckah's bright?' And that's how we found out, mastah."

Gabriel moved his eyes past Gabby's and René's. "They can't get out of her," Gabriel said, his tone a weapon, "who she's been with, which one of you—" His eyes stabbed Gabby, who shot back a venomous stare and said, in his meanest way, "I ain't laid a hand on the wench. If she says I did, she's a God-damned, lyin' black bitch."

Gabriel glared at René, but there was nothing on

René's carefully blank face. He was benumbed; he couldn't deny; he couldn't confess, he couldn't make his love filthy. He ached to cry over how cruel they were being to Rose.

"René," Gabriel said. "Your brother has spoken. I want to hear from you."

He shook his head, not in denial, but because he couldn't speak.

Suddenly, Hippolyte spoke, steadily and clearly. "Mastah," he said, "Hippolyte wants to marry Rose, suh."

Every eye flew to him. René's stunned heart called protest to this friend, this other self. Now everyone would know. For Hippolyte, known to hate Gabby, had, with the finger of love, pointed to the truth, had betrayed that it was René who had bedded Rose. He saw the stricken realization on Hippolyte's face.

"You see, Gabriel Leblanc!" Georgette exclaimed. "Enough!"

She quieted, glaring at René.

They stood, Hippolyte stricken; Manda silent; Ilene weeping; Hercules breathing hard; Georgette and Gabriel fiercely angry; René helpless; Gabby triumphant.

"How many know?" Gabriel demanded.

"Us, heah, mastah," Manda said. "And Sam."

"He's not to tell."

"He won't, mastah."

"Gabby, you'll not tell Sibille."

"I don't see why I can't tell my own—"

"Shut up! A rule of L'Acadie has been broken, and by one of the masters. There'll not be a 'bright' baby on this plantation."

There was silence until he spoke again. "There's a trading boat at the post, and it leaves in two hours. Hercules, you and Ilene and Rose will be on it. It is to be understood, here, that you are being sold as a family. The way you were bought."

"Sibille's father has a buck he's going to buy a wench for," Gabby said. "Why not Rose?"

Gabriel swung toward Gabby as if he would knock

him flat. Then, at Georgette's shrill, protesting cry, he visibly restrained himself. "No bright L'Acadie slave stays," he said, and despite the hardness of his face and the harshness of his tone, he felt an ache as he said the words.

René was lost in his own sense of doom. Thoughts were flying through his mind, each more impossible than the last. I'll stand up to him—defy Papa—refuse to let my baby be taken away. I'll—

"Get your things, Hercules," Gabriel ordered. "Meet me at the landing in fifteen minutes."

As the blacksmith and his sobbing wife moved through the door, Gabriel ordered Manda to help them pack.

After she had left, he looked at Gabby. "You will go to your garçonnière."

"Gabriel!" Georgette protested. "He's almost a married man!"

"I've seen him look at the wench. René, too. Both of them will go to their garçonnières—Hippolyte, too. Stay there until we're well downstream, around the bend. René, I'll deal with you later."

"I should hope so!" shrilled Georgette. "To sully the Leblanc name—"

"It's not going to be sullied, Georgette."

"He should be lashed! He should be—"

"I'm not going to whip him."

"Why not? If it'd been Gabby—"

"When I don't put the lash to my slaves, can I put it to my sons?" Still that towering rage. "We're not sure, beyond a doubt, that it was René."

René found his voice. "I—am the one, Papa."

He wished, but dared not ask that his father violate the rule.

"Eh!" Georgette snorted triumphantly. "He's admitted it! Are you going to let him—"

"He'll be punished, Georgette." Gabriel's voice sounded leaden.

As yet René had made no move to leave. His feet refused to stir, to leave this spot where Rose's fate had been named. Nor did Gabby depart, but moved his eyes alertly from face to face. Finally he focused on René. A fire came into his eyes, and it flamed. But for their father, René knew, his brother would lower his head and come at him like a maddened bull.

Gabriel made a chopping motion. "To the garçonnières!"

René and Hippolyte stood at the window from which they could see down the driveway to the landing. Gabriel was striding toward the bayou. There was no sign, yet, of Rose and her parents.

"Forgive me," Hippolyte said.

"It's not your fault. I got Rose into trouble."

"But I could have kept her out of it. If I'd agreed, if I'd spoken to your father early this morning."

"I was talking crazy. It would have been worse if the baby was 'bright.' Then he would have sold the three of you, and I'd have lost you, too. My owning you wouldn't count because I'm a minor."

"It was your right to ordah me to marry her."

"Stop that talk! You've got a right to use your own mind. You're my friend. I asked an awfully big favor, which was very foolish. But, hear this—I'm not going to have Rose sold!"

"How are you going to stop it?"

Now Rose and her parents, carrying bundles, came into sight, Manda with them. They plodded toward the bayou, shoulders not squared, but not drooping, either.

Watching Rose leave, René told Hippolyte exactly what he was going to do. He spoke wildly, he knew it was wild but said there was no other way.

Hippolyte listened, but made no comment.

The departing group reached the pirogue, and Gabriel stepped in, and picked up the first oar. Hercules loaded the bundles, then helped Ilene board. Rose stepped in unassisted. Manda stood on the bank.

Hercules shoved off, took the second oar. They rowed quickly, sending the pirogue skimming along. The last thing René saw, when they rounded the bend, was the scarlet of Rose's tignon, the gallant, queenly head.

"Well?" he asked, turning to Hippolyte.

"What do you mean?"

"Will you help me? After the place is settled to-night? Will you help me load, shove off for me?"

"I'm going with you."

"I'm not asking it."

"I'm going."

"Because of all the trouble."

"Because where you go, I go."

"You'd be leaving your parents forever."

"I know."

Suddenly, as they hadn't done since they were six, they embraced briefly, with some embarrassment.

"Did you want to go without me?"

"Do I want to go without my head? Don't be an ass!"

"You want me to pack now?"

"A change of clothes each, one bundle. Our rifles, flint, ax, knives. But not now—wait. Papa may come here when he gets back."

Silently they waited at the window. Their future held action, speed, and flight, none of which could really be mapped.

They were at the window when the pirogue, with only Gabriel in it, rounded the bend for home. They watched it nose into the landing, and saw Gabriel jump ashore and tie up. He walked purposefully toward the house, the walk of a man with things yet to settle. He went across the porch and into the house.

"We'll take that pirogue, the one he used," René said.

"The *best* one?"

"We need the best, the fastest."

"Yes. We have to overtake the trading boat."

"At night. We may have to hide on a side stream and then, very late, when they've tied up—"

"Won't they keep a guard? Especially when carrying slaves?"

"The guard can't watch every second."

"How will we get Rose?"

"We've got a signal. I'll make that. She'll slip off the boat and come swimming. I'll swim to meet her."

"And when you get back to our pirogue?"

"We paddle, fast. Downstream. Right down the Teche, on the other side. The moon—is there a moon now?"

"It's the dark side these nights."

Hope leapt in René. "Then we've got a chance!"

Hippolyte's eyes gleamed.

Just then they heard the clang of the supper bell. Like chastised youngsters, they hurried to the meal. René went into the big house and Hippolyte into the kitchen house.

"I will not," Georgette announced at table, "permit discussion of what has happened. It is ended, except for the punishment."

"Agreed," Gabriel said. "Eat."

René felt like he might vomit, but he forced himself to eat. If Hippolyte didn't bring food from the kitchen, which was unlikely under Manda's keen eye, they would have to live off the land.

He kept his eyes from his brother, who was eating heartily. Trouble, especially if it meant grief for the other party, always whetted Gabby's appetite. Tonight he ate voraciously, only occasionally shooting hate-filled looks at René.

Georgette tinkled the bell for coffee. When Gabriel growled that he would rather skip the coffee, she blazed. "We'll have coffee! Gabby, you can wait that long, eh?"

Alarm sprang in René. Sometimes Gabby took the fast pirogue to court Sibille.

"I ain't goin' tonight," Gabby said.

"Now what is it? Don't tell me you've quarreled?"

"No, we ain't. But after—and me not to tell—it's best I stay home."

"Isn't she expecting you?"

"I been goin' up every night, yes. But I didn't tell her for certain about tonight. If I go, she'll see something's happened, and she'll be after me. I can't tell, and then she'll get mad, and we *will* have a fight. I don't mean to go through that. By tomorrow I'll be cooled off some, and she won't see."

"How will you explain not going tonight?"

"I'll tell her Papa sold off a family and I had to help. Anything that looks to her like I'm havin' a chance to be master makes her happy."

When coffee was over, Gabby awkwardly excused himself—he'd never learned to do it to Georgette's liking—to retire to his garçonnière. René asked permission to leave, and it was granted.

"I'll be with you soon," Gabriel told him.

René found Hippolyte in the little sitting room. He had been unable to get any food to take along.

Almost immediately, Gabriel came in. René, inwardly trembling, both because of what he meant to do and because, after the next few hours, he would never see his father again, assumed what calmness he could.

Gabriel laid the slim volumes of his journal on the table.

"Hippolyte," he said, "wait outside."

When the door was closed, Gabriel spoke. "I'm not going to lecture you, René. You are fully aware of the wrong you have done, though you do not, as yet, appreciate it. Now, I wrote these journals for your eyes alone, to be read, if needed, when you were married with children for whose future you would be responsible. However. Read them tonight, every word, if it takes all night. When you've finished, you'll have the punishment—and more—that you have earned, though I don't give it as punishment, but as a guideline. And I ask that you be the one to write the journal from this day on."

Before René could speak, Gabriel turned on his heel and went into the night. There was the muffled thump of his shoes, then silence.

Hippolyte came back in, and René told him what his father had said. Then he took the volumes and set them in a gap on a shelf of schoolbooks.

"You're not going to read them?"

"I haven't time."

"I could put them in the bundle."

"No. They're about L'Acadie."

"Yes. And we're leaving L'Acadie."

"The packing. You can do it now."

Again they waited. The night bell rang. Down in the Quarters, the people would be closing themselves into their cabins and going to sleep. There were still lights in the big house.

At last, after the lights in the house went out, René and Hippolyte darkened their garçonnière. Gabby's quarters remained lighted.

A sigh from Hippolyte, foreign to him, sent a tinge of uneasiness through René. "What's wrong?" he asked.

"It's only me, I expect. But Mastah Gabby's been so moody since Rose came, and he hasn't been able to get at her. He's put the blame on you, been getting maddah and maddah. Now that he *knows*—"

"Well?"

"It's only a feeling, but I think he'll look for revenge. Some way, sometime. I'm anxious for him to put out his lights, for him to be asleep. So we'll be gone before he makes trouble."

"It's not liable to be tonight," René said, but he felt uneasy. "It takes Gabby awhile to think out a problem."

"He's been thinking all summah. He's been without—he's been waiting for his wedding. He's like a wild man inside. While you and Rose—"

René knew Hippolyte spoke the truth. Gabby had wanted Rose, and René had won her. And now Gabby knew. And Gabby would, somehow, seek revenge.

"It's just as well," he said, "that we're leaving."

Again they waited until, at last, Gabby's lights went out.

Still they waited. The night was alive with the swamp—the sound of a frog, the call of a bull alligator, the hoot of an owl, the piercing scream of a bird killed in the night, the whine of a mosquito hushed when a breeze ruffled up the long lane to finger the windows.

Even then they waited, peering into the darkness, looking for movement, but there was none.

Hippolyte whispered, "It must be past two."

"Let's go," René murmured.

They had put on their darkest clothes so as to blend into the night and now, as they stole onto the grass, René carrying one rifle, Hippolyte the other and the bundle, they were part of the night. Two noiseless shadows, they slipped along, passing over cushioning grass. Their bodies tense, their hearing alert, they were ready to dart speedily into the thickest heart of night if need be.

Here was the landing, the levee; downbank, the pirogues rocked gently. René's throat was dry. Only a few more cautious steps. Procedure had been agreed upon.

They had agreed that René would get in first, put down his rifle, get the oars ready, and while he was doing that, Hippolyte would toss the bundle into the boat, stand the other rifle in, shove off, grab his oar, and carefully, silently, they would push into the slow middle current, then downstream, silently and quickly.

In the blackness, René reached the levee, Hippolyte at his heels, ready for the descent to the pirogue. He took the first careful step.

Suddenly there was movement in the darkness and a voice growled, low and murderous. "Stop—stop in your tracks, you sons-of-bitches!"

NINE

René froze. "Gabby!" he breathed. Then he screamed, "Hippolyte, get back!"

But Hippolyte didn't move.

From the darkness Gabby yelled, "It's you I'm after, you sneakin', nigger-lovin' son-of-a-bitch! I know what you're doin'! It come to me at supper, I could see it on you! You're chasin' after that wench like she's a bitch in heat. What you aimin' to do, lay out in the swamp till her belly busts, then come home and sweet-talk Papa?"

René spun, dropped his rifle, and hurtled toward Gabby's voice in the blackness. He was ready to hit, slam, knee, beat, but when he reached the spot where he thought Gabby was, there was nothing, and he went at a staggering run to keep from falling.

Gabby roared, "Fool—baby! That how you got it into the wench, jab here, jab there?"

René turned in a three-quarter circle, listening, seeking where to attack in the blackness. Gabby would move about, slip from place to place, then come at full charge. René kept deathly quiet, knowing that if he couldn't see Gabby, neither could his brother see him. Then he heard Gabby's laugh, bold and taunting.

René hurtled at it, and again there was nothing. The shout now came from behind.

"Can't find me, ey? Not like you found her, eh? Here I am—ah, missed again! What'll you do if you find me? Naughty—that was too fast!"

René stopped, panting. Then he held his breath so he could gauge where Gabby was, so he could come to grips with him.

"You won't lay hand on me, nigger lover! *See!*"

The shout was everywhere in the darkness, dancing

from unseen spot to unseen spot; there was no touching it. "Ain't you gettin' dizzy? Things are goin' to be the other way—at my convenience. Now—tonight! The firstborn is goin' to clean up the dirt you made, and when Papa throws you off L'Acadie, you goin' to be nothin' but a chewed-up lump of meat!"

Drenched with sweat, jaws rigid, René tried finding that taunting bellow, then tried again. In one of his fruitless charges into nothing, he heard two bodies thud.

"I've got him!" Hippolyte screamed.

Even as René went headlong at the voice, Gabby yelled, something hurtled past and, as René crashed into his brother, there was the thump of something striking a tree. Hippolyte screamed in pain.

Gabby clasped René, trying to crush him. Throwing himself from side to side, forcing Gabby to weave. René managed to free one arm. He shot it upward, ramming his thumb into his brother's eye, then bore in and twisted.

Gabby howled, yanking his head back. But in the yanking, Gabby's grip loosened, and René jerked his other arm free. They staggered and weaved, and Gabby grabbed René around the neck. In turn, René squeezed Gabby's neck with both hands, digging his thumbs into Gabby's throat.

Still squeezing René's neck, Gabby jabbed a foot at René's leg; René sidestepped still holding on to Gabby's throat. Suddenly Gabby let go and grabbing René's wrists, ripped his hands off his neck. René tore free and brought up his fist, but a killer blow sent him staggering backward, up the levee.

Gabby hurtled onto him, and they flew off the levee into the bayou. They hit water, surfaced, and went for each other again. Struggling, rolling, thrashing in the water, each reached for the other's neck.

René's lungs took fire, he was being pushed under. His ears filled with water, and he swallowed water. From under the surface, in a death grip, in toiling, noiseless depth, he heard, impossibly, the sound of muted, shouting voices. He dug into Gabby's windpipe; his brother bored into his neck. They rolled, still under water, Gabby on top. René wrenched, and he was on top. They surfaced, then went under again.

Incredibly, abruptly, they were being dragged out of the water, up mud, up grass. There was light and there were hands, too strong to resist, tearing at their clamped fingers.

Gabriel was there, cursing. He pulled them apart and onto their feet, holding them each at arm's length as they heaved and gasped for air. Somewhere Georgette had a lantern, and somewhere else Manda was sobbing aloud to Sam and to Hippolyte. Over the other sounds came the agonized moans of Hippolyte.

Before a word could be spoken, Gabby broke free and went again for René. René sprang to meet him and they came together. Their father ripped them apart, throwing René aside, then held Gabby relentlessly as he lunged and bellowed.

"I'll kill the bastard—kill!" Gabby screamed.

"Shut up! It's over!"

"Not until he's dead!" screamed Gabby. In the wavering light of the lantern, his face was a devil's mask. It was clear that his mind had slipped. To kill was his only aim.

"Let me go! Or I'll kill you first!" he shouted at his father.

Gabriel crashed his fist into Gabby's nose. Gabby bellowed, and his hands shot around his father's neck, and Gabriel clamped him and wrenched at his grip as they staggered about.

René threw himself at them. Georgette came screaming, lantern in one hand, rifle in the other. Somehow she got herself between René and the struggling pair.

She pushed the rifle at him. "Point it—say you'll shoot! Go on. If you don't, he's going to kill him, he's going to kill my Gabby!"

René grabbed the weapon. "Stop!" he screamed.

But Gabriel and Gabby were locked, staggering up the levee. He leapt after them, kicked a foot and tripped another one. They crashed, but the hold they had never lessened.

"*Shoot!*" Georgette screamed.

René waited until Gabby was on top, took aim at his leg, then squeezed the trigger. Gabby's scream split the night, and he and Gabriel both rolled off the levee and crashed into the water.

Quickly René stepped to the edge of the water. Before he could make out who was who, they sank and did not rise. There was thrashing in the depths; suddenly there was another splash. It was Sam, diving in and going under the water. There René could see movement in the black bayou.

As he threw aside the rifle, his mother shrilled. "No! Stay!" She clutched his arm; her nails digging into his flesh. They waited in ominous silence that held only the sounds of thrashing water and, somewhere, soft moans.

The surface broke, but the light from the lantern did not yet reveal anything. Rifle again ready, René couldn't see where to shoot or whether to shoot. Though there was a struggle in the Teche, it had changed, and the sounds were different.

The light flickered on the water and at last René could see that two figures were bringing a third to shore. One figure doing the dragging could scarcely move, but the other could. The burden they dragged was heavy and inert.

Dropping his rifle, René went into the water. The light grew; Georgette had followed and was knee-deep in the bayou.

René went as fast as he could, but it seemed he was motionless. The figures doing the dragging, he made out, were his father and Sam. Taking his place beside his father, he hooked his arm under Gabriel's arm to help him walk, for it appeared as though he could hardly move. At last they pulled Gabby ashore and laid him on the grass.

Georgette knelt. "Gabby!" she screamed. "*Gabby!*"

When there was no response, she gripped his shoulders. "*Gabby!*"

"Georgette," Gabriel said. "Don't." Miraculously she hushed.

Gabriel knelt beside Gabby, laying two fingers in the hollow of Gabby's throat. René could see that there was something wrong with his father's leg as he moved. Georgette was breathing with a hard, sucking noise, and so was René. She was whispering a prayer. But Gabby made no stir. Gabriel laid his ear over Gabby's heart, and when he lifted his head, shook it.

"My son!" Georgette shrieked. "He's dead, my son is dead!" She whirled on René. "You did it! You shot him—you killed him!"

Gabriel looked the body over, then rolled up a trouser leg, revealing the wound at mid calf. "That's where René shot him, Georgette. René didn't kill Gabby," he shouted, blotting out her shrieks. "*I* killed him!"

Manda, who had crept up to them, put a hand on Georgette's shoulder. She jerked away, but she stopped shrieking. "Murderer!" she hissed at Gabriel. "Murderer!"

"Mastah," Manda wept, "they fightin' ovah that Rose. I don' know why, her gone, but Hippolyte say they was, and he got a bad hurt back and Mastah Gabby dead!" She began to rock and lament.

"Manda," Gabriel ordered. "Hush. Sam, carry Hippolyte to the house. René, help me carry Gabby. Georgette, light the way."

And so they went. Sam carried Hippolyte like a baby, Manda sobbing, murmuring, and walking alongside. René, using his remaining strength, lifted Gabby's legs, and Gabriel took Gabby's shoulders. They laid him on the porch despite Georgette's demanding he be put on her best bed. They also laid Hippolyte on the porch, where he was very still, having fainted.

"Sam," Gabriel said. "Go for Doctor Cline."

"What's the use?" Georgette cried. "He can't help Gabby!"

"There's Hippolyte. And me." Painfully, he sat down on the porch and rolled up his trouser leg. His ankle and leg were swollen and red. "One of those cottonmouths got me," he said. "While Gabby and I—in the bayou."

The doctor came at dawn, did what he could for the snakebite, and bound Hippolyte's back. By noon the body servant was in agony, and Gabriel Leblanc was dead. Rose, unaware and weeping on the trading boat, was enroute to the slave block.

❀

The hurricane, its front half having passed over the land, now swept madly down with its second, rear section. Its winds came from the opposite direction; it reached its second peak, higher than the first. It held and flailed L'Acadie relentlessly, devastatingly. Carita, in her sitting room in the great mansion, contained in her skull that thickened, tortured brain, and denied the lies, belabored by the merciless bits and shreds which flew and cleaved into the truth, which was an utter lie.

TEN

As René walked numbly from his father's death chamber, his first impulse was to rush to the trading boat and haul Rose and her parents back. He would take Sam, who was strong and fast with a pirogue; with Sam, he could get everything done that needed to be done—bring Rose back, himself back, before the bayou folk learned what had happened and came to pay their respects.

It was Georgette who stopped him. "Where are you going?" she cried.

When he told her, she screamed, 'No!"

"Who's to stop me?"

Her eyes were screaming. "*I'll* keep you from it. No-

331

body knows yet, only our own slaves, and of them only Sam and Hippolyte and Manda saw!"

"There's you. And me."

"So?"

"Surely you don't think you can hide this."

"Of course we can't! But we can choose what to tell."

"You mean you'll choose."

"We'll *not* tell that René Leblanc sinned with a wench! We'll *not* tell why the master of L'Acadie put his blacksmith and family for sale except the wench and the body servant weren't a match!"

"The fight. How can you explain that?"

"We'll *not* tell that Gabby caught you running away."

"What *will* you tell?"

"The pirogue. You both wanted it."

"At that time of night?"

"They know Gabby's wedding—and you going to college. And it's natural that a father, hearing the fight, would come."

"Is that what you told the doctor? How will he report it?"

"Accidental death, he said. Drowning and snake-bite."

"And Gabby's wound?"

"You tried to stop the fight."

René stood, the echo of the night's struggle in him. Had the wind been from the east, the Heberts would have heard. The L'Acadie slaves must have heard, but they could be kept in ignorance.

"Suppose the doctor—" he began.

"Doctors don't talk."

"They keep records. Report crimes."

"Whose crime? It's you—from the wench right up to the snake!"

It was true. That realization had struck him when he saw Gabby dead, more strongly as they carried the agonized Hippolyte, and finally the realization reached his heart when he saw his father's last breath shiver out.

Georgette spat. "You've got to carry out the wishes of your papa!"

Rose, his heart cried.

Georgette knew, somehow she did. "Before you follow that wench," she hissed, "bury your dead! Then weigh the dishonor to your father, the scandal on his name, against that black hussy."

"And the baby? What about it?"

"Pah! Blacks are blacks. That's why your father made the rule—which you broke and now, after all you've done, want to break again!"

"Papa and Gabby—everything's over for them. But for Rose and the baby, it's only beginning."

"You owe me!" she whispered viciously. "You'll never know!"

"Yes, Mama, yes. Life."

"More! The things I endured—no end! What I've borne for you!"

"And for Gabby!"

That silenced her. But her chin lifted.

He wished he was older than sixteen. He wished he had even a little wisdom. He wished his mother weren't so tiny, so ageless. She wasn't quite forty, yet forty was old and he had been taught to respect age. If only she wouldn't stand with those stricken but burning eyes.

"I'll wait," he said. "Do you want me to go across bayou and tell them?"

"I'll send Achilles."

"Then I'll go see Hippolyte."

"No. Doctor Cline gave him drops. You'll need another body servant."

"No."

Gabby had done that to Hippolyte. Gabby had injured, maybe broken, that frail, loyal back. Well, whatever his brother had done, he had now paid his score.

"Is there something you want me to do?" he asked.

"Yes! A thing for your papa. Open those journals, those foolish books he wrote in English. Read them. Now. Maybe you'll learn from what he wrote."

So she knew he had the journals. He refused, almost, but then he nodded. "It won't change anything," he said.

"We'll see."

She really thought that what his father had written about Le Grande Déportation would keep him from Rose, that it would open his eyes to some impossible realization and he would permit Rose to vanish.

He left Georgette and went to his garçonnière. Taking down the journals, he opened the first one and began to read. As he read, he was aware of people arriving, the Heberts and others. He heard shocked tones; bayou folk gathered until the whole plantation, all of L'Acadie, grew into a vast, sorrowful, murmuring hum.

The sun lowered and went. He lighted candles and read on, reading to the end. And then he turned back to certain pages, referred to specific volumes and read again, and some he read a third time.

Finally, he closed all the volumes, handling them with care that amounted to reverence. Then, being only sixteen, and regretting every inadequate year, he folded his arms on the table, laid his brow upon them, and wept.

Before meeting the bayou folk, René decided he needed to go to Hippolyte. And this was the safest time, with Manda scuttling between the kitchen house and dining room, with Sam busy and the other slaves huddled in their cabins, mourning. He picked up the journals and walked to Hippolyte's cabin.

There was a candle burning in the front room. In the back room, on the bunk, Hippolyte was sleeping. He moaned, but did not move, moaned again, but did not rouse.

René put the volumes between Hippolyte's face and the wall. The note he had written stuck out from the top journal.

He left the Quarters, hardly noticing how the children playing in the dust of the street backed away.

The area between kitchen house and big house was

swarming with whispering groups of friends, kinsmen and family connections. Women were patting their eyes with handkerchiefs; a man blew his nose. They gave René passage, hands clasping his as he moved. He went through the door and found the house filled with people. Beyond, on the front porch and in the area beyond, were people. He knew the faces. Some, who lived far from L'Acadie, must have been at the post when they heard.

Keeping his face blank, René passed among them with more speed than he would have expected. As he entered the sitting room, the banks of people opened and closed around him.

The polished oak coffins, made by L'Acadie carpenters working around the clock, were set out from the fireplace. Their tops were in place, pegs in tight.

Georgette, in black, her skin stark white, stood at the heads of the coffins. Her lips moved, and she began to speak. The people hushed so they might hear. Her lips were thinner than René had ever seen them; the dip of the lower one had vanished. From her tone, from its lack of variation, he knew that what she was now to say she had said before, had been repeating, and his presence would not change a word. He listened.

"I have lost my husband and my son through tragedy. Our sons quarreled, as brothers will do, and for no sensible reason, over a pirogue, only. They shouted and struck each other, waking their father, who ran to separate them.

"He tore them apart, but they would not stop. In the darkness my son, my Gabby, thinking he was hitting his brother, was fighting his papa, whose only thought was to make peace. They fell into the bayou and kept fighting under the water.

"When they came up, my husband was pulling Gabby with him. My Gabby was dead, drowned. Because the snake had bitten my husband, the drowning happened, for my husband could not move fast enough. It was the snake that killed them."

The silence pulsed.

"This is what happened," Georgette said finally. "I tell you because we are neighbors, because we have built this country. We all had a tragedy before. Now the Leblancs are in a new tragedy but will survive."

René watched the sharp chin, the white face, the erect body. Shameless, he thought. He glanced around the room, at the women's tears, at the believing faces of the men. By God, he thought, she's done it, she's convinced them all, even the doctor. Nobody'll come out of this wondering if Papa killed Gabby, nobody would dare. She was having things her way. Again.

His own chin set. He passed from group to group until he came to Jacqueline Hebert and her family, and there he paused.

Catherine was as white as her dress, but she held herself with that inborn presence. Her half brothers clustered around her.

"I'm sorry, René," she said.

He nodded. She didn't offer her hand, and he didn't want to touch it. Wearing white, with her hair floating past her shoulders, those fine bones, the chiseled features, the rosy lips, she was too dainty to touch. It came to him, again, that she was fragile. It must be the shock, he thought.

"Where's Sibille?" he asked.

"Oh, it's terrible, René! Aunt Yvonne told her, and do you know what Sibille did?"

He shook his head. What would a fourteen-year-old fiancée do on being told that her beloved was dead?

"She laughed, René, Sibille laughed! She thought Aunt Yvonne was joking. But then when Uncle Louis—she swooned. That's a thing she vowed she would never do. And they had a very hard time bringing her awake. The minute she would open her eyes and remember, she'd swoon again. Uncle Louis is here, but Aunt Yvonne and the children stayed at home. Mama thinks"—she lowered her voice, her lips against René's ear— "that she might go into a decline!"

"You mean—*die*?"

"It does happen. I think Mama's right."

"How do you know. How can you know?"

"Sibille and I are like twins. We've confided every little thing to each other. I know how she felt about Gabby, could almost have felt it myself if. . . . So I understand how she feels now."

"Maybe they can send her to school with you. A different place and people."

Catherine shook her head, her eyes brimming.

"Now chérie," Jacqueline interrupted. "Catherine feels too deeply, René. And that's dangerous." She probed him with her direct Acadian eyes. "You'll have to look out for yourself, in that respect."

He nodded, then moved to another group and another. Except for a brief greeting, he avoided the priest, letting his mother deal with him.

When people began to move toward the dining room where Manda and the other servants had set out food, he went, at last, to his mother and the coffins. He stood at the head of the box that held the remains of the man who had sired him. If he reached out, he could touch the box that held the remains of the sunny-haired Gabby who, as he had learned from the journal, may or may not have been his brother.

Georgette gave no sign she knew he was there. She was repeating her story. The listeners were a group of six whom René barely recognized, but he knew they had to be within bayou distance. They offered their hands and he shook them. His mother continued talking.

Mama, he thought, with a start.

The one who had given him life, who had loved him enough to leave him, he could think of only as Tonton. It was this one, with the knife-edge tone, the burning eyes, who was mama.

ELEVEN

Nearly all the people remained for the funeral the next morning, those from afar spending the night with friends and relatives. They came back in early morning, and René, told by Manda that Hippolyte was alternately suffering, sleeping, and trying to read, did not go to the cabin, though he was frantic to see him.

At the burial ground, long ago set apart, all stood gathered at the cypress ground-level bases over which L'Acadie carpenters had labored through the night. As the priest spoke his words, Georgette stood rigidly beside an equally rigid René. When his father's coffin was set onto the base and the heavy wooden top was lowered to cover it, a piece of René's heart went along. When Gabby's coffin was closed, he knew that he would miss the sunny hair, the swaggering strut.

When the funeral was over and the people were at last gone, René started for Hippolyte. Georgette seized his arm. "Where are you going?"

"To Hippolyte."

"Not now. Your Uncle Louis wants us in the sitting room. It is business."

He stared at her. She had shown no concern that Gabby had injured Hippolyte. She hadn't even, the night of the tragedy, told the doctor to attend the slave. It had been his father who had urged the physician to examine Hippolyte.

Well, he'd see what Uncle Louis wanted. But afterward he was going to his friend, and his mother and all hell couldn't stop him.

In the sitting room, Louis pulled up a chair for Georgette. To René he said, "Sit down, my son."

Uneasy, wondering if his mother had enlisted this thick-shouldered friend whom he always called "uncle" to lecture him on his duties, René complied. It wouldn't be about Rose. Mama, he was certain, would go to her own grave with that unrevealed. But it would be, if her hand was in it, designed to make him give up Rose.

Louis took a folded paper from the table. "This document," he said, his normally warm tone cooled by the solemn atmosphere, "is the Last Will and Testament of your husband, Georgette. Of your father, René. It is written in his own hand, signed by him, witnessed and signed by myself and my brother Étienne. It is legal and binding, and it is at Gabriel's request that I read it to his family as soon as possible."

René thought of the journal. "He didn't mention a will, sir."

Mama's thin lips revealed that he hadn't confided in her, either.

"No," Uncle Louis agreed. "He said that a will is a necessary evil, that a man's duty forces him to make disposal of his estate, that the document must be entrusted to an honest person. Now, with your permission—"

"Read!" Georgette snapped.

"This document is dated December 30, 1760. Early in Gabriel's life at L'Acadie, quite early."

Swiftly René tried to pinpoint dates in the journal. His father had married his mother in mid-February, 1758. Thus, he had made his will less than two years later.

The reading began.

" 'I, Gabriel René Leblanc, being of sound mind, do this day write my Last Will and Testament, to be witnessed by trusted friends.

" 'To my wife, Georgette, I bequeath for her lifetime, L'Acadie, which is the name of my house, and also of my plantation. To her I give the house and all its furnishings. I also bequeath to my wife one-third interest in all stock owned at the time of my death, including slaves, their cabins, as well as horses, mules, cows, and swine. To her I bequeath one-third interest in any investment made by myself and one-third of income therefrom. She is further to receive one-third of income from crops grown at L'Acadie. To her, I render recognition for being a good wife, for rearing our children, and for giving me any future sons and daughters.

" 'To my children, born and unborn, I bequeath equal shares of the remaining two-thirds of my holdings. To my sons, born and unborn, I assign the task of keeping L'Acadie lands intact during the lifetime of their mother and, hopefully, in perpetuity. To them I give and assign the duty of managing L'Acadie and its land.

" 'To my daughters, if born, I bequeath equal furnishings of linens, clothing, and a dowry of money to be provided, share and share alike, from the assets of their mother and brothers. The size of the dowries will be set after consideration of assets by an attorney and properly executed.

" 'Signed Gabriel René Leblanc
" 'Witnessed Étienne Hebert
Louis Hebert.' "

Louis folded the paper. There was a long silence, then Georgette's eyes swung to René. "It should all be mine, all of it! The boys were babies when he wrote that—babies with everything yet to be done!"

"He knew you'd manage."

"Pah!"

"It's a good will. Things are easy for you. Simple, too. You own one-third. René owns two-thirds."

"Which makes him master. Isn't that true?"

"Yes, Georgette. René is master."

"He is sixteen years old!"

If I'm master, René thought, I've the right to bring Rose home.

"Why can't I run L'Acadie, eh?"

"The will is specific. René knows how to run the plantation. Even if you went to lawyers—leave it, Georgette."

"Pah!"

"I know it's come too fast—for both of you." He frowned. "But René's got Sam, trained by Gabriel, in addition to what he himself knows. And he's got Étienne straight across-bayou, and myself almost as near. He'll grow into his father's shoes."

He stood and handed the will to René, who took it, bewildered. Too much was happening. Hippolyte. He had to talk to Hippolyte. He knew his servant lay reading, pondering as deeply as he could push his own sixteen-year-old mind about the journals. Now here he, René, stood holding the will, which demanded more thinking. It was all an impossible muddle.

After Louis had left, Georgette said, "I'm going into the fields."

"This is not a day for work."

"I'm going to work in the fields as I did before."

"Then I'll come with you," René said. The prospect of bending his back, using his hands, tiring himself beyond thought, was suddenly welcome. "First I've got to dispose of this will."

"I don't want you. I want to be alone. Tomorrow."

In this manner, she accepted Louis Hebert's advice. René was master. But she would give her opinion, she would argue; she would turn him to ashes with those black eyes. But always she would work.

After she had gone to change, René hurried to Hippolyte. Manda and Sam weren't at the cabin, but now it didn't matter, for he had authority to send them away if he wanted privacy.

Hippolyte was asleep, and René woke him. Hippolyte's big, dark eyes opened heavily. "Is it aftah suppah? Mama said—I haven't finished my thinking."

"You'll have to read this, too. It's Papa's will."

He put it into the tremulous black hands.

"Does your back hurt awfully, Hippolyte?"

"Not with the drops."

"Don't miss a dose. I need you well again."

"The doctah says I'll heal. I'll read this will and think some more."

René left promptly because his friend needed to do so much so fast—to rest, to heal, to read, to ponder and evaluate. The immediate issue was Rose, when and how to bring her back, how to arrange matters, with Mama sure to make trouble, to do some unthought of, impossible thing.

By the time he reached the garçonnière, he was trembling. His knees buckled as he climbed the stair to get into work clothes. He had to work; he couldn't just wait. Tears stung his eyes. Papa. He forced the tears away.

When he stood naked he looked at his bed. Suddenly, taken by overwhelming fatigue, he dropped onto the bed, on his belly, arms and legs outflung. He was master. If he wanted to lie here, the breeze covering and moving along his bare skin, he would, and for as long as he needed. Presently, he was aware that he was falling asleep, and he made no effort to resist.

It was dark when he awoke. He dressed and combed his hair. He had slept through the supper bell. He should be hungry, since he had eaten nothing since breakfast, but he was beyond hunger.

He went running straight to the Quarters. He didn't want to rout Manda out of bed; Sam would still be up, for he had the night bell to ring.

But both Manda and Sam were on their porch. Seeing René, they stood. "Mastah René," Sam said, "is somethin' wrong?"

"I must talk with Hippolyte."

"He in mis'ry, Mastah René," Manda said.

"There's a candle burning in his room."

"He want it, say he thinkin'. He always thinkin' 'bout dem books. But he think and stare at the candle and sleep."

"Manda," Sam said firmly.

"No. I his mama. I know what best. Mastah René don' want to wake up Hippolyte, do ya, suh?"

"That's what I want. Sam, ring the bell, then you and Manda go to the kitchen house so she can fix me a meal."

After they had gone, he went into the cabin, uncertain that he could wake Hippolyte up. But Hippolyte was fully awake. The journals and will were stacked on the mattress between himself and the wall.

"You sounded like your fathah. Your voice carried, a whispah, almost, but I heard. You gave orders like the mastah."

René almost winced. Then he asked, "Your back, how much does it hurt right now?"

"Hardly any. I had the drops."

"Not enough to interfere with your mind?"

"No."

"That will. What do you think of it?"

"It makes you mastah of L'Acadie."

"Whether I want to be or not."

"Your fathah didn't have that intention."

"No. There was Gabby and all those others, the ones who never got born. Because of some English sailor."

"You can't know that for certain."

"I know what Papa wrote. What he talked about with M. Dupiers when we studied medicine. How some disease in a man can rob the woman of her fruitfulness."

"Yes. It could have been."

"And she blamed *him*. And now, all of a sudden, I have to—"

"You want to be mastah. In your blood. Think."

He didn't need to think. He had been groomed for L'Acadie. It was engrained in him.

"So," he said angrily, "what I say is law."

"Will your mothah accept that?"

"She has to."

He told of his mother's reaction and repeated Louis Hebert's offer to advise him. Hippolyte started to nod, then stopped from pain.

"The advice part sounds good," he said.

"About every move?"

343

"Not to extremes, no."

"You mean about Rose?"

"You know what he'd say about her."

"What do you say?"

"Let her go."

René met Hippolyte's dark eyes. "My first act as master was when I ordered Sam and Manda to the kitchen house. My next will be tomorrow when I send Sam in the fastest pirogue to bring Rose and her parents home."

"To marry me?" There was a sadness, an ache, in Hippolyte's tone.

"You've changed your mind," René accused. "The will did it."

"Not the will—the journals. Parts of them. If you wish, Mastah René, I'll point them out to you."

"You know I hate that 'Mastah René' business!"

"I'm sorry. Sometimes it's hard. I'm your slave, even though we are friends, and, at serious moments, I do put mastah in front of your name."

"That's ridiculous! Don't you see, if Tonton hadn't run away, if she'd been caught, I'd be a slave, too!"

"But it didn't happen. Tonton was very intelligent. She left you so you'd be white."

"But I'm not white! It's all there, in the journals!"

"Until you read them you were white."

"Only because I didn't know."

"So now you know, and what has changed? You have three-quarters white blood, and the white is all that shows. Your fathah made a bargain with your mothah. She believes you white, and she has kept her bargain by allowing people to think you're her own son, born of her. Which you yourself believed until now."

"I'm not going to tell about Tonton."

"I know. You won't ruin what your fathah built, and you won't destroy your mothah's pride. This thing you're doing now, bringing Rose back, is what your fathah did when he rode after Tonton."

"So?"

"You can't tell Rose about Tonton. Even if you bring her back."

"What do you mean, 'if?' That you don't want to marry her?"

"I'd do it. I'd let people think your children are mine."

"She's coming back, understand? Our children will be more black than white, that's better than before I knew. She'll be my secret wife, they'll be my family!"

"And when you die?"

"I'll not marry to get an heir!"

Hippolyte selected a volume, found a page, then held it so the candle gave light. "Let me read.

" ' . . . with this journal in your hands, my son, know that the following is written with the blood of my heart and that of Tonton, my only love. Though in your veins you are quadroon, the life you have lived, the education, the property you will inherit, render you white and a man who bears inescapable responsibility.

" 'In this beautiful Louisiana, it is said that one drop of Negro blood makes a Negro. Your obligation is to take the first step to breed slave blood out of the Leblancs. Never be intimate with a wench.

" 'When your sons are born, they will be octoroon only. They, in turn, must shun wenches. You may need to show them the journal, though I pray not. This secret of blood will best be kept secret. Your grandchildren will have but one-sixteenth, their children but one thirty-second, and theirs a mere one sixty-fourth. By that time I defy the God I do not worship to find that "one drop."

" 'I have now realized that Tonton's thinking was sound. She tried to make me appreciate the aversion people have to black blood. She explained, to my stubborn ears, that the only chance you had to escape stigma was, that since you look white, you be raised so. But all I would consider was Tonton. My Tonton.

" 'I believe, at this point in time, that though she did mean to go with me to Mexico and become my wife, she would have, before taking the vows, reconsidered. For there was in her the terror that future babies would show the blackness. She was right. The only way for the Leblancs to enjoy respect in this new world in which I have established them is to breed in security.' "

Hippolyte stopped reading. The candle flickered; shadows danced. The room throbbed with silence, and the sound the journal made when Hippolyte closed it, all but made René start. The night bell rang, muted.

He was in a trap. L'Acadie was a trap, the journals, the will. Sixteen was a trap. His blood was a trap. Mama. Even Rose.

"Why would Papa do this to me?" he demanded.

"Because he loved you."

"He's telling me to marry someone I don't love!"

"He did that. For you."

"A girl wants love talk, and I haven't any of that."

"He didn't have love talk for your mothah."

"They made a bargain. They were in a trap, too."

"Name your trap."

"You know what it is. And it'll go on. I'll have to sneak to her cabin, lie to a wife—"

"You won't lie if you do the right thing."

"What right thing?"

"You won't sneak to the Quarters."

"Have you gone mad? Forgotten that you're to marry Rose?"

"No."

"Then what can I do?"

"Don't go aftah Rose. Let the family be sold."

"Your head must have hit that tree, too!"

"My head's fine, and it's got what your fathah went through and what he wanted for you in it sharp and clear. He's even outlined for you how to breed the black *out*."

It was then, with Hippolyte's emphasis on the one word, that the truth hit René. He trembled. Dropping his head into his hands, he sat on the edge of the bunk, trembling. His elbows quivered on his knees.

"Yes," he faltered. "If I keep on with Rose, I'll breed black *into*—oh, my God!"

He began to sob, feeling the tears running between his fingers. Hippolyte's hand came to his shoulder, not pressing, just there, in gentleness.

"Rose's baby," René said. "He's got white blood."

"But more black than white."

"God! The scale can go either way!"

"Yes."

"What of his sons, theirs? They'll have Leblanc blood."

"There'll be more black put into each generation."

"No! My God, no!"

"But not by you. By full Negroes, generation aftah generation until one year, long after Tonton is bred out of this line, all the Leblanc will be bred out of that one."

René lifted his head. In candlelight, his eyes met the steady eyes of his friend. His heart began to tear itself into shreds. The thought vaguely drifted across him that this had happened to the heart of his father.

"Damn it—damn Satan!" he said, his teeth clenched. "There's no justice in it, not one grain! But it has to be." His heart shattered. But he did not alter his decision.

TWELVE

He didn't sleep that night. He grieved, not for the dead, but for Rose. He recalled the wonderful blackness of her, the supple, giving beauty, and his love burned on, grief its companion.

At breakfast Georgette motioned for him to sit at the head of the table, and she took her usual place at the foot. It was unnatural that only two now sat where there had been four. It was too quiet, René thought, without his father's heavy, warm voice, without his mother's objections. He even missed Gabby's pucker-faced look. The two of them sat wordless while Manda served.

After she left, René searched Georgette's face. She was pale, her lips held tightly together, but not trembling.

"I'm taking Brandy for my valet while Hippolyte's mending," he said.

"He's supposed to work in the house. Your papa wanted a butler. Manda is to help train him."

"That's why I'm taking him. He'll get training at the garçonnière—"

"Garçonnière! You'll live in the house."

"No. When Brandy comes to the house, he'll soon be a good butler. Under Manda, and under you, Mama." She glared at him.

"What is it, Mama? What's wrong?"

"You! Not one word! Everything secret!"

"The cane will be harvested, taken to the sugar-house, and shipped to market. The ditches will be cleared. I'm going to have Sam run the place as it's been run, have him gather the people so I can tell them they'll not be sold off, that L'Acadie will be the same."

"What about that wench?"

"She's being sold."

"What about college?"

Her word struck him silent. He had forgotten.

"You can't go, you can't run off like a boy!"

He was about to assure her that he wouldn't, but she kept on.

"And all this insane talk of war—an American revolution! Pah! Your papa, except for me, might have gone, the way he talked, he might have revolted against the English."

"Acadians have reason for that, Mama."

"Still—you can't go, either. If those filthy colonies who treated us Acadians like slaves, want to revolt, let them do their own fighting!"

"Papa spoke of joining the militia, if it forms. I might do that much."

"Selfish! You will *not* join. Next is a gun and a battle. You can't leave L'Acadie on my shoulders! You have *got* to stay home from college and from war."

Suddenly anger was boiling up in him. He was about to retort, to shout that he was not her son, that the baby Rose carried would have black blood from himself, as well. But glaring into her flaming eyes, he suddenly realized the many tragedies already thrust upon her—rape, Gabby, another woman, himself. He saw also the grief and read, in the sharp chin and rigid body, the terror, the awful pride, which had brought her through enough torment. So he did not give her the truth.

His anger flattened. "I forgot about college," he said. "As to war, I'll not fight unless it comes to the bayou. I'll grow food for the army."

"And you'll marry."

"When the time comes, yes."

"There must be sons."

It was in the journal, and it was in her. He nodded. Because, willing or not, he owed her. He was all she had now.

At a certain phase in Brandy's training to be the first butler on the Teche, René moved into the house with Georgette. She had not let up on her campaign to get him inside and had finally convinced him.

He took the big upstairs corner room, twin to the one which his mother and father had shared. There was an alcove in which he installed a cot for Hippolyte to use once his back healed. He ordered Honeymoon House and both garçonnières closed, leaving the journals in the one that he vacated. He moved his big home-crafted desk into his chamber and, at times, wrote in his own journal.

He devoted time to studying the records his father had kept on every phase of planting, cultivating, drainage, harvesting, sugarhouse operations, and stock breeding. Though he knew the routine, he combed through the yearly program again and again to make certain he missed nothing, however minute.

He saw Étienne Hebert frequently. Out of courtesy he said one day, "When you write to Catherine, sir, please give her my respects. I hope she likes the school and that Sibille is reconciled to it and recovering from her grief."

"I'll do that," Étienne agreed, smiling. "You'd have thought they were going into exile when I took them to Vicksburg. The way Sibille used to chatter about going away to college before. . . . It's understandable, though."

"In Catherine, too, sir. What makes Sibille unhappy—"

"Yes. Jacqueline also thinks Catherine was homesick."

"She loves the Teche, sir."

"So she does."

René thought of the cousins, at a fine school. He thought of Rose, on the block.

"By the time they come home next summer, sir," he said, from courtesy, "they'll have so much to tell, they'll never stop talking."

Only such was not to be.

For the following June, when the boat on which the girls were to travel from New Orleans, accompanied by Étienne, who was to meet them in that city, put in at the post, he brought devastating news. Sibille, whose beauty had become breathtaking, had eloped with a handsome young man she met on the downriver boat and slipped right under the nose of Miss Merriweather's head mistress.

She left a note, and by the time the head mistress found it, Sibille was on the high seas, enroute to her bridegroom's native Paris. And Catherine had sunk into a total decline, due to protracted and painful homesickness.

Catherine Hebert, word swept the bayous, had to be carried off the boat and taken home, put to bed and slowly nursed back to health. This took well over a year, at the end of which, instead of returning to Miss Merriweather's, she held to her declaration that she would never again, for any reason, leave the bayou country.

THIRTEEN

During the three years following his father's death, René worked beyond any capacity he had known he possessed. Georgette worked just as long, planting sugar cane and clearing ditches like any slave. She worked until she was a wisp, at which time René ordered her to confine her labors to overseeing her house and the Quarters.

Her eyes snapped, but she no longer went to the fields. Now, sometimes, she would sit in the Grape House mending or knitting.

Hippolyte walked almost as well as before. He and René had resumed their reading and discussions, with the added exercise of keeping records of the plantation.

René seldom permitted himself to think of Rose. The agent's report, when it finally came, revealed that she had been sold, along with her parents, to an Alabama planter.

There were, however, nights when, bone-tired, he couldn't sleep from wanting Rose, from wanting a woman. But he took no woman, no wench, whore, widow. The Leblanc need, this time, was going to wait.

A militia was formed but he didn't join. He did, however, participate in hours of discussion with bayou men and with Hippolyte about the Revolution, and he trebled his food crops.

At supper one night when he had spent the afternoon at the post, talking about the war, Georgette, knowing where he had been, herself attacked as singlemindedly as a soldier bearing arms.

"You've been in war talk."

He told her about the Declaration of Independence.

"Pah!"

"It's a good thing, Mama, a needed move."

"And you, René Leblanc, are you thinking of breaking your promise to me, ey?"

"No. No."

"You think I don't feel, eh? If a man wants to keep his land, he's got to stay on it, not go miles away, leaving it to women and slaves!"

"Some men must go. Remember Acadia. The men didn't fight. They were peaceful, and when the English came to exterminate them, they still didn't fight. We won't let that happen the second time."

"Feed our army."

He was sick of hearing that.

Abruptly, she switched subjects. "Have you seen Catherine?" she demanded now.

He tried to remember. He had seen her once, but no more, in the long time of her illness. She had been at a window of her house when he had passed it on his way to the sugarhouse, and she had waved and he had lifted a hand in acknowledgment.

"Once," he replied to his waiting mother. "Why? Is something wrong—has she gone back into the decline?"

"She's as healthy as she ever was. More beautiful."

Catherine, he remembered, had never looked robust. She had always seemed dainty, slender, and frail.

"Her mother brought her across-bayou yesterday," Georgette said. "They spent the afternoon. I thought you might leave the fields, but no. Anyway, you weren't dressed."

René stared. What was she driving at? "I didn't need to come in," he said. "And I didn't know they were here. As to clothes, they've seen me all my life."

"Not Catherine. Not since she's grown."

"What's that got to do with it? What's different now?"

Georgette just looked at him, a long, sharp look.

He gazed back, bewildered. He had heard of a time women went through when they changed, and wondered if that applied to his mother.

And then he understood. "If you think I'm going to marry Catherine," he said, "you're mad! She's a schoolgirl—a child—"

"She's sixteen and you're—Gabby and Sibille—"

"They did their own courting!"

"Then you do yours!"

"When I get damned ready."

"You'll not curse in my presence, René Leblanc! I'm your mother, and you'll give me respect!"

He glared at her. "I apologize for the profanity. But not the other. You can't choose a wife for me, nor will you tell me where or when or why to get married!"

"Then I tell you not to marry Catherine!" she flamed. "She's too frail! You need a wife who is strong, like me."

"You'll not tell me what girl *not* to marry, either."

"Have your way. Your papa believed in early marriage."

"He was twenty-one, in Acadia. You were twenty-one. You didn't marry young."

"We had no choice. But your papa believed in it because of the way the Leblanc men are." She blurted it, her face suffused with color.

Angry though he was, the old sadness about Rose entered him. He felt an impatient sympathy for his mother. "Leave it," he said.

Later, he repeated the conversation he had had with his mother to Hippolyte, who listened without comment.

"Well?" René demanded. "Isn't it foolish? I've got this big plantation and that new land and new slaves and war food to grow, and now she says take a wife!"

"You'll always be buying land and slaves," Hippolyte said.

"But why should I get married now?"

"Why not? Have sons. Unless you don't want to keep L'Acadie—"

"I'm not letting L'Acadie out of the family. Even when we were going to run away that time, I didn't want to leave L'Acadie."

"You don't say if you'll build that mansion your father drew plans for."

"I suppose I will, some day."

"For your wife?" Hippolyte ventured.

René grinned. "You're worse than Mama!" The grin faded. "It's not all that easy. I don't know many girls, and when you think of those on the Teche, they're either engaged or too young. I'd have to go looking."

"And that takes time," Hippolyte said. "Don't you think you'd bettah begin?"

He plunged into his wife hunt in earnest, going to every dance, every party, every gathering that girls attended. Not one who had no fiancé appealed to him.

There came an afternoon during which he worked in the sugarhouse at Hebert Plantation. When he had finished, he started for his pirogue to go home.

Suddenly he spied a girl in a white dress sitting on the front porch of the weathered plantation house. It was Catherine. The only decent thing he could do, in view of the fact he had shied away from visiting her when she was ill, was to join her. Besides, he'd always liked her deeply; thought she was a special person. He should have come before.

Her delicate features lit up as he climbed the steps, and she got up from her chair and came to meet him, hands outstretched. "René!" she cried softly. "René Leblanc, after all this time!"

He took her slim, soft hands and held them. He gazed upon the perfection of her auburn hair, her dark eyes, her rosy, smiling lips. She was dressed in white; she looked like an angel.

He tried to speak, but couldn't. The thought that this was Catherine whom he had known all her life, had gone to school with, and had played children's games with, flitted through his mind and was lost.

She was new; she was different; she was grown.

354

She was, simply, an angel. And he had no idea how to treat an angel.

"Have you swallowed your tongue?" she laughed. "Say hello to me, René Leblanc! I want to hear your voice!"

"H-hello," he croaked.

"That's better! Now, come sit on the bench with me!" she said gaily. "Tell me what you've been doing, how you like being master of L'Acadie—tell me everything!"

Her white skirt touched his work clothes, and when he drew away to protect her skirt, she only laughed. "This is an old dress, and it launders," she declared. "Besides, you're clean as can be!"

"I've been working down at the sugarhouse."

"I know. I've been hoping you'd stop in and see me. And now you have! Go on—tell me all the things I want to know."

Because L'Acadie, sugar cane, slaves, and stock were his life, he spoke of these things. She listened, entranced, asked questions to learn his opinion of proper cane planting. Her questions were sensible; she had been raised on talk of sugar cane.

He found the courage to ask her about her time away at school. Her face clouded, then, swiftly, she smiled. "School itself was fine. I had Sibille, and she was fun, but all I wanted, the whole time, was to come home."

"You're not going back to the school, then?"

Her delicate face solemn, her eyes big and dark, she shook her head. He watched the red glint in her hair and swallowed a lump in his throat. He wanted, somehow, to capture her hands again, to comfort her, but he was too clumsy even to try. Instead, he decided he had better leave before she tired of having him there. He stood, feeling awkward.

She came to her feet with light grace. "You're—going?"

"Supper will be ready. Mama is strict about being on time."

She smiled and nodded. "But you'll come back? We'll talk again?"

"Yes," he promised, croaking anew, wondering how soon it would be decent to return.

He was back the next day and the next and every day after that. He was invited for supper more than once. One night her parents retired, leaving them together in the sitting room.

She was lovelier than he had ever seen her, ethereal yet healthy. She had on another white dress. He was bemused, his ears ringing.

Not knowing what he was going to do, he stammered, blurted, swallowed, then asked her if she would consider marrying him. "You see," he explained, because it was important that she know, "I love you, that's the reason."

She was in his arms, lifting her lips for what would be their first kiss. "René," she whispered, a breath before their lips came together, "ever since I was a little girl, I've been waiting for this moment!"

René Leblanc took as his bride Catherine Hebert on March 1, 1777. He would be twenty in June and she eighteen in November. They were totally in love. The wedding was held in the long salon that Étienne had created by having the wall between the original sitting room and bedroom knocked out. On the grounds that the bride had suffered delicate health, the new priest performed the ceremony before the families, with no other guests.

The truth was that Catherine refused to endure a reception, and no amount of reasoning moved her. She would have René's mother and the L'Acadie slaves; Uncle Louis, his family and slaves; her own family and slaves. None other.

"It's not that I mean to be stubborn," she told René. "We're having lots of people as it is. It's the *noise!*"

"I agree, dearest," he said. "Our wedding will be as all weddings should be, vows between two people, given in peace."

356

He thought of the journals and felt the guilt of the secret of his blood. He felt reverence and his abiding love for Catherine.

"After the ceremony," she said, "we'll have to stay awhile, for the cake. But as soon as you can, René, darling, without being rude—"

"I'll take my bride away. To Honeymoon House."

"We'll live on the Teche always," she murmured.

"But not forever in Honeymoon House, dearest."

"N-no. I realize that we'll need to entertain. It's that now, while the Attakapas is still—" She moved a hand.

"It'll be a wilderness for a long time, maybe all our lives. You'll have your Teche, have peace and quiet. I'll always take care of you, my love."

"René. Darling. I've always wanted to be your wife."

He had, suddenly, to cross his legs.

He made good his promise to spirit her away after the cake. They ran down to the bayou, families and slaves, calling out happiness. He lifted his bride into the pirogue and rowed across the bayou. They marveled at the beauty of the big moon, admiring its reflection in the black water, and once he stirred the water moon with his oar, and it rippled, and Catherine laughed.

Manda had lit candles in every room of Honeymoon House This meant she must have left the wedding the moment the vows were spoken rowed across-bayou, lit the candles then hurried to her own cabin.

Since Catherine had left her maid Dicey, behind until morning and Hippolyte would return to the old garçonnière the newlyweds entered a private world. Catherine laughed when René would have lifted her across the threshold and ran ahead stopping in the middle of the sitting room turning slowly.

"It's perfect!" she breathed "I'm glad I didn't change a lot of the things Sibill fixed when she was going to marry Gabby." The light stroked the mahogany furniture, wavering on the books—Catherine's books, René's books. The journals were in Hippolyte's keeping.

"Do you like the new curtains, darling?" she asked, anxious now. "See, they're the same blue as the carpet. Oh, I hope you like our house!"

"Of course I do, dearest." He did like it, now that she was in it.

Before, when it had been under construction, he had liked the distance it would put between himself and Gabby. He knew that the structure was sound, but as for admiring the generous size of the rooms, the grace of the windows, this had not, until now, entered his mind.

"Wait here!" she said breathlessly. "Come the instant I call!"

He was alone. The mantel clock swung its pendulum, the candles tossing their flames over the clock's golden hands. His heart began to swing in time to the pendulum. His desire, which he had fought without letup, grew. It throbbed, matching the stroking pendulum.

A bullfrog gave his call; farther off, another frog answered. Others joined and the chorus started, and he wondered if the song of frogs was one of the bayou features Catherine so loved.

Now the song got into his need. He didn't know how much longer he could wait. Though he was almost unable to contain his desires, he reminded himself that Catherine was a virgin and that she, of all virgins, must be approached with tenderness and must not be put to undue pain and must not, above all, be frightened.

At first he wasn't sure she had called. He strained to hear. The damned frogs!

"René, darling!" The words had come, they really had. When he opened the door, he sucked in his breath. She stood in front of the bed, her nude body like alabaster, one exquisite part flowing into another. She was beautiful beyond beauty, fragile beyond fragility.

He tried to speak, tried to go to her, but his feet wouldn't move.

Her hair floated to her waist, the red tinge enhanced by her white skin. She stood watching him, her lips trembling.

"You—don't like me?" she whispered. "I mean—Sibille's—told her this is the way a husband—"

He couldn't take his eyes off her. That this girl, in her purity, should be his wife, that she should have exchanged confidences with Sibille, and from what she had been told—"

"Alex told Sibille," she repeated. "René, darling—?"

"You honor me. I—"

He couldn't say more, couldn't take her into his arms. Because now he certainly could not trust himself, not one damned inch, not to frighten her. He undressed as fast as his clumsy fingers permitted.

As he walked toward her, she went to the bed and lay on her back. Her lips were still trembling, but she was smiling. "My husband," she murmured as he came onto her.

She gasped when he tried to enter and could not, but tightened her arms around him. He abandoned tenderness and thrust into her so hard she cried out. Her depths were tight and cool. He waited. This is Catherine, his being shouted. Let her get used to you.

She stirred, a small adjusting motion, and somehow he managed to hold back. She stirred again, and this time in an exploratory manner. He began to move. She was still tight, a wonderous tightness, an inner embrace that he had neither known nor expected. She was moistening. Then he began to move quickly; he couldn't help himself. Her breath sobbed in and out; her hands gripped his shoulders. He went into a frenzy, a contradictory state that was cool and soothing, yet was a hot, mounting climb to glory, a coming home and a completion that he must, would, attain.

Now she was moving, not in rhythm, but moving. In the end he cried out. He had never conceived, even in his most erotic dreams, that a miracle like this could be, that, in this manner, he would fully recognize his deep, abiding, reverent love.

She whispered, "Was I— will I be a good wife?"

"You're a perfect wife, my dearest."

"And you love me, even if—"

"Even if what, dearest?"

"Even if I did write—things—to Sibille and follow what she wrote back. The way I behaved tonight. Even after all that, you love me?"

"You couldn't have pleased me more, my darling. I've always loved you," he continued, speaking the truth. "When you were a baby, when you came to school, always. Now, more than ever."

Rose. He had loved Rose and loved her now. But he would not bring her back if he could. He would not do that to Catherine, whom he wronged by marriage, wronged with his very seed, his blood. She who must be treasured.

FOURTEEN

In due time another wedding was celebrated, this one in the Quarters, Catherine the instigator. Brandy, the young butler, had lost his wife and son at birth a week after René's marriage, and the sadness on him bore on Catherine so that she would fall quiet in the midst of her own joy. René knew what was troubling her, but knew of no way to lighten either it or Brandy's sorrow.

René and Catherine spent hours making love. Catherine, though shy about any unexpected new love play, invariably abandoned herself to it. Once, after a romp, he teased her about looking like a piece of fragile china when she was with others, then turning wanton in bed. A shadow crossed her face.

"Sibille—Alex says that's what a husband wants,"

she said earnestly. "Don't you like what we do, darling? We could—well, tame it down—but it's such fun—"
Realizing what she had said, she went scarlet.

"You're exactly what I want. If you get tired from every night and some afternoons, *I'll* do the taming down."

"No! That would be—neglect!"

They laughed, and then she mentioned Brandy.

"He needs a wench, darling. He's a young, strong buck, and—"

"I'll buy him a wench."

"You don't need to. There's Dicey."

"*Dicey!* Your wench? You've got to be joking!"

"She's as black as he is."

"She's older."

"Six years. His—Sue was too young."

"He was wild about her, asked for her, begged."

"And now Dicey wants him the same way. She's begged me to have you get them married. She isn't pretty, not with that nose, but she's smart and strong. Papa says she's built to have babies, one every year."

"Then why didn't he marry her to one of his bucks?"

"He was going to buy her one, but then I brought her here. Brandy needs a wife, and he's got a cabin."

"The one he had with Sue. Where she died."

"I know, darling. But death didn't spoil Honeymoon House."

"I'll have to think about it."

"She'll please him, darling. She knows how. With Sibille's letters—she's read them. Sibille describes things. You have reason, darling, to know how well. Dicey's ready."

"But Brandy isn't."

"He has no chance to know her. He's at the big house, and she's here."

"You want to move into the big house with my mother so they can get acquainted?" René asked, bewildered.

"Of course not. I thought you'd talk with Brandy."

"We don't order our people to marry, you know."

"I thought you bought bucks and wenches and paired them."

"Yes, but we never order them to marry. It's worked out that they take a liking to each other."

Except once. When Hippolyte and Rose had not wanted each other.

"This is the way we'll do it," Catherine said. "You point out to Brandy that he and Dicey are the only two single slaves here and that it's logical that they get to be friends—how does that sound?"

René laughed. "Like a lovely, conniving matchmaker! We'll try it. And if it works, if Dicey's as good at bed tricks as her mistress, it may turn out to be the best marriage in the Quarters."

René did speak to Brandy. He went so far as to tell the butler that Dicey was very much taken with him, that she both wanted and deserved a husband. Brandy listened.

"Yes, suh, Mastah René," he said. "I been passing Dicey, seein' her throw her eyes. Brandy need a little time—"

Dicey must have managed to give Brandy a foretaste of things to come, René decided, for, after a short period, the butler expressed his readiness to marry. "If we can wait," he added, "until it's been six months since Sue—"

René agreed. "Fair enough. All our people know how you felt about her, and they won't think you're showing her any disrespect."

"No, suh. And in the Quarters, they like Dicey," Brandy added with satisfaction.

For Dicey and Brandy's wedding, Catherine, despite her aversion to noise, instituted at L'Acadie the custom of making every slave wedding a social occasion. All the slaves from both Hebert Plantation and Double Oaks were invited, as well as the residents of the plantations.

The ceremony was held in the schoolhouse, which was decorated with blossoms and greenery. The Negro preacher from Hebert Plantation presided over the ceremony.

After the cake and initial dancing in the streets of the Quarters, the white masters retired to the big house. Here they chatted, the sounds of merrymaking muted.

At midnight the bell was rung, and it was over. The L'Acadie slaves escorted Brandy and Dicey to their cabin, the guest slaves to their pirogues. The white people also departed.

René and Catherine lingered a bit with Georgette.

"I was insane not to get out of the field sooner," she declared. "I should have entertained. I did some, but to think that the first big occasion, the very first, was for *slaves!*" She spat the word.

"That's easy to remedy," René said. "Catherine willing, we can entertain by the dozen. Have dancing, everything."

"Catherine doesn't want the whole bayou country. She hates crowds."

"Only when I must be the center of attention!" Catherine protested. "Tonight was fun. We'll entertain."

"Honeymoon House is too small, even for you to live in. Where will you put that new wench that's coming to take Dicey's place?"

"She can stay with Sam and Manda, then live in the cabin we've been building for Dicey," René said. "I suppose she'll want a husband, too."

Catherine laughed. "Lulu's fifty, her husband's dead, and she doesn't want another."

"The two of you," Georgette snapped, "should move in here. We can make a big salon like Étienne's and have space for entertaining."

René caught his bride's beseeching glance.

"You'll get your salon, Mama," he promised. "But we stay where we are."

"Pah! What you should do, is build the mansion. The time has come for it, a big house, a showplace."

He saw the shrinking look in Catherine's eyes.

"I can't afford it now, Mama," he said. "I've bought more land and need more slaves."

After they returned home, Catherine wandered through the rooms, touching the furniture, demurring when René would have extinguished the candles. "I just want to—love it," she said.

"We've got to sleep," he protested. Then he grinned wickedly. "And before sleep—we can't let Brandy and Dicey have all the fun!"

She smiled, but it was a troubled smile.

"What's wrong?" he asked.

"Nothing, really. Things are so exactly right that I don't want them to change. I don't ever have to go away to school again, don't have to leave the Teche. I don't want to leave Honeymoon House either, René, ever! Even after we have a baby, darling. Don't make me leave my house!"

"But where would we put a baby?"

"We'll manage."

"I could double the size of the house."

"No! Don't you see—to add even one room—"

"Yes, dearest," he agreed, and, holding her, he did understand. But where, he wondered, understanding or not, are we going to put our children—and their nurses? Then, comforting himself with the fact that future housing didn't have to be dealt with at this moment, he promised, recklessly, meaning it nevertheless, "We'll never do anything you don't want, my dearest!"

Nine months to the day after her marriage, Dicey bore a ten-pound baby boy. To Dicey's joy, he had Brandy's handsome nose. Following the birth of this one, which she named Oak, each year for the next seven years, she was to produce a sturdy male baby.

Settlements continued to grow in the bayou country, some acquiring names. Thibodaux, situated on Bayou Lafourche, was the first trading post established between New Orleans and the Teche. Except for these dim signs of habitation, the country remained a trackless, roadless wilderness, the only means of transportation being the network of bayous and the Atchafalaya River.

The war continued. The British had moved it south and were building forts all along the Mississippi. Two months after the birth of Dicey's second boy, couriers to the bayou country asked the Acadian militia to come forward and help fight. To René and others who stayed on their plantations, diligently producing food while their fellows marched off to war, some not to return, this was a period of strain, endurance, and work, ever increasing work.

On June 15, 1780, two months after Dicey produced her third child, Gabe Leblanc was born. It was an excruciating labor, a horrendous delivery that, at the end of fifty hours, mercilessly tore and ripped the flesh of the screaming girl on the bed in Honeymoon House. The screams winged over L'Acadie into the cabin of Dicey, who had to tend her children and wept that she could not go to her mistress.

When at last the baby shot into the world, Doctor Cline, his shirt plastered with sweat, tossed him to Lulu and fought for the spark of life yet in Catherine. He staunched and stemmed; he felt her blood spurt and go through his trousers. He sewed flesh, using boiled white linens to catch seeping blood. Behind him the cry of the newborn baby sounded. There was the smack of hand and the cry built to a tiny roar.

Hearing the cry, René stopped pacing his study. Étienne, who was waiting with him, stopped, too. Together, they stumbled into the sitting room, not knowing whether Catherine, whose screams had cut off so abruptly, had survived. Georgette and Jacqueline looked at them and shook their heads.

As René started for the bedroom, Georgette jumped in front of him. "Wait. You wait."

He wasn't going to wait a damned second; nobody was going to keep him from Catherine any longer. It was than that the door opened and the doctor came tiredly out. He was white and drawn. "She came through," he said, pulling the door shut. "She's got to rest."

365

"She'll be all right?" asked Jacqueline, her chin quivering.

"I believe so, madame. René, you have a son. He was too big for her. Her bones didn't give. She was fortunate. But her chance of coming through this again is nil."

"You're *sure* that she'll be all right?" René pressed.

"She's young, not yet twenty-one, didn't you say? That's in her favor. She's strong, to a point. Beyond that—" He spread his hands, and René recalled the decline into which she had once fallen.

Now Lulu appeared with the baby. René had never seen her look so tall and black or her cheekbones so sharp. "Youah son, mastah. Hold out youah arms, suh."

He extended them like sticks. The bundle came onto them, and he felt the weight, the tiny solidity of his seed, his living, vigorous son. There welled in him the feeling of carrying on a dynasty. Here, in his arms, lay the future for which his father had struggled, for which he had given so much.

The new grandparents surrounded him. Georgette opened the blanket, and, almost fearfully, René examined his son. For months he had brooded, discussed and speculated with Hippolyte, trying to figure the odds on the black blood. He peered at the face of his son. The more he looked, the more relieved he felt. This baby had fiery skin and bits of long, lank hair that were, by some miracle, straight, though dark. Somehow, the baby's face reminded him of Catherine.

Jacqueline lifted one tiny fist, straightening the tiny fingers but, before René could see the nails—he had heard you could tell if a baby was black by the nails—the fingers crumpled. Jacqueline said he had Catherine's nose and lips, no doubt about it. She found his ears to be replicas of René's ears.

It was his mother who caused him to panic.

"He may resemble Catherine," she said, "but"—and René began to sweat— "he's my Gabriel at the forehead and cheeks."

Relief swept over René. He had been in a panic, but not one wrong word had anyone spoken.

Lulu took possession of the baby. "He needs rest, too," she said with dignity, carrying him back into the bedroom.

"I'm staying forty-eight hours," the doctor said. "I'll use the couch in your study, René. I suggest that you ladies go somewhere and sleep. You too, Étienne. Lulu should go to her cabin and send Dicey. I understand she wants to be wet-nurse."

"Catherine wants to nurse her own baby," René said.

"Impossible. She can't let her strength go to milk." René asked if he could look in on Catherine.

"No. She'll ask for you when she's ready."

Thus René, at loose ends, escorted the chattering new grandmothers to the house, then walked to the bayou with Étienne, who said he had things to do at home. When René started toward the garçonnière, he saw Hippolyte coming to meet him. Only then did he realize that none of their people knew certainly that the baby had been born, knew nothing of Catherine's precarious state. He blurted out the story to Hippolyte.

"If she—I killed her."

"But if the doctah says she's out of dangah—"

"For the moment. The doctor's staying, going to use the couch. I'll have a pallet in the sitting room. He won't even let me look at her!"

"If there's immediate dangah, he would since you're the husband."

Hippolyte laid his hand on René's arm. "She won't have to suffah for you. She won't have to pay."

Thirty-six hours passed before he was permitted to see Catherine. She was lying flat, white as the sheet on her bed. She offered a tremulous joke. "Alone at last," she whispered. The words took her strength; there was none left for a smile.

His heart shook. He sat beside the bed, stroking her soft hair, smiling.

"A boy," she whispered. "We made him ourselves."

He lifted her hand tenderly.

"Isn't he beautiful, René? Perfect?"

"He must be. His grandmothers and Lulu and Dicey do nothing but boast."

Her eyes glowed. "Gabe. Gabe Leblanc. Imagine. A week ago—and now Gabe Leblanc, a person."

Before she had a chance—as she would do—to start planning the next baby, René said, "He's to be the only one, my dearest. Doctor Cline says—"

"Doctors say that. Midwives. And women prove them wrong."

He wouldn't argue, wouldn't upset her. But she had borne the only child he would permit. To keep her alive was the first consideration; to avoid risking the birth of a negroid child was the second.

It was a week before he could show his son to Hippolyte. Even then Lulu, who brought Gabe into the sitting room, tried to keep a distance between baby and valet.

"Step right up," René said. "Lulu, open the blanket, pull up the wrapper. Let Hippolyte have a good look."

In magnificent silence she obeyed.

René himself reached for one small fist, opening the fingers. "Like my hand, do you think, like his grandfather's?"

"The shape, yes. But the bones are slendah, like Miss Catherine's."

After Lulu left, Hippolyte was very quiet.

"You saw something," René accused. "Some sign."

"Nothing, you mean."

"You've never lied to me. What did you see?"

"I'm sorry. I was considering, putting the baby together in my mind, balancing his bone structure, skin, eyes, hair. There's not one sign on him but white."

FIFTEEN

It took Catherine over a year to recover, for she went into a decline worse than the one she had suffered earlier. Even after this time, she still had not recovered her full strength, though Doctor Cline said that she would be all right.

"Just no more babies," he repeated.

Now the war was raging in the Carolinas. René planted additional food crops, working in the fields every day.

As she grew stronger, Catherine fretted over abstinence from lovemaking until René, bursting with need, turned to her at night and gave her—almost— what she wanted. But always he managed to hold back until she achieved delight, at which time he would roll from her and spill his seed.

"That's no way," she chided.

"It's the only way I know."

"Sibille does say Alex has every confidence in it."

"Do you and Sibille—about *that*?"

"What other way can I find out? You've never told me anything, and my mother—she'd die of shame! But Alex, being Parisian, tells Sibille all those things. He says young Alex is enough, that he wants Sibille slim, and she wants what Alex wants, so—" She smiled, and there was a flash of the schoolgirl he had loved. "But I want more babies!"

"That," he told her, "will never be."

Eventually, after months of pleading and a few small quarrels, Catherine unwillingly accepted the situation. But she turned to him each night eager, abandoned, and he gave her love, taking for himself the inferior relief.

By March, 1782, frustrated by defeats, the British Commons authorized negotiations with the American rebels. Dicey pushed out her fifth baby, calling him Dock in honor of Doctor Cline, who attended her.

With the war on its way out, René again suggested they build the mansion, and again Catherine expressed her wish not to have such a large house. She did, however, admit they needed more room and consented to Georgette's sharp, oft-repeated litany that they move in with her.

Once this was done, Georgette talked baby words to Gabe when she thought no one was listening and rocked him to sleep at every opportunity. But she also slapped his hands when he meddled or toddled too near a fire and withheld comfort until he sobbed himself out.

"He must learn, Grandmother's baby must learn," she would admonish him. René, hearing her, was half convinced she had forgotten that Gabe wasn't actually her blood. Involved though she was with him, she allotted Jacqueline a full share of privileges, and never went against Catherine.

Gabe, at two, was the darling of both L'Acadie and the Hebert Plantation. He was tall for his age, slim, and strong. He had wide shoulders with a hint of thickness that Georgette never failed to point out. His skin was the pronounced white of Catherine's, his hair a warm brown, lighter than hers.

Though he played with all the black children, it was to Dicey's cabin he ran most, and it was Dicey's boys—Oak, Novy and Bran with whom he played. Teche, a year younger, he ignored and Dock he tried to push away from Dicey's big black breast, much to her delight.

"See dat!" she would crow. "Massa Gabe, he Dicey's baby!" Once, when René was present, she appealed to him. "You evah considah, Mastah René, what you goin' to do with Brandy's suckahs?"

"Not yet," René grinned, scooping the wriggling Gabe up. "What notion have you got in that head now?"

She laughed. "Mastah René know Dicey, yes he do!"

"Go ahead, speak out," René said, grinning still.

"Brandy, he proud could Oak, he de oldest, learn to be butlah," she ventured.

René considered. He had watched Oak; he studied all the suckers. Oak was a small replica of Brandy, bright for his age, obedient, and played nicely with Gabe. "It's possible," he said. "We'll see how he does in school."

Dicey broke into a wide grin. René watched her innocent, much too innocent eyes, search him. "What else, Dicey?"

"You ready foah a body servant for Massa Gabe, suh?"

He chuckled. "Your suckers are babies! How can one of them be valet to a two-year-old?"

"Dicey's Bran, he two. He suck right 'long with Massa Gabe. Dey like twins. Mastah René could give him to Massa Gabe like Mastah Gabriel give Hippolyte to you, suh!"

René sobered. If his father hadn't given him Hippolyte when both were six, if they hadn't grown up almost like brothers, he would never have found such a friend. He studied Dicey, who had asked so beseechingly, yet was so carefully not looking into his eyes.

He made his decision. "I'll have the papers drawn up. Bran will belong to Master Gabe—and so will Dock."

When Gabe was eight, René came into the salon to find his son sitting very straight, a stubborn look on his face. He was arguing with his grandmother.

"Listen to me, Gabe," Georgette said fiercely. "How long have you lived, eh? Seven years. And how long has your grandmother lived? Over half a century! With her eyes open and seeing."

"My eyes see," Gabe insisted. "They're not horses and cows—they're people!"

Georgette threw her hands apart. "Hear this fine son of yours!" she cried. "Don't you teach him, don't you *tell* him?"

"He's young to learn about sugar cane, Mama."

"Pah! He understands about Bran and Dock! He's too stubborn to admit the difference between house slaves and field hands."

"She says they're stock. Stock is horses and cows. Slaves are people! That's what you and Mama call them."

René pulled up a chair and drew his son to stand at his knee. "Some people do call slaves stock," he said. "They don't mean anything bad."

"But why?"

"Because we buy and sell them."

"But they *are* people?"

"Of course they are."

"Stock—people—what difference, eh? He's not to play in the Quarters, he's not to play with that Jewell wench!"

"Grandmother says Jewell's dirty."

"All wenches are dirty.

"Mama!"

She glared at René. "Gabe has Bran and Dock and cousins. There's no need for him to be familiar with any wench."

Rage and guilt mixed in René. On every score he knew she was right, and without knowing the true reason. Nevertheless, he would have liked nothing better than to grip those proud shoulders and shake her until that graying hair tumbled.

"Boys are more fun to play with, Gabe," he said. "You can play even rough games. With girls, white or black, you have to be careful."

"Yes. They cry."

"Exactly. Play as your grandmother said."

"Yes, sir."

"You may go now. Ask your grandmother to excuse you."

Gabe did as he was told.

"He's got to learn!" Georgette snapped when he had gone.

"Yes. But I won't have hatred put into him. You're to stay out of it. If you don't, I'll build another house and you'll not be permitted to see him except in the presence of Catherine or myself."

Surprisingly, Georgette dropped her efforts, and peace settled over L'Acadie.

One afternoon, on a day René was spending with Louis Hebert at Double Oaks, his mother asked to sit with Catherine in her rooms. Every line of her tiny, energetic figure betrayed purpose, and, after seeing that the older woman had a comfortable chair, Catherine waited.

"So," Georgette said, "René's going to New Orleans."

Puzzled, Catherine nodded. René went once a year on business, staying a month or more. She glanced at the great, blue-white diamond on her right hand; he had bought her that once, using money he should have invested in land.

"Did he ask you to go along?"

"He always asks me, Mama Leblanc."

"And you said no again."

"Yes, I did."

"Why? Because you still have that idea you can't leave the Teche?"

"That. And Gabe."

"Pah!"

Catherine remained silent.

"What will you do when he doesn't ask you to go?"

"I don't think that will happen. You've not made the trip either, Mama."

"There was the work. When Gabriel went, someone had to tend the plantation. It's different now. You're insane to send your husband away and deprive him of his rights."

Catherine's face burned. "I don't know what you mean," she murmured. But she did know. She had been married to René for ten years, and he had seldom failed to turn to her nightly except when she was ill or when he went to New Orleans. But when he returned, ah then! They renewed the honeymoon.

"If you send him alone, he'll find a woman in the city."

"René would never do that."

"He's done it once, and he'll do it again!"

"He hasn't! He would have told me!"

"Not now. It was before you went to Vicksburg. With a wench, the blackest one at L'Acadie. He was sixteen."

Catherine gasped.

"It's in the Leblancs, you can't take it out of them, that having a woman! And René wouldn't leave the wench alone, even after we'd taught him—"

"No," Catherine whispered. "*No!*"

"He got her enceinte, that Rose! He put Leblanc blood into a slave. My Gabriel—how he fought blood mixing—took Rose and her parents to the post and put them on a trading boat!"

"No," Catherine moaned.

"Do you know what René was going to do that night Rose was sent away, him and Hippolyte? They were going to get the wench and run away!"

"No—ah, please!"

"My Gabby, he caught them. That's when the fight began. You know what happened, and now you know why."

Catherine gazed numbly at René's mother. All the things she had said were whirling in her. She tore her look free, gazed at her wedding band, and at the diamond. She felt herself crumple and slide.

Later, after Georgette had revived her and gone and she lay on her bed, the weakness seemed to be pushing her through the mattress. She stared at the slow movement of the window curtains. The breeze will go away, she thought. The heat will clamp down and there'll be mosquitoes. Maybe there'll be a breeze again, and it will be the same as always.

Only nothing was the same. Nothing was as she had believed it to be, nor had ever been. It wasn't René's fault. He had been born a Leblanc.

When René came, she said that she was in bed with a headache, which she did in truth now have. After supper he returned to her, undressed, and lay beside her. He knew something was wrong and suspected that his mother was somehow involved.

"What's Mama up to? Tell."

"She urged me to go on the trip. She warned me."

"Warned?"

"That if I don't, you'll get a woman."

"I'll be damned! I'll be double damned! It's time we got out of her house, Catherine! What else did she say, dearest?"

She told him briefly.

"Hell's fire!"

"Then it is true."

"Every damning word!"

His mind flamed with the other truth that, except for Hippolyte, only he knew. With it he could destroy Georgette, but it would also destroy Gabe.

"Even that you loved—Rose?"

"Yes."

"And meant to keep her and the child?"

"That, too."

"What happened?"

"They went on the block."

"But you were the new master. You could have gotten them back."

"Not with Papa dying that way. Not with myself master of what he had built."

Silence.

He gazed at her pallor. "Dearest—you haven't—do you hate me?"

"I could never hate you."

"Can you forgive?"

"There's no question of that. When it happened, you didn't know that I had loved you always. You didn't betray me, darling, since Rose was first."

Taking her left hand, he lifted it to his lips, and kissed the wedding ring. He brought her hand to his naked chest and held it. When his finger touched her wrist, he could feel the flutter of her pulse.

She needs a tonic he thought.

"Dearest," he said, "when I come home, I'm going

to build you a house of your own design. Away from Mama."

They made love, long and sweetly, yet with sadness. That night they loved, and the nights to come. And then, Hippolyte in attendance, René went to New Orleans.

When he returned and went racing up the lane, he found his mother alone in the salon, knitting. She didn't speak, simply gave him a burning look, and continued knitting.

"Where's Catherine?" he asked. He turned, about to rush upstairs.

"She's not up there," Georgette said. "She moved back into Honeymoon House a week after you left."

Without another word, he ran for Honeymoon House. It was dark except for what had been his study. His hand was on the bedroom door when Lulu appeared with a candle, her finger to lips.

"Don't go in, mastah," she whispered. "She just went to sleep."

"What's wrong?" he whispered.

Lulu led him to the kitchen. Even with the door closed, she whispered. "Doctah Cline say it like when she went away to school, like when Mastah Gabe's born, suh."

"Is she in another decline?"

"The doctah don't say de-cline, suh. He talk to Miss Georgette an' Miss Jacqueline."

"What about the doctor, damn it?"

"He say she lonesome for you, suh. That when you git home, she blossom like a rose."

Self-accusation, rage at his mother, wild determination to change things fought in him. "I'm going in there," he said.

Though she had no right, she clutched his arm. "She got to sleep, mastah! She ain't slep' since she move into this house. She roam, just driftin' from one room to anothah, the whole five weeks you gone."

"Is she in pain?"

"Not body pain, suh."

"Didn't the doctor give her sleeping drops?"

"She won't take 'em. She say they make her fuzzy, that she rathah lay an' lissen to the bayou sing."

"Step aside—*move!*"

He grabbed her candle and went running for the bedroom. She wasn't in a decline; she was homesick for him, and once she knew he was here, she would sleep, she would mend.

He eased the door open. Even so, she woke. He set the candle down. She had risen to a sitting position. Her white gown shimmered; she was pale beyond pallor. She didn't speak, not even his name. He went to her and sat on the bed, drawing her into his arms. Putting his lips tenderly on hers, he tasted salt.

"Don't cry, dearest," he murmured.

Weeping, she began to tremble. There was no joy in her, only the weeping. He could feel her extreme thinness, her terrible fragility.

"It'll not happen again, dearest. I've engaged an agent. He'll come here, and we'll deal by mail. I'll never leave you again."

There was no change in the trembling, the weeping. Gently he lowered her to the pillows, and she lay, arms where they had fallen. He stripped faster than he had ever done, but when he would have taken off her gown, she would not allow it.

Fear took him. "Is it that you're not strong?"

"No," she whispered. "Darling. It is as your mother said."

"Go on, love, finish!"

"You're a Leblanc—you need—can't do without—"

"But I did, always have! Just because a malicious, spiteful old woman—"

"Your mother, darling. The woman who gave you life." He bit his tongue for silence. "She only made me realize, darling, that I was to blame. I knew you were in torture because, when you came home—"

"That shows I never. . . . Let me get that damned gown off! You'll see, you'll find out!"

She pushed against his chest, and her lack of strength appalled him. "You *are* ill!"

"Not the way you mean, darling, but within. The question. The doubt."

"That *this* time—*Catherine!*"

"That's why I moved back here. To where love began. So doubt would go away. And I thought it might, darling. I prayed it would."

"And now it will. Dearest, let me show you!"

She turned her face away and began to sob.

SIXTEEN

There was silence over all L'Acadie, silence over the empty fields, over the pastures and stables, over the Quarters, over the big house and the kitchen house, and over René's garçonnière, where he and Hippolyte now stayed.

There was silence in the other garçonnière, where Gabe and his young valets lived. It was Gabe's ninth birthday, and Gabe and his valets had gone to Double Oaks because his mother was too sick to notice his birthday and his grandmother was too busy to recognize it, other than to give him a kiss.

Outside Honeymoon House, Hippolyte waited on a bench under an oak. He had been there for hours, ready should his master need him. He sat in silence, displeased if a bee hummed, lest the sound penetrate the sickroom.

Inside, Lulu and Dicey, along with Georgette and Jacqueline, did the nursing. The doctor had been here two days. René, sleepless, lived only from one moment to the next, as did his beloved.

When she was wracked with coughing, the doctor bent over her and did his best, but still her life's blood hemorrhaged. René hovered with the doctor; tenderly, he touched Catherine's hand. When the wracking ceased, the women took over, doing the swabbing and washing up and René and the doctor went outside where Hippolyte sat at a distance.

"How did it really start, doctor?" René asked again. Did I do it? he ached to cry out, did I bring her to this?

"I've told you. It won't help to repeat it."

"I want you to, damn it! How did it begin?"

"It goes back to childhood."

"But she was active!"

"But she would get feverish and have to rest a day. There was always a basic weakness in her. The bayou country was good for her. When she had the first decline, the climate, with rest and food, pulled her back."

"Then giving birth undid everything."

"She almost got the lung fever then."

"And this time?"

"She would be on the verge, I've seen it, then she would grow better. Actually, she's been failing all the time, slowly."

"Weren't the hemorrhages worse yesterday than now?"

"One was, yes."

"She came out of that."

"Y-yes."

"Is she going to come out of this damned thing, doctor?"

"I don't know."

"Damn me that I didn't see before I left!"

"Nobody noticed until she had moved into this house. Your mother didn't like Catherine's color and sent for me. I found her headed for decline. She took her tonic, her eggnog, but she wouldn't take the drops, so she didn't get sleep."

"She's still not sleeping."

"Some. She's so weak."

"But not enough sleep! If we put the drops into her, she'll sleep! That'll do it, with the bayou and the eggnog."

The doctor's eyes were steady. Meeting René's, they misted.

"Damn you!" René cried. "You're giving up! Well, I

won't let you! What she needs are the drops—give her the drops!"

"They don't heal, they don't cure."

"But sleep does—and the will to live!" His own words struck him a blow. Brutally, he threw it off. She would find the will to live; for him, she would do it. "I've got the drops in that room, the strength to pour them into her. And I've got the will for her to live!"

He went racing for Catherine. He didn't know Hippolyte had gone into the house until the valet passed him on the way out, hurrying to the doctor. But he heard Hippolyte cry out in a manner that he had never before presumed to use to anyone but René himself. "Doctah, they want you inside, fast!"

Within ten minutes, the last of Catherine's lifeblood gushed past her lips and soaked into the sheet. The wedding ring glowed on one hand, the diamond on the other.

She hadn't opened her eyes. She had asked for nothing, for no one, not even for René, her husband, who took up the hand with the wedding ring, held it to his lips, and wept aloud with a hoarse and tearing sound.

SEVENTEEN

In September Gabe Leblanc was taken by his father to school in New Orleans. René knew he was happy to go; the summer had been awful. The plantation school was closed. His mother had died and he had wept, as had everyone at L'Acadie. None of the slaves sang, none of them smiled at him. Sometimes they looked at him and cried.

Georgette was very upset about his being sent away to school. Though René and Gabe lived in the garçonnières, they ate at the big house, and they were at the table when school was spoken of.

"Insane!" snapped Georgette. "Nobody sends a nine-year-old boy to college!"

"I'd meant to give him a year to get used to the idea," René said. "But now—it's better that he just go."

"Insane! Madness!"

"In Europe, Mama, a boy goes to school when he is eight. Catherine wanted this for Gabe so that, when he is grown, when this area is more civilized, he can take his place as a leader."

"And how will he learn to raise sugar cane?"

"It's bred into him. He'll learn the rest when he's a man."

"That's not the way your papa did it!"

"No. What about it, Gabe? You can take Bran and Dock."

"Will Henri and Leonard be there?"

"That they will, but in a higher class because they're older. You'll have cousins and new friends."

Gabe frowned. "I'll go."

"It means," Georgette said fiercely, "that you'll hardly ever be at L'Acadie. Not but two months in summer."

"That's a long time," Gabe said.

Gabe settled quickly into school life. He wrote René often about his close friend, Paul Belfontaine, two years older than himself, but in the same class because Paul saw no sense in study when his papa owned the biggest sugar-trading house in New Orleans, in the world, even. He shipped sugar on great vessels, acquiring much gold, so why should his heir batter his brains with dates in history books?

Paul had dark blonde hair and light brown eyes. He walked with a permanent limp caused by a fall from a horse. The limp seemed romantic to Gabe.

He made other friends, and judging from his letters he hardly missed L'Acadie, and if he did start to get homesick, there were Bran and Dock on pallets in his room.

The headmaster wrote glowing reports to René, commenting on how easily Gabe made friends.

> . . . *He also evidences deep interest in the city. No public institution goes unnoticed by him. He is one of our aptest scholars, retains what he learns, and gives promise of growing to be one of the most handsome, intelligent men it has been my privilege to know.*
>
> *You have reason, M. Leblanc, to take pride in your son. He keeps his body servants under control, is kind to them, and is tutoring them in some of the subjects. He is grooming himself to be a kind master who will be loved and respected by his slaves.*

René continued to take his meals with his mother and sit with her for a time each evening. Busy as she kept herself, driving Brandy and his son Oak, as well as the house servants, to distraction, darting up and down the streets, in and out of cabins, she was lonely. Sometimes Jacqueline spent an afternoon and, less often Yvonne, but she rarely returned their visits, refused invitations to social occasions, and did not herself entertain.

During the summer, when Gabe was at home, she was as near to seeming happy as ever René had known her to be. Each year when Gabe returned to college, happy, smiling, he promised to write and always kept his promise.

With his passion for learning, he was twenty before he finished his schooling. Paul had gone into his father's sugar-trading house two years earlier and found, to his amusement, that he liked to argue price, buy sugar, sell, and ship.

Thus, as Gabe's college days were ending, Paul argued in his gentle voice, trying to persuade him to take a position with the Belfontaines. "Just two years," he said. "It'll broaden you. You'll know sugar trading, then sugar production! You'll come out of it the best-rounded sugar man in the country!"

Gabe considered, frowning.

"Well? How does it strike you?"

"It's a stunning idea. But I've got to consider."

They gazed at each other. Paul, Gabe thought, was the epitome of the city man. Aesthetic and, like himself, six feet tall, with fine-drawn features. While Gabe wore his hair in a moderate cut, Paul's flowed to the nape of the neck, where it was clubbed and tied with a narrow black ribbon.

"Your father is strong, isn't he?" Paul asked.

"Sure. Never sick."

"And not really old."

"Forty-three or so."

"Well, there you have it! Ask if he'll run L'Acadie two more years. Put it up to him." His light brown eyes began to dance. "Think of the times we'll have! The first year, before Florence and I marry, we can do as we please. After that—well, she'll try her hand at matchmaking, I warn you."

"Just so long," Gabe said, laughing, "as she doesn't know I keep private rooms for a girl!" For a while he had kept an American girl named Wanda, then, when she married, had formed an alliance with another American. He found them outspoken but amusing and sexually delightful.

"My lips are sealed," Paul said. "As yours must be about Emilie."

"You're going to *keep* your quadroon?"

"Octoroon. No, I'm going to find her a new man. I'll be a proper husband to Florence. She's a real match and deserves respect. And it's not every day a man finds a girl with a dowry of over a hundred thousand *and* breeding."

Gabe made no comment. The one real quarrel he had had with Paul had been over the wench. Paul had taken one look at her and was besotted. Despite everything Gabe had said, Paul had set her up in a little house, and now that he had decided to break with her, Gabe was ready to drop the subject.

At L'Acadie and at Hebert Plantation that summer of 1800, the grandmothers fed Gabe, bossed him, sat and admired him, and he good-naturedly permitted all of this.

The day came when he talked Paul's proposition over with his father.

"It's a fine opportunity," René said at once.

"It would leave L'Acadie on you another two years."

"I'll manage, my son. Take the offer."

EIGHTEEN

In 1802, when Gabe was twenty-two, he returned to stay at L'Acadie. He plunged into learning to run the plantation, his joy in living transforming it from a quiet, workaday world into new life. In 1803, the United States bought the tremendous Louisiana province from Napoleon, and he took great satisfaction in this.

L'Acadie being the biggest plantation in the Attakapas and Gabe the handsomest bachelor, every girl and her mother was on the alert. Gabe, however, having no desire to marry soon, chose a New Orleans girl, Abigail Green, for a mistress. She was twenty-five, warm, happy, and intelligent. She came to the settlement to live in a small house for which he paid and where he visited her often and discreetly. She did fine sewing for customers who paid her.

But her main purpose, almost in the manner of a placée, was to please and entertain Gabe. She waited on him, discussed world matters seriously when he chose, but most of the time sported with him seductively, and he was highly pleased with the arrangement. If she hoped that Gabe might come to depend upon her to the point of marriage, she gave no sign, and for this he was thankful.

He was twenty-seven, staying with his grandmother in the big house, spending some evenings with his father and Hippolyte, others with Abigail. Dock was now his valet and Bran, under his father and Oak, was learning the duties of butler so that, later, he could serve Gabe.

It was at this time Gabe decided to build. At supper one night he said, "I'm going to put up that mansion with the pillars, the one that Grandfather drew the plans for."

"Then you'll need a wife!" his grandmother cried. Hardly a month had passed without her demand that he marry.

"Hold on," Gabe laughed. "No wife, not yet. But the house, yes! It's a showpiece and must be very carefully done. It's to be of the best seasoned cypress, the woodwork the best walnut, floors parquet. And the fittings—doorknobs, chandeliers and wall coverings—all imported."

He plunged into building the way he did into everything, joyfully and wholeheartedly. He brought the best slave carpenters and woodworkers in the bayou country to help, paying their masters well for their services, even though his own carpenters were good.

It was four years in the building, decorating and furnishing, and when it was completed, its greatness vied with that of the Teche itself. It dominated the bayou country, surpassing any plantation house on the Mississippi as well. It was the house his grandfather had dreamed of. In it Gabe lived alone with Bran, his butler, and Dock, his valet, his father and grandmother refusing to budge from their accustomed quarters.

The year was 1812, he was almost thirty-two years old, and fancy-free—until the trip he made to New Orleans to celebrate the fact that, on April thirtieth, Louisiana, with a population of over 76,000, had been granted statehood.

Paul had written to insist that Gabe come.

*There's no way out of it. You must be our
guest when Louisiana receives her cherished
statehood!*

*Florence is like a new woman. She seems to
have lost the ill health caused by the birth of
Francis nine years ago and has already given
one big dinner in honor of it.*

*She insists that you join us for late April and
early May. I must warn you that she has the
usual matchmaking on her mind. The young
lady, a kinswoman younger than herself, with
whom she means to entice you, has arrived and
is, I must confess, a real charmer.*

*Francis, alas, remains delicate. After this so-
cial whirl, I hope to persuade Florence to bring
him along and the three of us will at last accept
your repeated invitation to visit L'Acadie.*

> *Best regards,*
> *Paul*

*P.S. The charmer is not staying with us, but
in an apartment, chaperoned by her aunt, who
disapproves of our gay city. They are from St.
Louis.*

After he read this letter, Gabe laughed and put it
aside.

He didn't laugh, however, when he saw the blonde,
blue-eyed girl in Florence Belfontaine's elegant drawing room. Instead, he halted in the doorway and
stared through the crowd of exquisitely gowned ladies
and their escorts, and knew this was the girl he must
have.

They were introduced. She was as instantly drawn
to him as he to her and assumed no subterfuge. That
first evening, he spent not more than ten minutes apart

from her, and before leaving he managed to draw her aside for a word in private.

"I mean to see a great deal of you," he said openly.

"That's—delightful," she replied softly but clearly, her eyes meeting his.

"I suppose you think I'm impulsive," he said, vaguely aware that this was no way to court a fine-bred girl.

"I'm impulsive, too," she told him. Color washed faintly over her face. "My aunt is always chiding me for it."

"The reason I'm going to see you, and daily," he went stubbornly on, "is that I'm—well, you're the first girl I ever met, who—" He stopped, then went on. "My intention is to show you the city. To take you everywhere. To court you. So if you have any objections, make them now. So that I can talk them away."

She smiled, making her more beautiful. "Gabe Leblanc," she said, and it sounded as if her voice almost shook, "you can court me all you please."

It was all he could do to keep from taking her into his arms then and there, from kissing those wonderful lips, from burying his face in her hair, from letting happiness possess him for all to see.

Theirs was the most exclusive wedding in the city that year. The date was June 15, 1812, the birthday of the bridegroom. The marriage was solemnized in the home of Florence and Paul Belfontaine.

The bride, Octavie Gaboury, was nineteen and the most beautiful woman present. It was whispered that she was half Creole, half American. Gabe scarcely heard; everything was a blur to him. He wanted only to be away from the guests and alone with his bride.

At last Gabe and Octavie were able to escape to their third-floor suite. He escorted her to the marble fireplace of the sitting room, its mantel lined with silver bowls of white roses. He turned her to face him then backed away.

"Don't move," he said. "I want to lock you in my mind, a mental painting I can never lose."

"Anything, Gabe," she said. "Anything you want."

He gazed at her. She was tall, slender, exquisitely formed. Her ash blonde hair was thick, long, and straight. She wore it in a braided coronet with pearls wound through the braid. The effect was striking and totally unlike the current fashion. Her skin was fair, her dark-blue eyes framed by thick lashes. Her face was heart-shaped, with delicate features, and her lips, in repose, were themselves shaped like a heart.

She gazed back at him lovingly, and he felt that she was, in her turn, committing to memory the way he looked. He thought she would remember, always, how he looked on their wedding night, just as he would remember her in her simple white gown.

On her hand glittered the wedding ring he had designed, made of a circle of perfectly cut blue-white diamonds. Around her neck, suspended on a chain of the finest gold links, was his gift to her, a large, pear-shaped diamond pendant.

"You," he said, "are the most beautiful bride a man ever had."

"And you are the most beautiful groom!"

"I'm afraid to touch you."

"You needn't be afraid, my husband."

But he was afraid. This was no Wanda, Sue, Abigail. He couldn't toss Octavie onto a bed, leap at her, no matter how playfully, and enter into a joyful tussle.

She chose that moment to come into his arms. He kissed her, and the lips he caressed held warmth and tenderness such as he hadn't known. Though desire sprang in him, he prolonged the kiss. He must not offend, must not frighten, must not mar perfection.

It was she who ended the embrace. "You don't need to—worry—Gabe. I'm nineteen, and a few days ago Aunt Harriet told me—things."

Gabe swallowed. "She—did?"

Octavie nodded. "You can join me in about ten minutes, darling," she said. And then she went into the bedchamber and closed the door.

He paced, thinking, among other things, about Dock, off in the Belfontaine Quarters, almost wishing for him. But no, he had wanted absolute privacy and Octavie had felt the same and had dismissed her maid.

When she called, he entered the chamber hesitantly. Lamps were burning softly. She was sitting in the canopied bed, wearing a nightdress, the sheet drawn to her waist. Her hair hung loose and over her bosom, caressing it. She was smiling, her lips unsteady.

He undressed, stood naked, the evidence there to see. "Do you want me to put out the lamps?" he asked.

"No, Gabe. This is delightful. Let's keep it so."

But when he would have lifted off her gown, she demurred. "A lady doesn't allow her husband to see her. She keeps her gown on."

He folded back the sheet, then pulled up her gown. His pulse leapt at her perfection, at the blonde target of love.

"I'll try not to hurt you," he said and then, the old Gabe taking over, plunged, wholeheartedly and deeply. And he couldn't stop. He heard her gasp. Then her arms came around him and, before he finished, she was moving, at first tentatively, and at the last in a kind of rhythm. Later, when he would have withdrawn, she held him.

"Again," she whispered.

"But I hurt you."

"So? I—at the end—"

Her whispered confession stirred him instantly. This time, when they had finished, she was clinging, sobbing, murmuring.

They lay through the night, whispering, making love. Octavie herself discarded the nightgown. "It's in the way," she declared.

At rest, she stroked his smooth hair. "Can you know how happy I am that I waited? Something told me, something warned."

"That Gabe Leblanc exists?" he teased.

"Not exactly. Something told me that love is my life, that I'm so filled with love I must have a place to put it. And it has to be the right place."

God, he thought, cradling her, oh, thank God.

NINETEEN

As the boat carried them toward the Teche, Gabe discovered that his bride was interested in national affairs. They discussed the differences England and France were having, were pleased that the United States had seized the opportunity to expand its trade, and indignant that she was in trouble for doing so.

"It's wrong for the English," Octavie said, "to impress American seamen and enslave them on English ships."

"Yes. And it's leading to war."

"Between us and the English? Again?"

"Exactly."

"What will you do, Gabe, if war comes?"

He frowned. "Most of us in the bayous would fight. We're third generation Acadians, but we haven't forgotten what the English did to us."

"If you went to war, who would run L'Acadie?"

"Papa. He did before, during the Revolution."

On June 18, while they were still enroute to the Teche, war with England was declared. When the news came, Octavie went pale.

"Darling," Gabe said, "war or not., I'm going to be very busy on the land for some time. We've got sugar cane to grow and new acreage to put under cultivation for food for the army. I can't push the responsibility onto my father overnight, not until things are well set and we see what course the war's going to take."

"But you'd want to go," she whispered.

"When the time comes. Meanwhile, we've a honeymoon and dozens of relatives for you to become acquainted with and two grandmothers to handle!"

"Don't worry about the grandmothers," Octavie smiled. "I've had experience with Aunt Harriet."

To Gabe's joy and his father's relief, Octavie's presence at L'Acadie was a complete success. She and the grandmothers spent many afternoons together doing needlework and planning the round of entertainment that Octavie, upon meeting all the relatives and bayou folk, decided to institute.

Gabe, within two days, made a brief visit to Abigail, after which she soon returned to the city—a bit reluctantly, he felt, but on the whole pleased with the settlement he had given her, which would buy her a house and set her up as a seamstress.

As the first year progressed, Octavie embarked upon a program of entertaining. Not only that, but when her maid Opal married Dock, she revived his mother's custom of giving a wedding party for slave marriages.

All the while, she was laying plans for a house party to last a month. She, Georgette, and Jacqueline discussed the invitation list for weeks. By the time they had finished, they had filled, on paper, not only the L'Acadie mansion, but the two unoccupied garçonnières and Honeymoon House, along with every available room in the Quarters for maids and valets.

Some guests would be from Bayou Lafourche, others from the lower Teche, still others from all the bayous and the country between. The house party, Octavie assured Gabe, was the ideal mode of entertainment for this country.

"Being together a month," she said, "we'll all have time to visit. The men can ride, fish, hunt, and talk, the ladies can do needlework and chat, and all the children can play. We'll have a ball at the end and invite the countryside."

Consequently, in June, 1813, the great gathering took place. Even Paul and Florence Belfontaine and their delicate son made the trip from New Orleans. Once the guests began to arrive, they filled L'Acadie with laughter, high spirits, confusion, merriment and above all with the spirit of holiday.

The women and little girls were like butterflies in

gauzy summer dresses, the little boys immaculate, at least for moments, in white, as were their fathers.

Paul and Florence were the only guests who were not acquainted with everyone, so Gabe, one arm hooked through that of the handsome Paul, the other through the tense arm of Florence, devoted much time to them. He made certain that Florence chatted with each guest, but though she was gracious, something about her troubled him. Her color was high, and there was a tenseness about her.

Unexpectedly, with a playfully chiding attitude, she turned her attention to Gabe. "What kind of host are you, sir?" she demanded. "I heard you mention a special French wine, but I haven't seen a drop of it!"

"See it you shall!" returned Gabe, relieved there was something he could do for her. "Come into the library. I've only the one bottle left—Alex Duval sent a case to Uncle Louis when Sibille came to visit. We'll have to close the door because it couldn't begin to go around!"

He seated Florence and went to one of the bookcases. From behind some leather-bound volumes, he brought out the half-full bottle. From the same niche he produced glasses.

After filling them, he capped the bottle, and took a glass of white wine to Florence. He gave Paul his glass, then took his own. Paul sniffed his wine appreciatively; Florence gazed into hers as though she were expiring of thirst.

Paul lifted his glass. "To L'Acadie, he said, and they drank.

The glasses were lowered. The men's glasses were still half full, but Florence's glass was empty. Paul looked at her warningly.

"Dar-ling," she drawled. "Gabe! Come—drink up! Grant me the honor of proposing the next toast!"

Suddenly Gabe remembered Florence standing at the wedding with a wineglass in her hand. Silently, Gabe refilled her glass. She lifted it, and they lifted theirs. "To all of us!" she cried, and they drank.

Suddenly Octavie came into the room. Her look

flew from Gabe to Paul, to Florence, to the empty glass.

"I'm going up to my sitting room, Florence," she said. "Won't you come? We haven't been alone yet."

Florence set the glass down and carefully stood. "If that's alright, gentlemen?"

They bowed. Gabe didn't miss Paul's look of relief.

As Florence rarely left their rooms before noon, Paul devoted mornings to his son, Francis, undertaking to teach the boy to ride and to shoot and encouraging him to climb a particular oak with broad, low branches. At first Francis was white with fear, but soon he began to show an interest.

Octavie missed none of this. One morning she and Gabe went to the stables and watched them mount. Francis was laughing, his thin voice rising gaily in the clear air.

"Have you noticed," Octavie asked, "how much better Francis's color is, how he's beginning to fill out, and that he's begun to play with the other children freely?"

"He *is* livelier," Gabe agreed. "I admire Paul's patience with him. I've seen it in New Orleans. He tells me he's going to buy mounts when they get home, one for each of the three of them."

"I doubt that Florence will ride," Octavie said.

"How about you, sweetheart? What have I been thinking of? Riding myself, not even asking if you—"

"But you did ask, Gabe. Right away. I was so busy settling in, getting acquainted, and now the house party. To be honest, I don't find myself interested in riding."

"Then you shan't do it!" he declared.

Octavie smiled, gazing after the diminishing figures of father and son. "If Francis could spend every summer here," she mused, "I believe he'd grow stronger."

"Well, why not? The whole family could come. You'd have Florence, and I'd have Paul. What do you say we invite them?"

Throughout the month, when the men sat together, they mainly discussed the war. During one of these sessions, Paul voiced what was in all their minds.

"This year," he said, "England has reasserted her supremacy on the sea, and now she's got most of our ships either captured or bottled up in our ports."

"The English are always at us!" Gabe exploded. "We can't let it go on. I won't let it go on!"

There grew in him an ever stronger will to fight. Gradually, through the last days of the house party, this desire became stronger, and he cast about for a way to manage it without placing too heavy a burden on his father, and with Octavie's full and free agreement.

But even a week after the guests had departed, he hadn't settled on how to arrange matters. Daily Gabe mulled over his problem. For once in his life, he realized, he couldn't just jump into what he wanted to do.

One night, Octavie, lying spent in Gabe's arms, said softly. "Gabe, it's happened. I'm pregnant."

He couldn't speak or move or breathe.

She gave the little laugh he loved. "What's wrong?"

"A b-baby!" he stammered.

"Surely you didn't think we could carry on the way we have and not be faced with a baby!" she teased.

He tried to laugh with her, but couldn't. The fact that now, at this moment, his child was growing in her body was too overwhelming for laughter. It was more, his bewildered mind groped on, a moment for prayer, and he was no praying man. That out of nothing, out of nowhere, a seed had gone from him to her and created life was miraculous.

"An heir," he managed, and his heart thundered.

"One only," she laughed so delightedly she could scarcely speak. "One now, but we're going to have baby after baby. So you'll have to get used to hearing this news, over and over!"

They told René first, then the grandmothers. René told Hippolyte. In twenty-four hours word had traveled the bayou. L'Acadie was going to have an heir;

Gabe Leblanc hadn't wasted time, give him credit. Now he could go off to war; it was written on him that he yearned to go.

Octavie knew this and told him he must go. René agreed, and they engaged a white overseer to be trained in L'Acadie methods.

Georgette had her own ideas about the matter. "You can't go, not for certain!" she snapped. "How do you know the baby will be a son, eh? You can't leave L'Acadie without an heir," she decreed.

"He will be a son," Octavie said with confidence.

"Pah!"

"The English have got to be put in their place," Gabe insisted. "It's my duty, as a Leblanc, to help do it."

"Raise food," she shrilled. "Wait—see if it's a son!"

Listening, Octavie swung to Georgette's side.

"I know how you are, Gabe," she said. "You leap into things, heart and soul. Only now, if I may be selfish—"

"You, selfish? This is no time for jokes!"

"I'm not joking, Gabe. I really want you to stay until our baby is born. That's a long time to ask for, and many women don't ask, but I do. Because—" she faltered, then went on— "I want you to see your son before you go into battle, and I want him to feel his father's arms holding him. Is it too much, darling? Is it too long?"

He kissed her tenderly. "Of course I'll wait," he whispered.

But he promised only because he loved her deeply, because she wanted him, because he could deny her nothing.

L'Acadie's heir was born April 12, 1814. Christened Gabriel René, it was decided to call him René. The new grandfather immediately made an announcement.

"From this point on," he said, "my grandson will be addressed as René or Master René. As for myself, I'm to be referred to as Old René or Old Master."

Florence Belfontaine, who without Paul, but with Francis, had come to be present for the event, was delighted with old René's solution of the name problem. In fact, she seemed to be a happier woman, to smile more and to drink less now.

When Gabe mentioned this to Octavie she smiled, but he got the impression that Florence's abstinence had something to do with Paul's absence. This puzzled him momentarily, then he forgot about it.

On April 26, when René was two weeks old, Gabe Leblanc at last joined the army. He kissed his loved ones goodbye as many times as they wished, held his son in his arms a last moment, and then he and Dock, who had kissed his Opal and patted her swelling belly, were off to the war.

TWENTY

Gabe, René wrote in his journal, tears blotting the words, was killed in battle outside New Orleans on December 23, 1814. They didn't know of his death at L'Acadie until early January, when Paul Belfontaine's letter came. The official notice from the army arrived on the next boat.

Octavie kept to her bed for a month. She did not, could not, weep. Georgette, eyes fiercer than they had been in weeks, insisted that Jacqueline come across-bayou and they sat together with the young widow. Georgette never ceased to berate the villainous English who had done her and hers so much harm.

Old René suffered in private over the death of his son. The fact that a treaty was signed December 24, one day after Gabe gave his life, grieved the father, and the added irony that the final battle of the war was fought just fifteen days later rendered, for him, Gabe's loss an utter waste.

Paul came to L'Acadie that month, bringing a heartbroken Dock, who had been at his master's side in battle. Before Octavie knew of their arrival, the three of them—Old René, Paul and Dock—sat closed in the library. Paul related what he knew, saying that Old René must be the one to decide how much of it to relay to Octavie and Georgette.

"Gabe, as you knew from letters," Paul said, "was in Beale's rifles. Those Tennesseans were dressed any old way—loose hunting shirts and jackets—but they could fight. So Andrew Jackson, with the help of Jean LaFitte's pirates and a bunch of Tennessee coon hunters and volunteers like Gabe, just murdered those redcoats."

He put a hand on the heaving shoulders of Dock. "Tell. You saw."

"Mastah G-Gabe," sobbed the valet, "he wus leadin' a small party at a run from the swamp. He knew that terr'tory an' he nearly reached it, when he saw a line of men advancing from the swamp right at us.

"In that very second, Old Mastah, befoah the bullet tore through Mastah Gabe's face and plowed through his brain, he yell, 'It's the Tennesseans, Dock!' An' then he fall dead. An' it was them Tennesseans killed Dock's mastah!"

"Thank you, Dock," Old René said, his voice choked.

"What Dock do now, Old Mastah?"

"First, go to Opal. See your new daughter. Bran means to train you to help him right here, to be butler."

After the grieving Dock had gone, Paul asked, "About my laying Gabe to rest among the Belfontaines, did Octavie mind?"

"No. She realized it was the thing to do."

There was a tap at the door. "Who is it?" Old René called, not yet ready to end the conversation.

"It's Bran, suh. Miss Octavie wants to know if she can come in."

"Of course." Old René stood up.

He saw Paul spring up before the door opened. He saw the open, wounded look that had lived on Octavie since word had come, saw her eyes fly to Paul.

"Paul, oh, Paul!" she cried.

She was in his arms, and he held her.

"Octavie," he said. "Octavie."

And Old René knew that she was loved, knew that this man, dear friend of Gabe, dead and gone Gabe, was filled with love for the young and grieving widow.

TWENTY-ONE

From the journal of Old René:

Octavie grieved sorely for Gabe. She grew thin and wan; even her interest in her child, who was a fine baby, seemed to wane, and she left him to his nurse. On the occasions she had him in her presence, she was tender to him, though it was obvious that she was, without Gabe, an empty vessel.

She asked me to resume charge of L'Acadie, which I agreed to do, being as sturdy at fifty-eight as at forty. She implored me to move, with Hippolyte, into the master suite at L'Acadie. She had already vacated these rooms, unable to endure them without her husband. Because she needs a man in the house, I consented.

My mother, though also invited to reside in the mansion, refused, though she is eighty-one. She is accustomed to the old house and has, in her own manner, missed my father, and clings to her old place.

It is Ocatvie, now that summer approaches, about whom I am concerned. Her emptiness, which transcends grief, is a danger. The only spark of interest, and this was brief, was when she received a letter from Florence suggesting that she, and her son, and Paul come to L'Acadie June first and remain through August. I pray that Florence has bested her fondness for drink. In view of what I saw in Paul when he came to us after Gabe's death, along with the fact that Octavie needs—indeed must have—a man to love, I fear the summer.

Old René knew that Octavie waited on the landing the day her guests arrived. He knew in his bones that her breath was caught in her chest, that the world was coming alive.

Florence embraced her first. She smelled of wine, Octavie reported to him later. "To be with you, to touch you!" Florence cried. "No correspondence can take its place! We'll send Paul and Francis off and talk by the hour!"

"Of course," Octavie agreed.

And then Paul was there, and she was suddenly, achingly alive. It had been so that time she had first arrived in New Orleans and had seen him, only to learn he was married to the very kinswoman she had come to visit. Then, later, she had felt almost the same when first she had set eyes on Gabe. So it was all right to feel thus now, because seeing Paul brought her out of the leaden emptiness in which she had so long been immersed.

❀

Carita, swept up by the storm inside her, ears filled with the hurricane outside, began to read Octavie's private words in a book piled among Old René's journal. The book began the night Paul reentered Octavie's life.

❀

She fell into his embrace; it lasted a heartbeat. He let his arms fall, and she stepped back, fire in her cheeks. Was this what happened to widows? Did they all go weak with the strange emotion, which had no name, no importance?

She hugged Francis, but only briefly, since he was at the age when boys scorn any display of affection.

Now she put an arm around Florence's waist, and Florence put an arm around Octavie, and they started up the lane. Like girls, she thought. But it felt good, it really did, to have her arm around someone.

She had rooms across from her own ready for Florence and Paul. Francis was to occupy his favorite garçonnière.

After Florence had freshened up, she came to Octavie's sitting room for the chat they had promised themselves. She cast a look around the blue and white room, at the graceful furniture, and sank into a chair. "Charming," she said. "But it's time you moved back into the master suite, don't you think? Let Old René and his valet take other rooms."

"I'll never—I prefer these rooms, Florence."

"Well, when it's been a year."

"When René marries," Octavie corrected, managing a smile. "He can use that suite."

"Heavens, Octavie, that's years! You're a young woman—" She cut off as Opal appeared and awaited directions.

"Bring us coffee, Opal," Octavie said. "And some of those cakes Jewell made."

"Not for me," Florence said when Opal had gone. "I prefer just a bit of wine. Paul was tiresome about it on the boat; he said to wait until we got here."

"Of course. It's just that this early in the day, coffee is what came to mind."

"I'll rest after that. So, if the wine makes me drowsy, it'll take care of itself."

Octavie brought out a decanter of wine and a glass. After Opal had served Octavie coffee and left, she and Florence settled into talk. Florence immediately confided that she had problems it would take them all summer to talk about. Taking a sip of wine, she set the glass on the table beside her and began. "You don't know how fortunate you are, Octavie. To be a widow."

Octavie was speechless. The wine!

"Don't marry again. Don't let any man. . . . Don't put yourself in danger!"

"Danger?"

"You've been married, you know how a man is. If there's anything a man. . . . look how soon Gabe got you pregnant!"

"But we wanted a baby!"

"Oh, you innocent! Don't you *know* what it does to a woman? Don't you *see* what it did to me?"

"Paul's devoted to you, Florence."

"Oh, he's devoted! He's got his heir, but is he satisfied? No, he's always after me! Twice a week, never less than a week or ten days! And I won't—" She broke off, the pulse in her throat jumping.

"You don't mean—?"

"I deny him. Indeed I do."

"But if you turn him away—"

"It's been a month now—but he won't disgrace me. He won't take a wench. Because of Francis, too. He's just got to overcome the animal in himself."

Poor Florence, Octavie thought. She recalled again the first time she had seen Paul, how drawn to him she had been. To her eyes now, as then, he was matchless. Except for Gabe. Her eyes began to sting.

Florence asked, "Octavie, one more sip?"

Octavie brought the decanter. Oh, Paul, she thought as she poured. Paul.

At noon dinner she concentrated on being the hostess. Only Old René, Paul, and herself shared the meal. Francis was permitted, as a treat, to sit at table in the kitchen house with his valet, Ponch.

"Francis feels very grown-up staying in the garçonnière ordering Ponch around," Paul said. "He's wild about it all."

Octavie smiled. No one could possibly suspect the way her pulse was racing, the cradle of warmth around her heart. She kept her eyes from Paul. It's because he was Gabe's dear friend, she told herself, because having him here is the nearest thing to having Gabe.

"And Florence?" she asked. "Does she find the rooms comfortable?"

"So comfortable that she asked for a tray," Paul said, his tone flat.

Octavie inclined her head. She would never let him know that she noticed the wine. Or that she knew the other. She said, "Maybe Francis would like the same horse this year. Ponch might like to ride, too."

"That'll be splendid!" exclaimed Paul.

"Let all ride who will," Old René said. He frowned, then smiled. "In fact, you'll do me a favor if you exercise all our mounts. I use Prince exclusively. We're used to each other; he's a direct descendant of my father's stallion."

"Of course, sir," Paul agreed.

Octavie tried to keep her eyes off Paul lest her sympathy betray itself. However, courtesy demanded that she look at him occasionally and converse, for to rivet her eyes on her plate or on Old René would be as bad as to stare at Paul.

How could Florence feel as she did? Octavie had found glory in the arms of her husband—every night. Their bodies linked by that wondrous maleness that Florence hated, detested, rejected.

"Can you do that, Octavie?" she heard Paul ask.

"I'm sorry. I'm afraid I didn't hear."

"I thought perhaps, when Florence has rested from the trip, that the two of you might go for morning rides. If you're willing, I'll select the proper mount for her." He waited, his eyes gentle.

This was the man Florence called an animal. This thoughtful, civilized man who walked with a limp, who planned for the good of a wife who rejected him! Gazing at the finely drawn features of the man she might have loved, such a rage of longing for Gabe swept Octavie that her cheeks flamed.

"Yes, Paul," she said. "Oh, yes."

There. Let them think what they would of her blushing.

"Fine," Paul said. "Thank you, Octavie."

Then Old René turned the conversation to the subject of sugar prices. Octavie listened, picking up facts, knowing that in a day or so Paul would be devoting as much time to sugar cane as to horses.

Dinner and the evening were a torment for Octavie.

Every glance Florence flashed at Paul was a challenge; every time she looked at Old René, it was a challenge. She spotted the modest size of the wineglasses and flashed Octavie a mocking, but fond, glance.

Showing no effects of the wine she had had earlier, she sipped what she was given with the meal as sparingly as Octavie herself, but her eyes glittered. She was warm in conversation with Octavie, reserved with Old René. Paul she ignored.

It was both a relief and a worry when they retired to the drawing room. Octavie asked Florence to play the piano for them and she consented. "First, though, I must hurry to our rooms and have Jojo see to my hooks."

"Shall I go with you?" Octavie offered, noting Paul's slight frown.

"I wouldn't think of it! You take care of the gentlemen! I won't be two minutes."

Before Octavie could rise, Florence was gone.

It was twenty minutes before she rejoined them, her manner unusually spirited. She carried a glass, which she set carefully on the piano before seating herself and placing her long fingers on the keys. She caught Paul's look and tossed her head.

"Now," she chided, "it's family! I didn't want to delay our music, so"—she lifted her hands gracefully—"I had a sip while Jojo—and brought my glass along!"

"Just play, will you, Florence?" Paul responded.

She laughed gaily but, after the first notes of laughter, the sound acquired an edge. "You think I *can't*? Just sit down on that sofa, and you'll find out!"

Her fingers began to move on the keys. She had a vast memory for music and played on and on. She sipped at her glass, gaily demanding, when it was empty, that Octavie have Bran fetch a new decanter. "Music and wine!" she cried. "Especially Grape House wine!" She sang to improvised playing. "Music—wine—friends—!"

Short of causing a scene, there was no way to stop her. She played on until, finally, glass in hand, she stood and turned to Octavie. "Now it's your time, darling. Play some of those St. Louis songs, some of those river melodies!"

There was nothing else to do. Octavie was aware, as she played, that Florence had filled her glass again. It was with relief that she said goodnight to them at last and they all retired.

There was silence, except for night sounds, in Octavie's rooms, and she lay in bed, her eyes closed, but sleep would not come.

Unwanted, vivid pictures slid through her mind. Florence, warning against men; Florence with a wineglass; Florence, playing the piano, too gay, eyes too bright; Paul asking her to entice Florence into riding; Old René, face unreadable.

It'll be better tomorrow, she thought. I'll catch her early. I'll get her on a horse, and we'll ride so long she'll be too exhausted to do anything but eat dinner and take a nap.

It was then that she heard their voices. Through the doors, across the corridor, from beyond their own doors. They're quarreling, she thought. Oh, dear God, let it not be! Why were they quarreling? About the wine, or about—the other? It went on and on.

She couldn't bear it, couldn't lie there and listen. Putting on her slippers she stood, her sheer white nightgown falling to her ankles. Fingers unsteady, she put on her robe, and tied it, then drew her hair back and caught it with a ribbon. She hastened through her sitting room, quietly pulling the door closed behind her.

"I'm a lady, Paul Belfontaine, never forget!" she heard Florence cry. "A lady *knows* when to stop!"

There was a reply, inaudible. Then Florence excitedly spoke again. "There's no harm in wine, none!"

Octavie ran. Before she could hear more, before her own unhappy heart could be further torn, she ran silently down the great stairway, to the outer door, into the night.

She sped away from L'Acadie, past the old house. The grass was laden with dew; her slippers were wet. Only when she reached Grape House, did she stop.

She entered through the vine-edged opening and sat in her favorite wooden armchair, beside a window that in daylight looked out to Honeymoon House.

There was no moon, only stars. She could make out small vistas by their light. Now, more than ever, Grape House seemed a part of her.

She had begun to use it as a refuge when Gabe left. Here she had wept, here she had smiled over tender memories, here she had brought needlework and dreamed over what they would do together when he came home from the war.

It was here she had come that awful night after they had gotten Paul's letter. Here, lying on her face on the earthen floor, she had wept, resisted, denied that Gabe—handsome, beloved, eager, headstrong Gabe—could be dead. Yet, even while denying, she had known it to be the truth because Paul had written it.

Many a night she had wept here. Many an hour she had sat here, regretting that she would never feel Gabe's wonderful passion again, never laugh at one of his impulsive actions.

Now she sat in her chair hoping that soon Florence would sleep and, for Paul's sake, the quarrel would be over. Slowly her own tension, her aching grief, drained away, and the sound of night entered. It seemed that even the stars added a music of light to that of the bayou, that the beauty of the night promised, not happiness, but peace.

Into this starlit quiet there came, after an hour or

two, the sound of footsteps. She sat unmoving. One of the slaves, perhaps, coming late from courting at some bayou plantation. She tried to recall whether Old René had mentioned a courtship and wondered if he would approve of the lateness.

Then someone entered Grape House, and she sat erect. It was Paul.

He came toward her. "Octavie?"

"Yes."

"It's Paul."

"Paul. How did you—why?"

"I couldn't sleep and thought I'd sit awhile."

"Of course. Please do."

He took the chair opposite her at the window. Their knees were almost touching.

"You couldn't sleep?" he asked.

"No."

"You heard us, then?"

"Not really, Paul. Just your voices."

"Florence told me—she confided in you."

She remained silent. Her heart went into a heavy, hurting thrust.

"She's terrified of being—a wife. She accuses me—and she drinks. So she can sleep and forget."

"We shouldn't discuss her, Paul. She's your wife, my guest."

"Also your kinswoman. Please listen, Octavie."

Because he was Paul, because his trouble was deep, she listened. Swiftly, with all fairness to Florence, he told of their years together.

Her pulse was tearing her to pieces. She was trembling. How did he endure it? How had he controlled his need?

He spoke of that first day, long ago, in New Orleans. "I looked into your eyes, Octavie, and loved you. As simply as that. And you loved me."

"At first," she whispered. "Then there was Gabe."

"I saw, knew it had to be, that Gabe was good enough, even for you. God knows, I realized his worth. So I stood aside with Florence and watched you marry my dearest friend.

"I made every effort, after that, and to this day, to win Florence over. Because you *can* build a marriage. And we have Francis. But it has been of no use, and she accuses me of. . . . It's you who kept me faithful, Octavie. It's you I can't betray."

She sprang up, only to find that her legs were shaking so they barely held her. Paul, too, sprang up.

"Don't go, please, Octavie!"

"It's not right, it's not decent!" she whispered. "We can't stay, feeling—" She broke off, the realization of what she had admitted overwhelming her.

They were standing so close between the chairs that she felt his breath on her cheek. There was no way to step away without brushing against him. Her heart was rising, beating, the way it had done for Gabe, only more so now, transcending anything she had known for him. She realized that Paul knew this and understood, for now he took her chin in his hand and kissed her on the lips, lightly, gently.

But in the next kiss his lips pressed, hot, and hers caught fire, and then they parted. Suddenly it was as though she were drifting along warm, silken water, with ripples of delight flowing from their fused lips, caressing her back and into her loins. Paul's kisses, just his kisses, were making her a woman for the first time.

She didn't know how it came about, but it happened, miraculously and naturally. She was lying on the floor, the breeze was rustling music from the vines, she was staring up at Paul in the star-touched darkness. And his gentle fingers were working at the ribbons, and he was slipping her garments away, and she was naked. He gazed down, murmuring, and she closed her eyes with the exquisite agony of it.

Now he was also naked and lowering himself. Beneath him, in hot nakedness, her body curved to fit his, enveloped his need and she moved because he was moving, and she wanted to cry to the stars, to scream with the need that was rising, still rising, innundating her and him, too. But she did not scream, and the glory left them wound together, ecstatic.

Amazement overtook her. This man, this Paul, he was the real one, none other. And then she remembered Gabe. And Florence. "Oh, dear God, Paul!" she moaned. "What have we done?"

"What was meant," he whispered.

She reached for her garments and, trembling, put them on. Paul too was dressing. When she would have fled, he held her with a word.

"Wait."

She stopped. He stood beside her. "I have sullied you, who are my heart."

"You haven't!"

"I disagree."

"I didn't fight you off, Paul. You, the husband of my kinswoman, for whom I have true affection! A woman who trusts me, who is a guest in my home!"

He held her, and she couldn't resist.

"Tomorrow," he said, "I'll leave for home. I know that Florence will not, of her own desire, give me a divorce. However, when she returns at the end of the summer, she'll learn that her husband has so disported himself that the only thing she can do, being Florence, is to bring suit for divorce."

"No, Paul. Don't lower yourself."

"I'll not betray you with another woman, my darling. There'll be gossip and arranged proof, but that is all."

"It's—monstrous!" Her lips quivered on the word because this was Paul, the blood in her veins, the marrow of her bones. But what he planned was monstrous, their state was monstrous, and she had to tell him. "We have no rights, Paul. Such a thing would break Florence's heart."

"Her pride, yes. But the town house, her jewels, half my assets and an equal voice in rearing Francis will mend her pride faster than you know. She'll be a wealthy woman and entirely free of wifely duties. This, for Florence, is the ideal state."

"You speak as though you've planned—"

"Not what happened here, not that. But divorce, after you were bereaved. Yes, I've planned, despite

408

myself. Now I'll carry the plans through. And after the divorce—"

"No, Paul."

"You will marry me."

"Never, Paul," she said slowly, feeling her way. "I did love Gabe, and I bore his son. Florence—what I did. I don't know what that makes me."

"A woman who must love."

"But not a marriage achieved by such means. After tonight, I truly can never marry again. I won't marry you, divorced or not."

He was silent, then said, "You truly mean it."

"Truly."

"I'll wait. A year, five years, more. I'll not give up what we had tonight, my darling."

In silence, separately, they returned to the house. Octavie lay tossing. A future together was hopeless, but she knew that Paul would not leave tomorrow, that he would not pursue divorce. He would stay the summer, and she knew that she would not have the strength to resist tonight's glory when he offered it again.

TWENTY-TWO

Old René's journal, June, 1820:

After nearly five years, the love between Paul Belfontaine and my late son's widow continues. Though they reveal nothing of their feelings, there is everything between them. The Belfontaines summer at L'Acadie, but where those two rendezvous, I do not know, but that it is nightly, I am convinced. There is an aura of the beloved about Octavie but one also of sadness.

Florence's drinking worsens. Another problem is the manner in which Mama, though she is very old, is beginning to show her poisonous hatred of Negroes to René, a child of six. I shall warn Octavie of this, for she will gracefully put an end to it.

June, 1826:

I must write while this is fresh in mind, being sixty-nine and on the watch for any sign of forgetfulness. René, twelve, is visiting a friend in Vicksburg, and I have arranged for him to remain there until school opens so that he will not be at L'Acadie for a year.

Last night, being unable to sleep . . .

The journal account lengthened. That night he had been pondering crop rotation when he became aware of movement along the corridor. As his rooms were at the end of a wing, there was no reason for anyone to be there at that hour.

Thinking it might be Florence, inebriated and wandering, Old René put on his robe, told Hippolyte to stay behind, and went into the corridor, finding it empty. He passed to where it joined another corridor and saw that it was indeed Florence, in robe and slippers, who was making her way, unsteadily, down the staircase. He followed, reluctant to speak and startle her, but ready to give aid.

To his consternation, she staggered to the front door and outside. He continued to follow, having no idea of where she was going, though he held a strong suspicion of her reason. She went weaving across lawns, past the old house, and on. Finally, he saw her go into Grape House, and he heavily turned back. . . .

Octavie soared into the heavens, beyond the clouds. She moaned, and the first breath of her moan brought his to life, and they made of it a song. They moved together, his beloved body one with hers. Her full, round breasts fell and spread and rose from one position into another until, miraculously, they seemed themselves to be embracing him.

The gentle wind rustled the vines, carrying with it the smell of greenery. They lay on the earth, part of the earth, the whole of love. Then, abruptly, there was a difference in the sound of the vines; the rustling was at the door opening, rough and loud.

Octavie moved to sit up, Paul with her.

"Animals!" shrieked a voice. "*Animals!*"

Old René's journal, June, 1826:

The Belfontaines left at sunup. Francis, grown now, is touring Europe and thus fortunately was not present. Octavie did not appear at breakfast. Opal had cracked open the door and said her mistress slept.

And I, be there a God and may he forgive me, told the wench to let her mistress rest, knowing what she had been through. Before noon, Opal came sobbing that she could not rouse her mistress. Hippolyte and I hastened to her chamber. She was dead, her body stiff and cold, and with such a look of desolation on her lovely face I shudder at the remorse that put it there. Her bottle of sleeping drops was beside her.

Death, according to Doctor Gilbert, was from an accidental overdose of the drops. Before he left, my mother, who was ninety-two and still of fiery nature, upon learning of Octavie's death, suffered a heart seizure and, despite all efforts, expired. Thus, for the third time, there was held a funeral at L'Acadie with two or more departed from this life.

TWENTY-THREE

The hurricane was trying to wrench L'Acadie off the earth. The hurricane had gotten inside Carita now, possessing her, sending its whirlwind through her on the winds of the mad, diabolic Leblanc words. It raged in her veins and blew in the mad rhythm of the howling outer temptest, blasted the debris of insane Leblanc deeds into every cranny of her being.

She heard her own laughter, peal after peal, rush to meet the other hurricane. Frenziedly, she snatched up journal after journal and hurled them against walls, windows, furniture. Shrieking, she kicked the journals and stomped on them.

Suddenly she quieted and became crafty-eyed. She was aware of deep silence except for the hurricane. The house was asleep. Her eyes became wild as she fashioned her own hurricane that would now come upon L'Acadie, to level, strip, destroy, and punish.

This was as it had been with her uncle Unzaga, back in her family, that intrepid Unzaga, when he had put slaves on the rack, when he had exacted and wreaked just punishment. Sí, his justice had made him wild-eyed too, had sent his mind streaking and probing.

She rested one hand on her middle, her palm flat against the slenderness, which, but for her valor, would round out and swell until, in tortured, diabolic anguish, it would eject that which now lay invisible within.

The hand fell. Everything must be done in order. Old René. No—what more evil could he do? Euphemie. No—no sully to Nuñez blood there. Dolores. Fat, lovable, enchantress. But she's a suckah. She's Nuñez, but defiled; René had pumped defilement into pure Creole blood.

That was the order in which they must be handled. She must do as he—Unzaga—had done, in proper order. Only this time, silent as lightning and as fast and sure.

She moved.

She was aware of standing at Dolores's cot, of Lura snoring in the alcove, of Consuela, breathing heavily, on another cot. She gazed at the sleeping child.

The fat little chest rose and fell. Under the fat she was dainty, with skin so white it seemed translucent, her softly curling hair now the color of Carita's hair. She examined the false beauty, the veneer that could not hide the black, hopeless animal inside.

With steady hands she lifted the pillow, admiring her own magnificent calm as she lowered it over the child's face. When Dolores moved, asleep and seeking air, she pressed harder, even harder and longer, until enough time had passed. She laid the pillow aside and made sure.

Next, she was standing at a window, Unzaga dagger in hand. A shutter had ripped away, and she could see into the storm. She waited.

She sensed the opening of the door and turned. She saw René come into her sitting room, sodden, trickling water onto the carpet. She saw his haggard face.

Still she waited.

"Carita," he said, and his voice was different, though perhaps not. Maybe he had always had the voice of a buck. "What in hell are you doing with that dagger? Put the damn thing down. I know you've got the worst grievance a wife can have, but histrionics aren't going to help. We've a hell of a lot to discuss, decisions to make that I don't see any way right now to make. First, I've got to dry off."

She followed him into the bedchamber, carrying the dagger calmly, with grace.

He stripped off his wet coat, shirt, and undershirt. Even his skin was shining wet. She watched him sit on a chair, back to her and bend over to pull off his boots.

She gazed calmly at his wet skin. There. Near the left shoulder. She moved quickly.

She felt the jolt as the dagger plunged in. She felt his flesh try to keep the blade, but she dragged it out. Ignoring his low cry, she lifted her arm and drove the second time, the third. Once for each sucker and once for him.

She watched his body topple, face down. She watched the blood. After a time, she got a towel and cleaned the blood off the blade.

After laying the dagger on the bedtable, she removed her robe and her nightgown. She sat in the middle of the bed, pillows arranged about her. She reached for the dagger.

With Creole hand she guided the tapered, needle-sharp blade into the entrance so often violated by the now-slain buck. She held her breath. In the blade went, ever in, and when there was resistance, she drove it mercilessly. She swallowed a scream. A second time she jabbed. This time she screamed, then screamed again.

She felt herself going into darkness. And within the darkness, blood flowed and carried away the unborn.

Old René's journal, final entry:

Carita's screams saved her life, for they roused the household, and there were women who knew what to do. She lives, and when her mind has healed, she must face what lies in the future, and will.

I, who know all our history, cherish hope for the future. In the veins of Euphemie, René's daughter, runs Leblanc blood and in the veins of the Rivard baby, as well. Leblancs live, and L'Acadie sheds her beauty over all, and we will, one day, attain that for which my father, Gabriel, laid down the pattern.

ABOUT THE AUTHOR

SALIEE O'BRIEN has been writing for as long as she
can remember, and publishing stories since the age
of fourteen. She was lured, while in her twenties
by community theater and radio broadcasting; but
they couldn't keep her from her first love—writing.
Stories began appearing in a wide range of maga-
zines: *Saturday Evening Post*, *Collier's* and *Blue
Book*. Novels followed, and in abundance. *Bayou* is
her seventh novel published under the pseudonym
Saliee O'Brien; former titles include *Farewell the
Stranger*, *Too Swift the Tide* and *Heiress to Evil*.
Ms. O'Brien is married and lives in Florida.

SPECIAL MONEY SAVING OFFER

Now you can have an up-to-date listing of Bantam's hundreds of titles plus take advantage of our unique and exciting bonus book offer. A special offer which gives you the opportunity to purchase a Bantam book for only 50¢. Here's how!

By ordering any five books at the regular price per order, you can also choose any other single book listed (up to a $4.95 value) for just 50¢. Some restrictions do apply, but for further details why not send for Bantam's listing of titles today!

Just send us your name and address plus 50¢ to defray the postage and handling costs.

HISTORICAL ROMANCES

Read some of Bantam's Best in Historical Romances!

- ☐ 24429 **Blind Duty**—Frederick W. Nolan — $3.95
- ☐ 24701 **Tall Woman**—Harry S. Gibbons — $3.50
- ☐ 24592 **Chantal**—Claire Lorrimer — $3.95
- ☐ 23952 **Before the Summer Rain**—Anne Faul — $3.50
- ☐ 23988 **Farewell My South**—Cynthia Van Hazinga — $3.95
- ☐ 20352 **Promise of Glory**—F. Nolan — $3.50
- ☐ 23850 **The Fields**—Conrad Ritcher — $2.95
- ☐ 23802 **The Trees**—Conrad Ritcher — $2.95
- ☐ 23926 **The Town**—Conrad Richter — $3.50
- ☐ 23798 **Starflower**—Lynn Lowery — $3.50

THE LATEST BOOKS
IN THE BANTAM
BESTSELLING TRADITION

DON'T MISS
THESE CURRENT
Bantam Bestsellers